The Fugitive Queen

AN URSULA BLANCHARD MYSTERY AT QUEEN ELIZABETH I'S COURT

Fiona Buckley

SCRIBNER

New York   London   Toronto   Sydney   Singapore

SCRIBNER
1230 Avenue of the Americas
New York, NY 10020

SCRIBNER and design are trademarks of Macmillan Library Reference USA, Inc.,
used under license by Simon & Schuster, the publisher of this work.

For information regarding special discounts for bulk purchases,
please contact Simon & Schuster Special Sales at 1-800-456-6798
or *business@simonandschuster.com*

Designed by Brooke Koven
Text set in Bembo

Manufactured in the United States of America

1 3 5 7 9 10 8 6 4 2

Library of Congress Cataloging-in-Publication Data

Buckley, Fiona.
The fugitive queen: an Ursula Blanchard mystery at Queen Elizabeth I's court/
Fiona Buckley.
p. cm.
1. Blanchard, Ursula (Fictitious character)—Fiction. 2. Great Britain—History—
Elizabeth, 1558–1603—Fiction. 3. Elizabeth I, Queen of England, 1533–1603—Fiction.
4. Mary, Queen of Scots, 1542–1587—Fiction. 5. Women detectives—England—Fiction.
6. Courts and courtiers—Fiction. 7. Queens—Fiction. I. Title.

PR6052.U266F84 2003
823'.914—dc21
2003045736

ISBN 0-7432-3751-X

*This book is dedicated
to the memory of
my husband,
Dalip*

Author's Note

It is true that during Mary Stuart's short stay at Carlisle when she first arrived in England, she was allowed out on at least one hawking expedition. As far as I know, however, there is no record that when she was at Bolton, Sir Francis Knollys ever permitted such a thing. The English government was far too afraid of Mary escaping to France—and coming back with an army.

However, if by any chance he did relax his restrictions, perhaps through anxiety about Mary's health, and something went wrong, he might well have kept quiet about it. I have let him do just that. This is fiction, after all.

It is also true that Mary Stuart suffered from unexplained bouts of ill health, often involving a mysterious pain in her side and likely to occur when she was emotionally upset. It is now believed that she may have suffered from an inherited disease called porphyria, which produces symptoms of this kind.

The Fugitive Queen

Letter from Mistress Ann Mason of Lockhill in Berkshire, to Mistress Ursula Stannard of Withysham in Sussex.
Dated February 1568

Madam, I pray that you will forgive me for the liberty I take in writing to you and in making the request that will follow hereafter.

We last met under unhappy circumstances but all that is in the past and I well know that you did not wish to harm my family; nor did you do so. You only unmasked villainy which we were harboring unawares.

Since then, my life has changed greatly, with the death of my dear husband, Master Leonard Mason. I am left with the care of Lockhill and of my children. My sons George and Philip are now men grown and some years ago were sent by their father to good households to finish their education, but my eldest daughter, Penelope, who is at present in her nineteenth year, has remained at home with me and it is time to consider her future.

I have no desire to remarry and indeed, need not, for a few days since, George returned to take his place as the master of Lockhill. He and I, alas, are not altogether in agreement concerning the kind of marriage his sister should make but by the terms of my husband's will, I am her guardian and the choice is mine.

I would like Penelope, if possible, to go to court, perhaps as a Maid of Honor—to mix with the best society and thus to have a chance of finding a good match, with a man of position and means. You know, of course, that our family holds by the old religion and I would want Penelope's husband to share our opinions. I would not, however, wish him to be anything but a loyal subject of our sovereign lady, Queen Elizabeth. Such men may be found at court, I believe. Her dowry will only be modest, but I will do my best for her.

And so, dear madam, I come to the point and make bold to ask if you, being a former Lady of the Presence Chamber to Queen Elizabeth, would take charge of Penelope for me and use such influence as you have to find her a place at court and a suitable husband? I would then regard you as her guardian and leave her future entirely in your hands, asking only that I be informed of any betrothal, that I may attend the nuptials and wish her happy.

I hear that since our last meeting, you have yourself been widowed and have remarried and are now Mistress Hugh Stannard. This came to me from my cousin Bess, who was a Maid of Honor once and although now married and away from the court, still keeps in touch with friends there and hears news. She is however not in a very influential position. You, I think, may well be better placed. Penelope is a good girl, not a great beauty but pleasing nevertheless in her manners and person. Will you help?

The messenger who brings you this also brings a young female merlin, which I pray you will accept as a sign of my goodwill. The bird is trained and I hope will provide good sport. Her name is Joy, for when we fly her at game, she so loves the air.

Your most humble servant and supplicant, Ann Mason.

Letter from Mistress Ursula Stannard, at Hawkswood, to Mistress Ann Mason, Lockhill. Late February 1568

Madam, it gave both my husband and myself pleasure to receive your letter, which finally reached us at his house in Hawkswood, Surrey, having first gone to my old home at Withysham. I have always regretted that because of the trouble in your household when I was there, and your husband's very natural indignation over my own part in it, we were not able to pursue our friendship.

I heartily thank you for the gift of Joy, the merlin. The bird has settled well and I have presented her to my daughter, Meg. It is time that Meg learned something of the sport of falconry.

Both my husband, Master Stannard, and I were grieved to learn of your husband's death. This is a great loss for you and for your family and we pray that you may be able to sustain it with courage and are not in any want.

I remember Penelope and well recall how much I liked her. We will gladly welcome her to our home. Her presence, even for a short while, may be of benefit to my own daughter. Meg is growing up. She will turn thirteen this summer. She would take pleasure in the company of a friend who could be as it were, an elder sister, until such time as I can arrange for Penelope to attend at court. I daresay that such an arrangement can be made and I will put my best efforts forward for her.

Meanwhile, as long as she is with us, whether here or when we are at Withysham (as we sometimes are), Penelope will share in the society of the neighborhood. If she plays chess, my husband would enjoy having a new opponent for a while, and I and my gentlewoman companion Mistress Sybil Jester will provide her with every opportunity to practice music, needlework, and horsemanship, and to continue with whatever studies you recommend.

But let me assure you again, I will make every effort to secure a place at court for her and after that, a good marriage into a family that is not likely to fall foul of the law. The political and religious divisions within our land are a trouble to us all, alas.

By this messenger, we send you the gift of a puppy, ten weeks old. He is bred from a strain of good ratters, but with a gentle temperament, so that he will make a pet as well. With earnest good wishes to you and all your family, Ursula Stannard, formerly Ursula Blanchard.

Letter from Mistress Ursula Stannard to Mistress Ann Mason. Dated April 1568

My respected friend Mistress Mason: I write from the court at Greenwich, whither I lately brought your daughter, Penelope. She is now established as a Maid of Honor to Queen Elizabeth. She was very welcome in my household where her many excellent qualities won all hearts and I am sure that at court, it will be no different. My husband has most generously provided her with new gowns and some jewelry for her entrance into royal circles. She will be second to none in her style of dress and ornamentation and I trust it will not be difficult to find a husband for her.

I will take every care to see that she is guided toward the kind of match which will please you.

What strange times we live in! Three years ago, I briefly visited the court of Queen Mary Stuart of Scotland. Her marriage to Henry Lord Darnley had not yet taken place although its likelihood was becoming plain. But no one could have envisaged then, that by now, Darnley would have been mysteriously slain and Mary accused of complicity and cast from her throne accordingly. I think she is no threat to England now and that her supporters are no longer a threat, either. But I promise I will see to it that Pen is introduced only to families who, whatever their private observances, are steady and loyal to our queen. . . .

Letter to Mistress Ursula Stannard at Withysham, Sussex, by private messenger, from Sir William Cecil, Secretary of State, at Richmond Palace. Dated June 1568

My very dear Ursula, I write this reluctantly, but with the queen's knowledge—indeed at her behest. It is not usual for me to concern myself with the antics of her Maids of Honor, but one of them is your protégée and you, Ursula, are most highly valued by the queen and by me and my wife. Also, a member of my own household is involved.

We are anxious on account of your ward, Mistress Penelope Mason, who, while at court, has formed an unsuitable attachment to one of my gentlemen—a Master Rowan, who is a linguist and accompanies me to court to help me in conversing with French and Italian visitors, since I myself speak no tongue but English.

Master Rowan has a wife of great charm, and they have four children. He has, I assure you, no interest in Mistress Mason, but she is evidently smitten by his good looks and pleasant mien and I am sorry to say is making herself a nuisance to him, as well as appearing foolish in the eyes of others. It would be well if you could come to Richmond and speak with her, or perhaps take her away for a while.

You will have heard, of course, the latest news regarding Mary Stuart of Scotland. In May, much to our surprise and horror, she escaped from her imprisonment in Scotland with a tiny suite of sixteen people, landed at Workington on the Cumberland coast, and threw herself on the mercy of Elizabeth. She is at present in Carlisle, but plans are in hand to send her to Bolton Castle in Yorkshire, which is more secure. Sir Francis Knollys has gone north on the orders of Queen Elizabeth, to take charge of her and guard against any machinations on her part.

He also hopes to convert her to the Protestant faith although I suspect that he will find this a difficult task.

Master Rowan has just come to me with a sonnet in Penelope Mason's handwriting. He found it pinned into a cloak which he had left upon a bench. I enclose it for you to see. I hope that you and Master Stannard will not delay in coming to court to deal with this most embarrassing situation. . . .

1

A Dowry for a Wayward Maid

I married Hugh Stannard in 1565, the seventh year of Queen Elizabeth's reign. I was thirty-one, a little younger than the queen herself, and Hugh was more than twenty years my senior, but this suited me very well. I had had enough of passion. I had felt passion for both of my previous husbands and it had brought me more suffering than joy.

Well, it was true that my dear first husband, Gerald Blanchard, had given me my daughter, Meg, who was a blessing to me. But I had nearly lost my life in bearing her, and I had lost Gerald himself to smallpox while Meg was still small. Now my second husband, Matthew de la Roche, was dead of the plague and although I had been deep in love with him, we had never had any peace or lasting happiness together. I bore him a stillborn son whose birth brought me even nearer to the grave than Meg had, so that I learned to fear childbearing. And also, I was loyal to Queen Elizabeth of England while he had continually plotted against her on behalf of Mary Stuart, who was Queen of Scotland and in the eyes of ardent Catholics such as Matthew should have been Queen of England, too.

If I were tired of passion, I was even more tired of conspiracy. For many years I had served Elizabeth as a Lady of the Presence Chamber but I had been more than that. I had also worked for her as a spy, seeking out plots against her. For a while, I found the excitement exhilarating. It had called to me in a voice like the cry of the wild geese, winging across the sky. When I heard the geese something in me always longed to bound up into the air and follow them. In the same way, I had responded to the summons of adventure.

But my work divided me from Matthew and willy-nilly, it caused me to send men to their deaths. It put me in mortal danger too, once or twice. I continually worried and frightened my two good servants, Fran Dale, my tirewoman, and Roger Brockley, my steward; I more than once risked leaving Meg alone without either mother or father, and when my adventuring finally brought me perilously close to being forced into a disastrous third marriage, I knew I had had enough.

In Hugh Stannard, I found a refuge from conflict combined with freedom from the perils of childbirth. He was a widower and hadn't spent his widowhood like a monk, which meant that he had had every chance of siring children yet he had never succeeded in doing so. With him, I could be fairly sure that I would not have to face pregnancy again. He was also a decent, honest man, interested in chess and gardens, an uncomplicated Protestant, and a trustworthy subject of the queen. Life as Hugh's wife might be dull, I thought, but it would be quiet. I was glad to settle for that. I could do without excitement. I could even do without happiness, as long as I could have some peace.

I hoped that we would make a good partnership. I would retire from court and conspiracy alike. Hugh and I would live together in amity, dividing our time between our two homes, my Withysham in Sussex and his Hawkswood in Surrey. I would educate my daughter, cultivate my herb garden, enjoy the society of my recently acquired woman companion Sybil Jester; let Fran and Roger enjoy each other's society, too. They were married, though Fran was still usually known as Dale, out of habit.

And so, in businesslike fashion, I ceased to be Ursula Blanchard, and became instead Mistress Hugh Stannard and if, for a while, I secretly grieved for Matthew, and cried in private because I had not been with him to comfort him at the end as once I had comforted Gerald, I only did so when I was alone.

And time erodes sorrow. Presently, my private fits of weeping ceased. Then I found that I had entered into more happiness than I would ever have believed possible. Hugh's lovemaking, if not frequent, was perfectly satisfactory, and his temperament was a pleasing mixture of the competent and the generous. He took a kindly interest in Meg and it was Hugh who achieved what I had not, and found a tutor, Dr. Lambert, who could teach her Greek as well as Latin. I was especially pleased, as I wished to study Greek and to improve my own Latin. Then, in the third year of our marriage, he was perfectly ready to welcome Penelope Mason, the daughter of my former acquaintance Ann Mason, into our home.

This pleased me, too. Years ago, I had uncovered a conspiracy that was brewing in the Mason household although the Masons themselves were not involved. It was an unpleasant business, though, and keeping up any kind of friendship with the family seemed impossible afterward. Ann Mason's letter delighted me.

I was less delighted however when, after Pen had been with us for a month and I was exchanging messages with the court, prior to taking her there, Hugh observed that romantically speaking, she was susceptible. "You should urge the matter of her court appointment on," he said to me, "and get her away from here. I think she's falling for the tutor."

"For *Lambert*?" I said in astonishment. Dr. Henry Lambert was about Hugh's own age and his hair was already completely silver. "He's too old to interest a young girl, surely!" I said.

"Don't you believe it," said Hugh. "He's a fine-looking man, and since Pen is studying Greek with you and Meg, she sees him every day. It won't do. Even if he were younger, it wouldn't do. He has no property beyond a cottage in the town of Guildford. And he's Protestant. Her mother wouldn't like that." Hugh had Catholic relatives and was tolerant of their creed. "Get her to court and under the eye of the queen, *fast.*"

I did as he said. My happiness with Hugh was based as much as anything on his reliability. He was a clearheaded man and I trusted his judgment. It wasn't Hugh's fault that Pen's sojourn at court was less than successful. I certainly didn't blame him for that.

In all our life together, Hugh and I only quarreled once and that was for the most improbable of reasons.

Pen had only been at court for two months, when the letter came from Sir William Cecil to tell us that, having been removed from Dr. Lambert the tutor, she had now fallen in love with Master Rowan the interpreter and was causing embarrassment and would we come to court—now at Richmond—to deal with her.

"Oh, really!" grumbled Hugh. "And riding makes all my joints ache. I don't *want* to travel to Richmond. It's all of twenty-five miles. Why can't this Master Rowan fend her off without our help?"

I wondered, too. Among them—Master Rowan, Queen Elizabeth, Sir William Cecil, and the mistress in charge of the Maids of Honor—they really should have been able to call Pen to order. However, a summons from Cecil could not be ignored. Dutifully, we set out for Richmond Palace.

I had always liked Richmond. Of all Elizabeth's homes, it seemed to me the most charming, with its gardens and wind chimes, its delicately designed towers and its gracious rooms, so many of which looked out on the Thames. On days like this, when the sun was out and the gardens were full of scent and color, and the Thames sparkled under a mild breeze, it was at its most beguiling. I would have enjoyed this visit, my first in years, if only we hadn't had to cope with Pen.

Cecil had arranged lodgings in the palace for us and Pen was sent to us there. She stood miserably in front of us, and Hugh and I, enthroned side by side on a broad window seat, probably looked and sounded like a pair of judges as we took her to task over her behavior.

Penelope obviously felt both frightened and embarrassed. First of all she turned very red and indignantly denied the charge. Confronted by the evidence in the form of Cecil's letter to me and also the sonnet in her handwriting (it was technically rather good, as a matter of fact; Pen was a clever girl), she did the only thing left for her to do and burst into tears. Hugh, without speaking and with a most unsympathetic expression on his face, took a napkin from his sleeve and handed it to her.

Gazing at her as she snuffled into the napkin, I sighed. It is no light responsibility, taking charge of someone else's daughter.

As her mother had said, Pen was not a beauty. To be truthful, she was almost plain. Her forehead bulged too much and her chin was too square. Her hair, demurely folded into waves under a white cap with silver embroidery, was no more than mousey. Her best features were her dark gray eyes, which were beautifully set, and her complexion, which when not swollen with tears, was clear and pale. She held herself well, too, had good taste in dress, and she was intelligent, as that confounded sonnet demonstrated. I was sorry for her now but I hardened my heart. Pen was not going to spoil her reputation through girlish inexperience, or waste herself on the wrong man if I could save her, and I meant to do that for her sake as well as to please her mother.

"Dry your eyes," I said firmly. "And listen. You have fallen in love—well, it happens. Few of us, though, marry our first loves and most of us realize later what a good thing that is . . ."

"*You* married your first love," said Pen mutinously.

"And what would you know about that?" Hugh inquired. Soberly clad in a dark formal gown, his blue eyes icy with annoyance, my husband looked particularly judgmental. He also looked tired, I thought. We had taken two days over the ride from Hawkswood and his mare was an ambler, thus providing a very smooth and easy pace, but the rheumatic pains in his joints had troubled him badly. It gave me an extra reason to be angry with Pen.

"I heard about it when I was with you at Hawkswood," she said in a resentful voice. "Dale told me. You ran off with your cousin Mary's betrothed. *You* pleased yourself. Why can't I?"

"That is enough. You will not address either of us in this pert fashion," said Hugh.

"I should say," I observed, thinking that Dale had talked too much and that I would have to raise the matter with her, "that my circumstances and yours, Pen, are not the same. I was not living as a welcome guest with my aunt and uncle, as you were at

Hawkswood with us, but was there on sufferance—a poor relation with questionable origins. No one was going to arrange a marriage for me. I had to make a future for myself."

"There's no need to justify yourself, my dear," said Hugh.

"One moment," I said. "I've a reason for talking like this. Pen, I ran away with Gerald Blanchard, but he was a suitable choice for me and he cared for me as I did for him. It was mutual. Master Rowan, on the other hand, is married already, with a family of children. He has no interest in you. You have been annoying him." I rapped the last two sentences out with deliberate brutality and Hugh, on the point of intervening again, raised his eyebrows and didn't.

"We noticed at Hawkswood," I said, "that you were gazing after Dr. Lambert, too. It is clear that you need to be watched. We understand that the queen has released you from your duties for the time being and returned you to our charge. For the moment, you will remain here in our rooms. I will send Dale to bear you company though not to gossip with you. Master Stannard and I are to have an audience with the queen, in which your future will be further discussed, I daresay."

"Oh no!" It came out in a wail. "It's not . . . you're not going to tell the queen!"

"My dear girl," said Hugh impatiently, "she already knows. Mistress Stannard has just told you that she has released you to our care and your deplorable behavior is the reason why. I suspect that most of the court knows! It's hard to keep any kind of secret here and maybe it's time you began to understand that."

Dale was waiting in an outer room. Sybil Jester was not with her, having remained at Hawkswood to look after Meg, who was too young as yet for court. On returning to Dale, I eyed her severely. "You're to go in and keep an eye on Pen. You'd better both settle to some embroidery until we come back. And, Dale . . ."

"Yes, ma'am?" said Dale, scanning my face with her large, light blue eyes and realizing that in some way or other, she must have offended.

"In future," I said, "will you please not gossip to Pen about me! It seems that you told her how my first marriage arose. It's given her some very wrong ideas about the kind of behavior I will overlook!"

"Oh, ma'am! I'm sorry! I never expected . . . I didn't mean to gossip; I can't abide tittle-tattle. Only, nearly everyone that knows you knows about you and Master Blanchard and . . ."

"I know." I melted and smiled at her. I sometimes had to take Dale to task but I was at heart very fond of her and she of me. "It's just that Pen is so young. Be careful what you say to her, that's all. Only improving conversation, if you please!"

"Have a competition to see how many psalms each of you knows by heart," said Hugh, his normal sense of humor reasserting itself. "Meanwhile, we must attend upon Her Majesty."

"You almost frighten me sometimes," Hugh said as, having found a page to guide us, we made our way through the palace toward Elizabeth's apartments. "I thought for a moment that you were going to be too soft with Penelope. And then you descend on her like a stooping falcon. *Master Rowan has no interest in you. You've been annoying him.* It was more effective than if you'd thrown cold water over her. It will do her good, as of course you knew. But how you take me aback at times! You are so gentle, so compliant at home, that sometimes I forget what you've seen and done in your life—and what depths you have, and what skills."

"I didn't like doing it," I said somberly. "It was necessary, that's all. I used shock tactics because I thought they might succeed, and I did it because I'm very annoyed with her—but also worried about her. We're about to face the queen and I daresay she'll tell us that our ward is in disgrace and must be removed."

"Elizabeth is fond of you. She owes you much."

"She won't like *this*," I said.

The walk to Elizabeth's rooms took us through the lively bustle that pervaded all her palaces. Elizabeth was a human magnet who drew people to her. The wide passages and lofty galleries, the tapestried anterooms and winding staircases of Richmond were crowded. Page boys and servants hurried hither and thither and the Lord Steward's chief officials, carrying white staves as symbols of office, went hither and thither as well, in more measured fashion, transmitting orders and inspecting the work of underlings, ready at any moment to pounce on the page boy overheard being less than respectful or the maidservant caught dusting too carelessly, spilling the goblets on her tray, or getting out of her betters' path too slowly.

And, of course, there were the courtiers: queen's ladies and council members; the ever-present but ever-changing group of foreign emissaries (all moving as often as not in a cloud of their own clerks, secretaries, or interpreters such as Master Rowan); and numerous hopeful young men who had come to court to make their careers. By right of well-born or sometimes merely rich and influential fathers, they had the entrée to the public rooms of the palaces, and came there daily at their own expense, hoping to be noticed by the queen or one of her great men, and thus obtain employment or a patron for their poetry and music. The court was a world to itself and as busy as an ant heap, full of well-dressed ants.

We found the queen in a thronged gallery. It had deep window bays, almost small rooms in their own right, and she was standing in one of them, talking to a couple of her councilors. We caught her eye as we came to the entrance to the bay, and with a faint nod, she let us know that in a moment, she would beckon us in. While we waited, lingering where she could see us, I looked with interest at the little groups of men and women, strolling or standing all about us.

I absorbed, as I always did, the byplay of it all, especially the cheerful smiles and studiedly confident stance of people who were not quite as richly dressed as those to whom they were talking, but were trying to give the impression of belonging to some worthwhile inner circle—because to be an outsider is humiliating and besides, life is so perverse that it is easier to attract a patron if people think you already have one. Those who understood the signs could tell at a glance who really mattered and who did not.

A rich variety of perfumes scented the air and the whole gallery was full of murmuring voices and rustling silks. As my gaze moved around, I noticed a well-made man with a face both weather-beaten and intelligent, and a doublet cut differently from the doublets of the English courtiers, in earnest conversation with a dark-complexioned individual who had an agreeable smile and very good clothes, which I thought were in the Spanish style. I had been away from court affairs for so long that my memory of faces was rusty, yet I thought I had seen the weather-beaten man somewhere before and I was almost certain of his companion's identity, too. As I watched, I saw the probable-Spaniard attempt to detach himself, and then check politely as the other man laid a hand on his arm.

If I were looking about me, trying to recognize people, there were also those who recognized me. A tall and splendid figure in a mulberry taffeta doublet, the queen's friend Robin Dudley, now ennobled as the Earl of Leicester, bore down on us. When we had exchanged greetings, I indicated the pair I had noticed and said: "Who are those two? Is one of them the Spanish ambassador? I'm sure I remember him—De Silva, isn't it?"

"Dear Ursula," said Dudley, his own gypsy-brown face lighting up with amusement, "you never change. You arrive at court after a long absence and instantly tease out the important threads in the complex tapestry of political life. The dark man is indeed De Silva. He is a charming, and fortunately, a sensible man. It's just as well, because the fellow who is talking to him and won't let him get away is Lord Herries, emissary from Mary Stuart. He came to England with her."

"I *thought* I'd seen him before as well. It must have been when I was in Scotland a few years ago."

"No doubt. Ah. Her Majesty is beckoning to us. Come."

"Beckoning to *us*?" queried Hugh.

"Yes. I am concerned in the matter, as it happens." Dudley saw my face and laughed. "No, no, Ursula. Your naughty Penelope hasn't been making eyes at me, not that it would have done her any good if she had. I have a reputation," said Dudley, "for being irresponsible, but I'm not *that* irresponsible. The queen prefers me to concentrate on her. Follow me."

As we joined the queen, Cecil also arrived. Every time I saw him, I thought that he had aged since the last time. On this occasion, the gap was nearly three years long and the change was very noticeable. There was far more gray in his fair beard and the line between his alert blue eyes was now a deep furrow. Like Hugh, I thought, Cecil was tired.

Elizabeth was informally dressed and had now seated herself in casual fashion on a broad window seat. From these subtle signals, I gathered that Hugh and I were not going to receive a blistering public condemnation for Pen's foolishness but I knew that we wouldn't escape quite unscathed, nor did we.

"My Cecil! Ursula! And Master Stannard! Sweet Robin, you are welcome." As we made our courtesies, Elizabeth gave each of us in turn her hand to kiss. Then she fixed her golden-brown eyes on my face and came to the point at once. "You know what this is about, of course. The girl Penelope Mason cannot remain at court. We understand that you know why."

"Yes, ma'am," I said sadly. Elizabeth too looked older. Her pale, shield-shaped face had settled into mature lines; her mouth was less vulnerable. She was no longer the young girl she was when I first met her.

"We expect the Maids of Honor to be lively," she said, "even if they sing and dance in their rooms and irritate people in neighboring apartments. After all, they are young. We even expect them to flirt a little. We watch them for their own protection but allow them some latitude. Not to this extent, however. This blatant pursuit of a married man—sonnets pinned into his cloak, no less!—such things will not do. We understand that the girl's mother wants to find a match for her. We would recommend that this is done without loss of time—before she has a chance to misbehave again, perhaps disastrously for herself. And now," said Elizabeth, turning to Dudley, "my lord of Leicester has something to say."

Hugh and I looked at Dudley, puzzled. He smiled. "One of the problems the girl has is lack of dowry," he said. "We have inquired from her and from her mother, what her portion is likely to be and there is little to spare for her."

"The rents of one small sublet farm and the tiny hamlet that goes with it," said Cecil, speaking for the first time. "Not enough to attract a court gentleman unless he were to fall deeply in love with her—and that doesn't seem likely."

"No," I agreed regretfully, thinking of Pen's unremarkable looks. "With Pen—no, it isn't very likely."

"I, however," said Dudley, "am willing to help."

Hugh and I continued to gaze at him, but now it was with astonishment. Dudley was a very wealthy man and could be generous; he gambled a good deal but had a reputation for paying his debts on time. He was not, however, known as a philanthropist, and I had never heard before that he went about providing dowries for plain young women who had no connection with him.

"I have a parcel of land in the north of England, about fifteen miles from the castle of Bolton," he said smoothly. "It's on the edge of a wild place called Saddleworth Moor. I was left it by a former employee who had no family of his own to will it to. It's a fair-sized stretch of land, with arable fields, a big flock of sheep, and both meadowland and hill grazing for them. They're valuable. The wool is good. It all amounts to a very respectable piece of property or so I understand. I have had reports of it, although I haven't seen it myself. I have little time or, to be honest, inclination to travel north and inspect it personally. In fact, in many ways, it's a nuisance to me. I am willing, as it were, to donate it to a good cause. It might well help to attract a husband for the girl."

"We understand that her mother would prefer a household with Catholic beliefs," observed Cecil. "Provided, of course that he has a loyal reputation and attends Anglican services at least once a month, as the law states. There are many Catholic adherents in northern England. A suitable man might be easier to find there. Mistress Penelope should perhaps go to see her dowry lands in Yorkshire."

He finished on an odd, thoughtful intonation. I recognized it. I'd heard him use it before. I looked at Dudley. "The place is near Bolton, you say, my lord?"

"Reasonably near," Dudley agreed suavely.

As soon as the word *Bolton* was spoken, I had come alert.

Mary Stuart was about to be moved to Bolton Castle. Something was coming; I knew it. There was more to this than just making arrangements to marry off a wayward Maid of Honor.

"Mary Stuart of Scotland will shortly move to Bolton," said Elizabeth, echoing the words that were already in my head. "You met her, did you not, Ursula, when you went to Scotland a few years ago?"

"I . . . yes, ma'am. I did."

"And I believe she liked you? You were her guest at Holyrood in Edinburgh for a while?"

"Yes, ma'am," I said with caution.

"No doubt she is finding life strange and limited in my northern castles, compared with life as a queen," said Elizabeth gravely. "Her representative, Lord Herries, is at Richmond now and would like us to receive her here but my good Cecil is much against the idea of bringing her to London."

"She has a charge of murder hanging over her. She is not a fit person to associate with the Queen of England until her name is cleared," said Cecil, his voice now quite colorless. The words *over my dead body* were not spoken aloud but hung in the air like an overripe ham from a ceiling hook.

"We think," said Elizabeth, smiling sweetly, "that it would be an excellent idea, Ursula, if my lord of Leicester's generous gift could be signed over to Pen at once, and if you took the wench north to inspect it. You could look for a husband for her in that district—and while you are about it, you could visit Mary Stuart. We can arrange that Sir Francis Knollys, who has charge of her, will admit you, though I shall tell him only that you and she have met before, and that since you chance to be in the district because you are accompanying Mistress Penelope, I wish you to present my compliments to my cousin."

"I see," I said uncertainly. "Or—do I?"

"Not yet but I am about to explain," said Elizabeth. "In fact, Ursula, I want you to pass a confidential message to Mary Stuart, from one queen to another. I said confidential—it's more than that. It's personal—on an unofficial level, if you understand me."

I did. There are strange rules in the world of diplomacy. A

message passed on by an official personage may be confidential, but it is not personal. *Personal* means a far greater degree of secrecy. *Personal* means that no one will ever acknowledge that the message was ever passed at all.

"I know of it," said Cecil in a low voice, "and so does Leicester here . . ."

"Because I trust your discretion as I trust my own," said Elizabeth. "And the same applies to you and your husband, Ursula. But I wish the matter to be known to no one else, not even to Knollys. He is a man with opinions of his own and they are not the same as mine. He will obey orders, but a man carrying out commands he doesn't agree with can dilute the message without meaning to. A mere tone of voice can make a difference sometimes. So, you will be my mouthpiece instead, Ursula," said Elizabeth. "Cecil advises it, and I have agreed."

I glanced at Hugh but he was looking at the queen. His face told me nothing. "The message has to be by word of mouth, I take it, ma'am?" I said. "Nothing written down?"

"Exactly," said Elizabeth. Her eyes met mine again and held them. "There will be an inquiry," she said, "into the facts of how Henry Lord Darnley, the husband of my royal cousin Mary Stuart, met his death. We have received an emissary from James Stewart, Earl of Moray, her half brother and at present the Regent of Scotland, requesting us to hold such an inquiry and we can scarcely refuse him."

"The request is reasonable, in the circumstances," said Cecil.

"But . . ." Elizabeth's gaze was still fixed on mine. "There is a difficulty. Any such inquiry could well turn into something very like a trial. Representatives sent by Moray will attend and may demand that Mary give evidence herself and allow herself to be questioned. This must not happen. Knollys, who is an honest man but doesn't have the cares of kingship, believes that Mary ought to testify on her behalf to clear her name, but he is wrong. She must not. Mary is an anointed queen and if a monarch is treated like a subject and questioned like a felon, then it can happen to any monarch—especially to one who permitted such a thing to be done in the first place. That is the message you are to

take privily to Mary, Ursula. Tell her from me, her cousin, that the inquiry will probably have to proceed but that she must on no account whatsover agree to testify in person or to be questioned. That is all."

She smiled. "We will not demand an answer now, this moment, Ursula. Think about it." Her gaze moved to Hugh. "You must think about it, too. You and your wife must discuss it. Ursula can give me your answer tomorrow."

2

The Unlikely Quarrel

Dudley remained with the queen but Cecil left with us. As we threaded our way through the crowded gallery, he said softly: "Come with me to my study."

At Richmond, Cecil always used the same room for his work. Its square leaded windows overlooked the river, and the bright ripples made reflections on the ornate ceiling, where Tudor roses, painted red and white, were carved into the beams. Cecil went to sit behind his desk, waving us to a couple of other seats.

Without preamble, he said: "This business of Mary Stuart is a nightmare. No one invited her to England! Her presence could damage England's security and our relationships with other countries. She's a most embarrassing nuisance." We couldn't help looking amused and Cecil in turn resorted to grim humor. "She's like a drunken relative, arriving uninvited at a gathering where the host is trying to impress a visiting bishop or his daughter's future in-laws!"

Hugh said: "We live very quietly and have only a superficial knowledge of what happened to Queen Mary's husband. Gossip says many things and all of them may not be true. Can you enlighten us?"

"I trust so," said Cecil. He paused for a moment, and his eyes became remote. When they focused on us again, their expression was very grave. "It's an ugly story. Very ugly. No one could have foreseen such an appalling outcome to that marriage. It should have been a good political match. Henry Lord Darnley was descended from King Henry the Seventh, just as Elizabeth and Mary both are." We nodded. "It began well," he said. "It produced a son, of royal descent on both sides, who may one day be Elizabeth's heir. It should have been a safe match, too, because we have the young man's mother here in England to discourage him from any ideas of helping Mary to invade us.

"And then," said Cecil grimly, "what happens? He turns out to be dissolute and murderous. The gossip you have heard included the killing of David Riccio, I take it?"

"One of her secretaries," I said. "And a good musician, too. Yes. I met him when I was in Scotland. He struck me as a harmless little fellow. What we heard was that Darnley and his men burst into one of the queen's supper parties at Holyrood, where Riccio was one of those present, dragged him out screaming, and slaughtered him, and threatened Mary's own life."

I hesitated and then added: "I'm fairly sure that the supper room was the one where I once attended a gathering. It's quite small, intimate. When I saw it, there were wall hangings of red and green, and a fire in the hearth, and . . . there was music," I said in a low voice. "Riccio was playing the lute. Darnley was playing a spinet. They were accompanying each other, like friends. It was *all* friendly, almost domestic. I can't imagine it as a scene of carnage. And to think it was Darnley who . . ."

"Darnley was a fool and a villain," said Cecil. "He may have had ambitions to become the widower king of Scotland. That murder could have been aimed as much at Mary as at Riccio. She was about six months pregnant at the time. The shock could have caused a miscarriage and quite possibly killed her. I have eyes and ears at the Scottish court. . . ."

"According to Ursula, you have eyes and ears everywhere, Sir William," said Hugh.

"I make sure of it," said Cecil candidly. "My informants in Scotland reported to me that some of the Protestant nobles had convinced Darnley that the queen was having a love affair with poor

David Riccio. It was also reported to me that when the plot was first laid, Darnley actually wanted Riccio to be killed before the queen's eyes, though the other nobles, at least, had the decency to say no, he must be dragged out first. Even so, I believe the first dagger blow was struck in her presence. After the murder, Darnley panicked and seems to have thought that the nobles meant to kill both him and Mary and then rule Scotland themselves. Mary apparently agreed with him. She somehow came to terms with Darnley and they fled from Edinburgh together. I daresay she couldn't have escaped without his help. But she had had enough of him and up to that point," said Cecil, "one can sympathize with her. *But...*"

Hugh said slowly: "Darnley was assassinated, and the rumor that we heard points the finger at Mary. By the sound of it, she had every reason to want to get rid of Darnley."

"Quite. No one could have blamed her for seeking an annulment," Cecil said, "and she could have got one. She and Darnley were cousins and she married him without a papal dispensation. Annulment might have made their son illegitimate, though I should think that a way round that could have been found. Popes can give dispensations for other things besides the marriage of cousins. Better still, she could have charged Darnley with treason, and got rid of him that way. The killing of Riccio virtually in front of her when she was far gone in pregnancy *does* look like an attempt on her life and that would indeed have been treason. Annulment or arraignment; no one would have questioned either. And either would have been legal, correct in law. But murder—the murder of a king and a husband—and in such circumstances as these: that's different."

"Just what were the circumstances?" asked Hugh. "It was in Edinburgh and involved an explosion but we know little more than that."

"I can tell you the rest," said Cecil. "And as I said, it's an ugly tale. Darnley had been ill—probably with the French pox. He'd been consorting with whores. He was recuperating in a house in Edinburgh, a place called Kirk o' Field. He'd rented it himself, to convalesce in—it seems that he was nervous of entering any stronghold controlled by any of his wife's noblemen. I daresay he had his reasons, and a guilty conscience may well have been among them! At any rate, there he was, on the night of Sunday the ninth of February last year. Queen Mary had been with him part of the time but that evening she was at Holyrood at the wedding celebrations for one of her servants and stayed overnight. In the small hours of the morning, there was an explosion at Kirk o' Field. The house was blown up. Presumably the intention was to encompass Darnley's death. However, someone or something must have warned him, because he tried to escape, along with one servant . . ."

Cecil was a statesman, a man of dignity, and in the general way, his way of talking was calm and restrained. But beneath that controlled exterior were depths of emotion and imagination. He would not have been so able a statesman without them. Elizabeth knew them and drew on them. We experienced them now. Using words as a painter uses a brush, he created for us a picture, a dreadful picture, of that night at Kirk o' Field.

It was especially clear to me because I had met Darnley. I knew that he was not a pleasant young man, far from it. But I also knew that he was young. He had been still no more than twenty-one when he died, barely out of boyhood, and therefore inexperienced. It was unlikely but still possible that, had he lived longer, he might have learned from his mistakes. But he never had the chance.

Cecil made us see him—roused, probably, from his first sleep, by a frightened servant "who had either found barrels of gunpowder and a waiting fuse in the cellars of the house, or else seen unknown men gathering in a secretive way nearby. There certainly *were* men nearby, as you'll hear," Cecil said.

At any rate, whatever his servant told him must have terrified Darnley, for he got up so quickly that he didn't even put on a cloak though the servant had brought one, and the season was February. Darnley had been ill; he must have been shaky through weakness as well as fear. His man helped him to get out through a window. "The fellow must have brought a rope. He let Darnley down on a chair attached to the rope," Cecil said. "Those things were found afterwards."

The servant had got down to join his master somehow, and then the two of them fled through the garden in a state of panic, Darnley still wearing only his nightgown.

"A February night in Scotland is likely to be chilly, even for a fit man, which he wasn't. If he didn't even stop to throw his cloak round him, he must have been desperate," Cecil said.

I could believe it. I imagined the boy who had thought himself the King of Scotland, running for his life across the wintry grass in the darkness, gasping for breath, his teeth chattering from a mixture of weakness, cold, and terror.

Running straight into the arms of the assassins who were waiting to make sure that he should not escape.

"There were some women living in a house close to the garden," Cecil said. "They heard Darnley scream out to someone to pity him, for the sake of Jesus Christ who pitied all the world. The scream ended in a choking noise and what sounded like a struggle. The men who caught him strangled both him and his servant, and while they were doing it, the house blew up. The fuse was probably lit while Darnley was getting out of the window. The explosion killed some other servants who were sleeping in the house. The roar of it, and the flames going up, fetched a crowd to the scene and the bodies of Darnley and his man were found."

There was a silence. Then Cecil said: "When you were in Scotland, Ursula, did you encounter the Earl of Bothwell, by any chance?"

"James Hepburn. Yes," I said.

"He's the nobleman most strongly suspected of having arranged the murder," said Cecil. He was once more the dignified statesman. "Possibly with, possibly without, Mary Stuart's knowledge. Either way, it was hardly wise of her to marry him shortly afterwards. She claims that he abducted and ravished her and more or less compelled her to marry him, but there are strong rumors that she consented to the abduction and all that followed. The Scots people rose up against both of them." The statesman allowed himself a little dry wit. "Bothwell has fled overseas and *we've* got Mary and, as I said, it's a nightmare!"

Hugh inquired: "Is she a prisoner or a guest?"

"Half and half," said Cecil. "But I can tell you this—the nightmare isn't going to go away. Whatever the outcome of this wretched inquiry, or trial, or whatever it's called, we have no jurisdiction over her. She is, as Elizabeth says, an anointed queen. When it's finished, we shall be left with exactly the same set of alternatives as we have now and I don't like any of them! For one thing, if her name is cleared, she will ask us to raise an army to put her back on the throne of Scotland. That's out of the question, to begin with."

"Why?" asked Hugh..

"We don't *want* her back on the Scottish throne!" said Cecil irritably. "Innocent or guilty—and think what she's guilty *of,* if that's the case!—she's still Catholic! We're surrounded by Catholic nations as it is. There's Spain—and they rule the Netherlands as well—and there's France. We need a Protestant Scotland. We lost it the moment Mary landed there and now we've got it back and we're not going to let it go. Just now, her half brother James Stewart, who is Protestant, is ruling Scotland in the name of Mary's infant son, and rearing the child to be a Protestant, too. Elizabeth *cannot* back a Catholic ruler against a Protestant one. She might as well cut her own throat and be done with it!"

Hugh said soberly: "Today we saw Lord Herries, who is apparently Mary Stuart's representative, deep in talk with the Spanish ambassador—almost holding on to his sleeve to make him listen."

"Did you now? I'm not surprised. He no doubt wants Spain to make representations on her behalf if not to send an army to rescue her! I trust De Silva has more sense than to listen. In one way," said Cecil thoughtfully, "the suspicion of murder is a useful smear on the lady's reputation."

"What are the other alternatives?" I asked.

"Hah! One is to pass Mary on to her relatives and in-laws in

France. It was unlucky that her first husband died. She would have been happy as Queen of France and much less trouble to us. I'm surprised she didn't go to France in the first place, and the probable reason why she didn't makes my skin prickle. She really does believe that Elizabeth wasn't born of a legal marriage and that she herself is the rightful Queen of England. She may have had fantasies about coming here to claim her own. However, since she is here, we're not going to let her change her mind and slip off to France. We don't want her reinstated with the help of a French Catholic army, which would then be sitting on the other side of a land border instead of a nice width of English Channel and beautifully poised"—here Cecil waxed sarcastic—"to invade on behalf of poor dear Mary, cheated out of her right to the English crown by a heretic usurper! Need I write it on the wall in letters of fire? *We don't want Mary back on the Scottish throne.* Which leaves us the only other option: to keep her in England as—well, you put your finger on it, Master Stannard. As a cross between a guest and a captive. We can't set her free within England in case she escapes to France. I wouldn't put it past her to try. *That's* why we've shifted her to Bolton Castle. It's well away from the sea and I've ordered her to be kept close. Just in case."

Another silence fell.

Then Cecil said: "Mary is said to have a beguiling nature, as well as a superb head of red-gold hair. I understand that she cut her hair when she escaped from Scotland and that when Herries first brought her to England, he tried to hide her identity, but her hair gave her away, even though it was short: that and her height."

"They're both striking," I agreed. It was a long time since I had seen Mary, but I could remember well enough what she looked like.

"Herries took her to a friend's home," Cecil said. "Curwen, that was the friend's name. Herries put it about that she was an heiress that he had kidnapped from Scotland and brought south to be married to Curwen's son. But there was a man in Curwen's household who had been to Scotland and seen her. He recognized her at once. She's obviously a memorable woman. Which is another reason why I am determined that she mustn't be allowed to come here to work her wiles. I doubt if she would beguile Elizabeth, but this court is full of men who are quite as susceptible to the charms of the opposite sex as your ward Penelope is, Ursula. It isn't only the fact that she is suspected of husband-murder that convinces me she should be kept at a distance!"

He paused and then added: "As I mentioned just now, when we were with the queen, I have even worried about Sir Francis Knollys. I would have said that he was as impervious to the likes of Mary Stuart as a man can well be. He's no callow stripling. He's in his fifties! But in reports he has made to us, he expresses rather too much admiration for her. He calls her a notable woman, bold and pleasant. I'd replace him except that I can't think of anyone *less* susceptible or more loyal than Knollys has always been! Elizabeth took the warning to heart. God! Why couldn't the Scots keep hold of their prisoner? But all the same . . ."

Again he paused, with the anxious furrow between his eyes deepening to a fold. "I have to say," he told us, "that I am myself not easy in my mind about the rightness of keeping Mary captive when it may well be that the inquiry either clears her or is inconclusive. The last is most likely. Moray has sent me some letters said to be love letters from Mary to Bothwell, but even if they are, they don't actually order Bothwell to blow Lord Darnley up. They contain some suggestive phrases—*very* suggestive—but not an outright command to kill. I wish they did! I wish I knew the truth. It would clear my head. When you go to Yorkshire, Ursula, I have an errand of my own for you. This, too, is confidential—above all, nothing must reach the ears of Herries. Mary must not be put on her guard. I want you to talk to her, Ursula, as one woman to another, and try to reach the truth. Did she order Darnley's murder or did she not? And even if she didn't, if Bothwell was the chief agent, as I suspect, did she realize that and if so, did she marry him of her own free will?"

"But what difference will it make whether you know or not?" I asked. "The inquiry . . ."

"Will be hampered by lies, protocol, and the fact that the chief witness mustn't be allowed to speak," said Cecil. "By the queen's own wish, though I agree with her reasons and I haven't tried to dissuade her from sending the message you are taking to Mary. It will undermine the chance of getting anything worthwhile from the inquiry, though. It won't take place until October, so you have some time in hand for your tasks, but we need you to carry them out. Mary must be warned against unwise behavior, and as for me, well, frankly, I think we shall end up keeping her as a semi-prisoner for life and I'd feel a great deal happier if I knew for sure that she was as guilty as the devil."

We sent Penelope out to walk in the garden with Dale and Brockley, who had strict instructions not to let her speak to any man other than Brockley: neither page boy nor dotard or anything in between. Left in private with Hugh, I gave vent to my feelings. "It's outrageous! It's insufferable! They were planning it all along! No wonder we were called to Richmond! No wonder the queen and Cecil didn't feel equal to making Pen behave! She was the excuse to get us here and now she's an excuse to send us north. *And* they're taking it for granted that we'll go! *When* you go, Cecil said, not *if* you go! You heard him!"

"My dear girl," said Hugh calmly, "why such a to-do? It's hardly a dangerous mission. You pass a perfectly respectable message by word of mouth, to Mary from Elizabeth, and get her to talk to you and see if anything emerges that might interest Cecil. You also have a good chance of getting Pen off your hands. It all seems quite reasonable to me."

"Not a dangerous mission," I said exasperatedly. "That's what I'm told, every time. Just go to a Welsh castle, Ursula, and see if you can get the castellan to talk to you about his mysterious scheme for becoming wealthy: that was one splendid example of a safe errand for me. I hardly get there before I'm stubbing my toes on a corpse in the dark, and then I'm accused of murder and bundled into a dungeon myself!"

"Ursula . . ."

"You have only to deliver a private letter to the Queen of France: that was another one. The next I know, I'm escaping from a burning inn, and this time the poor soul who finds herself in the dungeon is my faithful, innocent Dale! That abominable priest Wilkins would have burned her alive if he had had his way. I'll never forget having to leave her there, clinging to the bars and gazing after me. In bad dreams, sometimes, I still see the terror in her eyes."

"Ursula . . . !"

". . . and you know what happened to me in Scotland, and what I had to do to escape. You know how often I have been used, by the queen and by Cecil, as a pawn. Even my daughter, Meg, has been used as a pawn! I want no more of it! Pen must manage without her dowry. She . . ."

I had been striding about the room, working myself into a fury. From the chest on which he had seated himself, Hugh said fiercely: "You are behaving like an angry lioness in the royal menagerie, pacing back and forth inside your cage! Sit down!"

Turning to him, I saw that he was angry. I had never before known his anger to be directed at me. The coldness in his eyes was frightening. I subsided onto the edge of the bed.

"I know all about your past adventures," said Hugh. "You've told me. You've told me about Wilkins. Now listen. Dr. Ignatius Wilkins would have liked to see the Inquisition back in England. Well, Ignatius now is at the bottom of the North Sea. His rib cage is covered with sand and weed and small fish swim through the eyeholes of his skull. He's dead. But what he represents is not. The Inquisition thrives in Spain and its tentacles will come coiling into England the moment a Catholic ruler sits upon our throne. And here, in Bolton, is Catholic Mary Stuart, who believes that the English crown belongs to her. That woman is as dangerous to England as the gunpowder in Kirk o' Field was to Darnley."

"I know! I know! And that's another thing. I've met Mary. I can't . . . I just *can't* believe that she conspired to commit a murder like the one Cecil's just described to us. But if she did . . . all right, however unreasonable you may think me, I just don't want to know!"

"That won't do. Hiding from the truth is never a good idea. Listen to me. Elizabeth is right. If Mary lets herself be ques-

tioned in public, it would set a perilous precedent. One foolish
queen could drag another down. And one pretender to our
throne, here in our midst, could be a focus for serious trouble.
We *need* to know whether or not she's guilty. The chances are
that she is, and just knowing that would go a long way towards
drawing her fangs."

"Well, I don't want to be the one who finds out!"

"Someone must, and who better than a lady she has met
already, who can talk to her and lead her to talk in turn? And is
used to working by stealth. It has to be done by stealth. Cecil can
hardly write and ask her! *Most honored lady, would you be kind
enough to tell me whether you did or did not have gunpowder planted in
the basement of Kirk o' Field on the night of the ninth of February 1567?*
Can you imagine it? That's better." I had emitted a snort of
laughter. "What are you afraid of?" Hugh asked me. "You might
find out that she's innocent, and by the sound of it, that would
please you, though I doubt if it would please the queen and
Cecil. But if she's guilty, well, as I said: hiding from the truth is
foolish. And you're *not* going into danger. Yorkshire isn't a foreign land . . ."

"Isn't it? Listen, Hugh. When I went to Scotland, I was nearly
married off by force because in Scotland, these things happen.
From what Cecil said today, they seem to be taken for granted in
the north of England as well! He said someone in Curwen's
house recognized Mary, not that no one could believe in the
story of a kidnapped heiress! The north *is* a foreign country and a
barbarous one, as far as I'm concerned."

"You are my wife now and in no danger of a forced marriage."

"Quite. I'm your wife. Most men wouldn't want their wives
rushing the length of England to do the work of a spy. And it will
be too hard on you. The ride will be so long . . ."

"Much too long," Hugh agreed. "Even the ride to court from
Hawkswood has left me feeling I've got rigor mortis before I'm
dead! I can't come with you. But you could send Brockley to
Hawkswood to fetch Meg and Mistress Jester, and then you
could all travel to Yorkshire as a family party. It will look all the

more innocent and Mistress Jester will help you keep an eye on Pen. You dislike being away from Meg, I know. Well, you need not be."

"But I shall have to leave you behind!"

"I shan't wither away because you're absent for a while. How do you think I managed before we were married? I daresay your Gladys Morgan will make me up a potion if I fall ill."

"Oh, Gladys!" I snorted.

Gladys was a terrible old crone whom I had once rescued from a charge of witchcraft and now kept about my household. She was gifted at making medicinal potions but she was a most ill-natured creature and liable to curse people she disliked and I lived in fear that her curses and her potions between them would one day bring another charge of witchcraft about her ears. I hoped I would be able to protect her until she died of natural causes but she was a constant worry to me.

"So," said Hugh. "You will go north."

"No," I said obstinately. "I don't want to. I don't *want* to."

"You sound like a spoiled child."

"That's not fair! Haven't you listened to me? I *said*—I've been used as a pawn, over and over, and I've seen others used too, and I want no more of it. I don't believe people when they say that it's quite safe. They *always* say that and it's *never* the truth. I don't want it, I tell you! I don't want to leave you. I don't want to investigate Mary. Don't make me go. Hugh, don't say I must go!"

His eyes were still bleak. I began to cry helplessly, impaled on that implacable gaze like a moth on a pin, furious with him, yet hating the thought of leaving him, of traveling far away without him, to a place I feared, to perform tasks I resented.

At that moment I loathed Cecil and loathed the queen and Hugh himself bewildered me.

"I can't understand you!" I said. "We've never quarreled before and now—to quarrel over *this*! Most husbands would be indignant if their wives went off without them, on secret missions for the queen and her Secretary of State! Most men would say it was unfitting, that a wife's business was to look after her husband and her household. But you . . . !"

Hugh slipped stiffly off the chest and came over to me. He sat down beside me and put an arm over my shoulders.

"Hush, now. It is only a journey within your own land, to hold a few conversations with a woman you already know, and at the same time to settle Penelope into a marriage, if a suitable man can be found. There is no need for all these tears."

"It's such an incredible thing for a husband and wife to quarrel *about*!" I wailed.

"You are an unusual woman, Ursula, and I, perhaps, am an unusual man. Most of the time, for instance, I'm unusually tolerant of other people's beliefs. But not when when they threaten the stability of the realm, and that could well be the case with this Mary Stuart. And when the realm needs to be protected, anyone who can help should do so. That is our duty."

"My duty, you mean."

"In this case, yes."

"One of the reasons why I married you was to escape from being a pawn for Cecil and the queen, to escape from secret missions. Now you want to throw me back into the arena, into the teeth of danger!"

"What danger? Really, Ursula, don't be so dramatic! I'm not Nero, throwing Christians to lions. You're going to visit your ward's dowry lands and pay a gracious call or two on a . . . a royal lady in Bolton Castle. That's all!"

I stopped crying, but sat dejectedly on the bed, my gaze on the floor. He didn't understand, or wouldn't, and he wasn't going to give in. I knew it.

"Ursula . . ." I looked up. His eyes were kinder now, but there was no yielding in them. "You have to go," said Hugh. "How can you refuse? Both of these errands need to be completed. Cecil is relying on you and so is Elizabeth. And she is your sister."

3

A Wild and Lawless Land

It was true, though few people knew it. From the start of our marriage, however, I had wished to have no secrets from Hugh and had sought the queen's permission to tell him that my father, the lover my mother would not name, had been King Henry VIII.

When she knew she was pregnant, my mother had left her post as one of Queen Anne Boleyn's ladies. She kept the secret of my paternity, I think out of loyalty to her mistress and to the king, wishing not to hurt the one or to cause scandal about the other. She had been sheltered, grumblingly, by her parents and later (just as grumblingly) by her brother and his wife, in our family home, Faldene, in Sussex. I had been brought up there.

While she lived, my mother did her best for me. She somehow succeeded in insisting that I should share my cousins' tutor and therefore their education; she had taught me needlework and music herself. She died, though, while I was still a young girl. In the days before King Henry closed the abbeys, I would probably have been packed off to a convent, but as it was, I just stayed at Faldene on sufferance, used—as I had said to Pen—as a dogsbody, running errands for my aunt by marriage, doing accounts for my uncle.

Until my cousin Mary was betrothed to Gerald Blanchard, and I caught Gerald's eye instead. We fell in love and fled together, to marry and to live in the Netherlands in the household of an English financier in the queen's employ, a man named Sir Thomas Gresham. When Gerald died, Gresham helped me to get a place at court.

I did not know for many years that my path to the queen's employment had been smoothed by something else as well—by the fact that although my mother had kept her secret, she had had a tirewoman who knew it too, and had made a memorandum that was found after her death many years later. Both the queen and Cecil knew what it contained. Eventually, when the time seemed right, they told me. I recognized at once that it was true. There had always been a curious rapport between myself and Elizabeth. I understood her, and now and then I caught myself behaving in ways that I had seen in her.

Such as, for instance, pacing up and down a room when I was in a temper, like an angry lioness in a cage.

The moment Hugh said *she is your sister,* I was defeated. That blood relationship made me the ideal choice to carry a message as private, as personal, as the one Elizabeth wished to pass to Mary. To Elizabeth, I owed the love of a sister as well as a subject. He was right. I would have to go to the north.

"Very well. I'll write to Pen's mother and tell her—well, that we're going to Yorkshire. She needn't know about Pen and Master Rowan! We'll pretend that we have provided the dowry. I think Ann will be pleased and I'm sure she won't object if I take Pen to see it. I'll carry out my errands," I said grimly. "If by then I've found a likely match for Pen, we'll stay on to conclude it. If I haven't, I'll bring her back. We'll leave as soon as possible. Let's get this over."

At least it promised to be an easier journey than the last northward ride I had undertaken, through the snow and fog of January. This was summer. The tracks were dry and fringed with cow parsley and meadowsweet, bramble and foxglove and wild dog roses. Bees murmured and grasshoppers creaked in the clover meadows, and the trees were heavy in leaf. Soft breezes whispered through them, which kept the days from being uncomfortably hot. Traveling was pleasant, except for the flies.

We were quite a large party. When Cecil summoned me to give me final instructions, I asked for a good escort.

"The north is lawless compared to the south," I said. "When I last went, Dale and I had only Brockley for escort and it was risky. I think we were lucky to get as far as Scotland unmolested! This time I have two young girls in my charge. Pen I have to take, but although I don't want to be parted from Meg, I'll leave her behind unless I'm sure we're well protected."

Cecil understood and conferred with Hugh. Brockley went to Hawkswood to fetch Meg and came back with two young men from the estate, a young groom called Harry Hobson (his father was Hugh's falconer) and a lad named Tom Smith, the son of one of Hugh's tenants. Hobson was fair, placid, and burly, while Smith was a dark and gangling fellow with an eye for the wenches and a cheeky tongue, but both were sensible lads, who had been taught swordplay. Tom had a sword supplied by Hugh, but Harry brought one that his grandfather had owned, a rather splendid affair with an amethyst in the hilt, probably loot from some bygone battlefield.

In addition, Cecil contributed two of his own men, a fatherly individual called John Ryder and a sturdy, sandy man named Dick Dodd. I already knew them and had always liked them. Ryder was completely gray by now, but seemed as fit as ever and was pleased to meet Brockley again, for they were good friends. With these four men and Brockley, I reckoned that we had an adequate retinue.

"The queen wants secrecy," said Cecil, "but that's a relative matter. Those in one's service have to be briefed to some extent. Ryder and Dodd are aware that you have a private errand to Mary Stuart, though they have no idea of its nature, nor will they seek to discover it. They are both trustworthy. I expect that you'll also tell Dale and Brockley a certain amount, though they should not know any details either. But avoid mentioning the errands to any of the others if you can."

Our company therefore consisted of five men and five ladies, the ladies being myself, Fran Dale, my good friend Mistress Sybil Jester, Pen, and Meg. We were all well mounted. Hugh and Cecil always made sure that their men had good horses. I had my own mare, a good-looking dapple gray called Roundel, a gift from Hugh. I had decided to breed from my former favorite, my pretty Bay Star. Her first foal, a charming filly, the image of her dam, was now a long-legged yearling and I hoped one day to present her to Meg, who was already a competent rider.

Meanwhile, Meg had her own pony, a new and bigger one, since she had just turned thirteen, and was growing. Pen, who also rode well, was on the black mare she had brought from Lockhill. Dale, however, disliked riding and these days was very wearied by it and was therefore traveling on Brockley's pillion.

Brockley's old cob, Speckle, was aging and was now keeping Bay Star company at grass. Speckle's replacement, Brown Berry, was heavily built and inconveniently hairy about the fetlocks (always a trouble to the grooms who have to keep their charges' feet clean), but more than equal to carrying double. Dick Dodd had a cob that was similarly strong, and since Sybil too was a poor rider, we put her up behind Dodd.

We also had Meg's merlin, Joy, full saddlebags, and two pack mules to carry everyone's belongings. I needed suitable wear for an audience with a queen, and since Pen might accompany me, I had provided the same for her. Also, in a fit of optimism, I had stowed Pen's very best blue velvet gown and a new lace-edged ruff in a separate hamper for use on her wedding day, if wedding day there should be. We were quite an impressive cavalcade, though hardly a speedy one, as Brockley remarked, just as we were starting.

"The village dominie who taught me my letters had traveled a bit when he was young, madam," he said to me in his calm voice with its slight country accent, and with no expression at all on his immobile face. His high brow with its dusting of gold freckles was unwrinkled, though he was over fifty. "He talked about it sometimes. He called them the three Perfidious P's— pillions, pack animals, and pets." There was just a trace of a smile in his blue-gray eyes. "Then he'd say that he learned to take two useful P's as a guide. *Porta parvum,* he'd say."

"Carry little? Did he teach you Latin, Brockley? I never knew that!"

"I don't know much, madam. Just a smattering. He did teach his class some dog Latin but I only had a year of it."

"You're full of surprises," I said, smiling. "Isn't he, Dale?" There had been a time when Brockley and I had had such a habit of exchanging expressionless pleasantries, that we had made Dale feel shut out and hurt her feelings. Nowadays, I tried to share the jokes with her. "I just wish," I said, "that we hadn't got to find our way."

Dudley had never visited his Yorkshire legacy and the agent he had sent to inspect it and make an inventory of its contents, six years ago when it first came into his hands, was now dead. Dudley still had the report and the inventory, however, and these he gave to me, along with a letter of introduction to the steward.

The name of the place was Tyesdale, in a parish called Fritton. It was the largest property in the parish. The adjoining estate, Fernthorpe, had once been bigger but the family had foolishly got into trouble back in the days of King Henry VIII and been involved in the Catholic rising known as the Pilgrimage of Grace. None of them had been hanged, but they had been heavily fined—or had negotiated a deal—and had paid by surrendering some of their land to the crown. Tyesdale was now the larger by a considerable margin.

"And has the better house," Dudley told me. "At some point, after the rising, the original house caught fire and the family couldn't afford to rebuild it properly. The replacement's not much better than a large hovel. Tyesdale, on the other hand, is said to have a good manor house. The steward there is called Magnus Whitely. By the way, the agent I sent didn't take to him. And so . . ." Dudley's smile was malicious ". . . I shan't send a courier ahead to announce your impending arrival. You can take him by surprise, Mistress Stannard."

To get to Tyesdale, our recommended route was north through the cities of Bedford, Northampton, Leicester, Nottingham, and Sheffield; then north-westward for about twenty miles to a place I had never heard of, called Glossop, and after that, to another place I hadn't heard of, a hamlet named Mossley. After Mossley, we must ask directions, for the way led across lonely moorland. We should try asking both for Fritton and for Tyesdale. In his report, the agent admitted to having got lost several times after Glossop, until at last he had hired a guide.

"On which I was reluctant to spend my master's money but it was better than wandering in the wilderness," he had written piously. Our journey was clearly going to involve a marked element of exploration.

Still, we did have good traveling conditions and plenty of daylight. The fact that I detested the whole business only made me more determined to get on with it, so I urged an early start each morning. I allowed a rest at midday and then I made us ride on through the later afternoon and early evening. We made the best speed we could and reached Sheffield after six days. The next day was Sunday and we rested, horses and humans alike.

The humans attended church and I instructed Brockley to see if he could find us a guide to see us to Glossop. On Monday, with a local hired man to show us the way, we set off again. The road was a well-frequented track with quite a good surface. It was then, though, that we noticed how the land was changing.

Pen commented on it first, which was a relief because it was almost the first spontaneous remark she had made since we started out. Although she had had kind and encouraging letters from both her mother and her brother George, expressing pleasure at her new dowry and thanking Hugh and myself earnestly for our supposed generosity, my ward had started the journey in a fit of sulks.

Pen, of course, knew nothing of the ulterior motives behind the long ride north. As far as she was concerned, she was being dragged to Yorkshire because she was in disgrace. Until we left Sheffield, Pen spoke only when she was spoken to, and then replied in the fewest possible words. Meg chattered all the time, agog with excitement, but even Meg could make no headway against Pen's obstinate silence.

What finally broke through to her, unexpectedly, was the way the land around us had risen into high moors and steep hillsides, growing wilder and lonelier, it seemed, with every mile we traveled.

"Are those mountains?" she asked suddenly, taking her left hand off her reins to point at a spectacular skyline. "And how can sheep graze on a slope like that? Do they have sticky pads on their feet?"

Everyone laughed. "Not they," said Dick Dodd. "Just surefooted, they are. My dad kept sheep, so I know."

"But don't they stray and get lost? The shepherds can't be up there with them all the time!"

Harry Hobson was a quiet fellow, but he had a jolly laugh on occasion and we heard it now. Our guide chuckled, too. He was one of those very tough elderly men who look as though they have been pickled in brine and then hardened by time like the ships' timbers so often used in house construction. His wiry pony looked similarly tough.

"True enough, lass," he said to her, "but t'sheep don't need all that much shepherding. They know their own ranges and t'owd yowes teach their lambs. They won't stray off t'land they know or get mixed up wi' other flocks. Shepherds mostly knows where t'look when they want to find t'flock."

He had a strong northern accent but Pen, inclining her head and paying close attention, managed to follow him and said: "But how clever! I didn't think sheep were as clever as that!"

A moment later, when the guide had gone ahead to lead us through a place where several tracks met, Meg said to her: "I couldn't understand him very well. What did he say, Pen?"

Pen told her, and then repeated her question about whether the hills could be called mountains. "Almost," I said. "But proper mountains are even higher. I've seen them in Wales."

After that, because having once emerged from her sulks, she couldn't very well sink back into them, Pen was easier company, though still at times inclined to be prickly.

"She'll get over it," said Sybil to me when we had found an inn at Glossop and she and I chanced to be alone together in the parlor. "New things to see and do will probably work wonders. I hope that we do find a good man for her in the north. It's what she needs."

"I hope she doesn't go and fall in love with Harry Hobson or Tom Smith," I said worriedly, but Sybil shook her head.

"So far it's always been older men, the kind she can look up to. Hobson and Smith are far too boyish for her—and well beneath her socially as well. She does have a sense of her position, you know. She's far from being a fool. She's just young, and at the mercy of longings she doesn't understand yet."

I looked at Sybil with affection. She was in her forties and by no means a beautiful woman, for the proportions of her face were wrong for that. They looked as though her features had been compressed between crown and chin. Her eyebrows swept out and upward too far beyond the corners of her eyes, and her nostrils were too splayed. Yet it was a face full of character, and the dark eyes under the remarkable eyebrows were always kind. "You understand young girls," I said.

"I have a grown-up daughter," said Sybil simply. "You'll be the same, when Meg is a little older."

The approaching voices of Pen and Meg, talking to each other, obliged us to change the subject. I said: "If we make good time tomorrow, I should think we would reach Tyesdale the day after."

Finding the way beyond Glossop presented a difficulty. Our guide had reached the limit of his range and could be of no more use to us, while the innkeeper was only mildly helpful. He was a stumpy fellow with a red face, probably due to too much of his own ale. Nay, he had no one he could spare to send with us in the morning; happen there was all to do for a fair in the town, wi' folk coming in from all about to sell their beasts and produce and he needed all his hands at home. Nay, he'd not heard of either Tyesdale or Fritton but he could direct us to Mossley.

After that we'd need to ask again. Road were rough but not hard to follow.

"Happen you miss your way, ask at a farm somewhere. They'll know at t'farms. Stop there overnight if you need to—no one'll refuse a drink of milk and a mouthful of bread and porridge. We're hospitable folk in these parts," he told us, giving us a grin from a mouthful of blackened teeth and leering at Pen. I saw young Hobson bristle. He seemed rather to like Pen, I thought, and sighed inwardly. It was bad enough worrying in case Pen fell for one of the men but I didn't want new complications in the form of them mooning after her instead.

We set off hopefully the next day, and at first all went well. Before midday we found ourselves in a village that wasn't Mossley but did at least have a modest inn where we could eat and rest the horses, and the landlord, more helpful than his counterpart in Glossop, assured us that we were going in the right direction. Mossley wasn't that much farther, we learned, and yes, he had heard of both Tyesdale Manor and Fritton Parish.

"Not that we see much of t'folk from those parts, but they come through now and again when there's a fair at Glossop." He gave us directions, though they were a trifle confusing. To make sure we were on the right road for Mossley, we were to watch out for a bewildering list of landmarks including a lightning-blasted oak and a ruined cottage. Once we were past Mossley, we should look for the outlaw Dickson Morley a-swingin' in his chains from an elm at a crossroad, and there the innkeeper thought that we should bear right—"half right, not full right; there's tracks for both"—and after that, it would be a matter of asking the way from whatever farms we came across. "But they'll knaw t'way, reet enough. Happen you'll be in Tyesdale by nightfall, God willing."

"Ah, but which night?" inquired Tom Smith pessimistically. I told him not to be depressing.

From then on, however, the road grew narrower and rougher, winding up and down the flanks of steep hills and moors. We found Mossley and rode through it, found the hanged outlaw and bore half right as instructed, but we were no longer making good time and Pen had fallen quiet again, and not, I thought, because her sulks had come back. This silence had a different quality.

As we made our way across a lonely moorland, so high and near to the drifting puffs of cloud that it felt as though we were riding across a colossal roof, I grew seriously concerned about her, and bringing Roundel alongside her, I said: "Pen? Are you feeling all right?"

"I've started my course," said Pen dismally.

"I thought so," I said. "I've seen you like this before. I'm sorry."

I had found out soon after Pen joined us from Lockhill that she was one of that unlucky band of women who have a truly difficult time once a month, when she was liable to violent cramps. I sympathized, for although I did not suffer in that particular way, I was prone to migraine headaches and they were more likely at those times. I knew that Pen needed rest.

I was anxious about the weather, too. The clouds were thickening and I had felt a few drops of rain. Ryder and Brockley now halted us, urging us all to get cloaks out of our baggage. Wet weather wouldn't be good for any of us, but above all it would be bad for Pen and also for Fran Dale, who took cold easily and especially when she was tired.

I spoke to Brockley and Ryder, telling them that Dale was exhausted and Pen not well, a polite euphemism that they immediately understood. Brockley pointed out a thin stream of hearth smoke in the distance, off to our left. "There's a house of some sort over there, madam. Maybe we could stop there overnight and finish the journey tomorrow."

We found a narrow track leading toward the place, but it was farther than we expected and the rain was coming down hard before we got there. When we did, what we found was discouraging. It was a thick-walled stone farmhouse huddling under the lee of a hill. Moss grew in the crevices of the stone and on the battered slate roof. The doors were low and the windows had shutters, but not a single pane of glass. "It looks more like a cave than a home," Tom Smith muttered.

It was true that the north country had a tradition of being willing to take travelers in. The inhabitants of the farmhouse didn't greet us effusively but they didn't turn us away either. Tom Smith's remark about a cave was fair comment, for inside, the farmhouse was so dark that we could scarcely see the faces of its occupants. One of them lit a frugal rush light, in fact, so as to take a look at us, and I sensed that this, to them, was a rare extravagance in the daytime.

Our hosts were the farmer—a short, unsmiling boulder of a man—and his wife, who might have been buxom if better fed, two grown sons with a marked resemblance to their father, and an aged woman whom the wife addressed as Mother. On account of the weather, the men had been occupying themselves in the byre, which virtually meant that they were in the house, for of its two ground-level rooms, one was a kitchen and living room combined, with pots over the fireplace and three hams hanging from the rafters, while the other was a byre for horses and cows. The men helped to make our animals comfortable there, while the women found benches and stools in the living room for us all, and the wife put a rack in front of her cooking fire and hung our damp cloaks on it to dry.

Presently, there was a meal, which we shared. The food consisted of a thick stew with beans and onions in it, and slices cut from one of the hams and fried. I noticed that between us all, we accounted for most of the ham in question, leaving the family only two. There was rye bread, too, with some kind of dripping. We were offered ale or milk to drink. It was all done with apparent willingness, and yet there was a dour edge.

"Happen thee've coom oop from t'south?" said the farmer, in a tone that implied faintly but unmistakably that he wished people from the south would stay there and not come knocking on his door and eating his provender.

I understood. This was a poor household. I told him that we realized that the arrival of ten people and their animals was a strain on their resources. We wouldn't have sought shelter there, except for the weather and the fact that Pen and Dale were too exhausted from traveling to go farther that day. I added that we would of course pay for our lodgings just as we would at any inn. The wife, who evidently had a friendly nature, demurred here but her mother dug an elbow into her ribs and her husband said: "Hush, lass," quite roughly.

Money, though, couldn't solve their immediate problem, which was to provide for us all and still have enough food left for themselves, until they could buy more from a market or a neighbor. We'd be off first thing in the morning, I promised, and when Sybil saw the younger woman getting out flour and yeast and preparing to make more bread, she offered to help.

The family, whose name turned out to be Grimsdale, were mildly curious when we asked about the way to Tyesdale. "Aye, I knows the place," the farmer said. "In Fritton Parish, that'll be— the next parish to this. There's no master at Tyesdale now, though; nobbut a steward. Owner's away down south."

I explained that Tyesdale had changed hands. Pen was now its owner, I said, and we had come to help her take possession of it. "And find her a Yorkshire husband!" piped up Meg, rather pertly.

"What—round here?" The elder of the two sons laughed. "Most o' t'folk in the big houses are Catholic hereabouts, even t'ones that pretend not to be. That won't suit, will it?"

"It will suit very well, provided there's no disloyal talk," I said.

The lad laughed again. "Well, there's the Moss boys, over north of Tyesdale, but they're promised to two of the Holme girls—your neighbors to the northeast, they'll be; all in Fritton Parish. There's three more Holme girls to settle and their mam reckons she's got first refusal of every likely lad for miles. If me brother and me were a bit nearer to gentry, she'd be sinking her claws in us. She could come to it yet!"

"Meg, you chatter too much," I said reprovingly. In my memory, something had stirred. "Holme—the family don't live at a place called Lapwings, by any chance, do they?"

"Aye, that'll be them. So thee knows them?"

"No, no—by chance, I've heard of them, that's all."

Heard was the wrong word. I had seen the name written down on a list. It was a list that had belonged to Mary Stuart, and three years ago, when I traveled to Scotland, part of my purpose had been to make sure that its latest version didn't reach her, for the names on it were those of families in England who supported her claim to the throne and would offer help if she ever made a bid for it; the more inaccurate her information on that subject was, the happier the English government would be. The updated list, happily, was destroyed before it got to Mary, but I had seen the original one, and since I had a good memory, I could recall many of the items on it. I could call up this particular entry in my mind. *Thomas Holme of Lapwings. Twenty miles from Bolton and about fifty miles from York. Not wealthy but would lend sword arm and horses.*

Ah, well. Mary, mewed up in Bolton wasn't likely to ask the Holmes to redeem their promise, and I needn't worry about them from that point of view. The locality didn't sound very rich in prospective bridegrooms, I thought, but we could cast more widely than the immediate district. I might hear of a likely prospect when I visited Bolton, and as I had said to Hugh, we could always take Pen home again if necessary.

The rain stopped after supper and the menfolk went outdoors again, to make use, presumably, of the light summer evening to finish whatever tasks the rain had interrupted earlier. The farmer's wife showed us to a room under the roof and we went to bed early.

We slept, all of us, in our clothes. The bedding consisted of fleeces with cloths thrown over them—on the grubby side and somewhat overwarm. Most of us fell asleep quickly, though, especially Dale, who was worn-out. Pen, however, was restless, and I too lay awake for some time, worrying about her.

In the morning, the weather was dull and misty but looked as though it would improve later. Pen, however, was pale with pain and unable to rise. There was no question whatever of getting her into the saddle that day.

"We can't all stay here," I said as we conferred in the attic chamber. "I suspect that these people just won't have enough to go round. Some of us at least have got to get out of the way."

"Fran and I can stay with Pen, madam," Brockley offered. "Fran will be the better of a full day's rest. Mistress Penelope will be better soon, I take it," he added in lower tones.

"She'll be all right by the end of today; she always is," Sybil said. "I'd stay, gladly, but if Dale is tired, then perhaps she should take the chance of breaking the journey. Brockley could bring them both to Tyesdale tomorrow. What do you think, Mistress Stannard?"

"That might be best," said Ryder, looking down at the stricken Pen in compassionate fashion. "Mistress Stannard can have Tyesdale made ready for you, Mistress Pen, before you get there."

I went down to talk to our hosts. It was very early still but only the farmer and the two women were in the kitchen. Their sons must be out on the farm already, mist or no mist. I explained that most of us were leaving at once but that one of our girls was too unwell to ride until the next day.

The women seemed sympathetic but worried. I suspected that the way we had accounted for nearly all of that ham had something to do with that. The farmer said bluntly that what that lass upstairs needed was to get herself up and on the move and that'ud shift the vapors fast enough. I myself wished that Pen could leave at once. I was sure her mother wouldn't have liked her to stay here.

However, there was nothing to be done. I worried about leaving Brockley to act as sole escort next day. One outlaw had been hanged but where there was one, there might be others. Grimsdale denied this quite passionately, assuring us that the district was quiet, but I decided to leave Tom Smith behind as well as Brockley. Grimsdale was visibly annoyed, even when I said we would buy a sheep from him, which he could slaughter for supper. "You've surely got one old ewe that's had her day!"

"Aye, happen I have, but . . ."

I insisted, however, and he subsided, grumbling. When we set off through the foggy morning, therefore, cloaked and hooded against the damp, we had an escort of three armed men—John Ryder, burly Harry Hobson, and Dick Dodd.

Three should have been enough but it wasn't. When the attack came out of the mist, there were seven of them at least. If we had had all our men with us, we would have had a chance. As it was, we were defeated from the beginning.

4

Abduction

We were riding at a walk, on a stony moorland track in a clinging hill mist that spangled our clothes and our horses' manes with gray droplets of water. Visibility was perhaps fifty yards; sufficient to show us the track stretching ahead and allow us to recognize landmarks. Master Grimsdale had told us more about these. After a couple of miles, he said, there was a fork where we must take the right-hand path.

"Though thee'd soon be put on t'right road again even if thee did go wrong. There's a farm or two over that way and a bit o' mining."

"Mining?" Ryder inquired.

"Aye. Sea coal," Grimsdale had said indifferently. "Not as much as on the east side o' t'Pennines—them's the hills away east of here—but some. At least, there's likely a lot more coal down deep where no one can get at it. Most o' the seams run off downward. I've an uncle who's a miner and that's what he says. But there's enough to make a living for them as likes t'notion. I'd sooner herd sheep up top, myself."

We had passed the fork, taking care to choose the right-hand way. We had seen no sign of mines or other farms, but could assume, we told each other, that we were on the right road and probably, if Grimsdale's directions were accurate, within four miles of our destination.

And then, without warning, there were shapes in the mistiness, shadowy forms that for a brief moment I took for upright stones or perhaps bushes, until I saw that they were moving. Then came hoarse shouts and a trampling of hooves, and out of the vapors burst a crowd of men on hairy ponies.

Sybil, on Dick Dodd's pillion, screamed. The merlin, which was in a hamper slung on a pack mule, bated inside the wickerwork with a furious beating of wings, and Meg's pony, which was alongside, plunged, frightened as much by the hamper as by our assailants. I caught at the pony's bridle, dragging it away from the mule. Our attackers were faceless beings with scarves wrapped around their faces and bodies swathed in thick mantles. They were also brandishing a haphazard but frightening collection of weapons. I glimpsed a sword or two, but most of them seemed to be carrying pikes and quarterstaves.

Our men had their own swords out on the instant but the sharpest blade is at a disadvantage when confronted with a longer weapon. A quarterstaff swept Harry Hobson clean out of his saddle and Ryder, lunging with his sword, had it struck from his hand by a pike. Dick Dodd, with Sybil clinging to his waist and still screaming, swung his horse between the attackers and the pack mules, which he was leading, and which he naturally assumed were the target. His blade was at the ready. But he and Sybil were ignored and so were the mules. It was my turn to scream as, too late, we saw that the enemy's real objective had nothing to do with ordinary robbery.

A bulky figure came up on the other side of Meg and hoisted her from her saddle, dumping her on his horse in front of him. In the same moment, Harry Hobson, who had scrambled to his feet and had kept hold of his sword, ran forward and lunged at Meg's captor. The man wheeled his mount deftly and then I screamed a second time for one of the swords I had glimpsed among our assailants was his, and he was swinging it.

It looked as though he were trying to parry Hobson's blade but if so, he missed. He struck Harry instead, between neck and shoulder. I heard the beginning of a hoarse outcry from Harry, but it was cut off short as his blood gushed out and a spatter of white bone came with it. Then his attacker wrenched the sword free and Harry fell, right in front of my mare, Roundel, who reared and squealed. Somehow I kept my seat though I let go of Meg's frightened pony. Meg's captor let out a shout, and then they were all spurring away, streaming off across the heather and into the grayness, taking Meg with them. I heard her shriek: "Mother, *Mother!*" and then she was gone.

"*Meg!*" I wailed. I tried to follow, but there were stone outcrops amid the heather and my good Roundel pecked and almost came down. She stopped short, trembling and sweating, and I found Ryder beside me, reaching for my bridle.

"Mistress, Mistress! There's Harry . . ."

"Leave me alone! I must follow Meg." I tried to push his hand off my rein, at the same time straining my ears, thinking I had heard voices in the fog, not far off, as though our enemies, or some of them, were still nearby, hidden only by the mist. But Ryder was turning Roundel, leading us back. Confusedly, I let him. Then he was helping me down and urging me forward, and a moment later I was kneeling at Harry Hobson's side.

He was dead. The sword had smashed into him at an angle that had nearly decapitated him and had gone like a meat cleaver deep into his breastbone. His blood was soaking into the wet heather. His eyes were open and glazed and his right hand was still clenched on the hilt of his own sword, the one with the amethyst in the hilt. That too was smeared with blood. He had died instantly. That at least was a mercy.

Ryder had disappeared, though I heard his voice close by, speaking to Dick Dodd. I could hear our horses, too, trampling and snorting, badly upset. I crouched, crying, dropping tears on poor Harry's body, and then stood up again and called into the fog: "But what are we to do? We can't wait! We've got to find Meg!"

Ryder emerged from the mist. "Dick and Mistress Sybil are holding our horses. Dick caught Meg's pony. But we'll not get them to come near the smell of blood. Quickly, now, mistress. I know we've got to get after Meg but first, can you help me move him? To shift him off the track and lay him beside that rock at the side of it?"

Numbly, I obeyed, though I shuddered, seeing my hands smeared with red and feeling the dead weight of Harry's body. It was warm, I remember, still as warm as it was in life. We laid him where Ryder said, and I closed his eyes myself. Ryder folded his hands.

"He's beside the path. We'll be able to find him again," he said. "I know we'll have to leave him while we go after Meg."

"She'll be terrified! Dear God, we can't even leave anyone here to guard him, because rescuing Meg may need all of us!"

"I know. God will have to take care of Harry while we're gone. See, I'll put his sword beside him. We know the direction they took. If only this mist would clear! Come, mistress, the horses are over here."

He led me away from Harry. We found Dick and Sybil holding the reins of all our mounts. There were tears pouring down Sybil's face, but she was trying to soothe the horses, who were wide-nostriled and showing the whites of their eyes, afraid of the scent of blood, which their keen senses had picked up, seeping through the mist. The two mules, equally uneasy, had been tethered by their leading reins to a couple of gorse bushes.

"They never touched the mules," Dick said in puzzled tones. "It's odd, for robbers."

"They wanted Meg," I said fiercely. I was already taking Roundel's reins from Sybil and reaching for my stirrup. "And they've got her. Come *on!*"

"Leave the mules," said Ryder, "and tether Harry's horse and Meg's pony with them. Damn this mist."

It was a bitter business. We had to pass close to where poor Harry lay and all the horses shied. It seemed cruel and disrespectful to leave him there, but there was nothing we could do for him, while Meg, small, terrified, and vulnerable, needed our help desperately.

I said: "They made off that way!" I pointed to hoofmarks in a patch of muddy ground where the heather was thin. Crouching forward, I peered down. "They've left a trail of sorts. But they'll be miles ahead by now! Though I did think I heard something not long ago . . ."

"Sound carries in mist," Ryder said. "Keep your own voice down, mistress. They can't see ahead any farther than we can and this ground nearly brought your mare down just now. They can't keep up any kind of speed for long. We'll catch them yet. The problem will be what to do then!"

"I'll grab that kidnapping brute by the ears and twist them off, that's what I'll do!" I blazed.

"I'll help you, mistress," said Ryder politely. Sybil said frantically: "Oh, why are we just talking? Poor, poor Meg!"

"Come on, then," said Ryder.

It was slow work, so agonizingly slow. I prayed for a wind to lift the mist but even when a breeze came it did no more than swirl the vapors. It thinned them a little but that was all. We went warily, leaning from our saddles to look for the spurt of thin earth, the crushed heather stems, the scattered pebbles, where the hooves of our assailants' mounts had passed. We rapidly lost all sense of direction. We eventually found ourselves on a track where the signs were clearer, and we put our horses into a trot, only to be delayed again when the path split into three and we found hoofmarks on two of them.

I sat on Roundel, seething with impatience, until Ryder and Dodd had concluded that one set of prints had rainwater in the deeper marks and therefore must be older. "It's the newer ones we want," said Ryder. "Come on. This way."

We pressed on. Every now and then Ryder raised a hand to halt us so that we could listen. We heard nothing, though, for a long time, not even the call of a bird. No skylarks; no peewits, no ravens. In such murky weather, even wild things are silent. The fourth time that Ryder stopped us, though, we did hear a sound. It was faint and we couldn't make out the direction very well but somewhere, a dog was barking. Then, distant but distinct, a door banged.

"We're coming to a house of some sort," said Ryder in a low voice. "I think I'd better get down and prowl on foot, mistress. If they've brought Meg here, we need to reconnoiter. Don't fear. We'll get her back, I swear it. Crazy! What do they think they're doing?"

"I expect they'll demand a ransom," I said shakily.

"If you want to be paid a ransom, you need to know who to ask for it and where to find them! I understood that no messenger went ahead of us to Tyesdale so how does anyone hereabouts know who we are?"

Sybil said: "We told the farmer yesterday and his sons were out after supper last night and again early this morning. It's such a poor household that maybe they'll seize any chance of making money. Maybe they've got friends who are outlaws. This seems a wild country to me."

"You've very likely put your finger on it, Mistress Jester," said Ryder grimly. "However, for the moment, I'll do some prowling, as I said. You'd better all wait here."

"Take care, sir," said Dodd. "There's a dog."

Ryder nodded, swung out of his saddle, handed his reins to me, and set off along the track on foot. He had only gone a few yards, however, and was still visible, when he stopped, raising a hand in warning to hold back and be silent. Then we saw what he had seen: a gray shadow on the path, coming toward us.

"It may be just a sheep," said Sybil uncertainly. Ryder made another *be silent* signal with his hand, but Sybil's voice had carried and been heard. There was a faint cry of *"Help!"* and the vague figure came on faster. Ryder ran forward to meet it. We heard him exclaim and then came another cry, this time with a sob of thankfulness in it. Then he was coming back, emerging from the fog, carrying something. He brought it straight to me and slipping from my saddle, I took my daughter in my arms.

For a good ten minutes, poor Meg just cried and shivered. We moved ourselves and our horses off the track so that the mist would hide us from anyone who might be chasing her back along it. Sitting on a stone outcrop, I tried to quieten her and at last, my dear daughter, who at heart was sensible enough, regained command of herself and tried to answer our questions. Unfortunately, there was little she could tell us.

"They just rode off with me. We seemed to go for miles and miles. I kept on struggling but I couldn't get away and in the end I stopped struggling, because even if I'd escaped, I'd just have fallen off and been lost on the moor in all this mist."

"But you must have got away in the end. I mean—we found you here, running back along the road," I said to her.

"No." She shook her head. "They let me go. No one's after me. We needn't have come off the track to hide. It's all right."

"Just what happened?" Ryder asked gently.

"We got to a house. A sort of farmhouse I think, but I couldn't see much, what with the mist. We went inside, into a passageway. There were oxen in a kind of barn on one side and a door on the other side that led into a room where there was a hearth . . . like the Grimsdales' farmhouse, only this was a different place . . ."

"Plenty of farmhouses like that, everywhere. Did they say anything to you? Or each other? Did you hear any names?" Ryder asked.

"I don't know. I mean yes, they spoke to each other but their mouths were muffled up with those scarves and they spoke— well, people up here almost speak a foreign language. I can't understand it," Meg said. "But they took me into the room with the hearth and one of them pulled my hood off and looked at me and then another one pushed forward and stared at me." A shudder went through her body and I held her more tightly. "I could only see his eyes but I didn't like them. He looked at me as if I were a *thing*. He got hold of my chin and turned my head this way and that and then he started shouting at the others. I understood some of what *he* said. He was saying I was too young."

"Too young! Bandits with a conscience apparently!" I said. "And then?"

"There was a lot of talking and muttering. I just stood there. I was so frightened. I was crying. Then I was taken outside again. The ponies were still there. One of the men got onto one and I was picked up and put in front of him, and off we went again, out onto the moor and onto the heather and then back onto a track—the one where you found me. I kept saying what was happening, where were we going, but the man wouldn't say anything until we got to the track. Then he stopped and put me down. He said something then. He pointed along the track and I *think* he said something like go that way in a straight line and I heard the words *last night*—I thought he might mean I'd get back to where I was last night. All I could do was run through the mist. I didn't know where I was. I was all alone and the mist was so cold. . . . Oh, Mother, I was so frightened . . . !"

"The bastards!" said Ryder. "Turning her out into the mist on her own! Anything could have happened to her! She could have wandered for hours; died of the cold; fallen into a bog!"

"Come," I said, getting to my feet. "We have your pony safe and sound, tethered some way back, with the mules, and . . . oh, my poor Meg. I'm so sorry. We'll have to tell you. Harry—Harry Hobson—he's . . ."

"He was killed," said Ryder somberly. Meg looked at him in horror and he put a gentle hand on her head. "We have to go back to where we left him. Then we shall have to take him with us, somehow. If we can wrap him so that his horse won't fret, we can put him across his saddle and I suppose then we'd better get on to Tyesdale if we can."

"Yes, let's get to Tyesdale before anything else goes wrong!" I said.

We retraced our steps with care but it was quite easy because now, at last, the mist was really lifting and besides, before long, the animals we had left tethered scented our horses, their erstwhile companions, and whinnied to them. Soon we were back at the place where we had left Harry. We made no mistake. His blood was still on the heather.

But of Harry himself there was no trace. His body, and the sword we had left lying beside it, had gone.

5

Tyesdale

"I knew I heard voices in the mist, when I first tried to go after Meg," I said. "I knew it! They left someone here to try and get hold of the body, if we gave them a chance—and that's exactly what we did."

"They weren't robbers in the ordinary sense," Ryder said thoughtfully. "We left the mules unguarded and still they didn't help themselves to them. It's odd. What do we do now?"

"But why take Harry away?" Sybil asked, distressed. "What was the point?"

Dodd said stolidly: "Very likely they never meant killing. But since they'd gone and done it just the same, maybe they wanted to get rid of the corpse. Be a bit difficult to make the authorities believe there's been a murder if we can't show them a body."

Sybil said: "But what *are* we to do? We ought to get Meg to shelter. She should rest."

And Meg, sitting in front of me on Roundel and still shivering, pressed her face against me and said: "I wish we could go home."

"There's no sense in going after them again, in search of Harry," Dodd said quietly. "Because they won't have taken him where they took Meg—at least, I wouldn't think so. I wouldn't, in their place. It must be their base—where they live. If they want to get rid of him, they'll bury him somewhere else, well away from anywhere that points to them."

I supposed that that made sense. Holding Meg close, I realized that I too was shivery, with shock and exhaustion. I too longed to go home. I thought of Hawkswood and Withysham, and above all, of Hugh. Then I thought of Pen and the Brockleys and Tom Smith, who were still with the Grimsdales.

"Should we go back to the Grimsdales?" I said. "If they sold information about us to someone then perhaps the others aren't safe there without us to back them up."

"If whoever did this killed Harry by mistake," said Dodd, "and stole his body to hide what they'd done, I'd reckon that they'll be a deal too scared to try anything else for a while. But I'll go back to reinforce Brockley and young Tom, if you like. I don't think that you ladies or little Meg should go back there, though. You should get to Tyesdale as soon as possible. Besides, the others are expecting to travel there tomorrow and find you there and the house ready."

"I agree," Ryder said briskly. "Yes, Dick, go back and make sure that the others are safe. But with your permission, Mistress Stannard, we'll press straight on to Tyesdale. It's our proper destination and once we're there, we're on home ground, so to speak. There's a lot to be said for that. That's my advice, anyhow."

I took it.

While we were talking, the mist had finally lifted, swept suddenly away by a strong, cold wind. Suddenly, there was blue sky above and we could see about us. Moorland spread in all directions, bathed in clear sunshine, though not as yet in warmth. The wind was chill and not in the least summery.

"I'll be on my way," Dick said. "I trust I'll be joining you at Tyesdale with the others tomorrow morning. I can find my way back to the Grimsdales, never fear. It must be less than three miles and I reckon I can see their hearth smoke from here." He pointed, and by shading my eyes, I made out the thin spire of smoke that he meant. He turned his horse and in a moment was cantering back the way we had come. He glanced back once to wave, and then was gone, over a crest of moorland and out of sight.

"We go the other way," said Ryder. "Mistress Meg, can you manage on your pony? The rest of us will each have to lead an animal—we've two mules and Harry's horse to cope with."

Meg nodded mutely and I set her in her saddle. The familiar feel of the reins in her hands seemed to encourage her, however. She sat up straight and gave me a pale smile. I took charge of one mule, Sylvia took the other, and Ryder took the reins of poor Harry's horse. We set off.

I hoped that we were going in the right direction, but fortune, at last, decided to smile on us. After a mile or so we encountered a couple of men, dressed in britches and sleeveless jerkins, tramping along with shovels over their shoulders. For some reason their clothes were dusted and their faces, hands, and arms were virtually blackened by what seemed to be soot. Ryder, coming up alongside me, said that they were miners. "That's coal dust. I've been north in bygone days and seen the like before. They'll be local. They'll probably know the way to Tyesdale."

They did, and once both sides had penetrated the difficult barrier of our respective dialects, they were able to tell us that we had only two miles to go and were on the right road. Soon after that, as we rode through a deep fold in the hills, we saw signs that the land was in use. Sheep were grazing on the slopes, and on the nearest hillside, I noticed old diggings, possibly attempts at mining, although by the look of them they had been abandoned some time ago, for the rounded humps of dug-out earth were covered now in grass.

Pressing on, we passed the mouth of a narrow vale that led away southwest and was filled by woodland, a solitary patch of thick green fleece in an otherwise open landscape. Then we were riding through cultivated land, with fields of oats and barley, divided by stone walls. The stone walls were sadly dilapidated and I clicked a disapproving tongue as we passed a barley field in which a broken plow was rusting in a corner.

If this were part of Tyesdale, then the place was sorely in need of a resident landlord, I thought. I was relieved, when at length we came in sight of a house, to see a paddock in which a gray cob and a mule were grazing and I noticed that they at least looked healthy. And then we were at the house itself.

I knew at once what kind of place it was. I had seen such buildings on my earlier visit to the north. This was a small northern manor house that had been built in bygone days with defense in mind. It had an encircling wall beyond which rose a lookout tower with a crenelated top, as though it were part of a miniature castle. The place even had a moat. We smelled it before we saw it, for it was stagnant, the surface more green weed than water. The drawbridge that must have been there originally, though, had been replaced by a permanent stone bridge, leading across to the gatehouse. This too was like a miniature castle entrance though the gate stood open, and no one came to ask our business. We rode straight in.

We found ourselves in a courtyard facing a solid, uncompromising house, with a windowless undercroft for animals and fodder storage, and steps up to the main door. The upstairs windows had been modernized, however. Once, they had probably been little more than slits, but now they had mullions and glazing, and were leaded in neat squares. The living rooms would be well lit.

Despite the lack of a porter, we were announced more than adequately by loud cacklings from the poultry in the yard and the noisy barking of two leggy gray dogs with menacing yellow eyes, which came galloping round the side of the house to inspect us. This brought a woman down the steps. She stared at us and then shouted at the dogs to be quiet, which they instantly were. She was small of stature and brick-red of face, with gingery hair escaping from an untidy cap, and her frankly grimy apron was tied on over a gown of a color that no one with a choleric complexion and ginger hair ought ever to wear, for it was crimson.

"Would this be Tyesdale?" Ryder called. She stared at us for a further moment before replying: "Aye, so it be!" and turned to dash back up the steps. She vanished inside, shouting: "Master

Whitely! Master Whitely!" A moment later, she reappeared with a man on her heels.

"There!" she said to him dramatically, pointing at us. "I told thee that my lord of Leicester 'ud be here one of these days and catch thee napping and now it's happened! Don't thee ever say I didn't warn thee!"

"I'll not say *that,* Mistress Appletree," he told her as he descended the steps, taking us in as he came. "It's been once a week at least these last three years."

This, presumably, was Magnus Whitely, the steward. He was a small man, plainly dressed in buff. He crossed the courtyard beside the woman and halted in front of us, brows raised inquiringly. He removed his cap courteously enough but his nondescript features—he had the kind of face and eyes that slip out of the memory the moment their owner is out of sight—were unsmiling.

"This is Tyesdale right enough," he said. "And who might you be?" His gaze traveled over us. "*Not* the Earl of Leicester, I fancy."

"No. Quite right, though I do have a letter of introduction from the earl." I had the letter ready in a pouch at my belt and now I drew it out and handed it to him.

The ride had calmed me. I still felt shaky, and the loss of Harry, whom I had gotten to know and like during the journey from Richmond, was like a dull ache inside me, but I was now able at least to appear normal. "We are sorry to arrive unannounced," I said. "The—er—decision to make the journey was taken at short notice and we had no time to send word ahead. My name is Mistress Ursula Stannard, and as you will see from the letter, Tyesdale has now changed hands. Ownership has been transferred to my ward, Mistress Penelope Mason. Mistress Mason was unwell on the journey and is resting at a farmhouse a few miles from here. We hope she will join us tomorrow. These people are my gentlewoman, Mistress Jester, my daughter, Margaret, and our escort, Master Ryder."

Whitely broke the seal on the letter and studied the contents. He looked up. "I *see.*" He had one striking characteristic and that was a mincing way of speech, with a trick of emphasizing words here and there, as if to make up for his unremarkable appearance. His accent was local but educated. "You all want to stay here, I take it?" He glanced at us as if counting heads and arriving at an unwelcome conclusion.

"Certainly," I said, allowing a slight chill to enter my voice. "The house is big enough, surely? When Mistress Mason arrives, there will be five more, as it happens. My tirewoman stayed with her, and three of our men to protect them when they follow us. This appears to be a lawless place! We were attacked on our way here!" I heard my voice quiver and controlled it with an effort. "And one of our number, a young man called Harry Hobson, was killed."

"*Attacked?*" Master Whitely looked astounded. "*Killed?*"

"Yes. Only a few miles from here," said Ryder briskly. "It's a long story. We shall need to send a report to the nearest place of authority and ask for some assistance. Not only was one of our men killed, but his body was taken away as well. And now, if we could dismount and come inside? Are there no grooms?"

While Ryder was speaking, the woman had been staring at us with her mouth open. She now recovered herself, however. "My man's somewhere about," she said and disappeared again, this time through a small door into the undercroft, returning a moment later with a broad, fair fellow, whose smile, I was glad to see, offered the friendly greeting that Magnus Whitely hadn't given us.

"This is Jamie Appletree," said Whitely. "And this is Mistress Agnes Appletree, his wife. She sees to the house. He'll help you with the animals. There's no staff at the house here except us three."

"What about the farm?" inquired Dick Dodd.

"Oh, the *farm,*" said Master Whitely sniffily. "There's a shepherd and a *handful* of men to work the fields, but they live in the cottages, half a mile off. If you'll get down and come inside, Mistress Appletree will see to some food for you." There is a surprisingly narrow edge between respect and insolence and he was right on that edge.

"I realize that our party will make extra work," I said as I dismounted. "Get more help in if you need it—perhaps the laborers have daughters or wives who would like to earn a penny or two?"

"Happen they would," Mistress Appletree agreed, clearly relieved now that we were talking of something that made sense to her. Her little red face, indeed, glowed at the notion of being given assistance. "I'll have a couple here by tomorrow, if thee can see they're paid right. Now, if thee'll come this way . . ."

As soon as we were inside, in the big, old-fashioned hall that was evidently the main room, Sybil took charge of Meg, found a settle on which she could rest, and tucked her up with cushions to lie on and a blanket over her.

Meanwhile, Ryder and I led Jamie Appletree, who looked as if he might be cooperative, to one side and asked him what we should do about reporting the attack on us. His recommendation was that we should apply at once to the constable in Fritton. "If he thinks fit, he'll send word to York, but it's him we ought to ask first." He offered to carry the message for us. "You'll be wanting Master Whitely to show you about t'place, no doubt."

Before I had even taken a glass of wine or shed my cloak, therefore, I asked Whitely for writing materials and was shown to his office, a cramped little room off the hall. Swiftly, I wrote a letter of explanation, sealed it, and handed it to Appletree, who departed with it at once.

I would have to send the news back to Hugh, as well, I thought, and he would have to tell Harry's parents, and it was a terrible thing that I couldn't even report that he had had decent Christian burial. But for the moment there was no more that I, or any of us, could do. I went to find Agnes. "We need food and drink," I said. "All of us." I had noticed that the interior of Tyesdale was far from satisfactory. I felt extremely tired, but before we could take our ease in this place, we would first have to inspect it. "After that," I said dispiritedly, "we would like to look over the house."

Dudley, of course, had never seen his legacy. I must be fair to

Dudley, though this wasn't easy, for I didn't like or trust him, an opinion shared by most of Elizabeth's council, and I knew that once at least he came near to betraying Elizabeth and all England with her. He was both ambitious and ruthless. Yet, by hindsight, I see that in the end he did Elizabeth more good than harm. If it was partly a case of knowing where his own best interests lay, well, never mind. She wasn't a fool. She knew him through and through, but she forgave him because for all his shortcomings, he was able to offer her the vigorous masculine friendship that she needed.

And for all his faults he wasn't shabby. He might well have had doubts about the steward, but if he had really known what Tyesdale was like, I don't think he would have handed it to Pen as a dowry.

Tyesdale, in fact, was in a deplorable mess.

Agnes brought us some ale and wine—it was unexpectedly good wine—and some food in the form of chopped ham cooked in beaten eggs, with bread on the side. I sat on the edge of Meg's settle to eat mine and watch her eat hers and drink her small ale. Afterward, I think we all felt better. Bracing myself for the effort, I got out the inventory that Dudley had provided and requested Whitely and Mistress Appletree to show us around. The degree of mess became instantly apparent.

The trouble was partly the lack of servants, of course. Mistress Appletree had obviously tried hard. Within the encircling wall there was a herb and vegetable plot, small and with very few herbs, but was properly weeded, and indoors, the floors were reasonably clean. The stores were low but there was a modest supply of salt and other foodstuffs, spare candles, and lengths of cloth and dyestuffs for making and coloring clothes and curtains at home. As I had noticed on arrival, however, most of the furniture was in a shocking state. Scratched tables, chipped benches, and wobbly stools had not been replaced; and the wall hangings were frankly moth-eaten.

We began the tour in the lookout tower. It contained three rooms, which Agnes had evidently decided were beyond her and had ignored. On the ground floor was a small, dusty chapel.

Here we found a gilded cross, a statue of a Virgin and Child in a wall niche, and a Latin Bible on a lectern. It was printed, but splendidly illuminated and probably valuable even though its leaves were spotted brown with damp. I fancied that there had once been a Catholic chaplain at Tyesdale. Indeed, when he rejoined us the following day, Brockley poked about in the chapel and in a cupboard found a cassock wrapped around a silver crucifix on a chain and a Latin prayerbook.

At the top of the tower was a music room and in between was a study. In them we found tables gray with dust, a lute and a spinet, both made useless by neglect and damp. Cobwebs festooned every corner. If cared for, the rooms could have been charming, which made their condition even sadder.

The big hall had a parlor adjoining it at one end. At the other was a small minstrels' gallery with the doors to the kitchen and to Whitely's office beneath it. The hall had probably been lofty to begin with but at some point an extra floor had been put in so that new rooms could be built above (as a result, the minstrels' gallery was now suitable only for rather short minstrels). A staircase led up from the hall, emerging into a passageway with windows at each end and doors leading to bedchambers, two at the back and two at the front. They were spacious and had been kept dusted; in fact, Whitely was using one of those at the back. The beds in the others were not made up, but each had a supply of linen in a window-seat chest.

A farther narrow staircase went on up to four small attic bedchambers under the slope of the roof. "Jamie and I sleep up here," Agnes said.

I led us back to the hall after that, because there, in addition to a scarred table and an array of battered-looking stools and benches, I had noticed a large sideboard. It was as scratched and unpolished as everything else, but I had been wondering what was in it.

Pulling it open, Sybil and I found silverware inside. We got it out for a closer look and compared it with the inventory. It hadn't been cleaned for a long time, and if the inventory was accurate, some of it was missing. "Where's the rest?" I said to Whitely.

"And *why* has none of this dreadful furniture or any of those out-worn hangings been replaced?"

Whitely was indignant. He couldn't, he said, *think* of taking it upon himself to authorize the purchase of new furniture or hangings unless the owner had inspected the old ones first, and as for the silver, what was in the sideboard was all of it. The missing items had never existed. Dudley's agent, whom he said he remembered very well, had been careless and apt to write things down twice.

"There never was but one of those ornate salts, Mistress Stannard. The old master wasn't such a wealthy man. The wealth of this place is in the sheep. And we *never* had but the half dozen silver candlesticks, not two dozen as it says here . . ."

I didn't believe him. It would be hard to prove that he had disposed of the absent items himself, but by this time I had taken in the fact that Master Whitely's plain buff garments were actually made of very good materials and had been cut by a highly competent tailor. A doublet that fit across the shoulders like a second skin was a telling sign. Like Dudley, I was beginning to feel suspicious of Master Whitely.

The inspection over, it was time to decide who was to sleep where. I chose one of the front bedchambers over the hall for myself, to share with Sybil. It was sunny and overlooked the courtyard. The rooms at the back also had a pleasant outlook, though, over the fields and moorland to the north and there was no outer wall at the back to interrupt the view. The wall we had seen on the way in only enclosed the courtyard and the sides of the house. At the rear, the house wall went virtually straight down into the moat.

Sybil and I helped Agnes to light a fire in the hall and put the bed linen to air, and we agreed with Ryder that when our party was reunited, he, Tom Smith, and the Brockleys should have the three spare attic rooms. Meg, by this time, had become restless and wanted to get up from her settle, so I set her to cleaning the surviving silver. A quiet manual occupation, I thought, might be steadying for her.

During the afternoon, the bright weather faded once more

and a rainstorm swept down. It cleared presently, however, and soon after that Jamie Appletree reappeared, accompanied by a large, loud-voiced man with a drooping ginger mustache and a workmanlike suit of russet brown, who announced himself as Master Toft, by trade a tiler, but for this year burdened with the duty of being the constable of Fritton, and what was all this about one of our men being murdered?

I looked at Master Toft and felt a terrible new weight of weariness descend on me. I knew his type. Constables are local men, usually with other trades to follow as well, who take on the task of upholding the law for a year or two, after which someone else replaces them. Some are good at the task, conscientious and intelligent. Some enjoy the power and become too zealous, arresting people for foolish reasons.

And some have too little experience of the world outside their town or village. They don't know what is important and what isn't, and automatically distrust all strangers, assuming that anything they say is only half as reliable as the testimony of local folk. They may be energetic but they're often ineffectual. On sight, I judged that Master Thomas Toft was one of that kind. And I was right.

6

Against the Wind

Jamie had taken the gray cob to Fritton. It apparently belonged to Whitely but was used by anyone who needed a horse, since Whitely himself spent most of his time at the house. Ryder borrowed it next, because our horses were all tired and he wished to show Toft the scene of Harry's death.

Ryder hurried Toft off straightaway and did not return until dusk. Ryder was visibly in a temper. Toft, unmoved, declared patronizingly to me that nothing had been found that could be investigated. He declined my request that he should speak to Meg about her kidnapping. "T'lass is back unharmed, and like enough they meant marriage, any road. That's nearly always the way of it and t'girls get husbands as good that way as any other." He then took himself off back to Fritton and his tiling business, and by that time, I was in a temper, too.

"The rainstorm did for us," Ryder told me bitterly, as we sat by the fire, glad of its warmth, for all that this was July. "The blood had all gone and even a lot of the hoofprints had been washed out. Toft, who is a complete fool, kept saying that if we didn't have Harry's body and there was no sign of bloodletting, how did he know Harry had ever existed? Well, we can all take oaths that he did and there are the Grimsdales and all the innkeepers between here and Richmond, but I don't think Toft thinks anywhere outside of Yorkshire really exists either!"

"The Grimsdales aren't outside of Yorkshire! Did you see them?"

"Yes, oh yes. And Mistress Pen is better and all the rest of our party will be here tomorrow. Dick's with them. Yes, the Grimsdales said they thought we'd had a third fellow with us when we set off in the morning, but they couldn't be sure. They hadn't counted the heads in our party and what with it being so dark inside their place . . ."

"Oh, for the love of heaven!"

"Quite. But that's what they said. At least, the men did. The women looked as if they might have said more, only they were too scared. The younger one did start to say something at one point but her husband told her to hold her tongue and not interfere in men's business. Toft, of course, thought nothing of it. That's the way these farming folk always treat their wives, he said, and it didn't mean anything. I thought it did, but . . . well, we went to other places, too, in the direction more or less that we went to find Meg. There're quite a few little farmsteads over that way; there's a sort of long valley with usable land in it—though not good land, by any standards—and farms, poor places, all of them, are dotted here and there. We didn't find anything suspicious in any of them. We didn't notice anything that might be a new grave anywhere, either. Toft says that unless we can prove to him there ever was a murder, there's not much he can do, and there have been no reports of robbers in this district since Dickson Morley. Why the devil he should think we'd made it all up, I can't imagine, but I really believe he does!"

I thumped an exasperated fist down on the arm of my chair, which creaked alarmingly. "So what next? What am I to write to Hugh about Harry's death? And what else can we do to find out what has happened to his body? I have all these other things to see to! I have to . . . to deliver a message to Mary Stuart in Bolton! And help Pen put this place in order and look for a husband for her and . . ."

Find out if the said Mary Stuart had tried to blow her husband up the February before last, as well! A hateful task and one which I couldn't for the life of me see a way of accomplishing. All this, and the disaster with Harry, too. It was too much.

I did not speak of that last errand to Ryder but he saw in my face that I felt as though I were being pushed beyond endurance. "Mistress Stannard," he said gently, "you should retire to your chamber. You need sleep. Mistress Jester and Meg are already asleep, I fancy."

"Yes. They went up before you came back."

"Join them. Things will look better in the morning."

That night, since it was our first in this unfamiliar place, I had sent Meg to share the same room as Sybil and myself. She slept well, to my relief. I slept soundly, too. I hadn't expected to, but sheer exhaustion saw to it for me. I can't say, however, that the outlook seemed any better when I woke in the morning. In fact, it seemed just as harassing as ever. I still had no idea what to do about Harry or how to carry out Cecil's impossible mission in Bolton. I felt as though I were struggling along, head down against a strong, cold wind.

Pen and the others reached Tyesdale by noon. I had sent Ryder back along the track to meet them and make sure that they found the way. They had, of course, already heard of Harry's death, and their mood was somber. Pen and Dale looked frightened, as well they might.

However, as it happened, there was something at Tyesdale to lighten the air for us all. Agnes Appletree had duly found a couple of girls and set them to cleaning the tower rooms. They were laborers' daughters, glad enough to earn a little and willing to work. "Feeb"—whose name was probably Phoebe though I never inquired into the matter—was only about thirteen and was lumpish and slow, almost to the point of being a lackwit, but wiry little Bess, who though so small was actually about seventeen, seemed bright enough. They both wore clogs all the time and we could tell from a distance whose footsteps were whose. Tom Smith, who had liked Harry well enough, but was too young and naturally lively to keep a sad face for long, found this amusing and said so.

"Feeb goes Clop, Clop, Clop," he said, "and Bess goes clip-clop, clip-clop. Don't you, Bess? If I nickname you Bess Clip-clop, will you mind?"

"Nay, I'll not mind. Been called worse than that when I annoy my da," Bess informed him with a grin.

Unlike Feeb, she didn't mind the Tyesdale dogs, either. I had by now made friends with the dogs and learned from the Apple-trees that their names were Gambol and Grumble. They weren't used for hunting, but were guard dogs and ratters. Feeb was scared of them but Bess liked them and said that they regularly sired puppies on her father's brindle bitch, Streaks. I gave her the job of feeding them.

Agnes chivvied the two girls cheerfully about and I had the impression that in contrast to Whitely, she enjoyed having some life and bustle about the house, to the point that she kept on for-getting that the rest of us were in a state of grief. I couldn't reprove her for that, for after all, she had never seen Harry, and if Tom Smith could smile then surely Agnes could.

For the time being, I decided, reluctantly and angrily, but of necessity, I must accept that I could do no more about Harry. Though I would find a way of inquiring further, somehow, sometime, I told myself. Information would reach me or I would stumble across something significant and I didn't intend to leave Yorkshire until it happened. It was plain that Ryder and Dodd felt the same.

Meanwhile, I must turn to my other tasks, whether I liked them or not. The one immediately to hand was Tyesdale itself. From the moment that Pen arrived, I had realized that the impe-tus for rescuing it would have to come from me. Pen, who was after all the official mistress of the house and should therefore be the one most concerned about its condition, wasn't interested.

Pen, in fact, had taken an instant dislike to her new posses-sion. She walked around it, wrinkling her nose with disapproval, and then told me bluntly that she thought it was a horrible place. She wanted to go home, to Lockhill or Hawkswood or

Withysham, she didn't mind which, as long as she didn't have to stay here. She didn't care if Tyesdale fell down around her ears; in fact she wished it would.

I sighed. Tyesdale was Pen's property and Pen was old enough to take charge. But now it seemed that I must shoulder the full weight of it, on top of all my other tasks. Well, I had better get on with it. I had brought a fair supply of money with me, but I would have to go into the Tyesdale finances, I thought. Dudley had told me that he had been receiving the profits from the wool and produce, and that he had allocated a sufficient sum to be kept back for the maintenance of the house and to pay its servants. I wondered how much of it had been used for that and how much had gone to Master Whitely's tailor.

In addition to all this, on our second night there, I sent Meg to share her bed with Pen, and Pen roused me at midnight because Meg was having bad dreams. I had to waken her gently and take her back to sleep with me. I had thought she was getting over her fright, but clearly it wasn't going to be as easy as that. During the night, she woke me twice more, crying out in distress, and I had to shake her back to consciousness and comfort her. I got up next morning feeling jaded. I hoped that I would at least find Pen in a more compliant mood but it was plain enough before we had broken our fasts that my irritating ward was still sulking.

And then, of course, the neighbors came to call.

7

A Surfeit of Company

The morning was bright and windy and I decided to try what fresh air and distraction could do for Meg. I called Brockley from the little chapel where he was interestedly peering into various cupboards and crannies and asked him to take her out for a ride. "Let her practice her falconry with the merlin, Joy."

Meg was nervous. "Suppose we meet those men again?"

"They sent you back," I reminded her gently. "I don't think you are in any danger. I'll tell Brockley not to go far from the house. See if you can bring down enough small birds to make a pie for supper."

Meg accepted that, and went out accordingly. I then told Whitely that as steward of Tyesdale, he should have made sure that the abandoned plow in the barley field was removed and would he do so at once, and after that I wrote a letter to Sir Francis Knollys at Bolton Castle.

I knew I should also write to Hugh but I shrank from putting the news concerning Harry down on paper yetawhile. Knollys, though, would be expecting to hear from me very soon. Though Dudley hadn't sent a courier ahead to Tyesdale, Elizabeth had sent one to Bolton to smooth the way into the castle for me. Ryder, borrowing the gray cob once more, took the letter to Bolton for me. "Now for Pen," I said to Sybil. "I must do something about her but I wish I knew how to deal with her."

"I think, Mistress Stannard, that Pen is still not really well. She wasn't truly fit for the ride yesterday, except that we could see we were a trouble to the farmer and his family. The way they all looked at us when we went downstairs yesterday morning..."

"Yes. I see. You think that her bad temper is partly because she still feels out of sorts?"

"Yes, I do. My daughter never had this particular problem, but as a young woman, I did and I know what it's like. It will pass presently."

"Very well." I was relieved to think that perhaps I need not rebuke Pen, for the prospect gave me no pleasure. I found her in the parlor, sitting by the empty hearth and staring miserably at the fire irons. She stood up politely as I came in, but her face was mutinous and she obviously expected a lecture. Instead, I smiled and signed to her to be seated again.

"Pen, I think you need some further rest and quiet. Now, I want to examine the account books this morning. They'll tell us a good deal about the estate—and about Master Whitely's honesty. Will you help? It won't be arduous. We can sit in here—it's pleasanter and quieter than the hall—and I'll have a fire lit here instead. It's supposed to be July but it's astonishingly cold."

Unlike most girls, Pen enjoyed figurework. For a moment, her desire to go on sulking visibly clashed with the prospect of an interesting task beside a comforting hearth. Then the accounts won and she agreed, if not altogether graciously.

I went to give orders about the fire and find the ledgers, taking Sybil with me for moral support in case Whitely proved difficult. But he had no doubt expected the request. He led the way to his office without demur.

I hadn't paid much attention to it when I wrote to the constable on the day of our arrival. Now I noted that it was a dull little room with plain, cheap paneling, and that its contents consisted only of a table, a writing set, a small coffer, and a shelf of ledgers, bound in brown leather, much like the ones my uncle Herbert had. "I keep a *little* money in the coffer," Whitely said in his mincing way, opening it to show us, "and a few unpaid bills, but I'm a tidy-minded man and I don't hold with keeping documents too long; they just get into a dusty muddle, to my way of thinking. I put the figures in the ledgers and that's where I look them up if I need to."

He pulled a ledger off the shelf. "This has the incomings and outgoings for the last three and a half years. I understand double-entry bookkeeping and I trust you'll find *everything* in order."

Thanking him, I carried it back to the parlor, where I found Agnes on her knees, encouraging the fire with bellows. As I came in, she rose, bobbed, and took herself off to the kitchen, leaving me and Pen alone. Knowing that we would have to go into estate matters, I had included an abacus in the baggage. Equipped with this, we settled down in the warmth to study the pages of notes and figures.

Sybil and Dale had gone upstairs to brush and press clothes that had become squashed in the pack-hampers. Bess and Feeb were cleaning the chapel. Smith and Dodd were outside with Jamie, tending the horses and mucking out the stables. For all of half an hour, the various members of the household worked undisturbed.

Pen and I found that the June wool clip had fetched less this year than last and wondered why, and we noted that the diggings I had observed when I arrived were indeed an abortive attempt at coal mining. Early in the ledger, three years before, we found a record of the payment to a company of prospectors. A note in the margin said that little coal had been found and the attempt had been abandoned.

Purchases of freshwater fish loomed annoyingly large. If Tyesdale's smelly, stagnant moat had been properly looked after, it could have supported a good population of tasty fish. There were no entries whatsoever concerning the repair or replacement of furnishings. The ledger seemed to be meticulously kept, but behind it was a picture that raised questions.

Then the peace was broken. The geese and hens in the court-yard started to cackle; Jamie's voice was heard raised in tones of inquiry; and then Agnes came knocking on the parlor door.

"If it please you, Mistress Stannard, there's folk to visit!"

* * *

"You're the hostess," I said to Pen, daring her to resume her sulks in front of company. She took the hint and accompanied me into the hall, where we were confronted by a large, hearty lady in a black-and-white outfit of impressive formality compared to the plain gowns and narrow ruffs we had donned for a working morning. She stood in the middle of the floor like the fabled Colossus: vast farthingale, elaborate ruff, huge puffed sleeves encasing arms as meaty as legs of mutton. With her were two equally large and hearty young men. The hall looked over-crowded.

The lady surged forward, brushing Agnes aside and booming that she was Mistress Cecily Moss, and these were her boys, Peter and Clem, short for Clement. They bowed. They too were carefully dressed but such mighty hulks of muscle would have looked better in farmers' britches and jerkins. They had broad faces, broad smiles, and round, ingenuous blue eyes. Amiable souls, I thought, but without much intellect. The younger one, Clem, might be fractionally brighter than his brother; that was all.

"Good Catholic names; I make no bones about it," bellowed Cecily. "We bow to t'law once a month in Fritton church but t'whole world knows what we think." Her surroundings were probably deafened regularly by Cecily Moss telling them what she thought. "Tyesdale was always a Catholic house, as well," thundered the lady. "Used to have its own chaplain till t'ould fellow died. Then there was an wandering priest that stayed here for a winter—there's always a few about; they come over from t'Continent to minister to t'faithful, and go from place to place, but they don't stop anywhere long in case t'law gets after them. Homegrown priests get winked at, but t'law doesn't like t'foreigners."

"Tyesdale is still Catholic," I told her. "This is the new owner, Mistress Penelope Mason, who is from a Catholic family in Berkshire."

"Thee's welcome among us!" roared Mistress Moss to Pen, who took a step backward in alarm.

I introduced myself as Penelope's guardian, asked Agnes to bring refreshments, and led us back to the parlor, where I gave the largest stool to Cecily. Her farthingale and her puffed and quilted arms overflowed it, bulging out in all directions. "How did you know we had arrived?" I asked as we seated ourselves.

"Stayed at Grimsdales', last stop before Tyesdale, didn't thee?" said Cecily. Agnes came in with oatcakes, a jug of ale, and some pewter mugs, and set them before us. "Word soon gets round. Master Grimsdale were out on t'hills yesterday and met our shepherd. You'll have others calling soon. We're always interested in new folk hereabouts—we don't get so many. Looking for a match for t'lass here, so I hear?" said Cecily, engulfing oatcakes with gusto.

I had been wondering how best to go about seeking a match for Pen. It seemed that I need wonder no more. We wouldn't have to search for prospects. They would come to us. This was the first contingent.

"Possibly," I said, glancing sideways at the boys. Peter and Clem, who had planted themselves on the window seat, had said scarcely anything, but seemed to be studying Pen, though not in an altogether pleasing fashion. To my eyes, they resembled farmers at a fair, considering the merits of a heifer. On her side, Pen was eyeing them as though they were strange specimens in a menagerie.

"No doubt thee'll find someone quick enough. Plenty of good Catholic houses in Yorkshire, even if this place is lonely," Mistress Moss told me. "Fritton's nobbut a village, though the church is fine enough. There's t'Thwaites of Fernthorpe, I suppose—their land marches with yours on the west. Their place used to be t'biggest round here till t'ould man made a fool of hisself—he were a young man then—and got mixed up in a rising and lost half his land. You know of t'Thwaites?"

"Not by name, Mistress Moss, though we've heard of their misfortunes. We had heard of you, though," Pen said, and then hesitated, glancing at me as if not sure whether she ought to have spoken or not. On receiving a nod of encouragement, she added: "We've heard of some people called Holme, too, at a place called Lapwings."

"Ah, yes, we know t'Holme family very well," said Cecily, and her two boys moved restlessly as though considering whether to say something or not, but seemed to decide against.

"T'Thwaites often get overlooked. Too unsociable," Cecily said, "and there's no Mistress Thwaite now. Will Thwaite's been a widower these many years. But t'son's a young fellow and I did hear they were looking for a lass for Andrew, though I fancy they're aiming high. Mighty keen on money, t'Thwaites are, ever since they lost so much. Will means Andrew to marry it! He was after one of t'Holme girls, till he found out their dowries weren't nowt to get excited about. Not to be wondered at, seeing there's five o' them. Hah! Likely enough Andrew'll end up with some smallholder's girl with a dozen chickens and half a pig to her name!"

From the window seat, Clem said: "And talk o' t'devil! Here t'Thwaites come now. Will and Andrew both. Just riding through t'gatehouse, they are."

Cecily heaved herself off the stool. "Time for us to leave, then. You've all to do here, that I can see, and you won't want crowds of guests all at one time."

"Before you go," I said swiftly, "we had a very bad experience on the way here." Briefly, I told her the tale of how Meg was kidnapped and Harry slain. "Would you have any idea who could have been responsible?"

All three Mosses exclaimed in horror, with shaking heads. "This whole district's been quiet this last year," Cecily told us. "There were the robber Morley, and he were a nuisance, but he was caught—they hanged him later—three months back and he worked alone, any road."

"And he didn't go in for kidnapping," said Clem. "Nor killing, neither. Just used t'hold folk up on t'road and take their valuables. That's shocking, that is. Nay, we've no idea who that could have been."

"But we'll warn all our neighbors," his brother said.

"See if t'Thwaites know owt," said Cecily. "We'll be off. We'll see ourselves out. We brought a groom and told him to leave t'horses saddled. Good day to you all, and God bless, and we'll meet again before long, I don't doubt. Come, boys."

We saw them to the main door. Whitely and the Thwaites, arriving at the foot of the steps at the same moment, stood aside while Cecily and her colossal skirts billowed down them, with her sons following. As our steward led the Thwaite family up to the door and we began welcoming our second batch of guests that morning, we could hear Cecily outside, bawling for her groom.

It was just chance that after exchanging greetings and introductions with the Thwaites, I lingered beside a window that chanced to be slightly open. As Cecily was being helped to mount her massive horse, which looked as though it had been bred to carry a knight in full armor, I heard her speak to her sons. If it had been anyone else, I probably wouldn't have caught the words, but Mistress Moss had a most exceptional larynx and didn't seem to be aware of it.

"She's a nice enough lass but t'poor thing's as plain as a yard of skim milk and I doubt she's got the strength to churn a pound of butter, and t'state that house has fallen into—you'll be better off with Kate and Mabel Holme, so we'll stick to t'ould arrangement. What do you say?"

Peter and Clem, who were mounting their own horses, didn't have quite the resounding voices of their mother, but their replies, though brief, were also resonant enough to reach my window. As they swung into their saddles, they both said the same thing at the same moment.

"Aye."

Pen was on the other side of the hall, taking her visitors' cloaks, behaving, thank goodness, like a dignified hostess. Sybil and Dale had come downstairs, and Pen handed the cloaks to Dale, asking her to hang them up. She had not overheard the Moss family's unflattering verdict on her charms. No one had heard but me. I smiled at her approvingly and went to join her.

Whitely had disappeared. Agnes, redder than ever with excitement, and apparently more pleased than otherwise at the prospect of providing refreshments for another set of guests, scurried off to the kitchen to fetch more oatcakes. I led the company back to the parlor.

Our few casual words at Grimsdales' farm must have swept across the neighborhood like the rainstorm two days ago. Maybe, I thought, the Grimsdales hadn't intentionally sold news of us—just gossiped to some chance-met acquaintance. First the Moss family, now the Thwaites. In view of Cecily Moss's comments, I couldn't doubt that father and son were here to introduce Andrew and inspect Pen. A few minutes later, I had decided that I didn't like it.

The Moss family had made me slightly uncomfortable but although I didn't think they were at all suitable for Pen—or Pen for them—I felt that they had warmth and honesty and would probably turn out to be good neighbors. Lacking in delicacy they certainly were, but they hadn't meant me to hear their parting remarks, and those remarks hadn't been spiteful, only realistic. They too had realized that Pen probably wouldn't fit into their family. The Thwaites, however, were different.

On the face of it, there was nothing amiss with them. The older man had white hair and a white beard and, as with so many older folk, half his teeth were missing and the rest were brown. He was obviously still active, though. His beaky-nosed face was bronzed with the sun and I had seen him dismount in athletic fashion, swinging his right leg straight over his saddle pommel and dropping easily to the ground.

Andrew was about twenty, and he too was lithe in his movements as well as being quite handsome in feature. He had escaped his father's nose. Their speech was Yorkshire but not to the point of being actually hard to understand, though Will Thwaite's teeth made his sibilants splutter. They were decently dressed, in a practical fashion, and were scandalized to hear of the attack on us. As Cecily had done, they insisted that the area had been perfectly quiet since Morley was apprehended. They could not for the life of them suggest who the perpetrators might have been.

Agnes then arrived with the oatcakes and some very respectable wine, and seeing that my visitors wished to change the subject, I tried to embark on small talk. I mentioned the ruined lute and spinet in the tower music room. Will Thwaite at once declared that he knew of an instrument maker in Bolton who could provide replacements, perhaps even carry out repairs. Meanwhile, he added—and at this point his gaze fixed noticeably on Pen—if any of us wanted to practice music, he had a lute that his wife, God rest her soul, used to play. "In fair condition; Andrew strums a bit now and then. Visitors from Tyesdale would always be welcome."

From that moment on, it was perfectly plain that they were here because they were interested in Pen. Andrew, agreeing with his father, and also staring at my ward, said he would be glad of a chance to practice dance steps. Did we know the latest London dances? Could Mistress Pen, perhaps, instruct him? There'd be a big dance when the Moss boys that we'd just met married the two Holme lasses they were betrothed to—did we know of that?—and he and his father would surely be invited but they didn't often go into company and he wished to acquit himself well. He'd much enjoy treading a measure with Mistress Penelope.

"Aye," his father said, "and why not? I've no prejudice against dancing. I met my wife when I dined wi' a merchant friend of mine in Bolton, and there was dancing afterwards." Then, without further delay, he came to the point. "Talking of wives—I hear you're after a match for t'lass there." He nodded toward Pen. "And I also hear you've no objection to a Catholic family. Heard all that from t'fellow that tutors the Holme lasses—he visits t'Mosses now and then and he got t'news from them. He's a priest in our persuasion. He saw t'Mosses yesterday and came on over to ours as he does once in a while . . ."

He hesitated. "He says Mass for you in private?" I asked, smiling. "Well, many a family does that." I added cautiously: "It's what Pen's mother would want for her, given that the family is law-abiding and loyal." Will Thwaite was presumably the man who had damaged his birthright by becoming involved in the Catholic rising thirty years or so ago. I wondered if he had truly mended his ways. "How people worship in private is their own business," I said. "The queen herself says so. As long as they remain her true subjects."

"We've naught to do with politics," said Will. "That's a game for fools, as I learned long since. We're just plain Yorkshire gentry wi' old-fashioned notions of prayer. We've been at Fernthorpe for generations and we're hoping for a few more generations still. My wife and I weren't lucky with our children, but Andrew we reared right enough and now it's time he took a wife himself."

It was normal talk for the circumstances and openness in these matters is usually accounted a sign of honorable intentions, but I found myself stiffening. Will Thwaite's gap-toothed smile was too assured and his chilly gray eyes were assessing the room, the furnishings, and Pen in a fashion that was much too proprietary for my liking.

Frankness is like many other virtues: usually admirable, until it goes too far. He had come to the point just a little too soon for my taste and he looked as though he thought it was for him to decide whether or not to take the merchandise on offer, rather than for us to decide whether we wished for his custom. As for Andrew . . .

One should not be blinded by prejudice, I said to myself. Just because Andrew Thwaite looked astonishingly like Henry Lord Darnley, the dissolute husband Mary Stuart had loved first and then hated and then quite possibly had murdered, didn't mean that Andrew too was foredoomed to turn into a vicious and promiscuous drunk.

Yet the resemblance was very strong. I had met Darnley in Scotland. He was taller than Andrew and Andrew was brown-haired instead of fair, but facially they were the same type. Like Darnley, Andrew Thwaite had wide eyes in slightly almond-shaped sockets, thin eyebrows in two perfectly matching curves, and pointed ears like a faun from Greek legend. The whole effect was curiously cold and pagan and the color of Andrew's eyes did nothing to offset this.

Darnley's eyes had been just blue but Andrew's were blue with a ring of yellow in them. In a different face with a different expression it wouldn't have mattered. But Darnley's pagan features combined with those eyes were unnerving.

I said that the matter of Pen's marriage was something I meant to approach with caution and that we were in no hurry. I then firmly changed the subject and discussed harvest prospects until our visitors, looking rather thwarted, took their leave. As they said farewell, Will Thwaite said in a persistent voice that he hoped they would see us again soon, and perhaps might entertain us at Fernthorpe before long. They bowed very low to Pen before they went. We stood at the top of the steps to watch them ride away and then turned back into the hall.

"Not him," said Pen, suddenly and passionately. "Not Andrew Thwaite. Mistress Stannard, *please,* not him! I . . . I don't like him! He makes me feel creepy!"

Pen, it seemed, could fall into aversion as easily and thoroughly as she had on previous occasions fallen into love. There was real fear, real loathing, in her voice and in her eyes.

"Don't worry," I said, putting an arm around her. "He has the same effect on me. I don't like him either. You're not going to marry Andrew Thwaite. Rest assured of that."

All the visitors had made me feel distracted. I couldn't settle to the account books again. From the windows, I could see Brockley and Meg cantering to and fro on a nearby hillside. Shadows raced across the hills and fields as a fresh wind drove brown and white puffs of cloud over the sky and I could see Meg snatching her cap off and waving it in excitement, while her dark hair streamed in the breeze.

Sybil understood accounts, too. I called her down, asked her to go on working with Pen, explained that my lord of Leicester had doubts about his steward's honesty and that she should look out for signs of this, and then, abandoning the figurework to the two of them, I had Roundel saddled, and went out to join the hawking party. I found Meg flushed with enjoyment and wind-burn, pleased with Joy's performance, and obviously much happier. We came back in time for dinner, and Brockley led the horses away to the stable while Meg and I took the bag containing Joy's catch up to the hall. At once, I heard voices from the parlor and realized that we had yet another set of guests.

"Take the bag to the kitchen," I said to Meg. "And then go and get tidy and come to the parlor. That's where I'll be."

My first impression was that the parlor was full of outsize kittens. Then I realized that the assembly awaiting me actually consisted of one very pretty little woman with dark hair and beautiful blue-green eyes with a sparkle in them, and five equally pretty girls, of ages between twelve and twenty, all diminutive like their mother, some dark and some auburn, but all with those same exceptionally lovely and sparkling eyes.

"Mistress Stannard," said Pen, rising, "this is Mistress Adeliza Holme and her five daughters."

We could hardly avoid asking them to dine. Agnes coped, augmenting the capons she had been roasting with a cold chicken pie and offering a custard as well as almond fritters. Adeliza Holme was full of neighborly assurances that she knew that Tyesdale had been sadly neglected and that if we needed anything, any help getting the house or land into good order, we had but to send to her and she would do her best. Like Mistress Moss, whom she believed we had met, she was a widow, her dear Thomas having been called to God two years since.

"Leaving me in fair circumstances, though with five girls to find portions for, I've still not much to spare. Luckily I think Kate and Mabel, my two eldest, are settled . . ."

She had come, undoubtedly, to inspect her daughters' opposition, meaning Pen. She was well mannered enough not to look relieved that Pen was comparatively plain, and Tyesdale run-down, but I guessed that she was. I understood. Five girls are a heavy responsibility. They were pleasant wenches, well spoken and lively, and I had no designs on the Moss boys. I wanted someone better than that for Pen.

I liked the family, even if it had, in the father's lifetime, featured on a list of Mary Stuart's supporters. That had probably faded out since Thomas's death. Mistress Holme had other things to worry about now. As with the Mosses and the Thwaites, I asked the Holmes for ideas about who might have attacked us in the mist, and like the Mosses and the Thwaites, they were horrified, full of commiseration for the poor young man who had died, and completely puzzled. "But grateful to be warned," Adeliza said. "My girls will be staying close to the house until the mystery is solved."

They rode off after dinner. In the evening, John Ryder came back from Bolton bearing a missive from Sir Francis Knollys. I was welcome at the castle whenever I chose to come. As requested in my note, he had told Mary Stuart that I was in Yorkshire, and explained that although I was now called Stannard, I had formerly been Ursula Blanchard. Lady Mary (he did not refer to her as a queen) remembered our meeting in Edinburgh three years ago and would be delighted to see me. I and any companions I brought were invited to spend two nights at Bolton.

I'd go the next day and take Pen with me; I decided. Meg could stay quietly at Tyesdale with Sybil. "You can go on with the account books. I think it's Meg's turn for instruction in interpreting such things," I told Sybil. "Keep looking out for any sign that Master Whitely has been up to something."

While I was delivering messages to Mary and trying to coax secrets out of her, I thought, I would also ask Sir Francis's advice on how to pursue the matter of Harry Hobson, and furthermore, I would explore the circles of society in which Sir Francis moved. I was more likely, I thought, to find someone suitable for Pen there than at Tyesdale.

I've made other mistakes in the course of my life but I doubt if I ever made a worse miscalculation than that.

8

The Enchanting Captive

Bolton Castle was lonely, well away from the town of the same name. Close to the castle, there was only a small hamlet. The castle itself had four square towers and a cramped courtyard and a curiously irrelevant air, as it frowned out across a landscape that no longer needed either its protection or its control and was mainly peopled by flocks of cud-chewing sheep and cattle.

However, it was bustling and lively enough inside. Sir Francis Knollys, grave, courteous, and neat, with a little pointed beard, came out to the courtyard in person to greet us and escort the ladies indoors and up to a sizable, well-appointed bedchamber.

Hot washing water, towels, a smoothing iron, and a tray of refreshments appeared shortly afterward. I had made sure that Pen and I had brought gowns suitable for calling on royalty. Dale unpacked our hampers, found a maids' room where there was a fire for heating the iron, and saw to the creases. Soon, we were ready to attend on Mary.

I was in satin, cream and tawny, a color scheme I have always liked. Pen was in dark blue summer-weight velvet. Pen, I had discovered, could wear colors that most young girls could not. The shades that suited Meg, such as white or crimson or apple green, somehow made Pen plainer than ever. Put her in the colors more commonly worn by older women, such as black, lavender, or dark blue, and an astonishing new Pen was revealed, a grave and intelligent young woman in whom an austere beauty was beginning to emerge.

The operative word, though, was *beginning*. Before that beauty could come fully into the light, she still had some maturing to do and I thought to myself that only marriage would achieve it. However, a little courtly gloss would help meanwhile, and since Pen had been ejected from Elizabeth's entourage, maybe Mary Stuart would provide it instead.

"Now," I said, "I'll find out if Queen Mary is ready to receive us."

On the way down to the hall to inquire, we met a young man in a clerk's dark gown, hurrying up the staircase toward us. He stopped, looking up at us, and asked if we were Mistress Stannard and Mistress Mason. If so, he said, Sir Francis had sent him to take us to the Lady Mary. "The Lady Mary knows you are here and is eager to see you. If you are ready, I am to take you both to her at once. Sir Francis has been caught up with a business matter. I am Tobias Littleton, undersecretary in the service of Sir Francis Knollys, at your service," he added, bowing.

"Thank you. Please lead the way," I said.

It was a complicated journey, to a different floor on the other side of the castle. As we went Littleton talked to us, particularly to Pen, for it appeared that he knew her brother George. George, it seemed, had been sent away to school for a couple of years and had made Littleton's acquaintance there.

"We still write to each other now and then. He will be most interested to know that I have met you," Littleton said.

Then, politely, he transferred his attention to me and talked about the remoteness of Bolton Castle and the difficulties of obtaining supplies of necessities. "We bought up all the local chandler's stock of candles in the first week we were here, and had to send to Bolton town, and as for getting silk thread for the Lady Mary's embroidery . . . !"

"*Lady* Mary?" I remembered that Sir Francis had referred to her in that way. "But surely—she's a queen."

"Sir Francis's orders, Mistress Stannard, on account of the fact that she has had to abandon her realm. She is to be known only by the title of lady. As I was saying, buying the right sewing silks for her is a challenge." He laughed, though in an indulgent fashion. "Embroidery is a pastime she much enjoys and she needs occupation, but she is so particular! When she first came here, we had to send nigh on seventy miles to York to get what she required. But I can understand her. This is a strange way of life for a woman who was once a monarch. Sir Francis does what he can and spends much time talking with her—about religion, as often as not. He has ambitions," said our guide, "to convert her to the Anglican church but she defies him. She is always gentle and sweet-mannered, but beneath that, she is as resolute as steel."

As we neared our destination, Littleton went ahead to speak to the guards outside Mary's door. "What a charming young man!" whispered Pen, as he receded out of hearing.

"Keep a watch on yourself," I muttered back. I too had been observing Littleton with attention but of a different kind. I had noticed that he had the indoor man's pale complexion, but that he was tall and well made, a personable young fellow. If he had been at school with George Mason, he was presumably from a similar level of society, as well. I saw why he appealed to Pen. Very likely, he appealed to Mary, too. "I fancy," I whispered, "that Queen—or Lady—Mary has made a friend of Master Littleton. Sir Francis may also be under her spell, even if he won't address her as royalty. Queen Elizabeth had some doubts about him."

"Oh, Mistress Stannard! Sometimes you are so . . . so down-to-earth!" Pen protested.

"Better than having your head in the clouds," I told her brusquely.

The brusqueness was because I was uncomfortably aware that I must keep my own head out of the clouds. I knew very well how easy it was to fall under Mary's spell. I had come here partly to find out what, if any, part she had played in the death of her husband and I was hating the task because I was so unwilling to think that perhaps she had.

A few moments later, I was even more unwilling. Over three years had gone by since I last saw Mary Stuart and much had happened to me during those years. I had never forgotten the effect she had had on me, but all the same, time had blurred it somewhat. Now, as I came face-to-face with her, it returned in a flood.

When we were shown in to her, she looked almost as she had the first time I met her, at Holyrood in Edinburgh. She was sitting in a good light, talking with another lady while they both worked at embroidery, and on a table beside them were two workboxes and a book and a scatter of bright silks. As Littleton announced us, Pen and I sank into curtsies, but at once, Mary was on her feet, casting her work aside, coming forward with hands outstretched, leaning down to us from her willowy height, raising us, exclaiming: "Come now, no ceremony. I am so glad to see you!"

And as I had been at that first meeting at Holyrood, I found myself bemused and enchanted. As I tried to reply, I stammered.

Mary laughed. "Oh, my dearest Ursula! Don't be tongue-tied! You are Mistress Stannard now, I believe; I have it right, have I not? And this is your ward, Penelope Mason? Sir Francis told me that Mistress Stannard was bringing you. You are so very welcome. Be seated, both of you. Marie, do you remember Ursula?"

She had lost not one whit of her old magic.

It was not just her musical voice, speaking in the mixture of French and Scots-cum-English that I had grown used to at Holyrood and found rather charming. Nor was it her beauty, for now that I saw her at close quarters, I realized with a pang of sympathy that some of that had been worn away, probably forever. She had seen trouble since we last met. Her golden-brown eyes were tired and new lines marred the once flawless complexion. The red-gold curls in front of her dainty pearl-edged cap were duller than I remembered, and very short. Cecil had said that she had cut her hair when she escaped from Scotland. It looked as though it hadn't grown very much.

What she retained, however, and in a greater measure than ever, it seemed, was that gift of making you believe when she spoke to you that you were the only person in her world or in her thoughts—that she had been waiting patiently for you, and you alone, to come to her.

In moments, we were all seated. The girl she had called Marie, using the French version of the name they both shared, greeted us as well and I remembered her as one of the ladies who had been with Mary at that first meeting in Edinburgh. She was a soft-voiced young woman whose real name was Mary Seton. She was one of four girls called Mary who had formed the Queen of Scotland's entourage of ladies, but the only one still with her, for the other three were now married.

"My last Marie has come to share my exile and these quarters," Mary told me as she settled into her chair again. She looked around the room, which although comfortable and well lit by mullioned and leaded windows, was sadly cramped. "We make the best of what little state I am allowed. She instructs my other maids—local girls, well meaning but untrained, mostly. We sew together, as you see, and Marie attends to my toilette. She has a great gift for dressing hair, even hair which has been roughly hacked short and soaked in seaspray. She has ordered some wigs for me, too. And now, Ursula . . ."

Then she was asking how my marriage had come about, and what my new home was like; what had brought me to the north, how long I expected to stay before returning home, and how had Mistress Mason come to be my ward?

For fifteen minutes, I talked with her, answering her questions, and admiring her needlework. I brought Pen into the conversation now and then, talking of Tyesdale, of my hopes of finding Pen a husband, of the merlin that Pen's mother had sent me. I did not mention Harry to her, for I knew that, being a sequestered prisoner, she could offer me no help there and would only be saddened. As it was, she seemed charmed with everything I told her, and I, Ursula Stannard, life-worn, experienced, and on occasion ruthless, found myself sinking into her kindness as though it were a feather bed.

Presently, a maidservant arrived with cakes and sweet wine. When she had gone, Tobias handed the tray around, remarking that he might as well make himself useful, since strictly speaking, he shouldn't leave the room. "I'm supposed to supervise your conversation," he said apologetically.

"I have few privileges, as you see," said Mary. "Even a peasant has the right to private talk, which I have not. I am not even allowed to be addressed as a queen!" She met my eyes sorrowfully. "But in my own eyes, I am still Queen of Scotland and, indeed, no one has ever said that I am not still a Queen Dowager of France. I am and will remain a queen even if I live a thousand years in captivity."

"Is it a very severe captivity?" I asked. One at least of my ulterior motives in coming here was nothing to be ashamed of. I felt no reluctance to pass on Elizabeth's message, but to do so, I needed more privacy than this. Master Littleton was horribly in the way. I looked toward the window and said: "There is open country out there. Are you not allowed out at all—to ride or to hawk? I am teaching my daughter to hawk at the moment—I have presented the merlin to her. Pen also likes falconry."

"I have been permitted a little such exercise. Sir Francis was concerned for my health. But he seems to be afraid to let me ride out often. As though I might suddenly sprout wings like one of the falcons, and fly away!" said Mary with asperity.

"I am sorry to hear it. I find open spaces pleasant, I confess, after being so lately at Elizabeth's court. Sometimes, in her palaces, I feel very enclosed. May I go over and look out at the vista?"

Despite the small size of the room, moving us to the window would give us a semblance of privacy. I would have to speak softly and hoped I could make it seem natural and not suspicious. As I said the words *Elizabeth's court,* I gazed very intently into Mary's eyes, which were so like Elizabeth's in color though their setting was different, and where Elizabeth's eyes were enigmatic, Mary's every thought and emotion could be seen in hers like the shadows of clouds passing across a hillside.

I kept up that hard, meaningful stare as I asked to go over to the window. Mary smiled at me and said: "But of course. Sometimes I stand there myself, for half an hour at a time, looking out at freedom."

There was nothing to do but go to the window, which I obediently did, thinking that she had not understood that I wished to speak to her apart. I had underestimated her, however. As I stood contemplating the pastures beyond the castle walls, she remarked: "Marie, you have had no breath of air at all today. Mistress Penelope is interested in falconry, it seems. Why not show her the mews? Master Littleton, please attend them—yes, yes, you are supposed to listen to all my conversations but the one I am about to have with Mistress Stannard will embarrass you. We are not going to brew sedition the moment your back is turned! Mistress Stannard is one of my royal cousin Elizabeth's own ladies and Sir Francis himself has welcomed her here! I have been much plagued of late by a pain in my side, as you know, and wish to ask Mistress Stannard's advice. I know that she is experienced in matters of women's health, and I suspect that my pain may have something to do with the miscarriage I suffered before I left Scotland. A young unmarried man should not overhear such details. And while I think of it, would you also return this book to Sir Francis?"

She had risen gracefully once more and picked up the book, which was lying on the table. "I have read it carefully, but I fear the arguments of the Reformers do not, to my mind, hold good."

Littleton, who had turned bright pink at the mention of obstetrics, looked from one of us to the other, visibly wobbled between obeying orders and outraging his sense of modesty, concluded that the orders couldn't really apply to anyone so definitely attached to Elizabeth's service as myself, took the book, and without further demur left the room at once with Mary Seton and Pen. Laughing softly, Mary Stuart came to join me at the window.

"It is true about the pain in my side," she said. "It happens now and then; it has done so all my life. I feel unwell when it comes, but then it leaves me again and I recover. It has nothing to do with the loss of my babies—I lost twins, did you know?"

"No. I'm so sorry!"

"They were my lord Bothwell's sons," said Mary. "Ah well. He is out of my life now, I fear, for good or ill. He abandoned me at the last and fled. I have been unlucky in my husbands, Ursula.

One too sickly to live, one—unkind; let us say no more about that—and one, to whom I looked for strength and protection, has proved false and left me to face my enemies alone. Is there any word from Elizabeth?"

"Yes, ma'am," I said. "A very private one."

"Ah. I *thought* that you wished to speak to me privily. This room is too small for the exchange of secrets if any third party is present. What is the message? Will she lend me an army to replace me on my throne? She is my cousin, after all, and a queen herself. She must surely understand . . . well, tell me!"

"It's nothing like that," I said compassionately. The eager hunger in her face was distressing. "I am sorry," I told her. "But no. It's a warning. Queen Elizabeth commanded me to deliver it to you privately, by word of mouth only. There is to be an inquiry into . . . into what happened to Lord Darnley."

"I know. I am not quite shut off from all news," said Mary. "Sir Francis tries to keep me so, but I am thankful to say that I have a few friends here. Some of them came with me from Scotland. I only see them now and then and we are always watched and spied upon, but they hear news from Scotland and they find ways to get information to me. My brother Moray has demanded the inquiry, and I know he wants to blacken my name. Go on."

"You may be asked to testify before the court of inquiry, and to allow yourself to be questioned. Queen Elizabeth says you must not, that you are an anointed queen and cannot be treated like a subject. She says it would set a perilous precedent and begs you to refuse either to testify or to answer questions."

"Well, well. So my cousin respects my title, at least, though apparently not to the point of lending me an army." Mary sighed. "I must be grateful for even small considerations, and so I am. When you go back to London, tell her that I have received her message and agree with it—though how I am ever to defend myself against the lies . . ."

Her voice died away. I saw an opportunity, loathed myself for taking it, but knew that I must. "Lies?" I said, and waited, wondering if she would go on, would say something to point toward the guilt or innocence that Cecil wished to establish. She said nothing, however. At length, forcing the words out, I said: "There have been many lies, madam?"

"Piled one on another, into a mountain," said Mary. "And what is one poor young woman to do, faced with such an edifice of calumny? I did my best, but everything I did was wrong. I trusted James Bothwell and learned too late that I should not have done. Oh well. Let us not talk of these things. They can be of no interest to you."

I couldn't force the conversation and didn't want to anyway. Indeed, I could hardly think how to do so. Hugh had pointed out the principal difficulty when he said that Cecil could hardly write to Mary saying *Most honored lady, would you be kind enough to tell me whether you did or did not have gunpowder planted in the basement of Kirk o' Field on the night of ninth of February, 1567?* Quite. Some questions can't be asked directly, and even they are, one would never get a reliable answer. The truth could not be reached that way. I must depend on encouraging her to talk, hoping it would emerge of itself, but if she didn't wish to discuss the subject, I had no means of insisting. Perhaps she might be more forthcoming another time.

I wished I could stop feeling afraid of what I might learn. Surely, surely, it would be an assurance of her innocence. Cecil wanted to be sure of her guilt, but a woman as gracious as Mary could not—could she?—have either blood or gunpowder on her hands.

For the moment, the subject was clearly closed. Mary led us back to our seats and once more took up her embroidery, remarking that she had been overwhelmed with joy to see her dear Seton again.

"Though I would like to see her married. All my other Maries are, and it is right that they should be. Seton, though, seems to have no desire for the married state. I think she would have done well as a nun! When Tobias Littleton joined Sir Francis's household—he has only just done so; he comes of a Bolton family—I did wonder. I thought he might come of good stock. Such young men often serve people like Sir Francis Knollys as part of their education. But I have since learned that Littleton, though well educated, has a humble background. His father is just a small cloth merchant in Bolton and Tobias himself is only a second son, at that. He has been equipped with good schooling to help him make his way, but make it he must. My dear Marie is the daughter of Lord Seton, one of Scotland's most noble families. It wouldn't do."

"Quite apart," I said, "from the religious matter. Tobias is an Anglican, I suppose."

"Unlike Sir Francis, Tobias never discusses such things," said Mary. "Tell me, Ursula—I know you are something of a needle-woman yourself—what do you think of this pattern which Seton has designed? It is for a cushion cover. I feel the silks should be chosen with great care, or some of these greens and blues will clash . . ."

Tobias, reappearing at that moment, having presumably decided that we had had long enough to discuss feminine problems, found us deep in a discussion about the delicate difference between colors that tone and colors that swear at each other. Nothing could have been more innocent.

I spent the whole of the next day at Bolton hoping to learn what Cecil wanted to know. I also asked to speak to Sir Francis and reported Harry's death and Meg's kidnapping to him.

Both projects failed dismally. Mary vouchsafed nothing of use; and Sir Francis, though gravely shocked by the attack on a party of innocent travelers, had no idea who could have been responsible and said that local law enforcement was not his task. He was Lady Mary's custodian and nothing else. If I had complained to the local constable and he had not found any clues that might lead to the perpetrators, then he did not see what else could be done. I could of course complain to the sheriff in York, but the scent of the quarry would be old by now in any case. The north was wild compared to the south and . . .

"I know *that*," I said grimly.

All this dimmed what would otherwise have been a pleasant Sunday, most of which Pen and I spent with Mary, whose company, as ever, was like warm sunshine. We were away from her only when I was talking to Sir Francis, attending the Anglican service held by the chaplain in the morning, and at meals.

Mary took hers in her quarters, but I and my party dined in the main hall, and here I met and talked with two amiable young men called Will and George Douglas, who had accompanied her from Scotland, and who were presumably among the friends Mary had mentioned.

I wondered if I might obtain information from them but I did not. They were good-natured, handsome, and devoted to Mary, but I soon realized that they knew no more than I did about Kirk o' Field and what had really happened there.

When we went back to Mary after dinner, Pen, with the frankness of youth, did actually ask a direct question about Kirk o' Field. But Mary only shook her head and said that some matters were too distressing to discuss. Tears came into her eyes as she spoke, and seeing them, I felt so uncomfortable that instead of encouraging Pen or following the subject up myself, as I should have done, I nudged my ward as a signal to be quiet.

Wiping her eyes, Mary said that in the end she had had to escape—yes, *escape,* from her own country! Then she told us how she had got away from where she was being held in a castle on an island called Lochleven, in the midst of a loch; how supporters had rallied to her but been defeated in a battle against her half brother James Stewart, Earl of Moray.

"He calls himself the Regent of Scotland and claims to be ruling in my son's name. I suppose it's one degree better than claiming the crown for himself," said Mary.

On Lochleven she had been in the charge of the Douglas family to which Will and George, the two young men I had met at dinner, belonged. "I admit it," she said contritely. "I used all my wiles and powers of persuasion to coax the Douglases into helping me. But what else could I do? I had only myself to rely on. I persuaded and smiled; I pleaded and cajoled; I wept aloud and sometimes I let myself be found weeping, and tried to hide my tears but not too quickly . . ."

She gave me a wry look. "Do I sound like a deceiver, a

woman full of cunning tricks? I expect I do, but what other weapons did I have? I hope that those who helped me will not suffer for it in time to come."

"I can only admire your determination and your courage," I said. I could imagine the loneliness of which she spoke, and I understood what she meant when she said she had only used what weapons she had. I knew about loneliness, too. I knew what it was to be forced, in self-defense, to go to lengths that once I would have said I would *never* go to. In my time, I had slept with a man I did not want; I had helped men to their deaths.

"One can't help but sympathize," I said to Pen, at the end of that day, when we had retired to our chamber. "Tell me, what do you think of the Queen of Scotland?"

This time to my surprise, Pen was the one who was not inclined to lose her head in the clouds. "She is very beautiful," she said. "She looks like a tired angel. I fancy that those two Douglases think she's *really* an angel! But I don't think she is."

I was on the whole relieved by the contempt in her voice when she spoke of the Douglases. They were probably too young to appeal to her, I thought, and a good thing, too. But I was startled by the way she had dismissed Mary.

Something of this must have shown in my face, for Pen said: "I keep thinking about that story that she tried to have her husband blown up. Everyone says he was very unpleasant, but all the same, that's a dreadful thing to do, and when I was at court, I heard that someone had been posted to keep watch in case he was somehow warned and tried to escape, and that he actually did, and was caught running away and strangled!"

"That's horrible!" Dale was with us, blending the water from an ewer of hot and an ewer of cold, so that we could wash before we went to bed. "I hadn't heard that. I thought—he just died in an explosion. I'd heard that much, no more. Is this true, ma'am?"

"Yes. Pen has the story correctly," I said. "And she's right. It was a dreadful plot."

"If she really ordered that . . . !" Pen said. "Well, how is one to know? She says the things that I would say in her place, and they all sound very innocent, but there's no way to be sure."

Then she startled me further by adding: "Have you got a private reason for wanting to talk to her? You used to do secret work for Queen Elizabeth, didn't you? Do you still? Is that really why we're here?"

"Now, then." Dale was disapproving. "That's not the way to talk to Mistress Stannard. Her business is her own."

"It was supposed to be confidential," I said. I hesitated and then decided that it might be wiser after all to admit some of it and make light of it, rather than let Pen imagine all kinds of dramatic secret missions and thus create curiosity and an unhealthy excitement.

"Since I was coming north," I said carefully, "both the queen and Cecil asked me to visit Mary Stuart and charged me with certain private messages for her. Not even Sir Francis is privy to them. He was asked to let me see Queen Mary, that's all. I've managed to deliver one but I still need to talk further to Mary. Sir Francis has only offered us lodgings for two nights, though, and I don't see how I can prolong it without making him wonder why. I may try to arrange a further visit later on."

"May I come too?" Pen asked. "I won't speak of your business to anyone—here or anywhere else; I promise."

"Do you want to visit Bolton again?"

"Oh yes, please!"

I think that at the time I wondered why she was so eager, but supposed that she found Bolton Castle and Mary interesting. I was quite sure that the attraction wasn't either of the Douglases.

The truth looks obvious now, by hindsight.

9

Accounting for Silken Velvet

I had still not written to Hugh. I knew I must tell him of our safe arrival at Tyesdale, but what was I to say of Harry's loss and our own failure to do anything about it? Also, I was worried about sending any of our men away. I felt we needed them. At Bolton, however, I seized the opportunity of asking to borrow one of Knollys's couriers and sent off a short letter, saying that we had arrived, that there was a good deal of news, but that I would write in more detail later. For the moment, it was all I could bring myself to say.

We reached Tyesdale in time for dinner on Monday. Meg, who looked much more like her usual lively self, greeted us with an air of suppressed excitement, and Sybil said that as soon as we had eaten, they would have something to show us. The moment dinner was over, they led me up to my chamber. Once there, Meg at once ran to pull some sheets of paper from concealment under the coverlet. She brandished them at me eagerly.

"Mother, you will never guess what we've got here! I thought I would burst, waiting all through dinner, but Mistress Jester said you would be tired and hungry and we must wait to tell you. But look at these!"

Sybil placed a hand on Meg's shoulder. "Gently, now. Let us begin at the beginning. Mistress Stannard, while you were away, I gave Meg lessons in bookkeeping, as you asked, and used the ledger that Master Whitely gave you. We remembered what you had said about looking out for anything amiss, but we couldn't find anything definite at first, though some of the figures seemed odd—too high or too low . . ."

I nodded. "Pen and I noticed that."

"Yes. But with nothing to check them against, we couldn't be sure that anything was wrong with them. However, we were working in the parlor and it happened that I glanced out and saw those two Thwaites, father and son, riding in."

"The Thwaites? Again?"

"Yes. Well, you were not here, but I had the feeling," said Sybil, "that you and Pen didn't greatly care for them."

"You were quite right. And so?" I said, wondering where all this was going.

"So I decided that Tyesdale should be, not inhospitable, but not effusively welcoming either," said Sybil. "I took Meg up to her room and then went in search of Whitely to tell him that I was not available and that I wished him to look after the guests and make our apologies. I met him straightaway, coming out of his own room, and while I was explaining to him—well, I suppose it was the first time I had ever really looked at him—I noticed his clothes. They're in dull colors—brown and dun and black, but the materials are too rich for a steward in a place like this."

"Ah. I've been thinking the same myself," I said.

"His shirt was silk, and he had a gold chain," said Sybil. "And his doublet was brown velvet—*silken* velvet. I know what it looks like. When I had sent him down to meet the Thwaites, I came back to Meg, and I spoke of it. And then Meg said . . . well, your turn has come, Meg. Tell your mother what you said. You spoke very intelligently."

"Mother," said Meg eagerly, still clutching the papers, "it just seemed to me to *prove* that Master Whitely was making extra money somewhere. I said to Mistress Jester, 'If he is wearing silk and gold, how can he afford it? His salary is in the accounts and it surely wouldn't stretch so far.'"

"I said that I agreed," Sybil said, "but that we couldn't be sure unless we could find other documents, bills, and receipts, to put against the figures in the ledger but then . . . go on, Meg."

"I suddenly thought," said my daughter, "that if I were falsifying accounts, I might still keep a note somewhere of the real figures in case I needed them. I might want to remind myself what was *really* paid for last year's wool clip, so that I could compare it with what I was offered this year. It would be easy to get muddled otherwise—and then people could cheat you. You might not be able to steal so much next time!"

"I've seen his office," Sybil said to me. "I was with you when you went to collect the ledger we've been studying, if you recall. I couldn't see anywhere there to hide anything, but if he *has* kept a separate record anywhere, he would take good care to hide it, I fancy. I said as much to Meg, thinking aloud, and . . ."

Once more, she paused to let Meg speak and my daughter said: "Well, if I was him, I'd keep it in my room." Her brown eyes, so luminous, so much the eyes of her father, my first husband, Gerald, were sparkling. "So," she said simply, "I said to Mistress Jester: 'He's downstairs talking to the Thwaites. I can hear him, and Mistress Appletree is offering meat pasties. They're busy. Why don't we look?'"

"So I told Meg to keep guard at the top of the stairs," said Sybil, "and I slipped into Whitely's room. I found what I wanted straightaway. He keeps a box under his bed. There's a lock but it wasn't fastened. Well, I don't suppose he expected us to search his room! Anyway, looking inside was easy. I found several bags of money and two bundles of papers. One seemed to be Tyesdale's copies of its invoices for last year's sales of wool and produce. The other bundle was receipted bills for things Tyesdale had bought."

"You mean that Tyesdale really does make purchases now and then?" I asked dryly. "Judging by the state of the furnishings . . ."

"Condiments, candles, sewing thread for Agnes, the services of a smith to shoe Whitely's cob," said Sybil briefly. "Even Whitely can't entirely avoid *some* household expenditures. I snatched up both bundles and ran back here with them and Meg and I compared some of them with the figures in the ledger. We were nervous and in a hurry so we could only check a few but the documents were in date order so it wasn't hard to trace the matching ledger entries. We worked for about half an hour—with our ears cocked for what was happening downstairs—and we made notes. Those are what Meg is holding. When I thought we'd done enough, I put the documents back. The Thwaites were still here at that time, talking to Whitely. He and they seem very friendly. He has no idea that his box has been found. He may well have locked it again by now, of course."

"I can open his lock if I need to," I said. In the course of my strange career as one of Elizabeth's agents, I had at times had to open other people's document boxes. I possessed a set of pick-locks, knew how to use them, and had never lost the habit of carrying them about with me. I had brought them to Tyesdale. "Let me see those papers."

Meg handed them to me. There were two sheets. Sybil came to my elbow to explain them. "This page has the income from some of the things Tyesdale has sold over the last two years, and for cottage rents; the other shows payments for things brought in. We've put the dates, and the amounts earned or spent according to the documents in Whitely's box, and according to the ledger. Most of the documents had some figures scribbled on the back. We didn't understand those at first, until Meg—Mistress Stannard, you really have a very bright-minded daughter."

I looked at Meg questioningly and also lovingly. With every year that passed, I thought, her resemblance to her father Gerald increased. Gerald had been employed by Elizabeth's financier, Sir Thomas Gresham, in the Netherlands, and Sir Thomas had had a brief to raise money for Elizabeth's coffers, by whatever means he could, which—since the Netherlands were controlled by England's archenemy Spain—didn't necessarily mean legal ones.

Gerald's principal task had been to bribe, bully, or blackmail various hapless clerks and keepers into handing over valuable plate from the Spanish treasury and armor and weapons from the Spanish armory, and to smuggle them to England. He had been very, very good at it and he had enjoyed it. In Meg's dancing eyes, he lived again.

"Mother, the scribbled figures are the difference between what Tyesdale really paid for the thing it bought or earned for something it sold and the figures in the ledger," she said. "The ledger is wrong. It pretends we paid more for candles and so on than we did, and it pretends that we were paid less than we really were for wool and produce. Look at this! We copied it from a receipt from a prospector who was paid to look for coal on Tyesdale land. The corresponding entry in the ledger is twice what Whitely really paid! And all for nothing because there wasn't any coal! There's a note about that in the ledger and I suppose *that's* true, because if there were any mining here, we'd surely know about it."

"I agree," I said grimly. "But if there isn't any coal here, Whitely's created his own little gold mine, hasn't he? Silk shirts and gold chains! He took a risk in keeping those bills."

"Not necessarily," said Sybil. "If he can show you ledgers that seem to be in perfect order, well, you might disapprove because he hadn't kept the original receipts and invoices, but as I said, he wouldn't expect us to go rooting in his room and finding the box under his bed."

"One of the things that made me suspicious," I said, "apart from missing silver, battered furniture, and silk velvet doublets, is the unnatural perfection of his accounts. I didn't see a single corrected figure in that ledger. It didn't look real, somehow. Pen must see these notes."

I folded the sheets thoughtfully. "Tyesdale belongs to her, after all," I said. "We shall have to admit that we've seen the source documents and challenge him about them. I think we'll have to dismiss Whitely. We had better wait until we can find a replacement, though. We'll do that first. Meanwhile, all bills and invoices must be seen by Pen and myself, beginning at once. Dudley should be informed, too. After all, Whitely has been cheating him most of the time. As if I hadn't enough to do!" I groaned in exasperation. "I still have to find a possible husband for Pen!"

I had mentioned the matter to Sir Francis during the interview I had had with him, and he had said he would make inquiries but he had nothing to suggest immediately. I had left it there, thinking that it might provide an excuse to visit Bolton Castle again. But it would all occupy a lot of time. I could have done without this.

I could have done without a lot of things, including the grievous letter I must send south, to report the loss of Hobson.

Hobson, though, was a tragedy. Whitely was just a nuisance.

10

Invitation to a Hawking Party

I had too many things on my mind. I hardly knew in which order to deal with them. I did know, however, that I must try once more to complete Cecil's errand, little as I liked it, and must therefore return to Bolton as soon as I could. I considered simply telling Cecil that it was impossible but my conscience wouldn't let me.

For the moment, I tackled the immediate problem of Whitely. I talked to Pen and found that although she was still unenthusiastic about Tyesdale, improved health and the visit to Bolton seemed to have taken the edge off her first dislike.

"We can't keep Whitely, can we?" she said. "But I don't like the idea of having him arrested. Mistress Stannard, everyone hereabouts seems to know everyone else. Look how people came visiting when we'd only been here five minutes. Whitely may have friends or relatives in the district—well, Mistress Jester says he and the Thwaites seemed friendly—and we're strangers. We don't want to make enemies." She considered me with a serious expression. "If we are ever to find out what really happened to poor Harry Hobson, we'll need help from people roundabout. You're going to inquire into that, aren't you, Mistress Stannard?"

"If I can, though heaven knows where I'll start. Sir Francis convinced me that sending a complaint to York would probably be a waste of time. But as things are, I can't even tell his family where his grave is! No, I can't just leave the matter."

"Then," said Pen practically, "I think we should be very careful in our dealings with people here. We do have to get rid of Whitely, but I think we should leave it at that, and get a local man as a replacement, someone who knows the ways of the district."

"You are quite right." I looked at her thoughtfully. "You seem to have sensed the atmosphere of the north."

"And I don't care for it much, Mistress Stannard. I don't think Meg does, either."

"Hardly surprising! But I think she's getting over her fright," I said. My daughter no longer needed to sleep in the same room with me and was now sharing with Pen as I had originally intended, while Sybil shared with me.

"She'll go home with you, though," said Pen. "I want to go home, too. Can't I go back to the south but still have Tyesdale as my dowry?"

She looked at me wistfully. I didn't remind her that she had been virtually thrown out of Richmond. "You won't be married off against your will," I said. "If we find the right man, you'll be only too eager to stay with him, I promise you! It's easier to find you a Catholic marriage in the north. I'm hoping to hear of possible prospects through Sir Francis at Bolton."

Pen smiled, which brightened her earnest face and made her almost pretty. "I liked the castle. But—Bolton Castle is *there* and I'm *here*," she said. "You said we might visit it again, but when?"

"As soon as we can," I told her. "Meanwhile, I suggest that we return the visits of Mistress Holme and Mistress Moss. I've explained the situation about Whitely to Brockley and he can escort us. I fancy that both those ladies know all there is to know about running a manor—we'll see if they can suggest anyone suitable to take over as steward. As soon as we've found someone . . ."

"Whitely can be off the premises the same day," said Pen, quite ruthlessly. She had the makings of a very good chatelaine, I thought, once she was settled as a wife, with roots, and no longer at the mercy of stray romantic breezes.

We visited the Holme and Moss families on the same day. The expedition took us through the village of Fritton, the first time we had seen it. I realized, seeing it, why Master Toft had such parochial attitudes. This, of course, was his world, and his world was little more than a hamlet, though it had a pond in the middle and a tiny green.

The church, though, was surprisingly big and well appointed, with some beautiful stained glass. For directions to the Holme and Moss houses, we called on the vicar, who was much less attractive than his church. He was a gloomy man in his middle years, who informed us that the Tyesdale district was a cesspool of popery and he hoped that we would set a good example by regular attendance at his services. We discovered that he knew Toft well and knew our story but wasn't surprised by it. "I know of nothing that may be useful. Such things happen in these wild places."

Short of scouring the moor for about ten miles in each direction, foot by foot, and searching every single farmstead, manor, cottage, hut, or cave we came across, I thought bitterly, there was nothing that could be done to find either Harry's body or Harry's killers. The gloomy vicar was still talking, saying that he himself came from Nottingham. He obviously wished he'd never had to leave it.

"I was appointed here when Queen Elizabeth acceded, and I suppose I have been called to do my best for the benighted souls here, but my best hasn't achieved much yet. Now, you need directions to Lapwings, where the Holmes live, and to Moss House. I can put you on the way to them. They're all popish, too. You'd think sometimes that the Act of Conformity didn't exist."

Lapwings and Moss House both proved to be sturdy, defensive buildings not unlike Tyesdale, although neither had a moat. Lapwings was well maintained, with a modern, timbered gatehouse, a black-and-white-tiled entrance hall, and a paneled dining room. The furnishings were bright and feminine, with embroidered cushions, scented rosemary amid the rushes underfoot, and a white damask cloth for the table.

The welcoming effect, though, was somewhat dampened by its mistress. Adeliza Holme was so protective of her kittenish daughters that I think it distorted her view of the world. She was relieved that Pen was comparatively plain and yet still resented her nearly as much as if Pen were Cleopatra in person. When, tactfully explaining that Whitely might be leaving, I asked if she could recommend a replacement, she merely shook her head.

"I can't say I know of anyone. If Whitely wants to go, why not leave the place in the care of the Appletrees? I daresay you'll not be staying long yourselves; Tyesdale's a depressing house if ever I saw one."

In other words, the sooner Tyesdale depressed us to the point of going home again to the south, the better, in her eyes.

Moss House was a more practical place than Lapwings, with few furbelows, though it too was well kept. The boys were out in the fields, but the overflowing Cecily Moss was indoors and was more helpful than Adeliza Holme. She might be able to suggest a possible steward, she said, just give her a week or two to think it over. I had the feeling that something useful might come of the visit, though I could not expect any news immediately.

On our return, we found a messenger from Bolton awaiting us. It seemed that I wouldn't after all need to invent excuses to visit Mary Stuart again. This was an invitation from Mary herself, endorsed by Sir Francis Knollys, to bring Pen and anyone else I chose from my household, to a hawking party the following Saturday.

There was no need for us to ride fifteen miles to Bolton, apparently. Sir Francis had decided that for the sake of her health, he should permit Lady Mary to ride out under guard for a little falconry, and we were asked to meet them halfway between Tyesdale and Bolton, beside a pool on the moors. We would enjoy a couple of hours of sport and a picnic, and then the two parties could return to their respective homes. The place was easy to find, since there was a twisted tree beside the pool, which was clearly visible from the main track to Bolton. Obviously, if the weather were inclement, no one would expect us to come and Mary herself would not set out.

I sent my acceptance back with the messenger at once. Whatever my secret reluctance, I must try to make good use of this further meeting with Mary.

Though I didn't think a hawking expedition would offer much opportunity for subtle conversation. I knew that from past experience. Oh well. I could but try.

11

The Sign of the Sword

"I feel like a pancake on a griddle," I said to Meg.

The moorland, that first Saturday in August, was swelteringly hot. I envied Dale and Sybil, who had stayed at home. But here we were, myself, Pen, and Meg (who was now very proficient with Joy, the merlin, and eager to practice), with Ryder and Tom Smith as escorts. Brockley had also stayed at Tyesdale, to keep an eye on Whitely, he said. From somewhere cool and shady, no doubt, I thought wryly, wiping my forehead.

Meg, who didn't mind the heat, just laughed. She was the only one from Tyesdale who had a hawk and was rather proud of it. Mary's party were well provided, however, with hawks and falconers alike. Sir Francis Knollys and the Douglases were there, all with goshawks, while Mary Stuart and Mary Seton, who was with her, had merlins, hen birds like Joy, with brown-gray backs and barred tails.

Mary was riding astride, in shirt and breeches and with a dashing feathered hat. Her party was at the meeting place before us and when we arrived, she greeted us effusively, leaning from her saddle to kiss both me and Pen, and blowing another kiss to Meg, but I saw that she was pale and that her smile was strained.

I could guess why. Even out here, she must feel like a prisoner, for she was as well supplied with guards as with hawks. As we set off, we were encircled by soldiers: in front, behind, and to either side. Even so, Francis Knollys seemed worried. Trotting beside me and Meg, he remarked in a low voice that he feared the expedition was ill-advised. "I let her go hare-coursing once from Carlisle but it made me nervous. My orders are to keep her close. But she has been ailing for lack of air and exercise and I also have to protect her health."

"She has a strong guard," I said. "What can possibly happen?"

"How could she have got herself out of Lochleven?" Knollys retorted. "I understand it to be a fortress on an island in the middle of a loch in the middle of nowhere. She is a clever woman." There was undoubtedly admiration in his voice, but it was clearly unwilling. Elizabeth and Cecil would have been relieved by that.

"She and the Douglases, who are her devoted slaves, could set spurs to their horses all of a sudden and ride for the coast," he said. "Or she might somehow arrange to get herself kidnapped as she was when Bothwell seized her, after that business at Kirk o' Field. I greatly fear she was party to that, so as to pretend that she was forced to marry Bothwell, when all the time she wanted to. She feared to do it openly because the whole of Scotland was whispering that it was he who organized the murder of Darnley. Ah well. I don't doubt that he had a persuasive way with a woman. Report says that of him. But a trick that worked once might be tried again. I must be wary."

"I'm sure you're right. Her presence in England is a worry to Sir William Cecil," I said.

"She is wishing now that she had made straight for France instead of coming to England," Knollys said. "She has even tried to send an emissary, though he was not allowed to leave England. I have no doubt that if she could find a way to flee to France, she would."

The moorland spread out around us: immense sunlit hillsides of heather and grass and gorse patches. A couple of ravens rose as we passed, and flew off croaking. A few fields and habitations and small patches of woodland lay in the folds of the land, but for the most part we were surrounded by empty, open country. Our little party was not only well guarded; it was also in the midst of a wilderness.

"The Douglases helped her to escape from Lochleven," I said. "But you allow two of them to stay with her?"

"I'd rather have them under my eye at Bolton than somewhere else, scheming," said Knollys. "I see to it that she never speaks with them unless I or some other trusted person is within hearing."

"Such as Tobias?" I said lightly.

"Sometimes," said Knollys. "Though I observe some caution, with Tobias. This is a mainly Protestant area, and he claims to be Protestant, but nevertheless, his father is a Catholic."

"It's a pity that these religious differences have to matter so much," I said. "They came between me and my second husband, and it was a great grief to me. Queen Elizabeth herself once said that we all worship the same God; the rest is a dispute about trifles."

"If she really said that, then I'm astounded to hear it. I should hardly call a dispute about Her Majesty's legitimacy a trifle," said Knollys acidly. "That is one of the biggest bones of contention. Ah well. With grave doubts, I have agreed to this hawking party, but she must not speak to anyone we happen to meet."

The queen and Cecil had no need to be anxious about Knollys, I thought. He had not been hopelessly beguiled. I glanced at Mary, thinking once again how unlike a ruthless plotter and murderess she seemed, and wondered if I were the one who had been beguiled instead.

One of the falconers rose in his stirrups, pointing into the air. Mary looked up, narrowing her eyes against the dazzling sky. There was a pigeon there, a big prey for a merlin. Mary, however, unhesitatingly loosed her bird and raised her wrist. The little hawk tautened, head stretching forward and body crouched, like the body of a stalking cat before the spring. Then she spread her wings and flew and we were off, in a splendid chase that swung us away from the track, galloping across the heather to keep up. We caught the prey, and then Sir Francis saw a rabbit in the distance and loosed his goshawk at it, and we were off again.

By the time we had caught the rabbit, it had become so very hot that the blue sky was twinkling with it, as though it were strewn with diamond dust. Mary Seton was complaining of a headache, so we stopped then to have our picnic meal.

We sat about, holding our reins and letting the horses graze, while flasks of wine and water were fetched out of saddlebags and handed around, along with cold chicken, fresh white bread, and cakes with raisins and honey in them, all neatly packed in napkins. In the quiet, without the sound of hoofbeats, the creak of grasshoppers and the twitter of the skylarks far above were like the very sound of scorching noonday.

Mary Stuart seemed better, as though the light and air were doing her good, and she clearly didn't mind the heat. I didn't greatly mind it, either, while Pen and Meg semed to be thriving on it. But Seton was streaming with sweat, runnels of it shining on her face and locks of soaked hair escaping from her hat and clinging to her neck. Mary noticed it and asked her if she was well. "You said your head ached, my Marie."

"It still does," Seton said ruefully, rubbing her temples.

"We should turn back to Bolton," Sir Francis said. "We have come farther than I meant. Let us remount. Mistress Meg hasn't flown her merlin yet, but there may be a chance on the way back."

Almost as soon as we were in our saddles again, Meg peered up into the sky and exclaimed that she had seen a bird. "It's drifting back westward, the way we want to go—can I . . . ?"

"Yes, yes!" said Sir Francis, and delightedly, Meg loosed Joy. The quarry, catching sight of her, fled. But not westward, or only for a moment. As Joy closed in, her intended prey veered into a swift climbing turn, changed direction, and sped eastward instead. Sir Francis swore, but Joy meanwhile had twisted in midair to give chase and the rest of us, perforce, had to do the same.

It was a longer chase even than the first, across acres of heather, over a crest and down into a moorland trough, in and out among gorse patches and small clumps of trees, in the full blaze of the sun. The horses were sweating heavily by now. Roundel's neck was dark with it and Meg's pony was blowing, as its short legs worked to keep up with the rest of us. The quarry, this time, escaped, by swooping down ahead of Joy, plunging into a small spinney. Among the tree branches it would be safe from any diving falcon. We pulled up and Joy returned resentfully to the lure that one of the falconers handed to Meg. "You never win them all, mistress," he said. "They don't in the wild, either." He smiled at her regretful face. "No need to be downcast."

"I know. I just feel for her disappointment," Meg said, gentling the bird and hooding her.

"Yes, such a pity," said Seton, in a valiant voice, and with that, closed her eyes and sagged forward over her pommel. Alarmed, I edged Roundel over to her. She looked up painfully, opening her eyes but narrowing them and flinching at the sunlight. "I . . . I'm sorry . . ."

I said quietly: "Is it migraine?"

"Yes. I don't have them often. It got better during the picnic, but this heat . . . it's like a band of steel round my head."

Mary and Sir Francis had trotted over to us. "This is my fault." Mary was contrite. "I have been selfish. I was the one who was ill, and wanted the sun and air and they have made me better." She threw her head back, breathing deeply. "Sitting in Bolton, I felt like a wild bird in a cage, a hawk trapped forever in a mews. Here, I can fly free. But I should have remembered that riding in the heat doesn't suit poor Seton."

"What's the trouble?" asked Knollys. "Sick headache? Out here?"

He looked worriedly about him as well he might, for there was not a vestige of shade to be seen. I was worried, too. I knew about migraine, for at times I suffered from it myself. In my case it was not brought on by hot weather but usually by difficult decisions, and so serene had my life with Hugh Stannard been that I had gone three years without an attack. Whatever their cause, though, most migraines shared certain hallmarks and one was that bright light was painful and would prolong the anguish. Mary Seton needed to rest somewhere cool and dim.

"We can't be all that far from Tyesdale," I said, "This looks familiar—we passed near here on the way to meet you all." I looked about me. We were in a trough in the hills and there were a few farms scattered about in it. Tyesdale, I thought, was just over the next hill, though it would still be a painful ride for someone with Seton's malady. Southward, I could see several hearth smokes, but they were all some distance off. Then, turning to look to the north, I saw with relief that there was one farmhouse quite close. I pointed. "We could take her there. They might let her rest until she feels better."

"In an emergency, I would allow the Lady Mary to go under your roof, Mistress Stannard, but not under that of any stranger. The same applies to Seton. She's devoted to her mistress. I am sorry, but . . ." began Knollys. I shook my head and stopped him.

"Please let me offer a suggestion."

"I wish you would!" said Knollys in a harassed voice.

"Take the Lady Mary back to Bolton, with her escort. I will take Mistress Seton to that farm to rest until she is better and I will engage for it that she lays no schemes, receives and passes no messages while she's there. She's beyond it, anyway," I added. "Her skin's the color of goat's cheese. No one can fake that."

Ryder came up to us. "Can I help, mistress?"

"You can take Mistress Seton up in front of you. I don't think she can keep her saddle. Smith, you can lead Mistress Seton's horse. She's ill. We're going to that farmhouse over there."

"Take Tobias!" said Mary. "Tobias, stay with Mistress Stannard and Seton and escort Seton back to Bolton when she is well again. Oh, my poor Marie." She looked ruefully at Seton and then at me. "We are parting rather hurriedly, are we not, Ursula? I hope you will come to Bolton again before you go home. But if not, will you carry a message to Queen Elizabeth for me? Will you tell her that I will do and say whatever she wishes, and assure her that I wish her well with all my heart and only long for her help and support in this time of trouble and false accusation?"

"Yes, of course," I said, "though I hope to visit Bolton again." I had better. Cecil's half of my errand was still to do. If I could.

Mary gave me her lovely smile and her hand to kiss, and was gone. I watched her go with a regret that had little to do with Cecil's commission and much more to do with feeling that the light was dimmed and the skylark music fainter because Mary Stuart wasn't there.

But Seton looked dreadfully ill. Both Pen and Meg were looking at her with concern. "That way," I said, pointing, and my own little party set off toward the thatched roof and the chimneys I had seen, perhaps half a mile away.

Ryder had put Seton into his own saddle so that its high pommel and cantle could support her, and was sitting behind, with an arm around her. She leaned against him, moaning a little. The only pace we could manage was funereal, and though it was not far, the journey to the farmhouse seemed very long.

When we did eventually get there, the place was depressing. This was no fortified manor farmhouse, but a sprawling, straw-thatched affair that looked as though it had been built for animals as much as people and the smell of middens and stables suffused the surrounding air.

The main door was open, and as I slipped out of my saddle in front of it, I saw that the house, like that of the Grimsdale family, was used for both people and animals. Inside, there was a cattle byre to the right and to the left, an inner doorway. The sun was shining in and I could make out a comfortless room with a floor of beaten earth, an uncushioned settle, a set of farming implements hanging on a rough stone wall, and a slatted wooden staircase leading upward.

Ryder called. Someone answered and a man emerged from the byre, carrying a broom. I recognized him at once, because of his white hair and beard and his aquiline nose. "Master Thwaite!" I said in surprise. "Is this Fernthorpe?"

"Aye. So it be." Will Thwaite favored me with his gap-toothed smile. "Why, Mistress Stannard! Thee've come to visit? Thee should have given us warning! Andrew's out in t'fields and . . ."

"We wouldn't normally have come without warning," I said, "but we need help. We've been hawking and . . ." I began to explain, though I was aware as I did so, of something going on at the back of our little party. It didn't concern Seton, for Ryder had already dismounted and with Tom Smith's help had lifted her down and was half-carrying her forward, ready to go inside the moment our host understood what we needed.

As I finished my explanation, I glanced over my shoulder, but still couldn't make out what was happening. Master Thwaite hadn't noticed. He was already leading the way indoors, telling Ryder to bring the sick lady in out of the sun.

Ryder carried Seton in after him and I had to concern myself with her first. Thwaite led us into the room on the left. It was kitchen and living room all in one, with a big fireplace, though the fire, for the moment, was out. As well as the wooden settle, there were a couple of stools and a table. Near the door, as well as the farm implements, a few businesslike weapons—a couple of swords, half a dozen pikes, and two muskets—hung on the wall. The animal smell was as strong in here as it was outside and a couple of hens were scratching about on the floor amid a scattering of grain and cabbage stalks. I wasn't surprised when a small door at the back was nosed open by a pink snout, and a small pig trotted in to help the hens clear the floor. I wasn't surprised either when the pig relieved itself in front of the empty hearth.

Thwaite uttered an angry shout at the sight of the animal life in the living room and kicked the pig, which removed itself with an indignant snort. He then swept its droppings into the hearth with his broom, and after that swept the chickens out of the back door in the wake of the pig.

Poor Seton had inhaled the smell and audibly choked. However, since there was nowhere else to put her, Ryder helped her to lie down on the settle. Master Thwaite vanished up the stairs and came back a few moments later, dragging a rustling straw pallet in one hand, while the other elbow clamped a pillow to his side. Neither pallet nor pillow looked very clean. "Happen this'll make t'poor lady more comfortable," he said. "I'll get some milk. T'girl's in t'dairy making butter; there'll be skim milk to be had."

He disappeared again, this time to the back regions, and I heard him shouting. Once more he reappeared, with a fat young woman at his heels, carrying a jug and some beakers. The girl had a dairymaid's good skin but also, unfortunately, a terrible squint. Somehow, she seemed to be just the sort of dairymaid that a place like Fernthorpe would have. No one, I felt, would work here if they could find somewhere better. When I got a closer look at her and saw that as well as a squint, she had the remains of a recent black eye, I was surer of that than ever. They obviously didn't starve her but they probably knocked her about. Pen's immediate aversion to Andrew Thwaite had come from a sound instinct.

She waddled around, offering skim milk to all of us. I accepted mine dubiously, hoping she hadn't had her grubby fingers in it. Everything in this place was grimy. The tools on the walls hadn't been cleaned before being hung up. Spade, rake, hoe, all had earth still caked on them. The pike heads were dull and I would have wagered that the muskets wouldn't fire and that if the swords were unsheathed, their blades would not be clear, either.

I was staring at the swords and gingerly sipping my milk, when Will Thwaite spoke to me. "Why are t'rest o' you still hanging about out there in t'sun? Fetch them in, lass. Horses can go in t'byre. Water them first—there's water in trough and happen they need some."

I put my milk beaker down on the table and hurried outside. As I came out of the door, Pen met me. She had dismounted and was leading her mare. "Mistress Stannard!"

"What is it, Pen? Master Thwaite says we can water the horses and . . ."

"We've watered them. We found a trough. Mistress Stannard, Meg won't come inside. She says . . ."

"Meg?" My daughter was still on her pony, hanging back from the house, with Tobias positioned as though he were shielding her from it. I hastened across the yard to her. "Meg, what's the matter?"

"Mother! Oh, Mother!" She was pale and trembling. "This house! That man!"

"That's Master Will Thwaite. He's visited us at Tyesdale—surely you saw him? No, perhaps you didn't; you were out with Brockley when he came the first time, of course, and the second time, you were upstairs with Sybil and Master Whitely entertained them. But . . ."

"I never saw him when he came to Tyesdale but, Mother, he came out of the house just now and spoke to you and I knew his voice! It's the way the gaps in his teeth make his *s*'s splutter!" Meg looked petrified. "He's one of the men who abducted me! I knew his eyes, too. I'll never forget how they looked at me. They were so cold. And that's not all. The sun was lighting up the passageway and I recognized this place. So I turned my pony and edged away before I was noticed. This is where they brought me and Master Thwaite's the man who said I was too young!"

My entire stomach did a somersault. "Oh, dear God!" I said. "And there's a sword on the wall in there that has an amethyst in the hilt just like the one Harry had! I didn't know—I wasn't sure—many swords have jewels in their hilts. But now . . ."

"They're the people who killed Harry," said Pen in a horrified whisper.

12

Matters of the Heart

"Tobias," I said, "and Tom. Take Meg and Pen home to Tyesdale. Now. At once. Into your saddle, Pen." I gave her a leg up myself. "We'll follow with Seton as soon as we can," I said. "I'll look after our horses. Pen and Meg must be got away from here immediately. Hurry!"

I put our horses—Ryder's, Seton's, and mine—into the byre with their tack still on, though I loosened their girths. Returning to Seton, I found that her migraine had reached the point of nausea, no doubt helped by the combination of pigsty stench and rather warm skim milk. The fat dairymaid was now holding a bucket for her, while Ryder hovered, looking anxious.

Facing Will Thwaite was difficult but somehow I managed to smile, and speak calmly as I said: "We are too large a party to descend on you without warning. I've sent the others home. Ryder and I will take Mistress Seton as soon as she can sit a horse again." I caught Ryder's eye and tried to convey with a meaningful stare that I had my reasons. He gave me a small nod, which I knew meant that he would back me up, whether or not he understood what I was about.

"Well, that'll not be yetawhile," said Thwaite, with a glance at the groaning Seton. Handing me my beaker of milk again, he gestured to me to take one of the stools, and then sat himself down on the other. "It's a pity maybe that Mistress Pen's not come in and I'm sorry my son Andrew's not here but happen it's as well. He insisted on coming when I called at Tyesdale t'other day but to my mind, some things are best talked over by parents and guardians when t'young folk aren't about."

"I beg your pardon?" I said.

Master Thwaite smiled. "Whitely and Mistress Appletree must have said that we called at Tyesdale when thee were away?"

"Yes. Yes, I knew that. But . . ."

"Master Whitely said thee were at Bolton Castle," Thwaite remarked. "And Mistress Pen as well. I like that. Visiting terms with castle folk—that's the kind of family I want for Andrew."

"I'm not sure I . . ."

"Oh, come now. We nearly came to t'point when we called on thee t'first time. I had it in mind from t'moment I heard that there was a young lass coming to take t'reins at Tyesdale. A girl can't run such a place all alone, so Mistress Pen needs a husband and rightly enough, thee's looking for one. Well, I want a wife for my Andrew. So—let's put t'cards ont table. How about making a match of it between them?"

This was hustling matters along, by anyone's standards. Standing where Thwaite couldn't see him, Ryder raised his eyebrows and pursed his lips into a silent *whew!*

My pulses were jumping with alarm. Had it been physically possible, I would have abandoned my beaker, dragged Ryder and Seton out, grabbed our horses, and fled from Fernthorpe as though it were infected with the plague. Only with great difficulty could I keep from turning my head and staring at the jeweled sword hilt that had caught my attention the moment I first entered the room.

But the retching Seton could not yet be moved so I was trapped where I was, fending off a proposal of marriage from the family that had struck down Harry, stolen his body away, abducted my daughter, and only rejected her because she was "too young." For breeding, presumably. No doubt the existence of a dowry had been assumed and was a further encouragement to kidnapping. Had Meg been just a little older, what might have befallen her before I found her? I quaked.

"Pen and your son have hardly seen each other," I said, keeping my eyes on Will Thwaite's face with difficulty. The sun was shining on the sword hilt and making the amethyst give off violet flashes. "They have had no time to get to know each other, to know whether they . . ."

"Oh, come now, Mistress Stannard. There's more to marriage than a couple of doves billing and cooing. T'pair can meet and talk before t'ceremony if you reckon that's important but nature's nature; it'll work out just as well if you leave it till after. In any case . . . ah, Andrew!"

"I saw horsemen," said Andrew Thwaite, stepping into the room and hanging a further hoe and a wide-brimmed hat up on the wall. He was dressed in loose, patched hose and a dirty shirt and had an old leather jerkin slung over one shoulder. In this farming gear he still looked as faun-like as ever, except that he now resembled a rustic English faun instead of a legend from classical Greece. He jerked his head at the fat dairymaid. "Get me some ale, Rosie, and be quick about it. It's hot as hell out there."

Rosie, glancing at him as though she were scared of him, which I could well believe, scurried away. I wondered if she were the only house servant here in this otherwise masculine household and whether she had other functions besides that of housemaid and cook. Very likely! I thought. There were methods of making sure that the farm wasn't cluttered up with accidental babies.

"I was telling Mistress Stannard here," said his father, "that we want to ask for Mistress Pen as a wife for thee. Mistress Stannard's talking about love, but as far as that goes, we're halfway there already, aren't we?"

"Indeed we are," Andrew said. "One glance at Mistress Pen was enough for me. She's charming, Mistress Stannard. I'll love her right enough; no fear that I won't." The corners of his mouth curved up in the most disquieting grin I had ever seen on a living human being, although I had seen grins like it on the masks that people sometimes wear at May Day fairs, especially when they're impersonating the Green Man of the Woods, who accompanies the hobbyhorse. And is eagerly touched by childless women because he is supposed to cure infertility. (Vicars of all persuasions are forever trying to forbid the more outrageously heathen aspects of May Day celebrations but they never succeed for long.)

I was in no doubt what the word *love* meant to Andrew. Not that there's anything amiss with that; but it shouldn't stop there. It is supposed to have a context of kindness and concern and anxiety for the loved one's well-being. I felt strongly that this context was as unknown to the Thwaites as it would be to any pagan forest god. Pen, to Andrew and his father, would be just a better-off, slimmer, and legalized version of Rosie.

I thought fast. "The fact is," I said confidingly and untruthfully, "that while we were at Bolton, Sir Francis Knollys suggested a possible match for Pen. Plans are in hand to introduce the young people. So you see, I am in an awkward position. Of course, if for one reason or another, the plan comes to nothing, then we will have to think further but . . ."

"I know what's wrong, Father," said Andrew, taking the far end of the settle from Mary Seton, who by now had sat gingerly upright and was leaning back, eyes closed, but complexion improving. "It's this place. It's so untidy. Mistress Stannard, we do realize that."

"Ah, that'll be it." The older Thwaite's smile was horridly reminiscent of old Gladys at home, with her witchlike fangs. "Mistress Stannard, what you see isn't what Fernthorpe ought to be. There was a fine enough house here once. This is what happens when a house gets burnt down and there's no money in the family to replace it rightly—and anyhow, it's just father and son and the likes of Rosie to keep order. Even at that, we're a bit more respectable upstairs than down. Up above"—he jerked his head at the ceiling—"we've a couple of decent enough bedchambers and a music room, too. Down here we just think of as t'farm buildings." He paused. Rosie came back with Andrew's ale and handed it to him, and he waved at her in a *go-away* signal. She went.

Then he said: "If Pen weds Andrew, she can have things as

she likes—it'll be up to her. She'll bring her own money, I take it, so she can make Fernthorpe whatever she wants; pretty it up, more servants; no pigs in the kitchen; she'll be t'mistress. But since Fernthorpe and Tyesdale adjoin, maybe she and Andrew'd rather live there and I'll stop here as steward, as it were. Leave the youngsters alone to make their lives and their babies. There's good blood in my family. Andrew takes after his mother and she were connected to the Lennox family—not close, but some sort o' cousin. You know who I mean? That husband o' Queen Mary, him that was murdered; his father were Earl of Lennox."

Andrew's resemblance to Darnley was clearly no accident. To my mind, looking like a Lennox was bad enough; actually being one was frightful. *Good blood?* Bad blood, I thought. Murderous blood. I made a vague noise to signify that I had indeed heard of the Lennoxes, and Ryder chipped in uninvited.

"It seems to me," he said, "that all this has come as a great surprise to Mistress Stannard and that she can hardly be expected to decide at this moment, even if there were not a prospect for Mistress Pen at Bolton." He spoke as smoothly as though he had been present at detailed marriage negotiations in the castle. "We only called here because Mistress Seton was ill. Mistress Seton, how are you now?"

"Better, thank you," said Seton. Her voice was faint, but she straightened her back, and glancing at her, I found her eyes fixed steadily on me, conveying a message just as mine had done to Ryder earlier on. She had sensed that I wanted to get us away. "I can't manage the ride to Bolton yet," she said bravely, "but I heard you say earlier that Tyesdale wasn't very far off, Mistress Stannard. I might get there, perhaps. I think I am a trouble to these good people."

"Just how far is Tyesdale from here?" I asked.

"Matter of a mile and a half, house to house," Andrew said. "My horse is in t'meadow but I can catch him and show the way."

"Our thanks, but there's no need," said Ryder, at his most fatherly and protective. "I've an eye for country. I can guide the ladies to Tyesdale. Master Thwaite, I think we should leave. Mistress Stannard and Mistress Pen should have a chance to talk over your most kind proposal in private and—er—compare it with the offer at Bolton."

"We're Catholics, as I've told thee," Thwaite said, "and if we haven't a chaplain, we do have a chapel, out at the back. Rites can be done twice—once by t'vicar in Fritton and once here, to make it sure. Wed in the eyes of God and Queen Elizabeth, they'll be, then."

"As Ryder says," I said, rising and laying my empty beaker aside, "I must consider the matter and speak to Pen. Mistress Seton, if you think you can endure a little more riding . . ."

"I'll get the horses," said Ryder.

I knew that the Thwaites wanted to keep us for longer but there was nothing they could do. At least, I thought, they hadn't seen Meg. They couldn't know that she had recognized them.

The fear that had kept my pulses hammering through every moment I spent in that house sank away when at last I got into Roundel's saddle. At that moment, anger took its place. I would have liked to seize Will Thwaite by his scrawny throat and pound his head on the farmhouse wall until he told me where Harry Hobson was buried.

But that was hardly possible. For the moment, I must say farewell in a polite voice and ride off. I yearned to give my feelings an outlet by leaving at a gallop, but for Seton's sake we still had to proceed at a funereal plod.

As we went, Ryder said: "I think I spoke out of turn in there, madam. I'm the escort; not the man in charge. Only, I thought you needed help. *Is* there a marriage prospect for Mistress Pen at Bolton?"

"Not yet. I invented that. I had to. You were right to think that I needed help but you've no idea how much! Meg wouldn't come in because she recognized the place and recognized Will Thwaite's voice as well. She'd come across them before. Can you guess when?"

Ryder's thick, graying eyebrows shot up again. "When she was kidnapped? Is that what you mean?" I turned my head to

THE FUGITIVE QUEEN • 129

look at his face and saw his eyes widen. "That sword on the wall! With that great big amethyst in the hilt! Was it—is it—?"

"I think so."

"Strewth!" said John Ryder, appalled.

It was still only the afternoon when we arrived back at Tyesdale, though the air was cooler. A breeze had sprung up and cloud was drifting from the west. As Ryder helped Seton down, Jamie Appletree and the Brockleys came out to meet us. Fran at once took charge of Seton, putting an arm round her and leading her indoors.

"I'm glad to be home, Brockley," I said to him as he handed me out of my saddle and Jamie led the horses away. "Where are the others? Are Pen and Meg back safely?" For some reason, Brockley's inexpressive face became more blank even than usual, which was a sign that he was disconcerted. "What's the matter?" I said in alarm. "I sent them off with two men to guard them and . . ."

"They're all here, madam—Master Littleton, Tom Smith, and the young ladies. I'm glad to see you safe. I would have come to find you before long, if you hadn't come home. Fernthorpe is no place for you, from what Mistress Meg had to tell us when she arrived. To think that *they*—our neighbors!—were responsible for . . . !"

"It was a blessing that they didn't realize Meg was there. But there's more, Brockley. While we were in the farmhouse and waiting for Mistress Seton to be well enough to leave, Will Thwaite made a formal proposal for a marriage between his son Andrew and Pen. I managed to put off giving him an answer and got us away. But I don't like it. They're not far away and now that we know what kind of people they are . . ."

"Desperate, by the sound of it, madam," Brockley said.

"And extraordinary," I said. "I can't understand why they tried to snatch a wife for Andrew when we were on our way to Tyesdale and could be approached in a perfectly normal manner—as indeed we were, in the end. We . . . Brockley?"

Brockley's air of being disconcerted, not to say distracted, had reappeared. "Madam, there's something else. Nothing to do with Fernthorpe. This is very difficult."

"What is? Brockley, what's the matter?"

"Well, it's nothing much," said Brockley awkwardly. "Only, when you go inside, you'll find them dancing."

"Dancing? Who's dancing?"

"You know what young folk are, madam. Your Meg was upset by finding herself at Fernthorpe, and what does Mistress Pen say to her, but *Oh, let's practice some dancing; it will give your thoughts a new direction, and what kind of music can we arrange?* The instruments we found in the music room here are useless, of course, but then it turned out that Master Whitely has a lute in working order, and that Dick Dodd had one in his luggage, and now they're both up in the minstrels' gallery, sitting on stools because of that low ceiling, and playing for them . . ."

"Playing for whom?"

"Mostly Mistress Pen and Master Littleton, madam. Mistress Sybil is there as well, of course, watching. Tom Smith is partnering Meg. Somewhere or other, Tom has learned to trip a pretty measure. But . . . I think you'd better go in."

I made for the steps. At the top, I was met by Agnes Appletree, looking anxious.

"Mistress Stannard!"

I could already hear the lutes and the slip-slide, pit-pat of dancing feet but Agnes was barring my way. I frowned. "Agnes? What is it?"

"I saw't with my own eyes," said Agnes, brisk and worried. "I never thought no harm when the dancin' started but now, well, I said to mysen: Mistress Stannard's the guardian of t'lass Pen and did ought to know . . ."

"Know *what*?" I demanded.

"Her and that man Littleton," said Agnes dramatically. "I *saw*. They were dancing and they got under t'shadow of t'gallery and t'others weren't looking and Littleton . . ."

"Yes, and Littleton what?"

"He kissed Mistress Pen, mam. I saw it. And t'lass were laughing. Then they danced across the hall and he did it again and that were no snatched kiss, neither—went on and on, he did, till Mistress Jester called out and chided him. Then he stopped but..."

I pushed past her and marched into the hall. There they were, as Agnes had said. Sybil was standing at the side of the hall, hands folded in front of her. Meg was dancing, hand in hand with Tom, and yes, there were Tobias and Pen. Pen was gazing up into his eyes. Littleton was still in the shirt and breeches in which he had gone hawking while Pen had changed into a charming gown of deep green embroidered with yellow flowers, but they danced with equal elegance, face-to-face, toes pointed, hands on hips, whirling away from each other and then back, to clasp hands and parade gracefully down the hall. I recognized the sequence. It was part of Leicester's Dance, which Robin Dudley had made so popular at court three years ago.

As I watched, Pen saw me and turned her smile toward me, and even though the hall was shadowy after the sunlit courtyard, I could see how her eyes were shining.

The Thwaites and their proposal were complication enough but here was another. Pen had done it again. It had even driven the horror of our discovery at Fernthorpe out of her head. The wretched girl was once more in love.

13

Credentials of a Suitor

My arrival broke the dancing up. I didn't like myself for it. Young people dancing are a charming sight and I spoiled it, like an attack of wheat rust on someone's harvest. But I was responsible for Pen and this would not do. I would have to speak to her. Feeling yet again that I had too much on my mind, too many problems of too many different kinds, so that I was like someone trying to travel to all four points of the compass at the same time, I told Pen to go to her room and wait for me, while I went first to my bedchamber. There Dale helped me to change out of my dusty riding dress and I sent for some wine and sat down to think.

I was soon interrupted, however. Meg came to me there and after one look at my daughter's small scared face, I decided that I would let Pen wait.

As Dale slipped tactfully away, I took Meg in my arms and said: "It's all right. You're perfectly safe here, and they didn't want you for Fernthorpe, anyway. They set you free—remember?"

"I was only dancing because Pen said I ought to think of something else. I didn't really feel like dancing! When I heard that man's voice and knew why that place seemed so familiar, I thought my knees would turn to water. When we got home, I just wanted to hide in my bed and cry, only Pen wouldn't let me. Oh, *Mother.*"

"She probably did you a service." Meg had only been an

excuse, but Pen had helped her even if it was by accident. "Darling, there is nothing for you to fear. And we've learned something. We know who killed Harry and we know what kind of people the Thwaites really are." Meg managed a watery smile and I gave her another hug. "You're here with me," I said, "and that's where you're staying."

"We didn't mean any harm, by dancing, Mother."

"Of course you didn't. It's a skill you need to practice."

"But it displeased you—everyone saw it."

"It wasn't the dancing that displeased me," I said. "It was something quite different. I daresay I shall arrange more dancing, now that I know we can have music. I wish I'd thought to pack my own lute. Now, find Mistress Jester and occupy yourself sensibly until supper. I must talk to Pen."

"Oh, she wants to talk to *you*, Mother. She wouldn't stay in her room. She's waiting to come in. I raced her to get to you first."

"Indeed?" I said. "Then tell her that I'm ready to give audience!"

Pen must have been just outside, for she virtually passed Meg in the doorway. I greeted her by standing in the middle of the room, and waiting, with a stern face, for her to approach. But if I were trying to convey the idea that she ought to have something on her conscience, I failed. She came eagerly up to me, bobbed a mere sketch of a curtsy and exclaimed: "Oh, Mistress Stannard, what an amazing day this has been! That dreadful business at Fernthorpe—but now, something so splendid has happened! You'll never guess what it is!"

"I have a strong suspicion," I said, "that it doesn't need much guesswork. However, just in case I'm wrong, you'd better tell me."

"It's Master Littleton—Tobias! Oh, Mistress Stannard, he is such a kind, interesting young man! We talked at Bolton, you know, when we went to look at the mews, and when we were leaving, he said he hoped we would soon meet again. Mistress Stannard, he's so well educated! He can speak and write Latin and Italian, and he likes the same poetry that I do. And he dances beautifully! He wants to offer for my hand! Oh, Mistress Stannard, it would be a perfect match, wouldn't it? My mother would approve, because Tobias says he's Catholic, though he makes no parade of it because he is working for Sir Francis Knollys. And Sir Francis is a courtier and we would go to court eventually, as part of his household. I expect I would be received back at court once I was married, wouldn't I?"

"Stop!" I said. "All this is happening far too quickly. Littleton had no business to make advances to you without obtaining my permission first. I shall have a few things to say to that gentleman."

"But, Mistress Stannard, we couldn't help it—it just overtook us! It began at Bolton, just tentatively, as it were, but Tobias wrote to my brother George about having met me and liked me, and George wrote back saying that he was agreeable to the match . . ."

"Did he now?" I said sharply. I remembered Ann Mason's words in her letter to me. She had said that she and George were not altogether in agreement concerning the kind of bridegroom his sister should take. She had also remarked that by the terms of her husband's will, she and not George had been made Pen's guardian.

Oblivious to my tone, Pen was rushing eagerly on. "Then today, on the way back from Fernthorpe, we rode side by side and talked further, and now we've danced together and . . ."

"You've gone too far and too fast for my liking. Pen, I saw you with him in the hall when you were dancing, and you were also seen to be kissing him openly. Your mother wouldn't approve of that! Sit down!" I sat down myself, on the edge of the bed and Pen came to sit beside me.

"I'm not a gorgon," I said. "In fact, I feel at the moment like nothing more than a very tired Mistress Stannard. I want your happiness. I am not here to stand in your way. But there *is* such a thing as checking a suitor's credentials. Your mother made it clear to me what manner of man she wished you to marry and I'm not sure that she'd choose Master Littleton. He has no property for one thing. And," I added, holding up a hand to stop Pen from interrupting, "there is such a thing as indiscreet behavior. What you were doing when I arrived was sadly indiscreet."

Pen's mouth drooped. "You are so young," I told her. "I'll talk to Littleton. He will stay here overnight, I think; it would be best for Mistress Seton to rest until tomorrow and then I have decided that we should both ride back to Bolton with them."

"Both?"

"Yes. It would be natural for me to ask Sir Francis Knollys's opinion of Tobias and I need an excuse to go to Bolton again as I still have to talk with Mary Stuart. The falconry gave me no chance. I want you to come because I want you under my eye. Pen, you are entitled to know this. While I was at Fernthorpe, Master Will Thwaite asked me formally for your hand, for Andrew . . ."

"What?" Pen whitened. "But . . . Mistress Stannard . . ."

"It's all right! Good God! There's no question whatsoever of an alliance with them, even if you liked the look of Andrew . . ."

"I don't!"

"Just as well. They're criminals and I intend to send Brockley to Fritton again to report what we have learned to Constable Toft. Perhaps he'll pay attention this time. Meanwhile, though, I think there's something very odd about this whole business. I can't understand why they're so eager for an alliance with us. That's another reason why I want to watch over you. You will be in Tobias's company on the journey to Bolton but there's to be no more talk of love until you have permission. Go along to your room, now. Read something improving!"

I sent her away, looking downcast, which I regretted, although I knew I was right to be firm with her. I secretly admitted to myself that I envied Pen's easy, youthful abandonment to passion. I had been like that, when I ran off with Gerald. But I had been lucky in my man. At Tyesdale, I felt that we were surrounded by unknown quantities and it is more alarming to be responsible for someone else than for oneself.

Before supper, I wrote a letter to Constable Toft and then called the Brockleys to me. However, when I told Brockley that I wished him to deliver it, his face at once became doubtful. "What is it?" I asked.

"Madam, if this is an order, I'll do your bidding. But I think it may be unwise just yet."

"Explain yourself, Brockley."

"Toft is a stupid and obstinate man, and what have we to tell him? Will he believe—or even listen to—the testimony of a child like Meg? She will tell him she recognizes Will Thwaite but she never actually saw his face. Apart from Meg, the only evidence we have that the Thwaites were concerned in Harry's death is the fact that they have a sword that looks like his. But such swords are not uncommon. I think," said Brockley, "that we need to find Harry's body. If it's on Fernthorpe land, that might make a difference. Toft would have to take notice of that. We should ride over that land and search, if we can."

I fumed, but Brockley was talking sense. I had no confidence in Toft, either. Something else had also occurred to me. I now told Brockley and Dale, in detail, everything that the Thwaites had said to me concerning a possible marriage between Andrew and Pen, both during the visit they had made to Tyesdale, and at Fernthorpe.

Before I had quite finished, Brockley was clearing his throat and obviously longing to speak. I paused inquiringly.

"Madam, it's clear to me that Master Thwaite not only wants a wife for his son, he also wants a well-dowered wife. Now, the morning you left the Grimsdale farm, if you recall, the farmer wasn't pleased that we were leaving Mistress Pen behind. And the Grimsdale sons were out before us that morning—and out the previous evening, after supper."

"And you think they may have told the Thwaites that a likely prospect for Andrew was in the district? Sybil wondered the same thing. She thought the Grimsdales might have sold news of us for money."

"They may well have done! But they're so eager to marry Andrew Thwaite to our Pen, that what *I'm* wondering is—did they try to cut a corner by grabbing her before we even got here, only they grabbed the wrong girl? If you remember, we thought Master Grimsdale resented Pen being left behind because they were short of provender but perhaps it was because he knew that his sons had gone to tell the Thwaites she was on the road and he couldn't let them know that she wasn't. Dear God, what a risk we took, leaving her there! Just as well Tom and I were both there with her and that Dick Dodd joined us. It's my belief that on the day of the attack, the Thwaites just snatched the only young girl we had with us—Meg—and it wasn't till they got to Fernthorpe and had a good look at her that they realized she couldn't be Mistress Pen. I daresay the Grimsdales had told them how old Mistress Pen is."

"So they turned Meg out to take her chance on the moors in the mist! And what kind of folk would do that?" Dale's blue eyes were fairly bulging with horror.

"How they must all have cursed," I said. "I suppose then they decided that Pen was too well protected and to go about things in a more decent fashion!"

"But why should they be so wild to marry her to Andrew?" Dale was puzzled. "Tyesdale's her dowry, but it's not much of a place, to my mind."

"That's exactly what I'm asking myself," I said. "It doesn't make sense. I've been thinking the same as you, Brockley—I mean that they mistook Meg for Pen. But for a place like Tyesdale, kidnapping the girl is going to ridiculous extremes." I passed a hand across my forehead. I had a slight headache and hoped that I wasn't about to follow Seton's unhappy example and develop a migraine. "Very well, Brockley. First of all, I have to go to Bolton to see Sir Francis about Tobias and, I hope, to see Mary Stuart, and Pen will come with me. I want both of you with me as well. When we return, we will try to find Harry's grave."

But before we left for Bolton, I thought, I really must talk to Tobias Littleton.

I interviewed him after supper, in the parlor, and came to the point without wasting time.

"Master Littleton, I gather that you have been making advances to my ward, Penelope Mason. Is that correct?"

Master Littleton, of course, was still in the clothes he had been wearing all day, in which he had hawked and danced. He had had a doublet with him and had put it on for supper but on his own admission it had been pushed into a saddlebag along with a water bottle and some cold chicken. It was creased and looked as though both the chicken and the water bottle had oozed. He had joked about it at supper, saying that he had undertaken to be a human larder, and this was what came of it, and I had caught Pen looking at him adoringly, as though this were the very height of wit.

"Mistress Pen," he said now, "is a most delightful girl. I have to admit that I am smitten. I have perhaps overstepped the mark but I have been in touch with her brother and . . ."

"As her guardian I principally represent her mother, whose views are not the same as those of George Mason. If you have actually spoken to Pen of marriage without first speaking to me, then you have indeed overstepped the mark. *Have* you spoken to her thus?"

"Yes, Mistress Stannard." He grinned at me. The sun and wind had worked on his clerk's indoor face, giving him bronzed cheekbones and a peeling nose. The effect was to make him both more handsome and more endearing. "But I did propose marriage," he said frankly. "I wasn't trifling. Matrimony is an honorable estate, or so we are told."

"And Pen is attractive to you?"

"Very much so."

"And Tyesdale? Tyesdale is her dowry, as you probably realize. I assume you are taking that into account."

"Do you mean am I proposing marriage to Mistress Mason in order to get my hands on her property, or am I proposing marriage to her in spite of the fact that her property needs a deal of work to be done on it?"

"I have no idea how you view it," I said. "Do you see it as an asset or a liability? Which?"

"An asset. It has great potential," said Tobias, "and both Mistress Pen and I are young. We can make something of it. Mistress Stannard, I cannot afford to marry a girl with no dower, but I am not looking for riches on a platter. I admit that on my side, I have no property and that my elder brother will inherit Father's business. However, Father has already made over some money to me and has made further provision for me in his will; I am not quite penniless and I have expectations. I also have a good position with Sir Francis Knollys."

I was beginning to soften, though I was careful not to show it so soon. This was just as well, because his next words startled me.

"I know Tyesdale a little, as it happens. I think that Magnus has had a difficult job, left alone here to take all the decisions and never sure if he was doing the right thing or not. I would be more helpful to him. I came to know Tyesdale through visiting him here. He's my cousin. He too was at school with me and George Mason. I could work with him."

"I . . . did not know that," I said, disconcerted, and instinctively scanning Tobias's features for some resemblance to Whitely. There was a faint one; they both had the same indeterminate-colored eyes. Otherwise, they were a contrast. Tobias was by no means nondescript.

I recovered myself. "I can't possibly give you an answer now. I must ask you, meanwhile, to keep a polite distance from Pen. No more stealing kisses, if you please, Master Littleton. If . . . if for any reason I felt I couldn't agree to this match, I don't want her to be hurt. If you steal kisses, you might also steal her heart, too soon."

"I do realize," said Tobias, "that there may be others in the field. I believe that the Thwaites are considering her as a match for Andrew."

"How on earth did you know that?" I was jolted out of my caution.

"Magnus told me. He knows everyone for miles."

"You and he aren't related to them as well, are you?"

"No. But people in this district have close bonds, Mistress Stannard."

"I've noticed," I said caustically. I thought of my party arriving at the Grimsdales' farm one evening, and being the targets of a kidnapping the very next morning. I was beginning to wonder if everyone in the vicinity of Tyesdale communicated with everyone else at dead of night by means of crystal balls, or possibly coven meetings, reached with the help of flying broomsticks.

"Have I your word, Master Littleton, that you will hold back until I finally make up my mind? I am coming to Bolton with you tomorrow. I shall speak to Sir Francis Knollys regarding your character and family. You realize that I am bound to do that?"

"Certainly, Mistress Stannard."

"Thank you." I moved toward the door. "I won't be too long in coming to a decision."

And how much difference, I wondered as I went upstairs to bed, would the fact that we were about to dismiss Magnus Whitely make to Tobias? I longed for Hugh's advice. Then I realized that I knew what he would say, and that I agreed with him.

Hugh would say: "Whitely is dishonest and there is no question of keeping him on. If that causes Tobias to take against Penelope, then it would be better to find that out now rather than later."

Quite. Added to which, I thought, as I reached the top of the stairs, a cousin as dishonest as Magnus Whitely must make one look twice, or even three times, at Tobias, and judging from Ann Mason's letter, the fact that George approved of Tobias as a match for Pen was another point against him. Implicit in that letter, to anyone who knew the Mason family, had been a hint that George was something of a Catholic hothead who would choose a similar husband for his sister if he could. Ann, wisely discreet, hadn't said so in so many words, but her insistence on finding a loyal and law-abiding match for Pen had made the point clear. She did not want Pen to marry into a family of potential traitors. Was Tobias really a harmless individual who looked on his Catholic faith as a private matter, or was he likely to let it lead him—and any wife of his—into trouble?

I needed to know a great deal more about Tobias. And his proposal could make no difference to Whitely's fate. I must find a replacement steward and get the dismissal of Whitely over. It was urgent.

The next day was fresh and bright. My headache had subsided during the night. Rain had fallen, cooling the air, and even the stagnant moat looked less repulsive than usual. Meg, intrigued by the sound of quacking, found a couple of ducks preening their plumage on the narrow ledge between the moat and the house wall and regretted that they were too big for Joy to tackle. Those of us who were going to Bolton were relieved that the rain had cleared and hoped that the day would stay fine.

I thought it likely that we would stay at least one night at the castle and must therefore take a change of clothes and some night gear. We were just assembling the hampers in the hall when a cheerful clatter of hooves and a halloo in a female voice as loud as a bugle announced that Mistress Cecily Moss had arrived. She was accompanied by one of her sons, and when they had dismounted and come inside, she announced that this one was Clem. "T'younger lad; I daresay you could hardly tell t'difference between 'em!" boomed Cecily.

"We haven't had time to get to know them yet," I said. "Come into the parlor."

"Makin' ready to go off somewhere, are you?" inquired Cecily, looking at the hampers. "I was at church in Fritton early this morning and saw you weren't there."

"Not this Sunday, no. We're going to Bolton and may hear the evening service there. Agnes, wine and some of your oat-cakes, please."

"Kind of you and welcome enough, I admit, but I'm here on business," Cecily announced as I led the visitors into the parlor. "So is Clem. Now, you're looking for a steward . . ."

"I must tell you, Mistress Moss," I said hastily, "that our present steward still doesn't know that . . . well . . . that we wish to replace him. Please keep your voice down." I thanked heaven that by this time we were safely in the parlor and that I had shut the door. Whitely was in his office at the opposite end of the hall and even Cecily's voice couldn't carry all the length of the hall and through two closed doors.

"Well, if thee's agreeable to what I propose, thee needn't hide it much longer," said Cecily, though to my relief, she dropped her voice to a normal level. She pushed Clem forward. "Here's your answer! Not permanent, maybe, and he'll have a wife before long, but t'arrangement ought to last long enough to do for t'time being. Peter's my heir and there's nowt spare for Clem here. He's got to make his way and he'd best set about it quick, now that he's betrothed to Mabel Holme. You'll not mind Mabel comin' with him? She can help Mistress Appletree and there's room here for when t'babes come along. No need for wages for her beyond all found. Hope that'll suit. Clem knows what's what in house or farm. Speak up, lad!"

"I reckon I could do t'job," said Clem calmly, and, to my relief, in a voice which didn't rattle the fire irons. "I can steward the house and I can oversee t'land as well. I'd save, as best I could, and with t'little dowry that Mabel's got, and whatever I can put together, I daresay after a few years I might rent a smallholding for her and me, but meanwhile, I'll serve thee as well as I can, Mistress Stannard. Would it do, mistress? With Mabel in t'bargain with me, like?"

"It's Mistress Mason you'd be serving," I said mildly. "Tyesdale belongs to her. She may live here with her husband when she's married—that isn't settled yet."

I recalled that when the Moss family paid us their first visit, they had thought of abandoning Mabel Holme in favor of Pen. I wondered if Clem would mind working for the young woman he might once have been asked to consider as a wife.

Clem, however, merely smiled. "I'll work for my wages honestly, for whoever's t'owner here. Don't matter about that."

"I've no objection to Mabel and I don't suppose Mistress Mason will have, either. Nor will Agnes, I think. She'll welcome the help. Can you keep reliable accounts?"

He nodded. "Aye, I can that. Peter and I have done t'accounting for our own place together these last few years."

"I've no patience with stewing over ledgers," boomed his mother. "I was right glad to pass them over to t'boys. But they can do more than that. Both my lads know a bit of Latin and they've read verse and books of travel, too. They're gentlemen, for all they've been reared to be practical on the land."

"I think," I said, "I really think—that we might do business."

14

Captive Bird

I parted Clem from his mother by calling Sybil and asking Cecily to advise her on a local supplier for some new wall hangings. Then I fetched Pen and let her ask Clem a few questions herself. It was the kind of thing she needed to learn.

She pleased me. The young are adaptable and willy-nilly, Pen, who had hated Tyesdale so much to begin with, was now developing the feelings of an owner. She asked sensible things, such as what Clem, as steward, would do if this or that should happen and what kinds of decisions he would be prepared to take on his own responsibility.

Clem in turn made sensible replies. In his mother's pres-ence, both he and his brother seemed tongue-tied but probably they just couldn't be bothered to shout for a hearing. Away from Cecily, Clem was both forthcoming and shrewd. Of his own accord, he remarked that he'd see that old plows weren't left rusting in the fields. "Did tha know there was one in t'barley field? That field's due to be left fallow next year and have cattle grazing in't. They'll fall over that old plow and hurt theirselves."

"You mean it's still there?" I said. "I told Whitely to have it removed."

"I saw't on t'way in," said Clem simply. "And if t'coffers'll run to't, I'd have that moat drained and refilled and stocked with fish. I saw a pair o' ducks there as we came in. No reason why you shouldn't have ducks in plenty and duckling for dinner whenever you fancy, but t'moat's too dirty as it is. There's a stream feeds it that's choked with weed and wants clearing but likely thee'd have to hire men in for t'job."

I exchanged small nods with Pen. After that, it was only a matter of settling when Clem should come. He wanted to go home, put his belongings together, and talk to his betrothed. "I can settle a date for t'wedding now. Peter'll be pleased. He's got a fancy for us two to get wed on t'same day. No reason why I shouldn't move in here beforehand, though. I can come in a week if that suits."

We all shook hands on the bargain. I went to tell Cecily and when she and Clem had gone, I explained to Pen that although one day dismissing unsatisfactory servants was another thing she must be prepared to face, I thought I'd better deal with Whitely on her behalf. Then I went to give that gentleman his marching orders. I sent Tobias out of earshot, saying that a domestic matter had delayed our departure for Bolton, and asking him to take Mary Seton for a walk outdoors. I also asked both Sybil and Brockley to attend me at the interview. At home I could have dealt with Whitely alone, but in the north I was permanently nervous.

It was unpleasant. Whitely first of all stared at me in disbelief, and then embarked on a stream of self-justification. He had been left to carry Tyesdale on his own for *years* on end. He had had to take *all* the decisions. He had never known how much of the profits he was expected to put back into the house and farm; he had never had *anyone* to give him orders, tell him when he'd gone wrong, or give him a word of praise—or a rise in wages—when he had done right. He'd lost heart, frankly. Men do when no one takes an interest in their work . . .

I asked him to bring me the box that he kept under his bed. At this point, the protests, which up to then had been expressed in a kind of whine, became a resentful shout. The box was private. If we'd been poking and prying in it, we ought to be *ashamed* of ourselves. It was no more than one might expect from a pack of women, peeping and sneaking, but it was a scandal and a *disgrace* and . . .

I sent Sybil for the box. When she brought it, Brockley invited Whitely to open it. He refused, so I opened it myself, with my lockpicks, while Whitely watched with amazement and fury struggling for supremacy in his face. When the bills and receipts were out on his desk, I myself took from its shelf the ledger which we had studied, and then let Sybil point out the discrepancies in the figures. Whitely began to bluster that women couldn't be expected to understand accounts. Sybil calmly produced the notes she and Meg had made, picked out a few specific cases of discrepancy, and asked him to explain them.

Whitely refused to answer. Brockley went to the door and called, which brought Ryder to join us. Brockley and Ryder then shoved the Tyesdale steward up against the wall and told him he'd better answer or else. Frightened and sulky, he admitted that yes, he'd paid himself a rise when he thought he'd earned it. Who else was there to authorize it? What if he *had* taken a bit of commission for haggling to get good prices for the wool clip and so on? Didn't most stewards do the same?

"While a plow rusts in a field and even when you're told to have it removed, you don't do so," said Sybil.

"You had better leave at once," I said. "I haven't yet written to the Earl of Leicester about you, and if you go quietly, I won't."

"Leave? Just like that? I've been here ten years and more! I've . . ."

"Don't worry, madam," said Brockley grimly. "I'll stand over him while he packs. The mule belongs to him as well as the gray cob, I gather. Whitely, you'll saddle the one and load your things on the other and go."

I will not repeat the language and the curses with which Whitely took his leave. Eventually, he shouted for Jamie Appletree to catch his animals and saddle up, and Brockley escorted him (still muttering imprecations) to his room, where we heard him banging about in a rage, throwing his belongings together.

Pen, in the hall, had watched wide-eyed as Whitely was marshaled upstairs. I sent her to her own room "to make sure you've packed everything you need for Bolton" and went in search of Tobias and Mary Seton. They and Agnes were looking at the vegetable plot and the scanty array of herbs at the side of the courtyard.

"I have to tell you," I said, "that I have just dismissed Magnus Whitely for cheating the estate. A new man is coming. Master Littleton, Pen doesn't know that Whitely is your kinsman. If this changes your feelings for her, please tell me now, before this matter goes any further."

"You've dismissed Magnus?" Tobias looked startled. "Well, I know he'd rather lost heart about his work. I don't know what to say."

"What has happened?" asked Mary Seton. I explained, and she smiled at Tobias. "So you have your eyes on Mistress Pen. Dear Master Littleton, don't let your cousin stand in your way. If you have touched Pen's heart, don't make her suffer."

At that moment, Whitely came down into the courtyard, where Jamie had the cob and the mule ready. He grabbed the cob's reins, mounted, and seized the mule's halter rope. Both cob and mule, sensing their owner's temper, laid back their ears and showed the whites of their eyes. At the sight of Tobias, staring at him from the vegetable patch, he scowled.

"I'm leaving! I'm going to friends. I'll see you before long!" Whitely shouted. Then he spurred his unfortunate mount, plunged into a canter, and clattered off through the gatehouse, the mule trailing resentfully after.

"I see no reason why this should make any difference," Tobias said to me. "I regret it, but perhaps after all it would be easier for me not to have my own cousin as my steward. May I ride with Mistress Pen on the way to Bolton, and talk with her?"

"Provided you don't talk of love," I said.

We reached Bolton Castle three hours later. I left Ryder and Dodd at Tyesdale to guard Sybil and Meg, who were also remaining there, but the rest came with me, Fran on Brockley's pillion.

As we dismounted in the courtyard, Sir Francis came hurrying out, looking harassed.

"Dear God, I'm thankful to see you, Mistress Seton. I can do nothing with the Lady Mary. Mistress Stannard and Mistress Mason, you're welcome, too. She likes you both; you may be able to help. Go in, go straight to her. Tobias, go to my office— my correspondence is falling behind and I have a report to dictate, to be sent to Queen Elizabeth . . ."

"But what's wrong? Is my lady ill?" Seton was alarmed.

"Yes, but it's more than that!" I could never have imagined that Sir Francis Knollys, that grave and dignified gentleman, could sound so distracted. "Someone has told her something she is not supposed to know," he said. "She came back from the hawking party and found a message in her workbox. One of the local girls who waits on her saw her find it and read it, and reported it to me. She's paid extra for looking out for such things. It was reading the message that made Lady Mary fall into such a frenzy. Go to her, go to her! She is frantic and she is suffering from that pain in her side again and my physician can find no cause . . ."

Mary Seton picked up her riding skirt and ran, with Pen and myself on her heels. We dashed through the main door, up two flights of stairs, and arrived headlong at Mary Stuart's suite. The guards on duty outside recognized us and let us pass. Mary was lying on her bed. A small dog was whimpering on the coverlet and one of the local girls Knollys had mentioned, possibly the very one who had spied on her, was vainly imploring Mary to drink this tisane, madam, please; it has valerian to soothe your nerves and eastern poppy for the pain . . .

Mary, her face flushed and blotchy with crying, was pushing her away and exclaiming fretfully that she could not bear the smell or the taste and that no tisanes on earth could heal her troubles and why would no one leave her alone to weep in peace? The girl looked thankful to see us.

"Thank you, my dear. We'll take over now," said Mary Seton, gently taking the cup. Mary heaved herself up on her pillow and said: "Oh, my dear Seton! Are you better? You find me in despair and so very glad to have you back. And Mistress Stannard, and

Penelope! I am sorry for such a poor welcome. Oh dear. Oh dear."

She rolled over, turned her back on us, buried her face in the pillow, and dissolved into helpless weeping while the small dog sat up on its hindquarters and started to howl.

We spent the next hour working on Mary, as grooms sometimes work on an exhausted and upset horse. Seton sent the maid for perfumed water and a sponge, coaxed Mary into turning over to have her forehead laved, and despatched Pen to commandeer mulled wine and egg custard. Pen sensibly came back not only with sustenance for Mary, but also with a bowl of meat for the dog, which quietened its whimpering. Seton coaxed wine and custard into the ex–Queen of Scotland, told the girl to take away the used dishes, and then she and I together gave Mary a massage. Pen found a lute on a window seat and played some soft music.

By the time we had finished, we were worn-out but Mary was much restored. Seton drew the thin coverlet over her, and said: "And now, tell us what the trouble is. My dearest lady, please tell us. Troubles grow smaller when they are shared."

"There's no mystery!" Mary sighed. "Why should I make a mystery of such things? I have known for more than a month that my half brother Moray meant to send Queen Elizabeth anything he could find that would injure my good name. I heard—in June—that he had found some letters of mine and meant to send them to her, but I write so many letters and I never wrote one with any harm in it that I could remember! I was not anxious, not then . . ."

"And now?" I said.

"For weeks, that was all I knew," said Mary, with a trace of petulance. "Then, a day or two ago, a messenger from Cecil to my half brother stayed here, on his way north; not that anyone told me of it then! I am kept mewed up in these rooms, a captive bird, and know hardly anything of who comes to the castle or leaves it or where they are going! Sir Francis would have me kept from all knowledge as though I were blindfolded, with plugs of wax in my ears! But oh, *this* knowledge! Sweet Virgin . . .when I came back from hawking and wanted to take up my embroidery, I opened my workbox and I found . . .I found . . . !"

She began to cry again. "The workbox is in the other room," she said. "On the window seat. Mistress Stannard . . ."

I fetched it. Mary took it distastefully, as though it might dirty her slender white fingers, opened it, and between finger and thumb, withdrew a folded sheet of paper. She looked at it with tearful loathing and then held it out, uncertainly, halfway between Seton and me. "It is so easy to doctor innocent letters or misinterpret them." She sobbed as she spoke. "There was no harm meant, no harm, but . . ."

My dear madam, said the letter, *a courier from Sir William Cecil to your brother Moray in Scotland rested here last night and I searched his baggage, and found the message he was carrying. I hadn't time to copy it all out, but it said that Cecil was pleased with the letters which Moray had sent to him and in particular with some of the phrases in the longest letter, this being one which, as Cecil understands it, was sent by yourself, madam, to James Hepburn of Bothwell just before your husband's unhappy death.*

Madam, I myself am sure that the letter was forged or written by someone else, or that the phrases have some harmless meaning. I am certain of you. But these are among the phrases.

. . . We are coupled with two false races; let the devil sunder us, and God knit us together forever for the most faithful couple that ever was united . . .

and

. . . I remit myself altogether to your will. Send me word what I shall do and whatever shall be the outcome, I will obey you.

and

. . . seeking to obey you, my dear love, I spare neither honor, conscience, hazard, nor greatness.

Also, there is in the letter (so Cecil says) a warning that once read, it should be burned, for it is over-dangerous.

Madam, take care, for if these phrases are read out at any inquiry, I fear they could do damage. You should be on your guard. T

"Who's T?" I asked. "That's not the initial of either of the Douglases." No one answered. A disagreeable thought popped into my head. "It isn't Tobias Littleton is it, by any chance?" I inquired.

"Tobias!" Pen gasped. "Oh no! It couldn't be!"

Seton, who was once more sponging Mary's forehead, paused involuntarily and I thought: *Oh yes, it could be. I knew straightaway that he was under her spell. It could be.*

"It is, isn't it?" I said.

"And why not?" Mary sat up sharply, knocking Seton's hand away just as Seton was about to resume her ministrations. Her tears had subsided. "Is it a sin to help a beleaguered woman, falsely accused and denied knowledge of what is being said and plotted behind her back? Tobias is a good friend to me! Yes, it's Master Littleton! Why *not*? Yes, I *do* know he is Catholic, though he has not told Sir Francis so. Tobias has been kind to me. He believes in me, God bless him. He wishes to help me. He must have put this in my workbox just before we all went off to the hawking. But you see how I am hounded? My words are to be twisted to use against me; my innocent letters turned into proof that I am a monster. I . . ."

"What did you intend the phrases to mean?" I asked. I spoke very mildly, but Mary's golden-brown eyes flashed such fury at me that I took an involuntary step back.

"Have they turned you against me already, my sweet Ursula? Yes, they were love letters. I admit it; Bothwell stole my heart in my husband's lifetime. He was all that Henry Darnley was not: capable, loyal to me—or so I thought then—a man I could lean on. I wrote to him, I confess it, as women in love will write. He was then wed to Jean Gordon, and I to Henry Darnley, but he was planning to have his marriage set aside and I hoped that mine too would soon end . . ."

"You were hoping for an annulment, I take it?" I said. There was a chilly feeling in the pit of my stomach. But she had presented me with the opportunity and I must take it. "I suppose it would be easy enough," I said in brisk tones. "You and Darnley were cousins and I believe you had no papal dispensation to marry."

It was an old trick, which I learned from Gerald long ago. He used it to help him discover things to the discredit of the clerks and treasury keepers he wanted to blackmail into lending their keys. "If you want someone to tell you something and they won't answer a direct question, then pretend you know the answer and put it to them as a statement. Seven times out of ten, they'll correct you, and then you'll have the truth."

I did it instinctively, pitying her, moved by her, detesting myself, but knowing that I must. And Gerald was right. It worked.

"Not an annulment," Mary said. "How could I do that? It would have made our son a bastard! No, it had to be some other way. A rebellion by my nobles, perhaps—Darnley might fall in a battle. Or a charge of treason. When my poor secretary David Riccio was killed almost in front of me while my son was still in my womb, the shock could have killed us both. I suppose that would count as treason. But who can say which way a trial will go? I didn't know what to do. I didn't arrange my own husband's death! That is what Cecil wants to prove but it's a lie—a stupid, wicked lie! How could I? The man I had slept with, cared for in illness? Besides, a woman can be burned for that." She shuddered, and I saw real terror in her eyes. "The mob in Edinburgh thought I *had* arranged it; they came raging round the place where I was, screaming, *Burn the whore!* I was so frightened . . ."

"You must have been," I said sympathetically. *Please,* I said within myself, *please return me the right answers. I don't want to do this. Don't disappoint me. Say what I want to hear.*

I had to go on with it. It was required of me. "It must have been horrifying—when the mob accused you, and earlier, when you were still wondering how to end your marriage. How *did* you decide to do it?"

The odious answer was already in my mind. I could only hope that Mary wouldn't confirm it. I prayed she would contradict it, but if it were true, I didn't want her to admit it. In her place, I wouldn't have done.

But she looked at me in surprise, as though taking it for granted that I already understood, and said, "Why, I put it in my nobles' hands, in Bothwell's hands, and bade them see to it. They were men; they would know what was best to do. That was all. I was only saying to James that I hoped our marriages would end soon so that we could wed each other—and that meanwhile I would take whatever advice he gave me—that I already saw myself as his wife and felt bound to be obedient to him as I would have to be once we were married. That was all! But who will believe me, whatever I say? I am a queen anointed; I will not testify or be questioned—what wise advice that was!—but what difference will it make? Others will speak evil of me and who will prevent them?"

She began to wail anew, and when Seton tried to put her arms around her to comfort her, cried out that the pain in her side had begun again. Seton glanced over her shoulder at me and with a movement of her head, signaled that Pen and I should go.

"Not a word," I said as we went through the outer chamber. "Not until we're private."

Brockley was hovering outside, waiting to tell me that we had been given a different suite of rooms from last time, and that he would show me the way. Dale was there, he said. We followed him to the rooms, and once inside, I closed the door, telling the Brockleys to stay.

"You have always been privy to my secrets," I said. "We have discovered that Tobias Littleton has been spying for Mary Stuart and reading other people's letters for her benefit. It's come as a shock." I looked at the silent Pen and saw from her white face how much of a shock it actually was. "Sit down, Pen," I said.

"I can't, I *won't*, believe he meant any harm!" said Pen.

"I think you must," I said soberly, and sadly. I had more on my mind than Tobias. The coldness in my guts was worse now, like an icy hand, squeezing them. Mary's spell was broken. I had looked at her blotchy face and angry eyes and seen not pathos but a tigress. I knew what had happened, as clearly as though I had been inside Mary's mind. I had Cecil's answer for him now.

She had told her nobles in general, and Bothwell in particular, that she wished to be rid of her marriage, by some means that would not make her son illegitimate. And then she had taken up her embroidery needle and gone on with her delicate stitching, leaving it to the important, clever, ruthless men of her court, the men who would know what to do just because they were men, to rescue her from Darnley, by whatever means seemed best to them.

They were the men who had murdered her secretary David Riccio. They were violent by nature. They turned to murder without hesitation. They would turn to it first, before the legal processes of treason or even the device of a carelessly swung sword in a battle-line. She could not have been surprised when they employed it to deal with Darnley. But she would never admit to herself that she had known in advance what they would do. She would hide behind the fact that she had given them no specific orders. They should have the blood, the gunpowder on their hands; she, sweet, feminine Mary, would keep her innocence, her right to wide-eyed horror. And, of her own choice, she had married Bothwell, knowing what he had done.

Suddenly, shockingly, it occurred to me to wonder what the outcome would have been if Mary had had the good sense, after the murder of David Riccio, to charge her husband Henry Darnley with high treason, for endangering her life and that of the child, the heir to the throne, that she was carrying. Cecil had remarked that she could well have done. If Darnley had been tried, found guilty, and executed, Mary, the ill-used wife and offended queen, would have remained safely on her throne, her credit unshaken. Or would it have been shaken?

Would people still have been shocked, I wondered, by the spectacle of a young woman, even one so wronged as Mary, sending her own husband to the block? Would they have whispered that perhaps she had been too intimate with Riccio and that perhaps, after all, Darnley was not such a villain and Mary not such a saint?

Maybe. But it might have been otherwise. Perhaps the wrongs of this virtuous young queen would have echoed around Europe! In which case, she would have been in a wonderful position to rally support for her claim to seize Elizabeth's throne as well as that of Scotland.

From England's point of view, the decisive mess that the

Queen of Scotland had made out of dealing with Henry Darnley could well have been a very good thing. It hurt seeing the truth of her, and yet I was also glad that I had. I am not one to take kindly to being fooled.

Meanwhile, here before me was Pen, her eyes full of pleading. I must deal with her first.

"There is no question now of you marrying Tobias," I said. "He has betrayed his master. He is supposed to be working for Sir Francis, after all! His business is to write and sometimes read his employer's correspondence, not to search the satchels of passing guests and copy out other men's letters for the benefit of Mary Stuart!"

"But he is Catholic, and he only wants to help Queen Mary! I don't like her very much myself, but if Tobias thought he was doing right—if he thinks of her as his queen . . . I know my brother George does . . ."

"He has fallen for the wiles of a murderess and betrayed both his employer and his *rightful* queen!" I snapped. "We shall leave Bolton at once. I will speak to Master Littleton before we go."

"Are you going to tell Sir Francis?" asked Pen, horrified.

"Of course," said Brockley. "What else can she do?"

"Quite. I have to, Pen. And yes, I daresay Master Littleton will soon be looking for new employment."

"Oh no, Mistress Stannard, please don't! Even if I can't marry him, don't ruin him! He'll be sent off without a character and . . ."

"His bad character will no doubt recommend him to some employer or other who shares his views," I said shortly. "Dale, help Pen to pack. Brockley, please saddle our horses. We won't be staying the night, after all. I am going to find Sir Francis."

15

Birds in Flight

Sir Francis saw me in his study. I told him what Littleton had been doing and his reply came as a surprise. "I know."

"You *know*?"

"Oh yes." Sir Francis, seated behind his desk, smiled in a kindly way, which checked me just as I was about to begin striding up and down the room. "It was bound to happen, of course."

"Bound to . . . ?"

"I have a kindness for Lady Mary. I think most men would feel the same, with the apparent exceptions of her husband and brother! I am glad that you and Seton came back today to help her. But I have always known that it was dangerous to trust her. If only I could have turned her toward the Reformed faith! But she has resisted all my efforts and she remains, alas, a danger to England, though she sees herself, of course, as England's savior. That being so, I quickly realized that if she could, she would suborn some unfortunate man or other and turn him into a spy. She has such a power to spellbind." He shook his head ruefully. "Did you know that the Duke of Norfolk wants to marry her?"

"The . . . ?" This conversation was taking an unforeseen turn. I hadn't expected the Duke of Norfolk to crop up. I knew who he was, of course. I had seen him at court, though I had never spoken to him as far as I could recall. He was one of Elizabeth's foremost noblemen. I looked in astonishment at Sir Francis, who gestured me considerately to a stool. "Has he been here?" I asked. "Has he met her? I thought he was married. And so is Mary married—to James Bothwell!"

"The marriage to Bothwell took place under irregular circumstances," said Sir Francis. "Well, perhaps not that irregular, the north being what it is, but ecclesiastical law still exists, in the north as much as in the south. She *can* claim that she was kidnapped and took her vows under duress. The marriage could probably be set aside. As for Norfolk, he's a widower now. He's only thirty-two; quite a suitable age. He hasn't met her but he has written to her. Norfolk's sister, Lady Scrope, was at Carlisle when Mary was there, and she may have put the idea into his head. Tobias smuggled the letter in. I knew all about that, too. *I've* met Norfolk, in London. He's ambitious. I think he has ideas of making himself King of Scotland or maybe—well, if Elizabeth never marries, Mary is the next in line."

"Or her son is. Mary's discredited."

"I fancy Norfolk hopes that Mary's credit will be restored, and that if they marry, he may one day be King Consort of Scotland. And later, perhaps, of England."

"But that's . . . !"

"Very nearly treason? Not quite. Not if it is done through the proper channels and Elizabeth were to consent."

"But that would be tantamount to setting up a rival court, and if Mary won't change her faith . . . Elizabeth would *never* consent!"

"No," agreed Sir Francis. "I don't think she would. But ambitious young noblemen have been known to convince themselves of extraordinary things before now, especially when there's a lady, reputedly beautiful and charming, in the bargain."

"My God!" I said, with feeling.

"Tobias has served me well, unknowingly," Sir Francis said. "I virtually arranged it, you know. It was easier to use him than to use the Douglases. They manage to whisper things to her sometimes, but I make sure they never have the chance to transmit letters, either from her or to her, and if I'd started being lax about that, she might become suspicious. Tobias I could appear to trust. Once I realized that his father was Catholic, I investigated a little further and found out that Tobias was, as well. That's when I saw my chance. I took to putting him in her way and it worked."

"Are you saying that you expected him to go through that courier's baggage?"

"Oh yes. I already knew what Cecil's letter contained. Cecil obliged me with a copy. I didn't mind if Tobias passed the gist of it on to Mary. I couldn't see that it would do any harm, and if I let it happen, they would feel safe. I wanted Tobias to feel sure he wasn't suspected. I suppose that's all over, now, since Mary went and let it out to you. Foolish of her!"

I gazed at him in wonder, seeing the grave, honest Sir Francis in an entirely new light. He chuckled.

"Deceit goes against the grain with me," he said, "especially when it concerns a lady as delightful as Mary Stuart. And yet, sometimes, I confess, I derive amusement from it, as though it were a game. One pits one's wits against the wits of others. It can be—entertaining."

I understood that very well. At one time, when I first began to be an agent, I had found entertainment in it, too. Since Sir Francis was unaware of my past, however, I limited my reply to a small nod.

"I soon knew that Tobias had done what I expected," he said. "Joan, the excellent maidservant who keeps an eye on Mary for me, saw him slip back into the castle just as the hawking party was preparing to leave. She followed and saw him put his note in her workbox. I had a full report of its contents from her. Joan also reported to me what happened when Lady Mary came back and found it! That *did* take me by surprise. I didn't expect her to fall into quite such a state of hysteria."

"She's still very upset," I said. "But Mistress Seton is looking after her. I imagine she'll recover."

"And I shall have to replace Tobias," said Knollys glumly.

"Sir Francis, I think I should tell you that Tobias has been making approaches to my ward, Pen Mason. I can't let the matter go any further. I am looking for a husband for her, as you know, but . . ."

"I wouldn't recommend Tobias, Mistress Stannard. At the moment I regret that I have no suitable name to suggest."

"Tobias is certainly not that," I said. "Forgive me, but I think it best that I should leave the castle at once and take Pen with me."

"I understand," said Knollys.

Back in my chamber, I found the hampers packed and Dale on her knees fastening a strap around the last one. Her face was red and she was muttering in disapproval, because over by the window, Pen and Tobias were clasped in each other's arms, kissing like mad things.

"Tobias!" I shouted.

He broke away from Pen. "Mistress Stannard. I beg your pardon."

"I should think so!"

"I'm sorry. I came to see Mistress Pen and she tells me that you have decided against the marriage. I imagine because I am Magnus Whitely's cousin. I am sorry for that. Nothing that he did, or failed to do, is my fault, Mistress Stannard."

Pen had evidently kept the real reason to herself. Mary would soon tell him, of course, that I now knew he was working for her and he would be a fool if he didn't know that I would pass the news on to Knollys. But Pen had decided not to tell him herself. She did have a sense of responsibility, I thought. She only needed to grow up a little more (and be partnered with the right man).

"We were saying good-bye," she said defiantly and began to cry.

"Now, hush," said Tobias. "Sometimes, these things have to be. Mistress Stannard, I have said my farewells. I'll go. Good-bye, dear Pen, and may your life be happy."

"I suppose you've told Sir Francis about him?" Pen asked bitterly when Tobias had left the room.

"Sir Francis is well aware of Tobias's indiscretions and

always has been. He has made use of them," I said quietly. "Dry your eyes. I am tired of this whole business. We're going back to Tyesdale, today."

We reached Tyesdale safely in the early evening. Pen sulked all the way. During the night, I heard her crying, but when I went into the room she now shared with Meg, she turned her head away and refused to talk to me.

In the morning, I was irritated to find that she had gone out, saddled her horse, and borrowed Meg's merlin, all without permission, and I caught a glimpse of her, cantering about on a nearby hillside, flying Joy at small birds. Meg was highly indignant and Brockley, who had intended, with John Ryder, to ride toward Fernthorpe and begin searching for signs of disturbed earth, left Ryder to go searching on his own and went to bring my ward home. He did so eventually, having had hard work to find her.

"When I got up the hill, she'd gone, madam," he said, coming into the hall while Pen took the merlin back to the mews. "I found her in a hollow, off her horse, sitting with her back to a tree, and letting the horse graze. I told her she was behaving like a silly wench. It isn't safe for a young woman to go about on her own hereabouts." Brockley's opinion of northern England was forcibly expressed in a snort.

I forbore to lecture Pen myself, feeling that Brockley had done it for me. I didn't want her to hate me.

Ryder came back disappointed, having found nothing useful. Jamie Appletree had also had an errand that morning, for I had sent him to the Moss family to ask if Clem could come sooner than he had suggested. He returned to say that Clem would be with us on Friday.

"He'll be speaking to Mistress Holme tomorrow about his marriage date. He's meeting her and the girls at Fritton Market."

The next few days passed quietly. Brockley and Ryder continued their search, though with caution and, alas, without result. They were taking pains to keep out of sight of the

Thwaites and couldn't pursue their business systematically. Meanwhile, my forbearance with Pen brought rewards. She came out of her sulks and asked, quite meekly, if she might ride on her own again provided she didn't go far from the house, and after a little hesitation, I agreed, thinking that perhaps she needed some freedom and privacy in order to get over her distress.

"Don't think I don't know what the loss of love feels like," I said to her. "But it's the future that matters. I was wildly in love with my second husband, Matthew de la Roche, but I suffered greatly because he was the enemy of my queen. I spent years in a state of conflict. I don't want that to happen to you. Nor do I want you being turned into an enemy of the queen yourself."

Pen said nothing in reply; just curtsied. She duly exercised her mare each morning after that, and stayed near the house as she had promised, as far as I could see, rarely out of sight of the windows and never for very long. When she came back, she remained very quiet, but was polite, and even apologized to Meg for taking the merlin.

On the Friday morning, Clem Moss arrived. He was accompanied by Peter, and they were leading a pack pony. "My belongings, mistress," he said, indicating the pony's hampers, when I went down the steps to greet him. "Peter will take the pony back when we've unloaded."

Mistress Appletree had made Whitely's old chamber ready for its new occupant and after helping to carry his brother's hampers in, Peter stayed for a tankard of ale and a pie. "Though I'll not linger after that," he said, "as there's all to do at home. I've a new chicken house to build. I picked up ten fine young birds at Fritton Market on Tuesday."

"It sounds like a successful market day for you," I said.

"Good enough," said Peter, "though . . ." At which point he broke off and he and Clem exchanged glances so meaningful that I said: "But what? Is something wrong?"

"Not about coming here, mistress," said Clem. "However, there's summat to tell you . . ."

He trailed off. I waited, and he said: "We'd fixed to meet Mistress Holme and the girls at t'market, and speak with Kate and Mabel and their mother about a double wedding date, now that I've a place and somewhere to bring Mabel, and a chance of a future. Only . . ."

Clem stopped and his round face suffused from outdoor pink to infuriated crimson. Then he said: "We met Mistress Holme and t'lasses, all among the crowds and t'stalls, and we were standin' together in t'road and I were tellin' Mabel and her mother what I'd got in mind, and Mabel stares at me as if I'm crazy and then bursts out that she doesn't want to be t'wife of a servant; she thought we'd rent a place we could look on as our own; maybe t'farm our new chickens come from."

"The old tenant died. That's why t'birds were for sale. Landlord's looking for another tenant," Peter put in.

"I know t'place," said Clem. "Out on t'moor, ten miles toward York. I wouldn't want it. T'land's too high and soil's too thin for good crops. We'd have a hard life there. I said we'd do better here till we could rent some good land in three or four years' time. That's what I said to Mabel. I never would have thought . . . !"

"T'fact is, Mistress Stannard," said Peter, "Clem here and Mistress Mabel had a bit of a disagreement, there and then, in the middle of t'fair. Mistress Mabel started crying . . ."

"A *bit* of a disagreement! Hah! I've never been that embarrassed, never in my life," said Clem. He looked it, too. As an act of mercy, I refilled his tankard for him. He buried his scarlet face in it and took a long gulp before raising his head to say: "She cried and created and carried on t'way I never thought to hear any girl go on, and there were people all round, gawping and laughing and *listening* . . ."

"As if it were a show, like the sword swallower they had there last May Day or t'freak they had the year before, with a face all skewed up," said Peter. "Mabel were gettin' a better audience than either on 'em."

"I saw that fellow Whitely, whose place I've taken, grinnin' in the crowd," said Clem resentfully. "Thinkin' I'd got my comeuppance for being after his place, I 'spect. And there's Mabel sayin' I'm pulling her down in the world, workin' for another man . . ."

"And then," said Peter, "her sister Kate—my Kate; she's great in t'dairy and pretty as a flower but there's no doubt she's got a way of tryin' to be clever—interrupts and says no, no, lass, he's not workin' for a man; he'll be workin' for Mistress Stannard and Mistress Penelope Mason."

"Then Mabel starts to shout that she s'poses it's all a trick to make her break off the betrothal so as I can go sweepin' my hat off to Mistress Pen and makin' up to her and her acres instead an' . . ." Poor Clem, quite overcome, gave up in mid-sentence and once more plunged his face into the sanctuary of his tankard.

"I know Mistress Holme sees Pen as a sort of rival," I said. "She still has three girls to settle and doesn't want any new young unmarried women in the district. I suppose she's infected your Mabel. Oh dear."

"Mistress Holme worries about t'lasses," said Peter tolerantly. "Five's a lot and she's been on her own with t'bother of it since her man died. Infected Mabel—aye, that'll be it, exactly. She'll have fussed and talked about it at home, and said that likely enough, Mistress Pen with her good dowry will mean one prospect less for t'three younger ones, and Mabel listened and took it all to heart and can't bear to think of havin' owt to do wi' Tyesdale. That'll be t'size of it."

"Fact is," said Clem glumly, emerging from his ale, "Mabel's a bit excitable-like and I've never been one for much billin' and cooin'; I've not been over to Lapwings makin' pretty speeches. I reckoned it were all arranged and there weren't no need for all that. We'd wed and then I'd be a good husband, I hope, but . . ."

"Oh dear," I said, again.

"T'fact is," Clem burst out, "I want a good sensible lass, not one that carries on in t'middle of a fair and pulls a crowd just like a bloody sword swallower! So I told Mabel that I hadn't thought of it up to now, but t'way she was actin' and shoutin', maybe I would do better elsewhere—though I said nowt about Mistress Mason," he added hastily. "I'm to be workin' for her and I know my right place and how to show respect. It's Mabel that wasn't showin' respect, mistress, and I'm sorry you should even know of it, except I knew I'd have to explain that Mabel wouldn't be coming here after all. I never meant to speak of it so frankly, but it just burst out of me, like. All I said to Mabel was, I might do better elsewhere. Then I said it was up to her; if she wanted to call it off, it was all right by me and she said yes she did . . ."

"What on earth did her mother say to that?" I asked.

"Mabel, now, don't be hasty," said Peter. "I think she saw things were gettin' out o' hand. But Mabel just bawled louder than ever and screamed at her mother that she wouldn't marry Clem now if he were t'last man on earth, so there!"

"Mistress Holme started apologizing to me and saying t'lass was upset, and maybe if I took her for a walk round t'stalls and we had a quiet talk, it could all be put right," said Clem. "But by then I didn't want to go walkin' wi' Mabel anywhere! So I said no thanks; I'd been dismissed in front o' witnesses and that was enough for me."

"He got on his dignity and said he hoped he'd allus be Mistress Mabel's friend and good neighbor but there was no more question of marriage," said Peter. "And then Mistress Holme smacked Mabel's head and told her she was a fool, and pushed Kate at me and told me at least to take *my* lass round t'market and not to let this spoil our plans. Which I did. I didn't even tell Kate off for interruptin' and upsettin' Mabel. Reckoned I ought to take it softly. I'm fond enough of Kate and she of me, and she *is* a great hand wi' t'butter and cream."

"And I just walked off on my own," said Clem. "But there it is. Mabel won't be comin' after all, mistress."

"It'll probably all come right," I said awkwardly. "Mistress Holme obviously wants the match to go ahead and I'm sure that when Mabel gets over her upset . . ."

"She can get over it or not as far as I'm concerned," said Clem. "She broke it off there in front of half Fritton and that's it. I'll not lay myself open to't twice over. I won't marry her now, no, not if she and her mother both come here together and go down on bended knee to me."

Peter set down his own tankard and stood up. "Time I took

my leave, mistress. I'll be over to see you, Clem, when I get time."

"I'll dance at your wedding," said Clem. "As long as Mabel's not my partner."

"Maybe if she were . . ." I began.

"No, mistress," said Clem quietly. "Beggin' your pardon, but not now. Truth to tell, her mother and mine fixed it up for me and Mabel. I'd been keen on another lass, over Bolton way, but her parents found her someone better off than me, so I didn't argue when Ma said she'd got Mabel for me. She didn't ask me my opinion. If she had, happen I'd have said I weren't that struck on Mabel. She's pretty but we all have our tastes and she's not that much to mine. Too much of a kitten-face and not *practical.* Kate's that, but not Mabel. I wouldn't have picked her, 'cept that at the time I didn't care much. Well, now I'm out of it, I'm staying out. Not Mabel now or ever."

Away from Cecily, both the Moss boys seemed to blossom into forceful characters in the most remarkable way. Clem's angry flush had subsided, but his round face, which at first had looked so ingenuous, had somehow acquired contours of firmness, and when he said *not Mabel now or ever,* he meant it. "You're welcome with or without a wife," I said.

Peter took his leave. Brockley and Ryder had just returned from another fruitless search for traces which might mean Harry's grave, so Brockley was in the house. I asked him to take Clem on a tour of the Tyesdale land. Then I took Pen and Meg out to discuss creating a proper herb garden next to the vegetable plot. As I had hoped, talking about the herb garden caught Pen's interest and when we went indoors again, she fetched writing things and made a list of the plants we wanted.

Ryder and Brockley were growing discouraged by their failure to find anything suspicious. I, too, now thought that our search would probably be in vain. I had still not written again to Hugh, but I couldn't put it off much longer. I must do it tomorrow, I thought. I must also talk with Brockley and decide how long we should go on looking before we gave up.

At least, life within Tyesdale was becoming more normal. We

had some music in the hall after supper that evening. Dick Dodd played his lute for us and everyone sang. Clem reported that he had removed the rusty old plow—"Broke it up, put it in sacks, in bits, mistress, and buried it in t'old diggings"—and assured me that his mother would be glad to let us have some herb plants.

I retired that night feeling quieter in my mind. I had performed my errands for the queen and Cecil. That at least was done. I ought to find a proper tenant for Tyesdale, who would pay a healthy rent to Pen. After that—well, perhaps we would have to give Harry up for lost. We knew who had killed him but what use was that if we couldn't prove it? I must, very soon, write that promised second letter to Hugh. When I did, I could ask if Harry's sword had had any other distinguishing mark besides the amethyst in the hilt. Meanwhile, I ought to think of sending Pen home, ahead of me if need be. I ought to get her away from here. I talked of these plans to Sybil for a while before we went to sleep and we agreed that they were good sense.

They were swept away within hours of being made. I was wakened by Meg, anxiously shaking me. "Mother—oh, Mother!"

"What is it?" I sat up in alarm. So did Sybil. It was daybreak and the birds were singing. "What's the matter, Meg?"

"Mother, I woke up and Pen was gone and I can't find her anywhere and then, on the window seat, weighed down with a workbox, I found *this,*" said my daughter, and thrust a note into my hand.

It was in Pen's writing. It was on the back of the list of herb plants. She was running away with Tobias. She had been meeting him when she rode out alone. Brief meetings, I gathered, but somehow they had managed it. Whenever she had been out of sight for ten minutes or so, she had not been simply on the other side of a stone wall or a fold of the land, but having a tryst with Tobias.

By the time I saw her again, said her note, she would be Mistress Tobias Littleton. She hoped I would understand and forgive her. She was sure I would. Had I not run away with my first husband? She was grateful for all my care of her, but she loved

Tobias. Like birds freed from a cage, they were taking flight together.

"She went during the night," said Meg. "She must have *crept* out. I suppose he was outside, waiting to meet her."

"My God," I said, "what will her mother say to *this*?"

16

Striking a Bargain

I left Meg at home, with Sybil, Dale, and the Appletrees. The rest of us rode off to hunt for the pair. Clem being new to the household, I told him how Meg had recognized the Thwaites at her kidnappers. Someone must go to Fernthorpe, I said, since Whitely knew the Thwaites and Tobias was his cousin. Clem at once volunteered, but he was so indignant that I sent Ryder and Dodd instead and despatched Clem to ask if the couple had approached the vicar at Fritton and to call at Moss House in case Cecily had news of them. Tom Smith I sent to Lapwings, while I took Brockley to Bolton.

We were all back home by sunset. There had been no trace of the missing lovers anywhere. The Thwaites said they hadn't set eyes on Whitely or Tobias in the last few days and had no idea where either of them might be. Ryder had asked bluntly if he might look upstairs "and they put on a show of being affronted but they let me. The bedchambers are better kept than the rooms downstairs, though not much, but there was no one up there."

At Fritton vicarage, Moss House, and Lapwings, it was apparently all shaking heads and no, sorry, we've seen nothing of Master Littleton or Mistress Pen. The vicar and Cecily Moss were both scandalized and promised to keep a sharp lookout, but Cecily reckoned the couple had probably put as much distance as possible between Tyesdale and themselves and had very likely made for York. She might well be right, I thought, in which case they had far too great a start.

At Bolton, Sir Francis had told me that Tobias had left the castle two days before. "Asked the Douglases to tell me on his behalf, packed his things, and went! Well, he must have thought he'd been caught out. I daresay he's annoyed with Lady Mary for being so indiscreet with you! I never said anything to him, you know. He must have wondered when I would! Maybe it's surprising he didn't go sooner. And now you say your ward's gone with him? What a way to behave!"

Sir Francis's inquiries into Tobias's background hadn't revealed that he was related to the Tyesdale steward. He did suggest that Tobias might have taken Pen to his own parents in Bolton, but a messenger who was sent off at speed to inquire came back to say that Tobias's family were very shocked to hear of the matter, knew nothing about it, and could not even suggest where Tobias might have taken Pen. They didn't know where Whitely might have gone, either.

Like Cecily, Sir Francis said that York was the couple's most probable destination. "I truly feel for you," he said. "This is a most distressing affair."

"Tomorrow," I said, when I had heard what all the other inquiries had brought forth, or rather, failed to bring forth, "we must ride to York. I'll make one of the party."

But in the morning, I was in no condition to go on a journey anywhere. The migraine, which had threatened me once already, had arrived. I awoke with iron pincers gripping my temples and an invisible demon plying a hammer just above my left eye. Migraine does no permanent harm, leaves no traces, but this was a violent attack and until it subsided, I wouldn't even be able to get out of bed, let alone into a saddle.

"Bring Brockley here," I said miserably to Dale. "He and Ryder will have to take charge of the hunt. It's got to go ahead, and at once. Even as things are, it's probably too late. What her mother is going to say . . ."

I tailed off, as the hammer blows increased in violence. "I'll make you a potion," said Dale in alarm. "I haven't the makings of the one that Gladys used to make for you, but there's chamomile in that apology for a herb patch outside. That used to work sometimes. I can't abide this place, and that's the truth. I'll be glad to see us home again."

"You're always glad to see us home again, wherever we go," I said, trying to smile. "Make me a potion, yes. But send Brockley first."

Brockley came in softly and stood beside the bed, looking concernedly down at me. Once more, I made an effort to smile.

My migraines always had anxiety of some kind behind them. This time, I knew it was guilt at my own failure, and my fear that I wouldn't be able to put it right. But more than once, Brockley had solved my dilemmas for me. For all his country accent and his life in service, he was an intelligent man and, as he had told me, he had had some schooling when he was a boy. He had been a soldier, too. He knew the world. I had a deep trust both in him and in Dale. They had been my constant companions for years. We had been in danger together; we had been afraid together; we had on occasion saved each other's lives. Such a bond is powerful, so powerful that we had no need of words to remind us that it was there.

Only one thing had ever imperiled it. Once, a long time ago now, Brockley and I had been so drawn to each other that we had come very near to crossing the line between mistress and servant and turning into lovers. We had drawn back from the brink but Dale had guessed and it was the reason why she didn't like our little shared jokes.

Matthew had guessed, as well. To Matthew, I had stoutly denied it. Dale, I had reassured by swearing that there had never been any such attraction between myself and Brockley (which was a lie), and that we had never been, and never intended to be, lovers (which was true).

Hugh had been a blessing, for, unlike Matthew, he never did things I couldn't bear—such as plotting the downfall of Elizabeth. I had no need to look for comfort elsewhere. But Hugh was far away and now Brockley's calm, high brow, with its dusting of gold freckles, and his bland gray-blue gaze, was the most steadying sight in my world.

"Brockley," I said, "if I don't get Pen back in time, I'll have let her mother down and let Pen down, too. I don't trust Tobias to be a good husband to her. Even if they're married when I catch up with them, I'll do my best to have it overturned. I hope if they do go through a ceremony, it's a thoroughly hole-in-the-corner affair with no witnesses and a dubious priest. Take Ryder with you and go to York. You'll have to inquire at inns and churches . . ."

"I'll do all I can, madam. I'll take Clem as well, if you agree—he's been to York before and knows the way. If we find a scent, we'll follow till we catch up with them."

"Like hounds," I said. I really did smile then and so did he. Dale wasn't by and we could afford one small shared jest.

"Exactly like hounds, madam," Brockley said.

"Thank you, Brockley. Is Brown Berry still fit after yesterday's hard riding? This is demanding for the horses but we can't waste time."

"Brown Berry will take me a fair way, madam. Clem says it's more than fifty miles from here but there are places where we can change horses. For the sake of speed, we'd better. I'll do my best, I promise. You must rest, madam. What Pen has done is not your fault."

"Well, it is. I should have watched her more closely and not given her permission to ride out alone. She was clever," I said grimly. "They both were. She didn't go far but they still found ways to meet." The hammer swung furiously again and I wrinkled my brow in pain. "I was a fool not to guess she might be up to something."

"You'd hardly have expected this from a modestly reared wench like Mistress Pen," said Brockley. "She needs a bit of stick, and when you get her back, you'd best see she gets it."

"I don't like doing that," I told him. "I had enough of that kind of thing from my dear aunt Tabitha. You'd better go and saddle up."

"The horses are being got ready now, madam. If you listen, you can hear the hooves down in the courtyard."

"Dear Brockley. Always a step ahead, thank heavens. Sybil will give you whatever money you need. I know you'll do your best; you hardly need to promise that. Is that Dale with my potion?"

But the footsteps approaching my door were not those of Dale. The two who appeared in the doorway were Agnes Appletree, looking extremely flustered, with a face as crimson as a woodpecker's crest, and behind her, incredibly, was Magnus Whitely.

"*You!*" said Brockley furiously. "What are you doing here?"

"Brockley . . ." I said weakly.

"He says he's got to see the mistress," said Agnes. "He says he's got news of Mistress Pen!"

I had known it from the moment I set eyes on him. After all, Tobias *was* his cousin. Painfully, I hitched myself up on my pillows, gritting my teeth as the pain crashed through my skull. "Good day, Master Whitely. As you see, I am indisposed but I am capable of hearing news. What have you to tell me? Do you know where Penelope Mason is?"

"Not *exactly*, at this moment, Mistress Stannard," said Whitely. He was as nondescript as ever in face and dress, but once again, if you looked at his clothing, you could see how good the materials were, and the cut. On the middle finger of his left hand, he wore a ruby ring. The sight of it made me want to grit my teeth even more. He came over to the bed and stood looking down at me. His expression wasn't sympathetic, which didn't surprise me.

"At this moment? What does that mean?" I asked him.

"It means, Mistress Stannard, that where she is *just* now is something I don't know. Better you don't know, my cousin Tobias said to me, then no one can bribe or beat it out of you. But where she'll be in a few days' time—that's *quite* another matter. That's for you to say. I'd like to speak to you in private."

Brockley bristled and so did Agnes but I shook my head at them. I regretted this at once and hoped that the nauseous climax of migraine wouldn't happen in the presence of Tyesdale's odious ex-steward.

"I'll be within call, madam," Brockley said as he marshaled Agnes out of the door. I hoped he would have the sense to put his ear to it. "Well?" I said, as soon as Whitely and I were apparently alone.

Uninvited, he sat down on the edge of my bed. "Penelope Mason is in the care of Tobias Littleton," he said. "But they are not married. Nor will they be. I'm charged to tell you that Queen Mary of Scotland is in *deep* distress over her future. She . . ."

"Queen Mary? What has she to do with Pen?"

"A lot, if you'll hear me out, mistress. You'll have seen her lately and you'll have seen for yourself what I've only heard of from Tobias. He says she's been foolish in some way but he doesn't blame her because she's *ill,* poor soul, with fear for her good name and her freedom. This latest news—you know of it, I think—of words taken from honest letters and used to condemn her, has *broken* her, her heart and her hope. She knows now that she was in error to come to England; that Elizabeth would rather be in Moray's pocket than stand her cousin's friend. She should have gone to France in the first place."

"I daresay." Migraine is a very strange illness. If there comes a demand for action that is imperative enough, it will yield. I sensed such a demand in the offing. I had known when I woke that I could send others to York in my stead, but something was coming now that would need me in person—and suddenly the breakers of anguish in my head were less violent, as though the tide were turning. I straightened myself more firmly against my pillows. *What has all this to do with Pen?*

"Simply this, mistress. Queen Mary's *friends,* among whom I and my cousin Tobias are *honored* to be numbered, have laid a plan to get her away from Bolton and off to France. It needs your help. If you give it, Penelope Mason will be returned to you *quite* unharmed—in all respects. She will no doubt," said Whitely sententiously, "be the wiser for the experience, if a little sadder."

I chose to ignore the moralizing. "And if I refuse?"

"The Thwaites badly want her as a wife for Andrew. They are not concerned in the plot to rescue the queen; we could not trust them for that. That family lost their taste for plots over thirty years ago when they lost half their land. But they are my friends. I have seen them and given them to understand that I *may* be able to bring her to them, and that they should have a priest ready. Tobias says that Mistress Pen has told him that she is afraid of the Thwaites and that they once tried to kidnap her. She even believes they had something to do with the death of one of your men. Nonsense, in my opinion—but marriage to Andrew wouldn't be to her taste."

"You're taking a risk," I said. "I might sacrifice her for the greater good."

"Penelope herself begs you not to, for her sake and her mother's. She knows what is planned for her. When I saw her last, this morning—in a shepherd's hut on the moors, just before Tobias took her on to another hiding place—she was in tears. *Floods* of them," said Whitely with satisfaction.

I regarded him with hatred.

"I believe you're fond of Queen Mary yourself," he said. "Do you *like* to think of her ill and frightened, a prisoner maybe forever?"

I didn't. Even though I now knew more about Mary than was at all comfortable, I didn't like that, no. She had certainly been foolish, in a number of ways. She had been too much a woman and not enough of a queen. She had handed Darnley's fate to her nobles, because they were the strong men she instinctively wanted to rely on. She had tried to pretend that because she had not actually said *kill him,* she was not responsible when they did precisely that, and finally, she had become hysterical when the guilt came winging home to her.

Yet still I was sorry for her, caught as she was in a trap of her own making. As for Pen . . .

"You had better tell me," I said, "what you want me to do."

Whitely smiled. "One thing you'd best *not* do, mistress, is try to get in touch with Bolton—or the queen or Cecil, either, or anyone else on their side. As for what *we* need from you—it doesn't amount to much. There is a *possibility* that Queen Mary may be allowed out of Bolton, under guard, to pay you a visit. Sir Francis is *extremely* worried about her health and *may* consent, against his better judgment—or his orders."

Yes, so he might, I thought. He was loyal to Elizabeth, but Mary's magic had touched him and clung to him, like a persistent cough after a bad cold.

"She may stay for a night," Whitely said. "This house has a spare bedchamber at the back. Give her that. It overlooks the moat—in fact the wall under the window goes almost straight down into the water. It's secure enough. No one will criticize you for putting her there. That is all. Meanwhile, you're to stay quiet in Tyesdale until you're called upon."

The pain was unquestionably fading. It had sunk down now to a dull throb. I would have to meet this challenge, whatever the outcome and in the face of it, migraine would surrender. "I see," I said. "And I have no time in which to decide? You want an answer now?"

"Yes."

I closed my eyes and pressed my head back into the pillow, as though the pain were still intense and had weakened my will. "I don't understand why the Thwaites are so mad for Andrew to marry Pen, but I don't intend them to have her. She'd never forgive me and nor would her mother. As for Mary—I'm sorry for her, you're right there. Poor silly woman. I'll do it. And hope to God I don't end up fleeing for my life to spend the rest of it in exile. Now will you go away? I'm likely to be sick in a minute. You won't want to be here for that."

Whitely got off the edge of my bed. "Best *not* try to deceive me, mistress. There'll be eyes watching Tyesdale. You won't see them but they'll be there. *No* messengers should leave the premises, if you please. *No one* is to ride beyond your boundaries. Once it's all over, and Her Grace is safe away, and Tobias and myself with her, you can do as you like. If you *really* fancy going to Sir Francis Knollys, or home to the queen and Sir William Cecil and confessing, then you'll be free to do so."

"Just leave, Whitely, please."

"I'll not say let's shake hands on it, mistress. We'll take *that* as done," said Whitely, and bowed to me most graciously, and went.

If Brockley had been listening at the door, he had taken himself quickly out of the way. Whitely found no one outside. As soon as I heard his feet going downstairs, I slid off the bed. My head gave a mild thud as I stood up, but I ignored it, knowing that the pain, now, would drain out of me like water through sand. I went to the window to look into the courtyard, and as I watched, Appletree brought Whitely's horse out, and Clem appeared, arms akimbo, to watch as well until my unpleasant visitor had mounted and ridden away.

I went to my bedchamber door and called. A moment later, Dale arrived with a beaker, exclaiming that here was my chamomile potion at last, and Sybil also appeared, with Meg. Since this was a Sunday, albeit a distracted one, they had been reading prayers together in Meg's room.

"Mother! You're better!" Meg cried.

"I'm thankful to say that I am, though I'll take the potion to be on the safe side. Come in here, all of you. I've something to tell you. Where's Brockley? Oh, here he is." Brockley and Agnes were coming upstairs after Dale. "Come in, Brockley—yes, and you too, Agnes."

"I know what's afoot, madam," said Brockley. "I listened at the door though I made myself scarce before Whitely came out."

"I thought you would," I said. "Well, you know what's happening, but I want all of you to know. Listen, everyone." They were silent and attentive while, sipping my beaker between sentences, I recounted my interview with Whitely.

"Well," said Sybil at the end, "what do you wish us to do, Mistress Stannard?"

"We *have* to get word to Sir Francis," I said. "Somehow! That goes without saying. Without risk to Pen, but it must be done. I *cannot* enter into a treasonable plot, even for her. Dear God, I must get her out of this muddle but not by that means."

"Well," said Dale, "it's a mercy that it's Sunday and we haven't got Bess Clipclop and Feeb here in the house. That

Whitely must know all the laborers' families. Maybe they're some of the eyes he was talking about—or ears."

"But the girls will be here tomorrow," I said, "possibly to spy on us. Even Feeb may not be as stupid as she looks. We shall have to be very careful!"

"You're recovering, I see, madam," Brockley said to me. That fugitive smile of his was in his eyes again. "I never thought of Magnus Whitely as a physician before, I must say."

"His treatment's not to be recommended, but it works, yes," I said grimly. "Now then. How do I get to Bolton unseen?"

"Ah," said Brockley.

"Brockley! You've got some ideas?"

"Hazy ones, madam, but after what I heard with my ear to the door, I started thinking. When I dodged downstairs to get out of the way when Whitely left you, I hid in the kitchen, and I heard the unctuous little brute saying good-bye to Clem in the courtyard and wishing Clem well in his new post."

"Did he?"

"He did. Smooth as you please. It reminded me of something—or someone, rather. A too-smooth chaplain that one of my former employers had, a fellow no one else in the house could stand. Thinking about him put another idea in my head, about a way to protect Mistress Pen. Or partly protect her, anyway. It may not work, but I can try. I'll have to get away from Tyesdale to do it, though, and I won't be going to Bolton. So there's two of us that'll have to make themselves invisible so as to get out of the house, but as I said, I do have a notion about that, too . . ."

"It's the worst problem," I said. "How *can* any of us get away from Tyesdale unseen?"

"Oh, I think it could be done," said Brockley. "Whitely's a fool. How he or anyone else proposes to watch Tyesdale after dark, I can't imagine."

17

"Go Through T'Wood"

I listened to what Brockley had to say and then added something of my own. "We need to know we can trust everyone in the house. We needn't worry about Cecil's men or Tom Smith, but—Agnes, fetch your husband. And Brockley, find Clem. The four of you are to come to the chapel. Sybil, you and Meg go back to your prayers—we may need them!"

I was first to reach the chapel. I still felt shaky, but the pain in my head had stopped and my stomach had settled. In my few moments of solitude before the others arrived, I knelt and said a private prayer.

I have never been sure that I believe in God. But I was so afraid for Pen that I wanted to pray for her and besides, I felt that I should be grateful to someone or something that I had learned the truth about Mary Stuart before I was faced with this. I would never have betrayed Elizabeth. Of that I am sure. But that morning, I was very glad that Mary's enchantment was gone and that I could shape my plans in the clean, plain light of day, untroubled by any goblin lures of magic.

A few moments later, Brockley, Clem, and the Appletrees came in, all together. I rose to my feet and took stock of them. Then I said: "You all saw Magnus Whitely. He brought news of Mistress Pen."

"Brockley's told us," Clem said.

I nodded, but briefly repeated it anyway. Jamie stood shaking his head in horrified disbelief. Clem's face was suffused with anger. "It's a disgrace, that's what it is. A decent young maid like Mistress Pen, used like . . . like just summat to bargain with! Aye, I know she walked into it, but she's young and too innocent to be wary of folk like that."

"Quite. Exactly," I said. "Now, listen carefully. The scheme in which Whitely wants to entangle me is treason. For me, it is doubly treason for I am attached to the court of Queen Elizabeth. I am also very frightened for Pen. She must not get into the hands of the Thwaites. She loathes them and for very good reasons. We all know *what* reasons."

They nodded. "Therefore," I said, "*somehow,* no matter how many watchers Whitely puts round Tyesdale, I have both to rescue Pen and to inform Sir Francis Knollys at Bolton of the plot. But first, let me be clear. I need not ask this of Brockley, but are you three, Clem, Agnes, Jamie, for me or against me?"

"High treason?" said Jamie Appletree in horror. "There's none of us want to get mixed up in owt of that kind! Or to do harm to Mistress Pen, neither! Besides, there was this young fellow of yours that lost his life on t'way here, that it seems these Thwaites spirited away!"

"Aye. That's right!" Agnes backed him up.

"I say the same," said Clem. "Even if we do hear mass at home, we're honest English right enough. Religion's private, but t'queen's t'queen. Even if there weren't Mistress Pen to think of. Poor maid."

"Very well," I said. "But this is serious business, so serious that I have to be sure." I moved to the lectern where the illuminated Latin Bible lay. "Come over here. I want you to swear."

They did as I asked. It was a makeshift ceremony, in a chapel that, though it had now been swept and polished, still had a desolate air, lacking the candles and incense that usually solemnize rites held in such places. Yet the light and scent and the solemnity were there in another fashion, for a shaft of sunlight was streaming in from the bright August day outside, catching the gold leaf cross on the front of the Bible, and the gravity of the oath they were taking created its own incense and was mirrored in their serious faces.

One by one, the Appletrees and Clem each laid a hand on the Bible and swore on it to be true subjects of Queen Elizabeth and to assist me as best they could both in foiling the present treasonous plot and saving Penelope from a detestable marriage. When all three had sworn, Brockley insisted not only on doing the same thing but also on fetching the other men and inviting them to take the oath. They did, which touched me.

"It makes us all one band, madam," Brockley explained.

After that, we went to the hall and got down to practical details.

One thing still stood out as a mystery. Brockley commented on it.

"Why," he said, "*are* the Thwaites so mad to marry their son to Pen? They snatched Meg in mistake for her. I'm sure that's true. The answer has to be in Tyesdale itself but *what* is it?"

No one, though, had any suggestions beyond the fact that Tyesdale was quite extensive and marched with Fernthorpe, and that the house, however much cleaning and repairing it needed, was a palace compared to the pigsty in which the Thwaites lived.

After a very short discussion, we gave up trying to solve the puzzle. Whatever the reason, Pen was in danger of being forcibly turned into a Thwaite and to prevent this we had somehow or other to get out of Tyesdale unseen.

"Eyes watching," Brockley said, "but watching where? If Whitely and Littleton had an ounce of sense they'd put their watchers at the other end, near Bolton Castle, because that's where we'd be bound to go. But maybe they've not had as much experience of conspiracy as we have. They may just try to put a cordon round Tyesdale. First of all, just how many pairs of eyes can they muster?"

"Possibly quite a few," I said. "Whitely knows the people round here and I daresay he can pay, damn him!"

"Quite a few doesn't necessarily mean an army," said Ryder. "What they're plotting is dangerous. Even if they don't explain the whole scheme to their hirelings, a lot of folk would be sharp enough to work out that it's something to do with Mary of Scotland, and they might be afraid to help. And some might wonder if Sir Francis Knollys wouldn't pay more for information than Whitely can pay for his scheming. Inexperienced or not, I fancy our friends won't want to drag too many people in."

"And even if someone is posted at the Bolton end," I said thoughtfully, "would it be all round the clock? In the depth of the night? Brockley, I think your idea is that we should try to get out after dark. I agree, and I think we should time our arrival at Bolton for just before daybreak. What about moonlight? The sky's clear at the moment."

"There'll be a half-moon," Clem said. "But it'll set before dawn."

"So if they put someone near Bolton, all the watcher would see would be shadowy figures riding to the castle," I said. "And that could happen at any time. The queen's messengers can arrive at any hour. There's always a guard at the castle, night and day, ready for such things. Once I'm there," I added, "I should get admittance all right. They'll know my name and probably my face as well."

"We can't worry about whether or not there'll be anyone posted at Bolton," said Dick Dodd. "You've got to go there, whatever happens, mistress. Just before dawn is the likeliest time to avoid being recognized; you're right there. At Bolton, we'll have to trust to luck or the goodness of God. We should concentrate on getting out of here."

Brockley turned to Appletree. "Jamie, if you let the dogs loose at dusk, will they warn us if anyone's hanging about close to the house?"

"Aye, they will that, unless I hush them. The which I shan't."

"All right," said Brockley. "It's risky just assuming things but I think we've got to. If Ryder here's right and they don't have that many people, they'll probably just guard the paths. They must have thought of us slipping out at night, but I think they'll expect us to use paths—westward ones. So we won't ride on tracks of any kind and we won't go westward, or not to start with. It'll take longer but it might work. All we need is someone to guide us who knows the land round here."

"I knows the land but I'm no horseman," said Jamie.

"Clem?" said Brockley.

"Aye. I reckon," said Clem. "See here. Look at this." And with that, grinning enthusiastically, he started to create a map on the hall table with the aid of the stray collection of objects that were lying on it: a hawking gauntlet, a chess set that Ryder and Brockley had been playing with, a book of verse, a pile of trenchers, and a few serving spoons that were used so often that we never put them away between meals.

"This," said Clem, setting out a trencher, "is t'bit of woodland that you'd have passed when you rode here from Grimsdales', mistress. It's in a valley that leads away southwest. And this . . ."—he put a gauntlet down beside the trencher—"is t'hump of hillside that's between t'woodland and here. It's mostly barley fields and pasture, with a few stone walls. As soon as we're a little way out of the house, we'll turn across that and make for the wood, keeping by t'walls when we can. Here, near t'house, is t'proper track for Bolton, leading westward . . ."

A spoon supplied the proper track.

"But if we go through t'wood, we won't be going west. That's what you had in mind, weren't it, Master Brockley? Well, once we're through t'wood, we come out on t'moor a good few miles south o' t'track for Bolton and on a path that wanders off southward. Who'll think we're going to go that way, for a start? Anyhow, we won't stop on t'path once it's in the open. We'll strike straight across t'moor. I hope I'll not lead us astray in t'dark, but I know the landmarks round here pretty well."

Another spoon supplied the line we would use. We would be riding across country, tiny figures lost in the night and the vast moor, traveling west and parallel with the official track but well away from it.

Clem frowned, chewed his lip, and borrowed a pawn from the chess set. "That's a tree that we ought t'see if we're on t'right road, except that it won't be a road, just moorland. T'land dips down into that long vale that has Fernthorpe at t'other end— there's other farms there but they're scattered and we needn't go near—then t'moor climbs and we're into t'worst part in t'dark, for there's no landmarks. There's a place where t'ground drops away to t'south, over a steepish fall. See it in daylight, it's sheer, almost—gray rock walls wi' moorland above and a river full o' boulders down below." Carefully, he placed another trencher. "There's t'river valley. We don't want to ride over t'edge o' that in t'dark. Maybe we'll be glad o' t'moonlight after all."

"Maybe we will!" I agreed with feeling.

Clem continued to ruminate over his map. "Farther on, over here"—he reached for a third trencher—"there's a pool and some trees . . ."

"I know it," I said. "We met Mary Stuart there when we went hawking."

"Aye, well, we've to pass that on t'south, but there's a beck . . ."

"A beck?" I queried.

"Aye, mistress." Clem grinned. "That's what we call a streamlet hereabouts. There's a beck—or a stream—flows out o' t'pool that we'll have to cross. Another mile or two after that and it'll be easier; we'll pick up a driftway track—one that drovers use, takin' sheep to market in Bolton. We'll be a good long way from Tyesdale by then; likely enough any watchers'll be closer in. Reckon we could risk the driftway. Once we're on that, there's less chance o' getting lost. It ends up joining t'main track between Bolton town and t'castle. I'm troubled not to lead you wrong, mistress."

He considered me gravely and it struck me that as the years wore on, Clem Moss might well develop a personality quite as strong as that of his mother, though with luck he wouldn't develop her booming voice, too.

"I hope it works," I said. "It's risky, but we must do something. I only hope to God I'm doing right. Now, who's coming? You, Clem. Ryder? And what about you, Brockley? You said you had a plan to help Pen and would need to get out of Tyesdale, though, not in order to go to Bolton?"

"That's right. I'll only come with you the first part of the way," Brockley said. "I'm going in the general direction of Fernthorpe." He gave me his rare smile and said reassuringly: "Don't worry. I shan't let on to them that they're being used in a plot to get Mary Stuart away. I wondered about suggesting that, since they're not privy to the plot, it seems. They might get scared and back out. But who's to know which way a cat will jump? They're supposed to be afraid of getting into conspiracies, but the way they're after Mistress Pen, well, I wouldn't place any bets. They might join Whitely and Littleton after all. The Pilgrimage of Grace was a long time back. Clem, what's the best route in order to pass near Fernthorpe?"

Clem showed him. Brockley nodded. "Branch off on a little path to the right, after the woodland, bear left round some deserted mine workings . . . very well."

"There are some real working mines hereabouts, aren't there?" I said. "We met some miners, the day we arrived. Who owns them?"

"T'queen," said Clem. "They're on t'land that Fernthorpe had to give to t'crown thirty years back. T'Thwaites have never got over it. Worth summat, these days, coal is."

"Brockley, just what are you intending to do?" I asked him.

"I'm not sure yet," Brockley said frankly. "But I've got a glimmering. Leave it to me."

There was a pause. Then I said: "We'd better dine early and rest. It'll be a long night."

The shadows were gathering when, having eaten and rested, we met again in the hall. A last shaft of sunlight was growing dull and changing from golden to coppery as the sun went down. Quite suddenly, it was hard to see the detail of Clem's makeshift map.

"It'll be full dark in half an hour," said Ryder. "Time to saddle up."

* * *

The dogs had been on guard for some time and we were sure that no one was near enough to the house to hear anything, but we brought the horses out quietly and kept our voices down. Farewells were said in low tones. The four of us who were going mounted quietly and moved off in single file to cross the bridge over the moat. I noticed that Brockley was encumbered with saddlebags, though when I asked him what was in them, he merely gazed at me in his most expressionless way and said: "Well, madam, a fellow must shave and change his linen sometimes," which told me nothing, as he evidently intended.

I was pleased to see that although the half-moon was out, it was yellowish rather than bright silver, and faintly hazy. There was a sharpness in the air, too, and I thought that there might be mist later on. Good, provided it wasn't so thick that we lost our way in it.

"You are all right, mistress?" Clem asked, bringing his horse alongside me. "It'll be a weary night for a lady."

"I shall survive," I said.

I didn't add that against all expectation, and despite my anxiety for Pen, I was very nearly enjoying myself. My head was perfectly clear and I didn't even feel tired. I sat straight in my sidesaddle, looking ahead between Roundel's pricked ears, and silently admitted it. It had happened again, the thing that I thought I had left behind when Hugh slid his wedding ring onto my hand.

My spirit had once more heard the cry of the wild geese and I was riding after them, into adventure.

18

The Scythe in the Moonlight

In the real world, that night, there were no wild geese but there were owls. They too had a haunting call, which moved something in my blood. As we turned off the track and began to walk the horses quietly in single file beside a drystone wall, I only wished that instead of this wary progress, we could ply our spurs and ride across the moors to Bolton at full gallop with the wind scouring our faces and the hoofbeats thundering like drums.

Clem, however, led us with steady caution and without him we could not have found the way in the dark. Our new steward, however, took us unhesitatingly along the edge first of the barley field and then of a wide pasture that lay like a grassy shawl over a shoulder of hillside, and on to a sheep track, which meandered down the hill again, conveniently sheltered by numerous clumps of gorse, and led into the wooded valley.

I had never been there before, even by day. By night, the place was disconcerting. There was a thin path but the trees met overhead and no moonlight penetrated. Roundel's ears vanished in the intense darkness. So did my companions. I could hear the footfalls of their horses and the faint clink of their bridles, but I rode an invisible horse through the wood in invisible company, and for a while the sense of adventure was drowned by an atavistic voice in my head, whispering that in the darkness, other things might walk abroad besides those of flesh and blood.

I could feel Roundel, though, even if I couldn't see her, and she didn't share human superstitions. Her untroubled plod was reassuring. I wondered if any of the men felt as I did, but I would never ask them, because I knew they would say that because they were men, they didn't fear the dark and if they were lying, they'd die before they admitted it.

We came out of the trees suddenly, emerging onto the moon-lit moor. We could make out darker clumps, which were gorse bushes, and here and there, the pale light caught the fleece of a few wandering sheep.

A few yards farther on, Clem halted and turned in his saddle. Brockley reined in beside him and they exchanged a few quiet words. Then Brockley moved off, taking a narrow track to the right. Brown Berry snorted and sidled, swishing an indignant tail, annoyed at being separated from his companions, but Brockley kneed him determinedly away. The rest of us rode on.

The path we were on now veered to the south, and after a short distance, Clem turned onto the heather to take a straight line westward, following the moon. Ryder came up beside me. "We're out in the open now," he murmured. "It's been a gamble from the start. But they can't be watching everywhere. Off the path is safer than on it, I reckon."

The moonlight showed us little detail, but it revealed distant skylines. This was a wide and lonely landscape. Presently, we reached the lone tree that Clem had mentioned. We passed it and rode on in silence for some time, going slightly downhill at first and then for a while on level ground. Once, in the distance, I caught sight of a thin spire of moonlit smoke from the banked fire in some lonely farmstead. We were crossing the vale where the scattered farms were. After an hour or so, we began to climb again. To the north, on our right, I saw that the moor sloped up more steeply still. Clem turned in his saddle and said: "T'proper road to Bolton's over t'other side of that crest to t'right. We're going parallel. We're where we should be."

"So far so good," said Ryder. "We've still got most of the night ahead of us. We need only keep up a steady pace. We can't risk any speed across rough heather in this light . . . Clem? What is it?"

Clem had pulled up sharply and his right hand, turned palm downward, made an urgent signal which unmistakably meant *stop and be quiet*. Ryder and I checked our horses. "What is it?" Ryder whispered.

"I saw summat, up there on the skyline," said Clem softly. "I could of sworn it. Something moved."

"Could be a sheep," said Ryder.

"That was no sheep. Didn't move right. Proper road's down t'other side o' t'crest, like I said. If anyone's keeping watch, that crest's a good place to post him, especially with this moon."

"What do we do?" I said urgently. "Can we be seen from there? We're not on a skyline and he'd be looking the other way, anyhow."

"Nothing we *can* do," Ryder muttered. "And we're not that visible, no. Reckon we'd better just press on. Just what did you see, Clem?"

"Summat moving, out o' t'tail of my eye. Summat tiny but upright-like and t'way it moved were like a man, not a sheep."

I cursed silently. I didn't doubt Clem for a moment. I knew those awful certainties, based on small details and instinctive reactions. He was almost certainly right.

There was nothing to do but keep moving and hope for the best. "How far are we from Tyesdale now?" I whispered.

"We're a good six or seven miles off Tyesdale land," said Clem.

Over eight miles still to go. But we had come far enough to ensure that a watcher couldn't instantly conclude that any movement he glimpsed in the night was a deputation from Tyesdale. "Let's ride on," I said. I added: "We could do with some mist now."

"Not just yet," muttered Clem. "We're coming to where t'drop's on t'left. I'd as soon be able to see where we're going just for a while."

"Single file, then," said Ryder quietly. "And go gently."

We went forward at a walk and I was glad to see that the moor was becoming less open. There were more gorse bushes here and some small trees as well. I glanced to my left and saw the drop that Clem had mentioned. We were riding, it seemed, perhaps fifty yards from the edge of an inland cliff. Here and there it curved and gave us glimpses of water glinting below, and a rocky wall, falling away in folds like a sculpted curtain, silvered by the moonlight.

The quiet was intense. There were no owls now, not even rustlings in the bushes; nothing at all but the footfalls of the horses and the soft clink of bridle rings. Because our pace was slow, the hooves would not be heard at any distance, but I hoped the clinking wouldn't carry.

Then Clem's horse suddenly pricked its ears and turned its head to the right and at the same moment, Roundel whinnied. Behind me, Ryder's horse trampled sideways, snorting. Ryder swore in a low voice, rose in his stirrups, and then spurred forward, straight at a gorse patch, drawing his sword and slashing at the bushes. We all saw the dark figure start up out of cover and run. Ryder galloped after it, overtook it, and swung his horse across the fugitive's path. The figure ducked and tried to veer away, but Ryder's horse was a soldier's trained mount. It was there again, barring the way, and the upraised sword shone in the moonlight.

Ryder said something, fiercely, and a frightened voice answered. Then they came back toward us, the fugitive stumbling ahead with Ryder's horse nudging at its shoulder and Ryder pricking his captive on with his swordpoint.

They emerged onto the path. Ryder slipped out of his saddle, leaving his horse to stand, and seized the figure by the arm, turning its face into the moonlight. "Who are you and what are you doing, skulking in the bushes and watching us?"

"Let me go! I've done nowt! Can't a fellow be late home from seeing his lass without being ridden down like a bloody felon? Let me *go*!"

"I know him!" said Clem. "Johnnie Grimsdale!"

"Grimsdale?" I said. I rode up close and recognized one of Grimsdale's sons. "Well, well," I said. "One of the fellows we rather fancy went and told the Thwaites that Tyesdale's new owner was on her way and she was a young unmarried girl and were they interested? Which led to Harry Hobson being killed and my daughter being kidnapped by mistake and frightened half to death. What have you to say for yourself, young Grimsdale?"

There was no reply. Ryder shook his captive. "And now he's prowling about in the night and watching us. If you were just an innocent lad coming home from a bit of courting, why were you hiding from us?"

"Didn't know who thee were, did I? Could have been anyone. Robbers, maybe. Honest folk don't go riding through t'night."

Ryder sheathed his sword but almost in the same movement, he grasped Johnnie Grimsdale from behind, twisted an arm up his back and put the other around his throat. "Just let's have the truth out of you. Who set you to spy on us?"

"No one! No one! Let me *go* . . . !"

"Tell the truth. Who sent you here?"

"Don't! Don't!" I couldn't see what Ryder had done to produce that anguished cry but whatever it was, it broke Johnnie's resistance. "Master Whitely, it were Master Whitely! Come to our place yesterday and said he'd pay us good money to watch t'road to Bolton an' report if anyone from Tyesdale tried to set out toward it! My brother's watching t'road nigh to Tyesdale. I were farther along t'way, up on t'crest, and I saw nothing on t'main track but I did catch sight o' summat moving down here. Only . . . no, sir, don't, don't! . . . I couldn't make out just what I were seeing so I cut across t'hillside to get here ahead o' thee an' get a closer look. I didn't think o' t'horses whinnying like that . . . !"

I believe, so hushed was the night, that I heard the snap as Ryder broke his neck. I saw Johnnie Grimsdale's body sag. I heard myself gasp. Ryder lowered him to the ground and crouched beside him, pressing his fingers into his victim's neck and then laying a palm on his chest.

"Dead," he said calmly. Then he heaved the body up, settling it across his shoulders, and walked away toward the cliff edge.

It happened so quickly that there was no time to protest. After my first appalled indrawing of breath, I sat on my horse, paralyzed with horror, and watched while Ryder dropped his load on the brink, crouched, and pushed. I heard a series of thuds and the rattle of small stones as the body fell over the cliff. Faintly, from below, there came a splash.

As Ryder came back, I said: "You *killed* him!" My voice had gone high-pitched with shock.

"There was nothing else to do," Ryder said coolly. "We couldn't let him go. If we could have marched him to Bolton with us and had him put in a castle dungeon, I'd have done that, but he was a strong lad and what if he got loose? Where would we be then? He'd report that we'd left Tyesdale. The conspirators could have got away, maybe to conspire again one day—and what of Mistress Pen? As it is, he'll be found in the stream and it'll look like an accident. He was out on the moors at night and maybe lost his way in mist . . ."

"There isn't any mist."

"There will be. Can't you smell it? He lost his way and his footing. He'll have a broken neck and the fall will account for that. There'll be no fingers pointing at Tyesdale. All we have to do is not to mention him to anyone, ever. He didn't suffer. He didn't know it was happening until it already had."

"But . . . !"

"Mistress," said John Ryder quietly, "there's more at stake than Mistress Pen. There's a foreign queen with a delusion that she ought to be Queen of England and a desire to bring a French army into Scotland. Sir William Cecil put it to me and to Dodd before we left the south. Queen Elizabeth doesn't care to admit it, but we're at war."

"But—just to kill him—just like that . . . ! We *should* have taken him to Bolton as a prisoner. We could have done it."

"He'd have been a danger to us. Master Ryder's in the right of it," said Clem. "Whitely and his friends, they mustn't be warned."

"Mistress Stannard," said Ryder. "I know, from Sir William, how you got yourself out of Scotland three years ago. Can you say that you have never guided the scythe-hand of Death?"

I said: "It still gives me nightmares."

"Soldiers learn not to have them," said Ryder briefly.

✳   ✳   ✳

His horse, which was indeed very well trained, was waiting patiently for him. He remounted and Clem, without further comment, once more led us on our way. The cliff edge seemed to veer southward, away from us, but we continued in a straight line and began to go downhill. On the skyline to the right, against the pallidly luminous sky, we glimpsed another lone tree, which Clem said was the one beside the pool. The downhill slope grew steeper, difficult to cope with, for the moon had become hazy once more.

And then, at last, there came the expected mist, ghostly wisps of it, drifting around us. Soon it was thick enough to slow us down, and when we reached the streamlet that ran from the pool, we didn't see it until the horses almost walked into it. We pulled up short.

It was not wide, but the banks were very steep and we had to ride downstream for some way to find a ford. The silvered vapors were thicker still near the water and gathered close about us as we left the ford behind. We journeyed through the fog like ghosts and once again I was thankful for Clem's guidance, for he knew his way. After a time, as he had promised, we struck the drovers' track. The mist began to lift. As the first grayness was beginning in the east, we reached the gate of Bolton Castle.

The night watch were yawning at their posts and quite glad to have visitors. I was recognized and we were let in. Ryder and Clem went to see to the horses and someone made haste to tell Sir Francis that Mistress Stannard had arrived with urgent news. It was so early that even the kitchens were not yet astir, but one of the guards fetched us some food from them.

Sir Francis, with a brocade robe pulled on over his night gear, broke his fast along with me in his study. Our cold pork chops, small ale, yesterday's bread, and dishes of butter and honey shared his desk with his writing set and document boxes, while I told him of the scheme to get his prisoner-cum-guest out of his hands and en route to France.

I also told him that we had made our escape from Tyesdale

and the journey to Bolton without incident. As far as anyone ever knew, Johnnie Grimsdale went out that night onto the moors, and there in the shifting mists and unreliable moonlight, lost his life in an accidental fall.

Ryder had done right according to his own set of rules. I understood them. But the call of the wild geese had faded away. Yet again, I longed with all my heart for Hugh, for Hawkswood and Withysham and home.

19

The Necessary Sacrifice

"An interesting story," Sir Francis said.

I applied butter and honey to a piece of bread and said: "I only hope you believe me!"

"Oh yes. It explains a great deal. For one thing, I now know why Lady Mary has spent the last few days alternately lying on her bed and sighing, and flinging herself about her rooms in tears, exclaiming that she feels ill and will never be well until she has more freedom and that her glimpse of the outside world when she went hawking was as good as any physic. She cries out to do that again. She longs for the simple pleasure, denied only to her among all the people of England, to ride out and visit a friend. Can she not visit dear Ursula Stannard? Surely Mistress Stannard is above suspicion? She can return the same day, but such a simple, ordinary thing would give her light and air and exercise and a sense of being, once again, a simple, ordinary woman . . ."

"She's never been that in her life," I said.

"I agree. But you should hear her. On and on; and yes, I have pitied her, though in the light of what you are telling me now—I fear I have become sarcastic. I dislike sarcasm, but really! All the same, I think that she really is unwell, though I don't know what the trouble is. It worries me because I *am* responsible for her health."

"She says she wants to visit me, and that she could return to Bolton the same day," I said thoughtfully. "But I've been told to prepare to put her up overnight and put her in a particular room."

"I fancy that the idea is for her to use an attack of illness to ensure that she stays overnight, I should think. Then something will happen. Rescuers will try to remove her."

"Yes, I see that. I was thinking of something else."

"Which is?"

"All they want me to do is make her welcome for one night and put her in a specified room. It hardly seems worthwhile to force me into it. I would hardly refuse to shelter her if she were unwell and Mary Stuart would only have to ask to have a certain bedchamber because she liked the view from the window and I don't suppose I'd refuse that either. I think," I said, "that in all this there is a good deal of Magnus Whitely taking revenge on me."

"I daresay, but what of it? For whatever reason, you *have* been asked to perform this service. Let us consider what it means. You've been asked to give her a particular room. Where is it, precisely?"

"At the back of the house. Quite high up. The moat is just below."

Sir Francis opened a box, brought out a sheet of paper, and pushed his writing set toward me. "Can you draw a plan of the house for me?"

"Sir Francis . . ."

"Yes?"

I said slowly: "I don't quite know what's in your mind—but wouldn't the best thing, now that I've succeeded in reaching you, be to send a squad of men to Fernthorpe and wait for the conspirators to bring Pen there? If Mary doesn't go to Tyesdale and therefore can't be rescued, I suppose Whitely and Littleton will carry out their threat. We'd catch them and save Pen at one and the same time."

"We might," Knollys agreed. "But in that case, what could we arrest them for? Any charges would rest only on your word and that of your manservant Brockley—who had his ear to the door. Pretty behavior in a servant, and anyway, he's been your trusted helper for years, has he not? No doubt he would say whatever you asked him to say."

"But . . ." I stopped, speechless.

"You and Whitely," said Sir Francis, "are in dispute. What if he complains that your talk of plots is only a fabrication made out of spite against him?"

"Sir Francis!"

"I didn't say I believed that. I don't. But *he* might say it. After all, the only thing he would be caught doing would be bringing a bride to Fernthorpe. An unwilling bride, perhaps, but in fact the Thwaites are of good blood and the marriage is reasonable by many people's standards. It may sound harsh to you, but Penelope Mason is not my responsibility. My task is to keep Mary Stuart in English hands and bring to book anyone who tries to get her out of them. I want these conspirators caught in the act. Now, if you please, Mistress Stannard, would you make the sketch?"

Silently, my hand shaking a little, I did as I was told, making separate sketches for each floor and then doing a plan of the house, moat, and courtyard. He examined the result thoughtfully. "There's no outer wall at the back, then. Beyond the moat is open ground?"

"Yes. There are some sheep pens there, and a little path in between, leading out to a pasture."

"I see. So the house could be easily approached from the rear—especially at night?"

"I would think so." I tried not to speak sullenly. "You can see the laborers' cottages—where our two maidservants live—from those back bedchambers, but they're not directly to the rear or very near. They're a good distance off to the right and there's a wide meadow and a stone wall or two in between. After dark, no one in the cottages would notice anything. But no one could get in or out from the back of Tyesdale, Sir Francis. The wall goes sheer down from the bedchamber windows to the moat. And the windows really are high off the ground."

"So the only way out is through the house?"

"Yes, through an upper passage and then down the stairs and through the main hall. There's a front door with steps leading down to the courtyard . . ." I pointed to where I had marked these things on my plan ". . . and a kitchen door with a few narrow steps, round at the side."

"If she did stay a night with you, there would be guards posted in the hall and the courtyard and at both the main and the kitchen doors," said Knollys. "But at the rear . . . how wide is the moat?"

I tried to thrust away the thought of Pen, alone and afraid and wondering what I was doing to save her and attempted to visualize the moat. "Twenty feet, perhaps. With a steep drop from the edge to the water level."

"And the house wall at the back really goes straight down into it?"

"I believe there's a very narrow ledge. Yes, there is. We saw a couple of ducks squatting on it only the other day."

"How big is the window of the bedchamber?"

"The windows on that floor are mullions, modern ones. I think I could squeeze through them," I said. "If so, Mary Stuart could, too."

"We're guessing," Sir Francis said. "But you have been told that Mary Stuart may make an overnight stay with you, and that she is to have that bedchamber. I would make sure that she couldn't escape through the door and our schemers would surely foresee that. If they think otherwise, their brains have gone begging. But if she had outside help, the window sounds possible. Our plotters will be gambling on the assumption that you will be too frightened for Mistress Mason's sake to betray them, and that we won't therefore be expecting an attempt at rescuing Lady Mary. So we may not do much about patrolling the back of the house. If we did, they'd no doubt start some sort of diversion in the front. But I fancy they'll expect us to look on the moat as an adequate obstacle."

Toothpicks had been provided with breakfast. He took one from its pot and absentmindedly prodded at his front teeth.

"Without outside help," he said, "the moat would indeed be a difficult obstacle. But *with* help—that's different. They'd only need a light boat and a rope ladder."

"How would they get the ladder up to her?"

"That's easy. Any soldier knows that one. You fasten a length of thin, strong twine to the end of your rope and a more slender thread still to the end of that, and fix the other end of the thread to a blunt arrow, and shoot the arrow through the window. Whoever is in the room just hauls everything in. I'm assuming a rope ladder. She's quite athletic enough to manage one, and since they'll presumably arrive on horseback, a real ladder will be difficult to carry."

"*Will* be?" I queried.

"Ah. You are sharp, mistress. Yes. Will be." Sir Francis sprang up and began to walk about the room. "I've let her beguile me; I know I have, but it's over now. Well, there's no harm done. You realize what I want, I think? We should let the plot proceed and catch them red-handed. I don't care for the idea that there are people at large in Her Majesty's realm who are willing to act against her in this fashion. If Mary Stuart once gets to France, she will certainly find sympathetic kinfolk there, by blood and by marriage. Before we know it, she'll be back in Scotland and . . ."

He threw himself back into his chair and stared at me. "You think that I am indifferent to the fate of your ward, Mistress Mason. It isn't that. But they aren't proposing to murder her. Just to marry her off. And here in the north . . ."

"I know. Here in the north, marriage by capture is still winked at," I said bitterly.

"Yes. I am sorry, Ursula, but Pen Mason *cannot* be my first concern and shouldn't be yours, either. What if Mary were forcibly restored to her throne by a French army? They'd have to invade Scotland to do it. What would happen next? If the said French army were then to go meekly home like a bunch of farm laborers after a good day's harvesting, then I am the King of Cathay. They'd be over the Scottish border in no time, annexing pieces of England, gathering support among the Catholics here in the north, and fomenting a rising to put Mary where Elizabeth is now. I'm not leaving these conspirators at large. I want to net them all."

"You mean you want to grant her wish and let her come to Tyesdale?"

"And we will have men on watch so that whoever comes to fetch her will walk straight into a trap. A far better trap than any we could set at Fernthorpe. They'll try to get her out through that window, sure as sunrise. I'll send an official request to Tyesdale this morning, asking if you will receive her tomorrow. You can ride back as part of my deputation."

"I've got to get back unseen," I said.

"You can borrow a set of breeches and a helmet, and ride astride, looking like a young soldier. That dappled mare of yours is a trifle distinctive; I'll find you another horse. You can travel in the middle of the group. The men who came with you can stay here until tomorrow and then accompany the escort that brings Mary to Tyesdale. I'll have them helmeted to avoid recognition, too. I'll keep the mare until it's all over."

"I understand. But . . ."

"Yes, Mistress Stannard, I know. Penelope! But once we have these traitors in our hands, they will tell us where she is. I can assure you," said Sir Francis, "that they *will* tell us. Within half an hour of their capture, we will have the information."

I was silent again, thinking of the fatherly and reliable Ryder, who last night had shown a very different aspect of his nature, and thinking too of things I had heard Cecil say. Ryder, Cecil, Knollys. The three of them were similar in many ways: civilized and essentially good-hearted. When they revealed their capacity for ruthlessness, it was astonishingly chilling.

At length I said: "I would like to borrow one of your couriers and send a letter to Pen's eldest brother George, at Lockhill, asking him to come at once to Tyesdale. Just that, no more. That way, her mother won't be alarmed. But I think her brother should be fetched to Yorkshire."

"By all means. I can have a man ready to go within the hour, if you will write the letter and provide him with directions. I will protect your ward as far as I can. If she has been forcibly married before we reach her, no doubt a way can be found to annul it. She will have had a distressing experience, very likely, but Mistress Stannard, the danger, if Mary Stuart gets away to France, is so great . . ."

"I know. Penelope may have to be sacrificed. I understand," I said wearily, and hoped to heaven that whatever scheme for her protection Brockley had in mind, he would carry through successfully.

20

The Heartbroken Enchantress

We spent a little more time on the details, but I was back at Tyesdale by midday, wearing borrowed man's clothing and accompanied by four men-at-arms and a captain. Knowing that Feeb and Bess Clipclop were probably in the house and might not be trustworthy, I waited, still in the saddle, among the men-at-arms until I had sent the captain in to fetch Sybil. She hurried out and came to my stirrup.

"I'm so glad to see you. We've been worrying ourselves to death. Dale was afraid the maidservants would notice you weren't here. She's making them clean the chapel again. They've been told not to go near your room—you're supposed to be in bed with another migraine and I said that the noise of their clogs might make you feel worse."

"Bless you all," I said. "Now, if I can get up to my room unseen, I can emerge in a few minutes' time, looking normal but wan, which shouldn't be difficult, as I've been up all night, riding to Bolton, and I've just ridden the fifteen miles back. In the meantime, you can be the hostess and look after this deputation from Sir Francis. Where's Dale now?"

But Dale was already at the top of the steps. I swung out of the saddle and ran up to meet her. Within a few minutes I was safe in my bedchamber and Dale was helping me out of my boots and breeches. I seized the chance to say: "Is there any word from Brockley?" but she only shook her head dolefully.

"Nothing, ma'am, nothing and I'm worried as I can be. I can't abide this waiting, not hearing, not knowing, but what else can I do?"

"Brockley is capable; he'll look after himself." My heart was as heavy for Pen as hers was for Brockley but I tried to encourage us both. "He only left last night. Give him time. Now, be quick. I want to be seen as soon as possible, by Feeb and Bess, looking like myself."

Soon, dressed in housewifely fashion, I was making my way down to the hall, declaring that my head was better and I was ready to "receive my visitors." Sybil had called the maidservants from the chapel to attend to the refreshments and in their interested presence, I pretended to learn (to my flustered surprise, of course) that Sir Francis Knollys wished to dine with me on the morrow and would be bringing his illustrious guest Lady Mary Stuart. Under heavy guard, naturally, and I would have to be prepared to feed numerous extra mouths.

Sir Francis's men, who knew all about it, thought the whole thing as amusing as a masque, and their captain, who was young, slightly foppish, and regrettably mischievous, grinned so outrageously that I feared that even Feeb, let alone the much brighter Bess, would notice and become suspicious. I frowned at him fiercely and also vainly, for all he did was pretend to look frightened.

Fortunately, Tom Smith had come into the hall to listen and was sharp enough to distract Bess with a flirtatious remark, which made her giggle, while Feeb was luckily preoccupied with pouring ale and not dribbling it. They noticed nothing and, mercifully, the rest of the Bolton men had the good sense to remove the grins from their faces.

The captain and his men went off after dinner, ostensibly to carry my acceptance back to Bolton. I announced that my headache had returned and retired to bed for some sleep. Sybil and Agnes told our two maids that they weren't needed next day, as Sir Francis would bring his own servants. Before dinner the following morning, he arrived, with Mary.

*   *   *

As promised, the party was accompanied by a whole squad of armed men, but no ladies. "Seton decided not to come in case this turned out to be another hot day, as indeed it has," Sir Francis said to me expressionlessly, preceding the others up the steps to where I stood waiting to welcome the arrivals, "and Lady Mary herself said that she did not need attendants, just to ride out and visit a friend informally. She sounded," he added with a sigh, "as innocent as a baby."

"Mary Seton knows what's afoot?" I asked in an undertone.

"One would imagine so."

"Well, she can't be blamed. Her loyalty is with her mistress, as one would expect. Please come in."

Mary Stuart followed him up, lifted me as usual from my polite curtsy, and put her arm about me as we went into the hall. "This is so kind of you, dear Ursula. I have been so far from well with that wearisome pain in my side, for which there is never any explanation, except that it often comes when I am unhappy. To live in a cage is unbearable to me."

And then, as we moved across the hall and into the parlor, she turned me a little so as to look into my face. "I believe," she whispered, "that you know the plan. Tobias said that if you agreed to receive me here, it would mean that you did. Oh, my dearest Ursula, you can never know how grateful I am for such a friend. One day, when I am a queen again, I will show my gratitude, believe me."

Her charm was like a sweet scent or a touching melody. It still moved me, despite the knowledge I now had. "Your Majesty," I said solemnly, aware of being a hypocrite, and not liking it.

"Dear, dear Ursula. I so much miss even being addressed as I should be. Queen of France and Scotland—and all I get from Sir Francis is a miserable 'my lady.' Is this your parlor? What a delightful room."

It was nothing of the kind, though it was better than it had been. Cecily Moss had told us where to buy new tapestries, but so far we hadn't had time to see to it. Two of the least moth-eaten hangings had been put on the walls in the meantime and I had had the scratched old settles polished and found some respectable cushions for them. There were fresh rushes on the floor. "It's not luxurious, but we haven't been here long enough to do more," I said. "I hope the dinner will please you, however."

Feeding so many mouths at short notice could have been difficult, but fortunately, Agnes had onions and cabbages enough in her vegetable patch and Sir Francis had had the forethought to help me out. The escort had brought some useful supplies, loaded onto a packhorse. I didn't have to slaughter Tyesdale chickens or make drastic inroads into its limited supply of hams or its modest stores of flour and sugar and raisins.

Except for a minor contretemps when Agnes caught the dog Gambol in the kitchen, trying to steal a capon, and chased him out into the hall, calling him names and brandishing a broom, the dinner was all it should be and was conducted with the decorum befitting a royal guest.

It was as the meal was finishing, when a sweet white wine (provided by Sir Francis) was being served as an accompaniment to a marchpane confection shaped (by Sybil, who was good with her fingers) to look like a little manor house, that Mary put her hand to her side and said in a weak voice: "I am sorry. I feel unwell again. I must withdraw. Please, you are all to finish dining. This is no time for ceremony, or for me to say that because I can eat no more, no one else must take a mouthful either. I am not so royal as that. Dear Mistress Stannard, if I might rest upstairs for a while . . . ?"

I showed her to my own room. She lay down on the bed and Dale came to help me loosen her stays and remove her shoes. She appeared to sleep and I left her with Fran Dale to watch over her. "I'll bring the rest of your dinner up to you, Dale," I said.

I went back to the hall to finish my own meal. When it was over, Sir Francis and I exchanged glances and he said: "I had better see her. It will be the next scene in our pretty play."

I took him upstairs. We found Mary awake again, tossing restlessly in my four-poster and complaining to Dale that her pain was worse and that she felt feverish and could not face the long ride back to Bolton.

Sir Francis stood by the bed, looking thoughtfully down at her. His face bore exactly the right expression of worry and responsibility. He had no mandate to allow Mary to spend a night away from Bolton, he said sternly. He had in fact allowed her far more latitude than he should. She must make an effort, for it was his duty to see that she returned to the castle that same night. Mary allowed a few tears to fall—I noticed with admiration that she could apparently cry at will—and obediently rose from the bed, only to stumble with her hand to her head, complaining that she felt giddy, that the whole room was going around and around . . . she was so very sorry; she was embarrassing good Sir Francis, but . . .

"You have men enough with you," I said helpfully. "Surely she can be as well guarded here as at Bolton. It will only be for one night, I trust. If Her Grace is still unwell tomorrow, we will fetch a physician."

Sir Francis appeared to hesitate. Mary lay down on the bed again and moaned artistically. "Well . . ." said Sir Francis slowly.

"What else can you do?" I asked in reasonable tones. "What if she were to collapse altogether on the way back to Bolton? It's a long way, even if she were carried in a litter, and we haven't got a litter."

Leaving Dale to watch the invalid, he drew me outside and out of hearing. "I can't keep this performance up for long. We must let her assume that you have talked me into it. We'll go back presently and say so. Meanwhile, show me the room that Whitely wants her to have."

I did so. He examined the width of the window, and leaning out of the casement, he studied the surroundings and the moat below with a knowledgeable eye. "I think we've guessed right," he said, drawing his head in again at last. "It could be done. We'll take them in the act of doing it. You are sure you can impersonate Mary by standing at the window to encourage them to proceed?"

"I'll hide my hair. I've a hooded cloak that will shadow my face, too. I think I can look convincing."

"Very well. We'll go back to her and tell her that she can stay the night—but not in the room she expects. She presumably knows the details of the plot. I hope she doesn't make a great outcry."

"Even if she does, there's no one in the house who might betray us," I said. "The maidservants were the likeliest for that and we made them stay at home today."

We returned to Mary, who was now lying on her back with her eyes closed. As I went to her bedside and looked at her, I thought that her claim of ill-health was probably not altogether false. She was much too pale and there were violet shadows beneath those lidded eyes.

A surge of the old sympathy overtook me. She was still only in her mid-twenties, and she had been through experiences for which nothing in her petted, luxurious life as a princess and then a royal bride in France could have prepared her. She had not expected to find herself coping in person with the rough Scots nobility; still less had she expected to fall into the hands of a dissolute husband who arranged for a murder to take place virtually in front of her.

I remembered David Riccio very well, as harmless a fellow as ever I saw. She had heard his terrified pleas for his life and his screams as they stabbed him. She had ridden headlong for safety although she was six months gone with child. Perhaps she had believed herself justified in leaving Darnley to the mercy of her nobles. God knew, she had suffered for it since; vilified and threatened by angry mobs, cast from her throne, imprisoned, hunted . . .

Looking at those beautifully modeled features, already worn despite her youth, I wondered at the strangeness of blood relationship. Since I shared a father with Elizabeth, I realized suddenly, I also shared her cousinship with Mary. She was my kinswoman as well as Elizabeth's. I lacked her beauty, but there was a trace of resemblance in our features. I thought of the wild rides she had made, after Riccio's death and again after her escape from Lochleven, and after the loss of the battle that Bothwell had tried to fight for her. Like me, I thought, she had a love of adventure. She too, surely, had heard the call of the wild geese.

Whereas Elizabeth, to whom I felt much closer, had not, as far as I was aware. What I shared with Elizabeth was something very different and possibly less admirable than Mary's capacity for dramatic gambles.

Deep in Elizabeth was a core of ice. I believed that it had been made icier, less amenable to any kind of melting, by the fact that when she was small, her father, King Henry, had had her mother, Anne Boleyn, executed—and later on, as though determined that his daughter should fully understand what it meant, had executed her young stepmother Catherine Howard as well.

All the same, I did not think that that was the whole story. That icy core had always been there in some degree, probably inherited from King Henry himself. One would need a cold heart, surely, to send to the block even one wife, someone with whom one had lain, and made love; with whom one had shared pet names and private jokes and breakfast times; had comforted or been comforted by after a bad dream.

But Henry had condemned not one wife, but two. Oh, Mary Stuart had probably looked through her fingers at Darnley's death, but she had not written her name at the foot of his death warrant or ignored his screams as Henry had ignored Catherine Howard's. She was not Henry's daughter and she did not possess that cold splinter. That was Elizabeth's inheritance—and mine.

Yes, mine as well. It had enabled me to carry out the ruthless duties of a spy; it had enabled me to send men to their death. I disapproved of the killing of Johnnie Grimsdale, but I had also accepted it. Perhaps Mary, foolish and vulnerable, was still the better woman.

Sir Francis, puzzled by my silence, cleared his throat. Mary's eyes opened. "Ursula! I am sorry to be a nuisance. But I feel dreadful."

"It's all right, Lady Mary. Sir Francis realizes that you can't ride back to Bolton like this. You must rest here overnight. You can have this room—it's the best in the house."

At once, as I had feared, a shadow passed over her face. She hoisted herself higher on the pillows. Sir Francis saw the signs, too, and hastily declared that he was sorry he had disturbed her. "Try to go back to sleep, dear lady. Come, Mistress Stannard."

Anxious to be gone before the storm broke, he was out of the door before he had finished the sentence, and in response to a movement of my head, Dale followed him, but before I too had moved out of Mary's reach, her hand shot out and closed on my wrist. "Ursula! This is the wrong room. It looks out to the front. The arrangement was that I should have a room at the back. Tobias told me. We planned it before he left Bolton."

Core of ice. Sometimes that core was like a second personality inside me, someone who now and then took over my body, my tongue. My feelings of sympathy didn't vanish, but they were elbowed aside. Without warning, surprising me as much as Mary, that other Ursula spoke.

"Did Tobias also tell you how he proposed to persuade me?" I drew my wrist out of her grasp. "I am a servant of Queen Elizabeth. Do you think I could be induced to take part in such a scheme as this simply for the asking?"

Mary's mouth dropped open. I saw that she had lost several teeth. "*Did* you know how he worked on me?" I persisted.

There were tears in Mary's eyes. "I asked Tobias if he was sure you would agree, and he said yes, because he would entice your ward Penelope away from Tyesdale and tell you that . . . that . . ."

"That he would have her forcibly married to a man called Andrew Thwaite. She is rightly terrified of him. He is a criminal," I said bluntly. "He is wild to have her but he never will if I have anything to do with it. That was the lever that Tobias and his cousin Magnus Whitely—a steward whom I dismissed from Tyesdale for milking the estate—employed to make me help them."

Mary, meeting my eyes, shrank against the pillows. "Tobias swore that no harm would come to Mistress Pen. He said that she is of a Catholic family. He said his threats were all pretense and that he would explain it all to Pen and that probably she would be thrilled at the chance to help me."

"And you believed him?" I asked.

"Yes, why should I not?" The indignation was a little too righteous. I continued to stare at her steadily and she twisted as though my gaze were a spike. "Yes, I *did*! Why should Tobias want to harm Penelope? He told me that when we leave here, he will take me first to a friendly house where I can rest in hiding until the hunt subsides. And he said that I will find Pen there and talk to her myself. Besides, I *have* to get to France! I don't believe my cousin Elizabeth will ever help me. I *must* get away. I *must*!"

"Even if Tobias is lying and really means to carry out his threat unless I help you? If it came to it, were you ready to sacrifice Pen?"

"Why are you talking like this? I'm here. You let me come. I'm staying the night. It's only that this can't be the room I'm meant to have. Tobias said, a room at the back, and they would rescue me from . . ."

"The window." I felt no sympathy now. "We guessed."

"We?"

"It's time to be frank with you." I heard the harshness in my voice. "You would have had to know at some point. I too have had to put Penelope at risk, though I will do what I can to save her. Sir Francis knows all about it. I got word to him . . ."

"Oh, I see! *You* can put your ward in peril for your purposes, but if I do it . . . !"

"You agreed to put Pen in danger in the first place. I have to deal with the situation you've created. And while you're trying to start an invasion, I'm trying to prevent one. So is Sir Francis. You are here as bait. I shall impersonate you at that back window, to tempt your rescuers into advancing with their ladder. They will be seized in the act. You will stay locked in this room until it's all over."

"No!" Mary was scrambling from the bed, clutching once more at my hands. "No, Ursula, please! I am sorry about Pen but I was sure—I am sure—that they mean her no ill! Let me go free! I can't live as a prisoner; I shall die for lack of liberty, for lack of the wind in my face; for lack of my purpose in life! I was born to be a queen, and queens are appointed by God. I . . ."

Her short hair was in a distracted tangle. Her face had crumpled into that of a frustrated and heartbroken child. She fell on her knees, staring up at me with eyes so desperate that for a moment that treacherous pity that she was so good at inspiring woke in me yet again.

Then I remembered what Cecil had told me, of that depraved but pitiful young man Darnley, also scrambling out of bed, in such fear that he didn't stop to put on a cloak against the February night, and his last plea for pity when his murderers caught him in the garden, just before they strangled him. And I thought of Pen, facing a nightmare wedding and wondering what had happened to the protection that I, her guardian, owed her. I wondered where Brockley was and what he was doing, and whether he had yet achieved anything toward saving her. With that, once more, and this time forever, my sympathy for Mary Stuart died.

"What Sir Francis has planned will be carried out," I said coldly. "There is nothing you can do about it. You will be back in Bolton tomorrow and your conspirators will be in custody. I shall rescue Pen if I can. Which is more than you undertook to do."

Her mouth stretched and she began to wail. Tearing myself free of her, though she tried to keep me by grabbing at my gown, I fled from the room. I found Sir Francis and Dale standing outside, their faces aghast.

"We heard," he said. He stepped forward and turned the key in the lock of the bedchamber, shutting her in. "Most of it. Oh, dear God!"

The last exclamation was a comment on the pitiful howling that we could hear inside the room. The door handle rattled and the door shook as Mary beat on it with her fists. Dale, her hand to her mouth, rushed away downstairs. Sir Francis beckoned to me to follow.

"Come away!" he said. "Just come away. Let her wear herself down until she's calm again."

"Sir Francis," I said, "I want to talk to you. She mentioned a friendly house where she would be taken first. Now, I have an idea . . ."

21

Scented Pebbles

"It's a mad idea," said Sir Francis. "Unthinkable."

"But if it worked, if I could keep up the impersonation for long enough, it would take me straight to Penelope—and it would also lead your men to this friendly house that Lady Mary has mentioned, and maybe bring some extra conspirators into the net."

"They'll be brought in anyway. Believe me. Once I get my hands on the so-called rescuers, they'll tell everything they know, and name every fellow conspirator that they know."

"But it might take time," I said. "They may be more obstinate than you expect—or less truthful. And meanwhile, those at the friendly house might realize that something had gone amiss. They could flee—and they might take Pen with them, as a hostage. She must be frightened to death! Sir Francis, she may not be your responsibility, but she is most certainly mine. I want to reach her. I *should* go, for her sake."

"You don't resemble Mary! You're not tall enough!"

"They'll bring a horse for me, surely. They won't see me standing on my feet for long and it'll be dark; they won't see clearly. I've a pair of boots with quite high heels. I'll use those."

"I suppose you *might* get away with it. If you can make yourself look tall and hide the fact that your hair isn't ginger . . ."

"I'm sure Mary wouldn't like to hear her hair described as merely ginger."

"This isn't the moment for pleasantries," said Sir Francis disapprovingly. The term *Puritan* was not yet in common use but looking back, I see that it fitted him well. "Your eyes are much darker than hers," he said, "but it will be night, as you say." He studied my face. "Your chin is more pointed than Mary's but the way your eyes are set is similar and your nose and cheekbones are similar, too. Surprising. You could almost be related."

"That's a piece of luck," I said carefully.

"But . . ."

"Sir Francis, once we reach this friendly house, wherever it is, your men can swoop at once. They have only to keep on our tracks."

"*If* I agree, my men will be as hard on your heels as they can be, as long as they avoid being seen," said Sir Francis worriedly. He cocked his head. We had followed Dale down the stairs and were now in the hall, standing near the foot of the stairs. Above us, the wailing and hammering from my bedchamber had not abated. "She's still hysterical. We shall have to put a stop to that or she might warn them yet, by making such a racket that they can hear it when you open your window."

"I have a sedative I can give her. She introduced me to it herself," I said, "when I was in Scotland. When I paid a visit to London with Hugh, I found an apothecary who recognized it and now I always have some to hand. He said it was unsafe to use it often because it can gain a hold on one, like wine, if you drink it too much, but it's useful now and then. If someone is ill or has toothache and can't sleep, it can be a blessing. I'll put some in a posset and I hope she'll drink it willingly. If she doesn't, well, I suppose we can use force."

"Very well." He sighed. "I cannot forbid you, not with Mistress Pen at such risk, and with so much to gain. We should have a pretty haul of traitors by the end of the night, and no need to wring their names out of anyone, which is a disagreeable business anyway."

He frowned, as a new idea came to him. "I wish I had

brought my hounds from Bolton! But you have dogs, have you not? They could help in following you."

"They'd be better than hounds," I said. "Hounds give tongue. With Gambol and Grumble, you can follow a scent without making a noise. They're good watchdogs, but they stop baying on command. Say *quiet* to them, when you first set out, and they won't bark."

"If we use the dogs, my men could keep far enough back to be safely out of sight. Can we provide a good strong scent?" Sir Francis was becoming interested. "What about a sponge soaked in something pungent? If you can rub it over your horse's hooves . . ."

"That could be difficult," I said. "I could only do it by pretending to inspect or polish my horse's feet. Someone escaping from captivity, with a throne at stake, isn't going to stop for that! It would seem very odd and might arouse suspicion." I considered. "Suppose I were to carry a supply of small pebbles? Very small—gravel, really—not too heavy but soaked in something smelly beforehand. I could drop them along the way. Sparingly, because I don't know how far we'll be going, but they could act as markers to help the dogs along."

"Aye," said Sir Francis, unexpectedly falling into the local accent in excitement. He saw me looking at him quizzically and smiled. "If I stay in Yorkshire much longer, I shall turn into a complete Yorkshireman. The smell mustn't be so strong that anyone will notice, but dogs have sharper noses than people."

He paused. I looked at him. "What is it, Sir Francis?"

"I shouldn't allow this. It's wrong."

"If all goes well, they won't know I'm not Mary until I'm inside the house. When they find out, there'll no doubt be uproar, but I can tell them that I've been followed and that harming me or Pen, if she's there, as I pray she will be, will only make things worse for them. I think I can keep them paralyzed with panic for long enough for your men to arrive and rescue us. If Pen isn't there, Sir Francis, I must ask you to see that they wring her whereabouts out of their captives, immediately. Will you promise me that?"

"Yes. Yes, they will. I agree. Don't worry, Mistress Stannard—we won't forget Penelope."

"Sir Francis, I've . . . taken chances like this before."

"As a matter of fact," he said, "I was aware of that, Mistress Stannard. It has never been officially said; indeed, there is an understanding that it should not be discussed, but it is quite widely known at court. If I had thought you were simply an . . . an ordinary young woman, do you think I would consider this mad scheme for a single moment? But as things are . . ."

"Just say, *and God go with you,*" I said.

He inclined his head. "You have the sedative in your baggage?" he said.

The warm day was followed by another fine night. The sky was clear and the moon was three-quarters full, blanching out the stars around it.

Since Mary was in the room that Sybil and I had shared, Sybil went in with Meg for the night. Meg, who knew some of the plan, though not its latest addition, was nervous at the idea of violence breaking out around the house and was upset by the noise Mary was making. I let her stay up later than usual, until the time came to prepare Mary's doctored drink. Then I poured out a small dose for Meg as well. She would sleep, and when she woke, I hoped the night's adventures would all be over.

Mary's drink consisted of a caudle of hot red wine, with an egg and some melted honey beaten into it along with a good spoonful of my sedative. I didn't want to see her again, and Sir Francis took the caudle to her himself, along with a dish of food and a book of devotional essays.

He had to shout and pound on the door, because Mary was still hammering at it from within. When at last he induced her to step back and let him enter, he found her not only distraught but also exhausted, so white and tearstained that he was alarmed.

"I recommended her to pray and to calm her mind with reading," he told me afterward. "At least she took the food and the caudle. She wept into them—*wailed* into them—but she took them."

Sybil and Dale went to her after a while and found her quieter. She let them put her back to bed. Judging from the silence as darkness fell, the dose had worked and she was asleep.

The quiet alone was a blessing. If I had had to listen to much more of Mary's lamentations, I thought, I would become as upset as Meg and might even develop a headache and that wouldn't do. I had other things on my mind.

Such as keeping vigil by an open window, cloaked and hooded in black, with a dark scarf over my hair beneath the hood, a masculine outfit of jerkin, shirt, and breeches under the cloak, and high-heeled boots on my feet, waiting for something to happen. I had a candle burning on the sill. At the front of the house, a guard was obtrusively on the watch, but here at the back, all was hushed. There was nothing to show that saddled horses were waiting in the stable or dogs tied in the yard, ready to be taken out at a moment's notice.

Or that Sir Francis was sitting behind me, waiting to see me leave before hurrying off to set the riders and dogs in motion.

I had my lockpicks with me, along with a small dagger, in a pouch fastened to my belt and pushed inside my breeches. Also, tied at my waist, under my cloak, were three small leather bags of tiny pebbles that had been rolled in a mix of manure, mint, and crushed garlic.

We had been careful about it. The cloak and the leather kept the odor of the pebbles from being too noticeable, though dogs would detect it easily when the pebbles were dropped. We had introduced them to it and given them a practice run along a trail of the same scent, using long leashes in the hands of horsemen, and they had followed it with ease, tails blithely wagging. They evidently took it for a new game.

All that remained now was for Mary's rescuers to arrive.

I was both tired and scared. Though I had slept after dinner the previous day and had also slept well enough the following night, I still felt weary, and ahead of me was a long and nerve-racking ordeal.

Which would presumably begin with a long and nerve-racking descent down some sort of ladder, to the fetid moat below. Until I was actually at my post, I hadn't realized how high the window really was. The drop below was terrifying. I couldn't imagine how I would ever negotiate it.

I sat staring tensely into the night. For a while, a faint candle-light had burned in one of the laborers' cottages in the distance, but this had now been snuffed. Except for my own candle burning on the sill, there was nothing to be seen but the moonlight on the pasture and the moorland beyond. Nothing moved except, here and there, the pale forms of sheep. Nothing . . .

They came so quietly that they were near the house before I was aware of them. Horses. Five or six of them, in single file, approaching the rear of Tyesdale just as we had foreseen. They came at a walk, and their bridle rings must have been muffled, for even when they drew up just beyond the moat, I did not hear the faintest chink.

Picking up the candle, I leaned out of the window and moved it to and fro. A dim figure dismounted from the foremost horse and raised a hand in answer. Others then got down and began to unload things from what at first looked like a weirdly misshapen creature but which I now saw was a packhorse with a curious burden on its back.

The first figure unslung something from his shoulder, stooped over one of the bundles taken from the packhorse, and then, straightening up, made a *keep back* gesture at me. I drew aside from the window, leaving the light there as a mark and signaling to Sir Francis to get himself out of the way as well. He moved quickly back into a corner. A moment later, an arrow whizzed past the candle and landed on the floor. I crouched, found the line attached to it, stood up, and hauled it in. Sir Francis had been completely right. The thin line led to a cord, the cord to a length of rope, and the rope to a rope ladder. Opening a second casement, I fastened the line around a mullion.

The moment to begin the descent was almost here. My heart pounded. The ladder seemed horridly frail. Below, our silent visitors were carrying something to the moat and putting it on the water. Yes, a little boat. That was why the load on the packhorse had been such an extraordinary shape. Someone was getting into it. Someone else was handing him a paddle. Very softly, he began to scull across the moat.

I glanced over my shoulder and gave Sir Francis a nod. Below, the nose of the dinghy grated faintly as it touched the ledge between the wall and the water. I looked at the drop, took a deep breath, and without stopping to think too much, hitched my cloak up, put a knee on the sill, and twisted awkwardly around, so as to reach down behind me with a foot and grope for the first rung.

I hadn't foreseen that my boot heels would make this awkward. I almost panicked, swaying at the top of the ladder, until I felt someone on the ladder below me, and a hand, gripping my ankle, guided my foot to the springy rope tread. I hoped to heaven that he hadn't paid any attention to the heels of my boots.

Whispering my thanks, I slid my second foot down and mercifully put it straight onto the tread. Once I had the feel of the ladder, I found that I could manage. I was going down backward, which meant that I couldn't see the drop, although I couldn't stop imagining it. Now that I was on it, I realized that the ladder was sturdier than it looked. It was made of thick, rough rope, which gave a firm grip for my fingers, while the rungs, if difficult to detect through my boots, were at regular intervals and the guiding hand was always there to help me and to hold the next tread away from the wall to give me a better foothold and keep my boot toes from scraping against the wall.

I went down safely if nervously and finally stepped onto the ledge beside my helper, who at once gripped my arm and guided me into the boat. In the moonlight, I recognized Tobias.

"Your Majesty!" he breathed, as I sat down.

I put my finger to my lips, fearing any kind of lengthy exchange, even in whispers, in case I didn't sound enough like Mary. I was glad of the hood, which concealed the outline of my face and shadowed my eyes. I pretended to be untangling my cloak from my feet, which allowed me to drop my eyes and turn my head a little away from him, before he had a chance to study me too closely.

The boat was tiny, and unlike the ladder, it really was insubstantial. It seemed to be made partly of lightweight wood and partly of some kind of fabric—leather or canvas, perhaps. There was barely room in it for the two of us. However, it seemed to be watertight. It had been borrowed or stolen, I supposed, from someone who used it for trips on a river or a pool.

We moved back across the moat. The rope ladder, presumably, was just being abandoned. As we reached the farther bank, there were further helpful hands. My rescuers, like me, were all swathed in dark cloaks but the moonlight showed me two faces that I knew. The farmer Grimsdale and his surviving son were there. I felt sorry for his wife. I had thought she was essentially a good-hearted woman and it was more than likely that she would lose all her menfolk before long. I hoped that her mother would be of some comfort to her.

A horse was led up to me. I put a foot in the stirrup and swung myself up, glad to be on something I was used to. I sincerely hoped that my first experience of a rope ladder would be my last.

The boat was abandoned just like the ladder. Someone adjusted my girth and stirrups for me. He patted my horse and murmured: "Welcome, Your Majesty," to me. To be addressed as Your Majesty felt very strange and had a curious effect. I felt as though I had actually been elevated in some way, hoisted up onto a pedestal. Monarchs, I thought, must be faced with temptations of which their subjects knew nothing. To fill the position of queen without having one's head turned must need remarkable strength of mind. I wondered if Mary possessed it.

For the moment, however, I must be Mary, and queenly. I bowed toward my well-wisher and for the second time that evening risked a word or two of thanks, and had the happy thought of extending my hand to be kissed. I had removed all my rings, since Mary had been wearing none when she arrived.

Then there was a low-toned order from Tobias, who by now had mounted his own horse, and we were turning and moving off, slowly at first, so that we might melt into the night unheard and unseen.

I settled into my saddle. There were certainly advantages to riding astride. One was a firmer balance over the horse's spine; with its body between one's knees, it was easier to use one's legs to steer. The high pommel in front of me gave an added sense of security. The night air smelled sweet and I would have liked to push back my hood and feel the cool breeze in my hair.

I would have been able to hear better that way, too. It was likely that the dogs would give a bark or two before they were hushed and I would have liked to hear that. As it was, I thought I did hear it, faint and far away. It sounded like Gambol. My guardians would be following by now. I visualized them, giving the dogs a piece of cloth, scented like my pebbles, to sniff, mounting and riding their horses out across the bridge, with the dogs pulling at their leashes. I fumbled under my cloak, found one of the bags of pebbles, eased the drawstring and drew out a handful of stones. I let one or two of them fall. The dogs must not lose the scent and leave me alone among enemies. Even as it was, I was afraid. Nothing would have made me take such a risk, except that I was going to Pen, and Pen had need of me.

We rode slowly for quite a long time though I could feel the impatience in my escort. It transmitted itself to the horses, which jogged and threw their heads about. The farmer Grimsdale swore. Neither he nor his son were accomplished horsemen; they bumped in their saddles and jagged their horses' mouths. The moonlight showed us the track ahead and at length, when we had put some space between ourselves and the house, we broke into a trot and then into a canter, with the Grimsdales clearly struggling to hold their mounts back. I hoped one of them would fall off and delay us, but unfortunately, neither did.

The track divided here and there and whenever it did so, I let some pebbles fall to guide the dogs aright. At one point, I was startled to hear a dog barking excitedly somewhere behind us, though I thought it was also well over to the right. Grimsdale said something in a sharp, questioning tone, but Tobias laughed. "That's a dog in one of the farm cottages. We heard it bark on the way here. Nothing to worry about."

We rode on in silence for a few more minutes. The path we were on left the fields and pastures of Tyesdale behind and began to climb a moorland slope. Tobias pushed his horse to the front and suddenly turned off the path, to take a line across a stretch of heather. Anxiously, I dropped pebbles to mark the place where we abandoned the path. I was beginning to fear that my supply wouldn't hold out. I had brought as many as I thought I could carry without attracting attention, using three small bags rather than one bigger one so that, for instance, someone who chivalrously helped me on or off a horse, wouldn't easily notice them. I was already on to the second bag and I didn't know how far we had to go.

I wanted to ask but I must speak as little as possible, for Tobias at least must know Mary's voice very well. We went over the shoulder of the moor, broke into a canter along a path that slanted downward to the left, and in a few moments were riding into what Clem Moss would have called a beck and what I called a stream.

We didn't ford it, but instead, waded our mounts along it farther to the left. After going for some way upstream, with the current foaming round the horses' knees, we left the water on the same side as we had entered it. It had evidently occurred to Mary's rescuers that they might be followed by our scent. I dedicated more of my small store of pebbles to mark the place where we emerged from the water again, and hoped to heaven that Sir Francis's men would make the dogs cast far enough along the bank and in the right direction.

A few more minutes brought us once more over a hump of moorland, and back onto a track that presently forked. We swung to the left. I dropped some more pebbles. I had started the third bag by now. The change of direction gave me a chance to turn my head and look about me in a natural manner, as though simply glancing at the landscape.

I could see quite a long way. There was no mist tonight. The moon was high and clear, whitening the world around us. Dawn could not be far off. I could make out, far away, the thin white scar of the track we had ridden on before we turned off to ride over the heath, and I could see the long shoulder of moorland that we had now crossed twice. Nothing stirred anywhere. There were no tiny, moving dots in the distance, no friendly glint of moonlight on pikes far away but following. The silvered world was empty of life.

My guardians might still be behind me. They might be out of sight behind the moorland, casting along the river. They might . . .

I do not know quite why I was so sickeningly sure that they were not, but I did know it. I felt as though I were reaching out with my mind, trying to make contact with them, and failing. They were not there. They had lost me. I was on my own, and I was finally about to run out of pebbles.

22

The Camp of the Enemy

We were nearing the end of the journey. We had settled into a purposeful canter and I heard someone murmur *Come on now, your stable's not far away,* to his horse. I wondered frantically what I should do when we arrived. Tobias would recognize me as soon as he got a good look at me. So, very likely, would the Grimsdales. In any case, they'd know at once that I wasn't Mary Stuart. If only Knollys's men had been where they should be, which was hard behind me. As things were . . .

It was just barely possible that if I could get out of their sight quickly enough, I might keep up the deception with someone who had never seen either Ursula Stannard or Mary Stuart. I was a woman. Could I use that? If there was a woman to greet us, perhaps I could whisper to her, *Madam, forgive me, but I have such need of the necessary house . . .*

She would show me the way and I would be separated at once from my male escort. After that, I must snatch whatever opportunities arose. If I could get back to the horses and seize one . . .

Pen would suffer. But I could not save her now that I had mislaid the men who were to have rescued us both. I had made a complete pig's ear of this. God alone knew what would happen to us now.

I had wanted to retrieve Pen before she had to endure a

honeymoon with Andrew Thwaite. Sir Francis had not understood what it would mean for her. I *must* escape from my escort
if I could. Suppose I were to veer off now, immediately, and ride
headlong? But even if I did, I thought, falling back into despon-
dency, I had no idea where I was or which way to gallop. I had
long since lost my sense of direction. I would find myself hopelessly lost on the moors.

I peered about me, seeking for a helpful landmark. A clump
of trees and a rocky outcrop did have a vague familiarity. How far
had we come from Tyesdale? We had taken a circuitous route,
but I didn't think that as the crow flew, we had traveled a great
distance. Looking at the moon, I tried to estimate our direction.
Northeast, I thought. I ran feverishly over the position of the
main houses in the district. Surely . . .

Oh no. Oh *no,* please, *no.* Because if we were going where I
suddenly feared we were going, I would have no chance of pretending to the lady of the house, no chance at all of escape. She
would know me at once, just as Tobias would. She . . .

A black and white timbered gatehouse loomed up on our
right, appearing as suddenly as if it had been conjured by enchantment. I looked at it in despair, recognizing it instantly. I had been
right. Lapwings. Oh, dear God, *Lapwings.* Whose late master,
Thomas Holme, had been on Mary Stuart's list of English supporters. His wife must be keeping up the tradition after all.

We were expected and the gate was set wide. We were
through it and in the courtyard. An elderly man with a dark gown
flapping around his ankles scurried down the steps from the
main door to greet us, holding up a flaring torch. Behind him
were candlelit windows. Before we had drawn rein, grooms had
come to take the bridles and the Holme daughters were coming
down the steps as well, also bearing torches.

At least I now knew where I was. I must swing my horse
around and charge for the gatehouse. I gathered my reins.

Too late. A groom had my horse's bridle and the gate was
being shut behind me. The dark-clad man was extending a hand
to help me down. The torchlight showed me gentle blue eyes
and a priest's tonsure, gray with years. Helplessly, I dismounted.

He bowed. He took my arm and led me to the house, up the steps and into the vestibule, brightly lit by torches in wall sconces and half a dozen branched candelabra standing about on tables.

And there, awaiting me in the middle of the black-and-white-tiled floor, which I remembered all too well, was the hostess, whom I also remembered all too well.

"Mistress Holme," said the priest gravely, "may I present Her Majesty, Queen Mary of Scotland."

"Your Majesty," said Mistress Adeliza Holme, stepping forward and sinking before me into a deeply respectful curtsy.

From which lowly position, she looked up, no doubt expecting me to offer her my hand to kiss, and looked straight into my face. I saw her mouth drop open.

My escorts were hanging back a little, allowing Mistress Holme to greet me without interference. I made one last effort. Leaning down, I took her hands and raised her and whispered: "If you value your life, keep up the pretense."

It was no use. She tore her hands away from me. "This isn't Queen Mary! Tobias—Father Robinson—we're betrayed!" It came out in a shriek and I did the only thing remaining that offered me the faintest hope, the faintest chance of rescuing Pen, or the faintest chance even of retaining any dignity myself.

I threw back my hood, tore off my scarf, shook my dark hair loose, looked Mistress Holme in the eyes and declared: "Mary Stuart is still at Tyesdale. I am Ursula Stannard, Lady of Queen Elizabeth's Presence Chamber and the guardian of Mistress Penelope Mason. I have come to fetch her home."

There was a horrified silence. I was encircled by staring eyes. For the first time I saw my escort clearly. Judging from the soot engrained in their faces, the three I did not know were probably miners. One, the eldest, had a marked resemblance to Grimsdale and I remembered the farmer saying that he had an uncle who was a miner.

The elderly priest—this must be the one who tutored the Holme girls—stepped away from me, his face blanching. The

Holme girls retreated too, in a bunch, as though I had suddenly sprouted horns or plague spots. Tobias seized my elbow, swung me around, and stared into my eyes. *"You!"* he said. *"You!"*

Then he hit me. I went reeling and collided with the elder Grimsdale, who grabbed my upper arms, peered into my face in turn, and shouted: "God's teeth, it's true! Saw thee when thee stayed at t'farm not long back! What t'hell's thee about, playing at queens? Where's t'Queen of Scotland? Well?" He shook me. *"Well?"*

"She's just told you. Still at Tyesdale," said Tobias. He sounded as though he was having trouble breathing. "My God, she's probably broken her word and put Knollys on our track! Grimsdale, go to the lookout tower and see if anyone's coming. The moon's still out."

Grimsdale let go of me and ran for the stairs. Gasping, I leaned against the nearby wall, a hand to my bruised face. "You bitch!" Tobias spat at me. The well-bred, well-mannered secretary had disappeared. His face was twisted, as much, I thought, with fear as anger. "If you're being followed . . ."

"I'm not!" I told him, glumly aware that this was almost certainly true, and wishing with all my heart that Sir Francis and his men were about to burst in on us. "If you'd let me explain . . ."

"Yes, I'd like an explanation! Let's hear what she has to say!" Adeliza was completely terrified. Her kittenish face had gone feral with fear. "We'd better hear! We'd better know what we're dealing with before she gets us all burned as traitors, me and my daughters!"

From the huddled group of girls at the foot of the stairs, there came an outburst of whimpers, which were echoed from above. Glancing up, I saw several servants, male and female, leaning over the upstairs banister. Tobias looked up as well.

"Back to bed, every one of you!" His voice shook, but he was regaining command of himself. "You girls—go upstairs and get into your beds, quickly! If anyone comes here, what they've got to find is a normal household, fast asleep as all good folk should be at this hour. Father Robinson, you are the tutor in this household—take your charges away and try to keep everyone calm."

The priest hurried up the stairs, shepherding the girls before him. They were sobbing and I heard him trying to reassure them, not very successfully, for his own voice was trembling.

"Queen Mary lost her nerve," I said loudly. "She has been ill. She has a pain in her side. She couldn't face it."

I hoped that Tobias didn't understand Mary well enough to realize that whatever her other weaknesses and shortcomings, she was nevertheless capable of facing almost anything that offered a chance of getting out of captivity and back into power.

"But she told me that where she was going, she would find Penelope Mason. She knows about Penelope. I disguised myself and came in Queen Mary's stead in order to find Penelope. I am responsible for her. I have *not*," I said, determinedly lying, "revealed anything to Knollys."

"Happen she'd say that any road!" said the eldest miner ominously and both the younger miners said: "Aye, Dad, that's right," in unison. His sons, I supposed. Grimsdale cousins.

"Sir Francis is at Tyesdale but I have told him *nothing*." As a good liar should, I tried to make myself believe it. "Tomorrow I will not be there, of course, but my woman will tell him I am sick and confined to my room."

Grimsdale came thumping down the stairs again. "There's no sign of owt moving. Tha can see for miles in this moonlight. Bit of ground mist drifting about to t'north, but not much of it yet, and Tyesdale's not that way, any road. No one's abroad."

"Good." Tobias relaxed fractionally. I drew a long breath and once more said: "Where is Penelope? Queen Mary said . . ."

"Ah well. I had to practice a small deception on Her Majesty to ease her conscience," Tobias informed me. "Pen, of course, could not be allowed to know that her abduction—yes, I admit that it was that—had anything to do with the Queen of Scotland. If Penelope knows too much, she might later on betray my friends, the Grimsdales and Mistress Holme here. My cousin Whitely and I were going to France with the queen, but the others did not wish to leave their homes. They must not be endangered. Your ward, Mistress Stannard, is not here and never has been. She is in another hiding place, awaiting her marriage tomorrow to Andrew Thwaite. Father Robinson is to officiate. I have, as it were, hired his services from Mistress Holme—at a good price."

"At a price?" I didn't understand.

"I have five girls to settle, as you well know!" Adeliza was angry and frightened both at once. "I haven't money enough to dower them all." Her head came up. "I would have helped Her Majesty of Scotland for nothing, but I was glad to be paid and glad as well to be paid extra for Father Robinson's services. Though he's been frightened of the whole thing from the start and, my God, I think he was right! How do we know for sure you've not been followed?" She glared at me. "Or won't be missed tomorrow? There'll be a search if you are. Oh, why are you all still here?" She looked fearfully around her as though she expected Sir Francis Knollys and his men to materialize out of the wall hangings. "Tobias, go away and take this . . . this person away with you! If anyone comes here, searching, I want them to find nothing to incriminate us, nothing at all!"

"Gently, gently. Look, Mistress Holme, we are all very weary and so are our horses. You have a hiding place, I know, because you said that Her Majesty could use it if necessary . . ."

"It's naught but a little room behind a panel! You can't all crowd into it and, anyway, I won't let you! I won't let you stay here! I don't care how tired you are, or your horses!" Adeliza's voice became shrill. "Go away from here! I want no more to do with this! The queen's not here; she isn't coming; it's all been for nothing and I'll not risk my life and my daughters' lives anymore. I don't even care about the money now! *Go away!* You can still take Father Robinson if you want—and if you'll pay for using him, I'll call him. That much, but no more."

"Mistress Holme, there's no need to be hysterical . . ."

"Yes, there is!" Adeliza shouted.

"What about Penelope?" Doggedly I clung to the story I had told, that I was here only to find Pen. "Where is she? I must go to her."

"Take the Stannard woman to her!" shouted Adeliza. "What are you waiting for? Go on! Go to her wedding! Father Robinson! Father Robinson! Come down here again! At once!" She ended with a wild laugh, which turned into a hiccup.

The priest came hurrying down the stairs, carrying a candle. He looked old and exhausted.

"What is all this about a wedding?" I demanded. "The agreement was that Pen would be married by force only if I betrayed you and I haven't. I want to take her home!"

"Ah. Well." Tobias managed a smile, which did nothing to reassure me. "Whitely and I practiced a small deception on you, too, I'm afraid, Mistress Stannard. There was never any question of Penelope returning home. You threw my cousin out of his employment without a character, after all. The Thwaites are his very good friends and are willing to pay commissions to him and to me if we can bring about a match between Andrew and Penelope. Pen, with the help of good Mistress Holme's chaplain and tutor, will marry Andrew Thwaite tomorrow—no, let me correct myself. It's this morning now, is it not? That was always intended, whether Mary Stuart escaped from her imprisonment or not."

"Revenge," I said bitterly. I had said that to Sir Francis. I had been right.

"Will you all just *go!*" wailed Adeliza.

"The Thwaites didn't want one of your girls, so it's no loss to you if Pen is married to Andrew," I said to her, "and I suppose that to you, Pen is a rival that you want out of the way. Poor, poor Pen. Father Robinson . . ."

"Will do as he is told," Adeliza informed me. "I feed, house, and clothe him. If he wishes that to continue, he will undertake this simple errand, which falls well within his natural duties as a priest. Father Robinson! Master Littleton and his companions are leaving to see to the marriage. You're to go with them and do their bidding. Get your horse. Master Tobias, the queen's cause is lost and I do not expect you to pay me for it, but with respect to Father Robinson . . ."

"I'm an honest man," said Tobias outrageously. He undid his belt pouch and took out a handful of coins. I watched him count ten sovereigns into Adeliza's outstretched palm. "I am sure that

Magnus will want the marriage to proceed, so there you are—payment for the priest's services and something more, for being willing at least to help Her Majesty of Scotland. It'll add something worthwhile to your fund for the girls' dowries."

"Thirty pieces of silver would have been even more appropriate," I remarked. Tobias laughed and Father Robinson looked at me sadly.

"I'm too old to go out into a world where priests of my kind are treated as criminals. I'm past the age for seeking lodgings door-to-door and sleeping under a hedge if the doors are slammed in my face," he said. He went out of the front door, shoulders bowed, and I heard his feet drag their way down the steps.

I looked at Tobias with hatred, and in return, he smiled unpleasantly. "I do seem to be making a career of deception," he said. He sounded quite debonair. "Penelope, you, and even Queen Mary. It's the way of the world, alas."

"If this marriage takes place, I'll see it's broken!" I said with fury.

Tobias's smile did not change. Swallowing my rage, I tried to speak reasonably. "Tobias, you have no quarrel with Pen. She thought you loved her. Surely you couldn't have pretended that so well if you hadn't at least liked her a little! She doesn't want to marry Andrew Thwaite. Why must you force her? Please let her go. You say she knows nothing of the plot concerning Queen Mary, so . . ."

"I offered Mistress Adeliza a good price to help me," said Tobias, "but I'm still in profit. The Thwaites are paying both Magnus and me rather well. More than they can afford, I suspect. However, that isn't our problem. I fancy we shall still be going to France now, even without Queen Mary—though of course it depends on what Magnus says when I rejoin him. If we do go, we'll be glad of the money."

"But why? *Why* are the Thwaites so mad to marry Pen? Tyesdale isn't that much of a dowry! We thought it was, before we came here, but when we saw it . . ."

"It's strange, isn't it? I think the answer," said Tobias, "is that

Andrew has fallen in love." The three miners burst out laughing and I was inclined to agree with them. I did not think that Andrew Thwaite was capable of any such thing.

Adeliza, who had been listening to us with mounting exasperation, now interrupted. "Will you stop talking and *go. Go!*"

"We are upsetting Mistress Holme," said Tobias reprovingly to me. "We'll be on our way at once. Come, Mistress Stannard!"

23

The Rattle of Chains

"Where are we going?" I asked as I was hustled out the door.

"You wanted to see Mistress Penelope, didn't you?" said Tobias. "Well, so you shall. We're going to her now. Magnus is with her."

"But where is she?"

"You'll see when we get there. You're to ride behind me. Come along, quickly. Mistress Holme doesn't want us here."

I did as I was told. I was beyond arguing by now, for a terrible longing for sleep had swept over me. It overcame almost everything else. In the courtyard, Father Robinson was already getting into his saddle and other horses were being led in. As I was pushed toward them, I noticed that there was a pillion behind the priest and also on two of the other horses. One was Tobias's animal, and I was now made to mount behind him. I wondered vaguely who the other two pillions were for but couldn't concentrate. My brain wasn't working properly.

The mist, which earlier in the night had been absent, was now swirling over the moor, and the moon, sinking westward, was a hazy circle in the sky. I wondered when, if ever, I would have a chance to sleep. How far away was this unknown place where Pen was being held? And what would happen when we got there?

I would die, I thought as we set off. Or fall asleep in the saddle and simply slip off into the heather. The thought of lying curled up even in the damp heather was positively enticing. To lie down, to close my eyes, to let my consciousness go . . .

"Mistress Stannard?" said Tobias.

I roused myself, assisted by anger. "Yes? What is it?" I said coldly.

He glanced at me over his shoulder. "You think I am a heartless monster, do you not?" Tobias said.

I saw no point in denying it. "Yes. Heartless and a deceiver. What has Pen ever done to you that you should use her like this—and after professing to love her!"

"Love? Believe me," said Tobias, "I am a man who loves strongly, with passion. I will do anything, anything at all, for those I love. But there are degrees of it. Pen is attractive to me; I like her intelligence. In other circumstances I might well have fallen deeply for her, but as things are, others stand in her way. Magnus, George Mason, and myself were all at school together. George was much the youngest, but we were all good friends and we shared a common devotion to Mary Stuart, whose claim to the English throne has been so roughly put aside. We always told each other that one day we would stand shoulder to shoulder and fight for her. Also, to me, Magnus was more like a brother than a cousin. I did not like to see him flung out of his employment at Tyesdale."

"He'd been cheating his employer," I said icily.

"Who took no interest in him and left him to run the estate without instructions. No, I understand Magnus's desire for revenge, and as for Pen, she is not being as badly treated as you think. What's wrong with the Thwaites? They're as good as anyone. If she's a sensible girl and looks after Andrew as a wife should, it'll work as well as any other marriage."

I was too exhausted to embark on the reasons why Andrew Thwaite was a quite unsuitable match for any respectable young woman. "She doesn't like him! He repels her!"

"Female megrims. She'll soon get over those."

"Which would rather seem to undermine Magnus's revenge!"

"The revenge is against you, mistress. *You* don't want this marriage. Now you must stomach it."

I was silent.

"But above all," said Tobias, "by using Pen and helping Magnus, I could also help Queen Mary and I love her far more, truth to tell, than I could ever love Pen or any other girl. Mistress Stannard, you have seen her—you know her! You have seen for yourself her grief at being abused and accused, at being cast out of her country and deprived of her power and dignity! She was once a princess in the gracious French court. She did not understand how to live among such rough men as the Scottish nobles mostly are. No wonder she lost her way! Will no one understand? Will no one pity her? Or help her?"

"I do pity her," I said. "And I do understand. But I cannot accept what she did. Or what she wants to do here in England. She believes that the crown of England should be hers. I do not, and I would fight, personally, knife in hand, to keep it from her."

"Poor Mary. She has been ill-used all the way, from the time she came to Scotland, from the moment she married that cretin Henry Darnley . . ."

"Who is actually related to Andrew Thwaite," I remarked. "Andrew resembles him quite markedly. I wonder if he will make the same kind of husband?"

"Why should he? It's not a close relationship. I know about it," said Tobias dismissively. "Magnus told me—the Thwaites told him long ago. Mistress Stannard, if I were not so far below her that I know I must not think of such a thing, I would wed Mary Stuart tomorrow. As it is, I can only kneel at her feet and serve her in any way that I can find. She has enthralled me, like a sorceress in a castle, deep in a forest, spinning a spell on an enchanted wheel, to draw men into the shadows of the wood and through it to her fastness and her arms."

"You are quite a poet, Master Littleton."

"She has made me so. I think perhaps that that was the downfall of Henry Darnley; that she enchanted him too and yet would not quite give herself to him. I don't believe she ever gives herself completely. Enchantresses never do. Perhaps that was why Bothwell felt he must use force, to take what she would not ever willingly yield."

"We are talking, Master Littleton, of a dissolute, drunken, and diseased man whose wife wished to be free of him, but instead of using legal means, left the matter to a pack of practiced murderers. And then married the chief of them afterwards."

This time Tobias was the silent one, until he said: "We shall never agree. I am sorry. I am not a monster, Mistress Stannard, but I do not think as you do. As I see it, I have tried to serve those I care for most, as best I can. I cannot regret it," said Tobias. "In time, even Penelope herself may come to thank us. The Thwaite match is as good as any, to my mind."

It seemed an interminable journey, though when I worked it out later, we only went about three miles. I wondered if there were any chance that Sir Francis and his men were still riding about in the fog and prayed that they would suddenly loom up in front of us but they didn't. What loomed up instead, apparently solidifying from the vapors, was a wall of rock with a cave mouth in it. We halted before it and, peering at it, I saw that it was regular in shape, rounded at the top, and almost certainly man-made, a tunnel rather than a natural cavern. Tobias whistled softly.

There was an answering whistle and a figure appeared at the entrance, carrying a flambeau. Its light danced over his face and I recognized Magnus Whitely. "Tobias?" he said. "Is that you?"

Tobias jumped out of his saddle, threw his reins to the younger Grimsdale, and went forward. He seized Whitely's arm and steered him a few yards away. I heard Tobias talking rapidly and then Whitely's voice raised in question and exclamation. It went on for some time and at one point sounded like an argument. But the indignant tone subsided presently and they came back to us. Whitely approached me and stood looking up at me. I have rarely seen such hatred in anyone's face.

"*You!* I'm thrown out of my employment because of you and now Queen Mary has failed to take the chance we offered her and I wonder how much you had to do with that. Bad luck, *that's* what you are! For Tyesdale, for me, for the Queen of Scotland ,and for your own damned ward as well. Get down!"

"Do as he says," said Tobias. "He wants you to have the privilege of preparing Mistress Pen for her wedding. It's to be hurried on."

"The idea," said Whitely, "*was* that the Grimsdales should take Mistress Pen to Fernthorpe and that they would have the marriage performed some time today but we wouldn't be there. I was to hand Mistress Pen over to the Grimsdales and go at once to Lapwings, where Tobias was waiting with the queen. We would hide there all day and then, if it seemed safe, to travel on the next night. But *now,* there is no Queen Mary to look after, only you."

"And ourselves," said Tobias urgently. "We stopped Mistress Stannard from sending word to Knollys, but he was bound to come to Tyesdale with the queen. There always was a weak point there. It's my belief that he knows."

"Maybe, but he hasn't *followed* her, you say." Whitely jerked a discourteous thumb toward me as I slowly obeyed orders and clambered down from Tobias's pillion. Once down, I found myself face-to-face with Whitely, which was frightening. His rage was so very palpable. Combined with the crimson torchlight it made his features, usually so nondescript, look almost demonic.

"Knollys hasn't lost the queen, has he?" Whitely said. "She's still his captive. The only person missing from Tyesdale is Mistress Stannard here and maybe no one's noticed yet that she's gone. Maybe she really didn't dare to give us away. We'd still be wise to make for France, but I think we can spare just an hour or two. I want to see the knot tied between Andrew Thwaite and Mistress Pen, and I want Mistress Stannard to see it too; and I want to watch her seeing it."

"It's wasting time!"

"Not much. It's not dawn yet. Come with me, mistress!"

Whitely seized my arm and hurried me into the tunnel. "What is this place?" I demanded, stumbling on the uneven floor.

"It's an abandoned mine," said Whitely. There were some unlit torches lying in a pile. He picked one up, lit it from the one he was holding, and shoved it into an iron bracket on the wall just inside the entrance. "On Fernthorpe land. They'd lost their *original* mines, but a year or two back they thought they'd found a new one. Only the seam ran out. They often do, round here. Now. Before we go any farther . . ."

His grip on my arm was painful. He twisted me around so that he could stare into my face and spoke in a low voice and without any affected emphases. "Not one word about Mary Stuart, do you hear? Penelope knows nothing of the plot and must not be told. If she *is* told then there will be no marriage because we would have to kill her. Understand?"

My guts went cold. I understood all too well, and more than he realized. "Yes. I do. Is Pen *here*?" I tried not to let my voice shake. "What's been happening to her?"

"Nothing that shouldn't. An older woman has been with her constantly. She's had food, clean water, wine, and a warm bed." Whitely's voice was mocking. "No one has molested her. She is Andrew Thwaite's promised bride and we undertook to deliver her intact to her bridegroom. I have guarded her virtue as though she were my own daughter. Now. You understand? Not *one word* about Mary Stuart."

"Very well."

"Good. Come this way."

He marched me on along the tunnel and then turned sharply into a side chamber. "Mistress Penelope! Wake up!"

In the darkness beyond the torchlight, I heard someone stir and there was a faint clanking sound. A woman's voice said: "What's to do?" and then Pen's voice came, slurred with sleep but shaky with fear as well. "What is it? What's happening?" Whitely walked forward, torch held high, and then I saw.

The side chamber was small, perhaps eight feet by ten. The walls and floor were of rock and there was no door. There was a wide pallet on the floor and on it, two women were sitting up. The older one looked vaguely familiar but in the uncertain light I couldn't make out her features clearly enough to recognize her properly. The other, however, was Pen.

The pallet was adequately covered, with fur rugs of some

kind. There was a table, with a basin and facecloth on it, and a stool, on which some outer clothes were piled. There was a bucket with a lid and even a couple of books lying beside the basin. The place was dirty, though. A dark dust filmed every-thing, and as Pen reached to pull her rugs up around her, I saw that the shift in which she had been trying to sleep was grubby.

As she moved, the clanking sound came again. Then I real-ized what it was and if hearts can truly bleed, mine did at that moment. Her left wrist was encircled by a bracelet made of iron, to which a chain was fastened. It was long and lay piled in loops between her pallet and the wall, but the other end of it was pad-locked to a staple in the wall. It would let her move freely enough about the little chamber but she had no chance of escap-ing from it.

I darted forward. "Pen!"

"Mistress Stannard!" With a gasp of joy, she threw herself off the pallet and into my arms. I held her while her tears soaked my shoulder.

"As you see, she's well enough." Tobias had followed us in. "Her duenna, by the way, is Madge Grimsdale. You've met, I believe."

I knew her then. Here was our hostess at Grimsdale's farm, on our last night before we reached Tyesdale.

"I've takken good care o' t'lass," she said anxiously.

"I'm sure you have," I said. She had had to do what Grims-dale told her, I supposed, and at least Pen had had her company. Mistress Grimsdale might be under her husband's thumb and could never be an ally, but I thought she was essentially kind.

Pen, snuffling, drew back to look up into my face. "Mistress Stannard! The trouble I've caused! I am so sorry. So very very sorry. If you can't forgive me, I'll understand, but I thought . . . I believed . . ." Her eyes shifted to Tobias, standing in the doorway. Through her tears, she glared at him. "I can't believe I ever thought I loved you!" she threw at him. "You betrayed me! You're evil!"

"You may not always think so," Tobias informed her coolly.

"Have you come to take me home?" Her eyes returned to

mine, and then glanced around as though expecting friendly support to appear from somewhere. If only it could! I thought. But instead, I must draw her to me again and hold her fast, to give her what comfort I could, as I said: "No, Pen darling. I am a prisoner, just as you are. I'm sorry. I'm so very sorry. But I have seriously offended Master Whitely here and . . ."

"You are to be *immediately* married to Andrew Thwaite," said Whitely. "In my presence and that of your guardian, Mistress Stannard. Tobias! Here's the key to that pretty bracelet."

"In my opinion," said Tobias, taking the key that Whitely held out to him and undoing the fetter around Pen's wrist, "we should send the young lady to her future husband and leave at once, but since you're so determined . . . there we are."

The iron was off. Pen rubbed her wrist. I said: "Where in God's name did you get those fetters from?"

"The basement of Bolton before I left," said Tobias. "There were all sorts of unregarded oddments lying about down there. These came in very useful. Pen, we have a priest with us who will acccompany us to Fernthorpe. Magnus and I will now leave you ladies for a short time. Mistress Stannard, get your ward dressed and convince her that she should resign herself to her future as Mistress Thwaite. Madge, take note of everything that Mistress Stannard says to Mistress Penelope, and report her words to me. You have fifteen minutes. Then we ride for Fernthorpe."

24

Grimy and Reluctant Bride

Pen was not prepared to resign herself to her marriage, and not only because the Thwaites were guilty of kidnapping and murder. I knew that she was repelled by Andrew Thwaite, yet even I had underestimated the strength of her feelings. The violence of her resistance astounded me.

Even if the Thwaite family had been law-abiding, with a testimonial from an archangel and a home as comfortable as Richmond Palace, it would have made no difference. She didn't merely distrust the look of Andrew Thwaite, it seemed; she had glanced at him once and been seized by the kind of physical loathing that many people feel for snakes or spiders.

Pen's protest was worse even than Mary Stuart's outburst when she learned that her escape plans were canceled. Pen cried and screamed, threw herself onto the pallet, and pounded it with her fists; then, when I begged her to be calm, promising her that somehow or other, eventually, I would get the marriage annulled, she flew at me and her fists pummeled me instead.

"What's the good of that? I'll have been pushed into bed with him first and it'll be legal, *legal*! He'll have rights over me; he'll own me! I can't do this, I won't! He's horrible! He's . . . he's . . . like a reptile! I won't . . . I can't . . . !"

It was the kind of situation, I thought, still fighting against my own weariness, in which lockpicks and a dagger are no use whatsoever. Indeed, at one point, when I was trying to hold her, to steady her, she felt the outline of the dagger sheath and tried to get at it in order, she said, to stab herself.

Madge Grimsdale, appalled, intervened at that point to help me quieten my frantic ward, who at that stage actually had my dagger halfway out of its sheath. Between us, we broke her grip and made her sit down on the pallet. Hardening my heart, I took her by the shoulders and shook her until I had startled the hysteria out of her.

"This must stop!" I told her. "I cannot save you from this ceremony, Pen. It's no use attacking me. *Be quiet! Listen!* Willing or not, you will have no option. You . . ."

"Brides are supposed to say *I will*. Well, I shan't say it!"

"You will be pronounced man and wife with Andrew Thwaite no matter what you say. It's been done before. Rules can be bent and I have no doubt that the Thwaites and Magnus Whitely are prepared to bend them into figures of eight. You have one simple choice and that is to keep your dignity or lose it. Stop all this noise. Let us help you dress and . . ."

"I can't do it!"

"You'd be wiser if you did. Go through with it. Say *I won't* instead of *I will* if you like. I'm a witness; the day may come when I shall speak for you before a tribunal to get the marriage annulled and that will be useful evidence. As for what happens afterwards; shut your eyes and imagine you're a log of wood."

"With *him*? With that . . . !"

"I said: shut your eyes. And, thereafter, keep your wits about you. I don't know . . . I may not be at Tyesdale for a while. I'm a prisoner, as I said . . ." I must not endanger Pen by speaking even obliquely of Mary Stuart. If I did, Mrs. Grimsdale would report it. But I was grimly sure of one thing; my captors would not let me go tamely back to tell all I knew to Sir Francis Knollys. What they intended to do with me instead was something I was trying not to think about. I doubted very much if I ever would testify on Pen's behalf at an annulment tribunal. Aloud, I said: "Your brother George may come to see you and . . ."

Pen interrupted me, with scorn. "George! He'd just say, 'Are they Catholic?' And when he knows they are . . ."

"Your mother will have something to say in the matter. She'll want to know who you've married and how you are. Once she knows how you feel, you can trust her to act." I thought hearteningly of Ann Mason, whose apparently gentle nature had much in common with the soft paws of a cat, which conceal a lethal set of claws. If I were not there, Ann would rescue her daughter. I knew it, which was more than Tobias Littleton or Magnus Whitely did.

"Whatever happens, it won't last forever," I said. "Smile and be pleasant and maybe it won't be so bad." Because of Madge Grimsdale's presence I did not say openly: *smile to allay their suspicions and bolt for Tyesdale the first chance you get* but I stared hard into Pen's face and I saw comprehension in her eyes. "Now then. *Get dressed!* Tobias will be back in a moment. Do you want to be carried screaming to the horses or will you walk on your own feet with your head high?"

In the end she let us dress her. There were a couple of iron torch brackets with torches in them in the chamber, and before leaving us, Tobias had used his own to kindle them. We could see well enough. Her gown was as grubby as everything else; as a bride, she cut a very strange figure. I thought sadly of her best blue dress, which I had brought to Yorkshire in the hope that she would wear it on a happy wedding day. However, despite the pervading grime and the whiteness of her face beneath it, she did at least walk out of the little rock room on her own feet. I took one of the torches and lit the way for her.

It was a good torch, burning more clearly and brightly than the one from which Tobias had lit it. As we left the chamber, its light showed me more of the passage than I had seen before. In one direction was the way out, with a light burning at the entrance and the night still dark beyond it. In the other, the passage ran on to end abruptly in a wall of hacked and tool-marked rock with a pile of small rubble at its feet. I glanced at it, began to turn away, and then turned back, halting for a moment.

The pile of rubble lay across the width of the passage, and there was something odd, something suggestive about its shape. I said: "Wait!" and walked away from Pen for a closer look. It only took me a moment to see that this was no accidental heap of fallen rock, but had been piled by human hands. I stirred the edge of it with a foot, and then, stooping, clawed some of it aside. It was loose and small enough to move fairly easily.

I straightened up quickly, feeling sick, and went back to Pen, who was standing rigidly in the chamber entrance. "What is it?" she asked. Her voice was high with strain.

"I wondered if there was another way out. I should have known better," I said. "Come. Keep up your courage."

Whitely and Tobias were waiting for us at the entrance. Whitely took her away from me and put her up behind Father Robinson, whose pillion, evidently, had been intended for her.

Wordlessly, she allowed it. But there was no more resignation in her than there ever had been. I knew it, and watched her with misgiving.

While Whitely was settling Pen in her saddle, Tobias caught hold of Madge Grimsdale and I realized that he was asking her what I had said while Penelope was being dressed. He looked relieved by her answers.

The third pillion turned out to be for Madge. Her husband and son, however, seemed to have disappeared. Disagreeable as it was to speak to Tobias, I asked him where they had gone.

"On ahead," he said shortly. "To make sure that the Thwaites are up and ready for us when we get there."

It was a brief ride; the abandoned mine was only half a mile or so from Fernthorpe's farmhouse. When Ryder and Dodd went there in search of Pen, they had been quite near to her, but no one had thought of looking for the eloping pair in a disused mine. We had all thought in terms of a house somewhere, with friends or Tobias's parents or in a city like York. Nor had the search for Harry's body ever brought anyone close to the mine. Perhaps it would have done in the end. We would never know. Well, I thought, if I survived long enough to report that mound of rubble to anyone, we knew where to look for him now. Under the stones I had scraped aside I had seen a human hand.

The mists were clearing when we reached the farmhouse and dawn was not far off. In the east, the stars were fading. The rooms were lit, however, and Will Thwaite, wrapped in a brocade dressing gown, came out to greet us with a flambeau held high, a broad and gap-toothed grin, and a stream of words. He spluttered vigorously every time he used one with an *s* in it.

"Fine turn of events this is! There was t'Grimsdales a'hammering on t'door—lucky we don't shut t'gatehouse these days—and shouting fit t'wake a whole churchyard full o' dead, and when I put my head out o' t'window and shouted down to ask them what t'blazes they think they're at, they tell me that t'marriage party's on its way, at this hour! Not that we're complainin'—my son's ready to jump t'moon. Puttin' on bridegroom's finery this minute, he is."

He handed Pen down from her saddle himself, grinning all the more when she shuddered away from him. "And here's summat comic," he added. "From not having a priest at all, it seems we've ended up with a choice! Good of you to come, Father Robinson, but we've got a fellow here already."

"You've got a priest?" Whitely was surprised. "How did that come about?"

"One o' t'wanderers that come around these days," said Thwaite. "From Italy, so he says. Sent over to comfort t'faithful, so he tells us, and test t'water, as it were, see what support a Catholic rule 'ud have in northern England. Been travelin' round and then got into trouble, askin' too many questions in t'wrong sort of household. Turned up t'other day, looking for shelter. Good fellow, speaks fair English. Says he'll gladly marry my son to Mistress Mason. Don't want to offend you, Father Robinson, but . . ."

"You won't offend me," said Father Robinson, with unaffected relief. "I will tell you frankly, Master Thwaite, that I don't approve of this marriage, which I know very well isn't to the mind of the bride. I'm only here because I've had orders from my employer. She has been paid for my services, but since I have made the journey here and would have done as she bade me if necessary, I feel that I have fulfilled the bargain. I need not insist upon actually performing the ceremony if someone else is ready to do so. If I can have a little rest before I go home . . ."

"Oh o'course, and welcome. Hope thee'll at least drink to t'couple. Get down and come inside, the lot o' you."

For the third time in the course of that awful night, I got stiffly out of my saddle. Pen's eyes met mine with frantic pleading, but all I could do was shake my head. We were pushed in at the door. The horses were brought in as well and put in the byre on the right of the passage. One horse was there already. As the only light in the passage was from Will Thwaite's torch, I couldn't see it very well, but its coat had a gloss and peering at it, I saw that though its fetlocks were hairy, they were clean. For a change, something at Fernthorpe was being cared for properly.

In the short interval since the Grimsdales had disturbed the household by pounding and shouting, preparations had been made. The kitchen-cum-living-room had been hurriedly tidied and made ready for a celebration. New candles glowed in what looked like the best candlesticks and a white cloth covered the table. Some pewter dishes and tankards had been set out, along with a couple of ale jugs, a cold cooked fowl, and a large cold pie. The squint-eyed Rosie was evidently up and working in the kitchen, for I could hear what sounded like eggs being beaten in a furious hurry, and a pleasant smell of baking bread mingled with the sharp smell of the horses.

A wooden crucifix had been hung on the wall of the living room and below it, a second small table, draped with an embroidered cloth and set with more candles, seemed to be doing duty as an altar. The Italian priest, in a black cassock and with another crucifix, this one silver, on a chain around his neck, was waiting beside it. The wavering candlelight made everyone's features indistinct but this was as swarthy a fellow as I'd ever seen, with a jet-black tonsure.

"This is Father Bruno, who's said he'll officiate," said Will Thwaite, spraying saliva liberally over everyone close to him.

"Eet will be my gritest pleesure," said Father Bruno graciously. "To starta younga pair on the holee road of matreemony; eet ees always a joy. I have not had soocha joy since I stepped ona the shores of theesa island."

Pen ran forward and threw herself on her knees before him, clutching at his cassock. "Please help me! Please! I don't want to be married! I don't . . ."

Gently, he lifted her up and held her, facing him. "Come now—*pax vobiscum,* my leetle one. Let us praya, you and I, *si*?"

He turned her toward the makeshift altar and with a hand on her shoulders pressed her to her knees. To my surprise, she yielded. They knelt side by side, and drawing his hand away from her, he laid his palms together in an attitude of reverence. So did Pen. I heard him murmuring his prayer. It went on for some time. Pen seemed to droop, but she did not interrupt or try to get up until he said *amen.* He said it in a firm voice and she echoed him, her own voice small and sad. He looked at her and smiled, and then they both rose to their feet. She came back to me. Her face was still dreadfully pale but she seemed calm. I opened my mouth to ask her what he had said in his prayer, but at that moment, Andrew Thwaite appeared, descending the stairs from the upper regions.

He was dressed in what was presumably his best suit, of dark blue with red slashings, and puffed breeches to match, and a clean ruff. He was wearing a sword. With a rage so intense that it actually overwhelmed my exhaustion, I saw the amethyst in its hilt.

The outfit made the best of his looks, though. He was undoubtedly handsome in his fashion. His father, greeting him, looked at him with such a doting approval that for a brief instant I saw him as Will Thwaite did; an only son, a bridegroom, the next generation, with the future and the potency that his father no longer had. Will Thwaite's one chance to perpetuate himself.

Pen didn't see him like that, though. As he stepped into the room, he bowed most graciously to us all, and especially to her, but she turned her head away. For an instant, he seemed disconcerted but then, turning to me, he said: "Mistress Stannard, as the representative of my bride's parents, would you care to inspect the bridal chamber?"

Apparently, we were expected to go through the motions of a normal marriage. It was like being on a river in a current. There didn't seem to be anything else to do except go upstairs to see what preparations had been made there. They were fairly satisfactory. The marital bedchamber was comparatively clean, and some lavender had been strewn among the floor rushes and on the coverlet of the big bed. There were clean sheets on the bed and an empty clothespress had been provided, which, Andrew said, was for Pen's belongings. "We'll send for them from Tyesdale." There was a washstand, too, with an earthenware basin and an ewer.

"You have taken some trouble," I said, detaching my gaze from the amethyst in Andrew's sword hilt and forcing myself to be polite. There was no point in antagonizing the people in whose power Pen would shortly be.

"I mean well by t'lass," said Andrew. "She's a pretty piece. This is honest marriage; nowt less."

"Treat her kindly, that's all I ask," I said.

We went downstairs again without exchanging any further words. We found everyone in their places for the ceremony. Father Bruno stood in front of the makeshift altar and facing him was Pen, with Magnus Whitely gripping her left arm. The rest were in a group behind them. Rosie had been fetched from the kitchen and was standing with the Grimsdales, wiping her hands on her apron. The light was still poor but I could make out that her black eye was better, although I thought there was a fresh bruise on the other side of her face.

Treat her kindly, I had said. I had said it to people who ill-used their maidservant and had left a girl of thirteen to fare as best she could in a moorland fog, miles from anywhere.

And after Pen had been made legally a part of it, what would happen to me? The fog of exhaustion had descended on me again, but within it, I was shuddering with dread for myself as well as for her.

Will Thwaite strode out of the group to meet us, frowning.

"At last! We're all waitin'! Master Littleton says we've to get on with it; summat might happen to stop it if we don't. That's what all this rush is about. There'll be folk out, huntin' all over for Mistress Pen again if not for Mistress Stannard too, as soon as t'sun's up, he says. And t'bridegroom ditherin' about upstairs without t'bride! Just you tak your place alongside t'lass, Andrew, on her right hand. Mistress Stannard, you're her attendant. You stand behind her. Master Whitely'll give her hand t'Andrew. Come on, now."

Bemusedly, miserably, I placed myself as told. Andrew went to stand on Pen's right. Father Bruno cleared his throat and in his thick Italian accent, began the marriage service.

It was a weird, nervous kind of wedding. Outside, the dawn had still barely gathered strength, and here within this shadowy room most of the light still came from the candles, but if an artist had been present to paint the scene they revealed, anyone seeing the canvas would have said at once: *this is a clandestine affair. Everyone looks furtive and most of them look as if they've spent the night in a cobwebby cupboard or under a hedge, and the bride looks about as happy as the chief participant in an execution.*

The service proceeded. I was aware that Magnus Whitely, after he had given Pen's hand to Andrew, had stepped to one side and was watching me with malevolent satisfaction. The smell of the horses in the byre across the passage permeated everything and some of Father Bruno's words were lost in their snorts and rustlings. To the last moment I had gone on hoping that Sir Francis Knollys would somehow find my trail and arrive after all, but he had not. Despite the bad light, I noticed that although the priest was so dark, he had unexpectedly light eyes. His command of English words seemed competent enough; it was just that he pronounced them so badly.

Andrew took his vows in a clear, strong voice. Pen denied hers in an equally strong one, saying *I won't* where she should have said *I will* in tones that fairly echoed through the room. No one took any notice, and neither the rustlings of the horses nor

Father Bruno's terrible accent prevented us from hearing it plainly when he said: "I pronounce that Andrew and Penelope are man and wife together."

Andrew kissed the bride. I saw her standing in his arms and shivering as she stood. Wretchedly, I went over in my mind all the events of the last few hours and wondered if there was anything, anything, I could have done to get her away but could not think what.

If she hadn't been brought here on a pillion, I might have grabbed her bridle, spurred my horse, and ridden off into the mist with her, I thought, or upstairs with Andrew, inspecting the wedding bed, I might have snatched out my dagger and attacked him. But he was bigger than I was and had a sword. Besides, if it came to the point, I would rather Pen went to bed, however unwillingly, with Andrew than expose myself to the risk of getting hanged. Though whether that would better or worse than whatever Whitely and Tobias had in mind for me, I didn't know.

The food was being offered and although Tobias was obviously ill at ease and by now Whitely was himself growing impatient to be away, we all needed to eat. I found a platter containing a piece of pie and a few slices of chicken being thrust at me by Tobias.

"We've to get to the east coast and it's a long way," he said in an undertone. "Magnus was so determined to see the wedding and make you watch it too that we're late setting out. You realize that we shall have to take you with us? There won't be time to waste on food or sleep. It's the last meal you'll have for a long while."

He turned away, coming face-to-face with Whitely, who glanced toward me and then said something. In the general murmur of talk, it shouldn't have been possible for me to hear what he said but danger sharpens the senses. I heard Whitely quite clearly. "You're a fool, Tobias. She's dangerous. It's the last meal she'll ever have, and if you say different, you're out of your mind. Leave it to me."

I didn't hear Tobias's answer. But I saw him shrug. And nod.

25

The Bereft Barbarian

I had expected it, of course. I had been trying not to face it, that was all—or else I was just too tired. It had been perfectly obvious since Whitely had threatened that if Pen knew too much, it would cost her her life. Instead of being married, she would end up buried in the abandoned mine, bedded not with Andrew Thwaite but—I was fairly sure of it—with Harry Hobson.

And if they were prepared to murder Pen, then they would be prepared to dispose of me, too, rather than burden themselves with me on a long journey, during which I might escape them. No. I wouldn't be going to France. Instead, I would be the one to share Harry's last bed.

I had done my best, and it hadn't been good enough. I had stopped Mary from escaping, yes. And I had found Pen. But I hadn't saved her and now I was going to die. I didn't collapse or burst into loud screams only because the shock of hearing it confirmed in words was so great that it was unreal, as though I were trapped in a terrible dream.

Where, I thought frantically, *had* Sir Francis Knollys got to? Why had the dogs lost my scent? Those who should have protected me had vanished into the moonlit night and I had heard and seen nothing of them since. And where was Brockley? Brockley, on whom I had so often relied and who had never before failed me, had also vanished into nothingness. I was alone among enemies and . . .

So was Pen. Standing there, rigid with hopelessness, I looked across the room and saw that Andrew Thwaite had her by the hand and was leading her toward the stairs. He called to his father: "It's a strange time of day to be off to my bed, but it's a special occasion. Maybe you'll see to my jobs for me, just this once? Getting a son's just as important as t'milking."

Pen was going with him, perforce, but her face was terrified. Will Thwaite was laughing and saying he would see to the cows, never fear. Over the couple, he sketched the movements of a blessing. At the foot of the stairs, Pen balked, crying out that she had taken no vows; she had said *I won't* not *I will*. She didn't want this marriage. She *wasn't* married. She wasn't going up those stairs with Andrew. She wasn't . . . !

Andrew laughed and picked her up bodily. She struggled and cried but in vain. He carried her easily up the stairs and when Rosie and some of the Grimsdale family made to follow them up, presumably to see them bedded in traditional fashion, Will Thwaite barred the way.

"Best they make friends on their own. Leave Andrew t'it. He knows his business," said Andrew's father with a dreadful grin and another spray of saliva.

Even in my own extremity, I stared after Pen with pity. She was still crying; I could hear her. Poor child. Poor, poor child. Happy is the bride who is so in love with her groom and desires him so intensely that she melts to him without fear or pain at their first joining. Happy is the maid whose first lover knows how to awaken that desire.

Pen had no desire for Andrew and I did not think he was the man to create it. Oh, Pen. Poor Pen.

And now, very soon, poor Ursula. Surreptitiously, I put my hand over the outline of my dagger. I would fight for my life, to the very last moment. I edged a little, toward the door to the passage. The horses in the byre were still saddled. If I could slip out and loose a horse and get astride it, I might just manage to bolt out of the byre and across the courtyard before anyone could stop me. If only the gatehouse had been left open. I inched another step or two.

I was close to the wall now but the door was still several paces away, on my left. Turning my head a fraction, I could see through into the passage. The outer door was open and the light of daybreak was now pouring in. Another step and I could see a segment of the courtyard, and part of the gatehouse. And the gate.

It was closed. My heart sank in renewed despair. I would never do it. Whitely was already looking my way.

I'd got to try! Undoing a gate can be tricky from the back of a horse, especially a horse one doesn't know well. The problem was to slow down the pursuit. Could I create a distraction . . . overturn some furniture, perhaps . . . enough to confuse people and get in their way while I rushed across the passage, slashed a halter rope with my dagger, scrambled up, clattered to the gate, undid the bolts, and made a dash for freedom?

Not very likely. But I was still going to attempt it. If I flung down the platter I was holding, caught hold of the table and threw it over, and all the wedding breakfast dishes were strewn over the floor . . .

In the byre, one of the horses whinnied. And then, with a surge of thankfulness so great that it weakened my knees and almost caused me to do what I hadn't done when I first realized Whitely's intention which was to keel over in a faint, I heard another horse whinny from beyond the gate, and a stentorian voice shouted: "Open in the name of the queen!" and someone began a thunderous hammering.

The wedding party froze. Full mouths stopped chewing; chicken legs and slices of pie and tankards of ale were halted halfway to people's lips. A horn blew commandingly and the command to open was repeated, even more loudly than before.

"Huh!" said Will Thwaite. "Thee said they'd be out lookin' for Mistress Pen, Master Littleton. Seems thee were right. Well, well, they're too late. And there's nothing against t'law in a young pair gettin' wed. As well you and Master Whitely hurried things on. God's teeth, they'll have that gate down in a minute! Better let them through afore they knock it flat."

The shouting outside was being repeated yet again and a further furious pounding on the gate was making it shake. Brushing past Tobias and Whitely, who appeared to be stricken immobile, Thwaite strode out to the courtyard, bellowing: "Wait! Wait! I'll undo t'door!"

The hammering stopped. Thwaite unbarred the entrance and as I stood there, leaning on the wall now for support, Sir Francis Knollys in person rode through. Crowding after him, fully armed and looking as impressive as an army, were a dozen of his own men, plus John Ryder, Tom Smith, and Clem Moss.

Whitely, regaining his powers of movement, suddenly made toward me, perhaps with some notion of using me as a shield while he made his escape, but I hurled my platter at him, dodged through the door, and sprinted for the courtyard, shouting: "I'm here! I'm here!" and a moment later was being thankfully embraced by Ryder as he threw himself off his horse and grabbed hold of me.

"You lost my scent? What happened? They were furious when they found I wasn't Mary. They've married Pen to Andrew Thwaite by force. Tobias's cousin Magnus Whitely, who I dismissed from being Tyesdale's steward, was going to murder me!" I said, putting it as succinctly as possible. For the moment, for the sake of brevity, I left out Lapwings and Mistress Holme.

"Going to murder you, was he?" said Sir Francis grimly, descending from his own horse. The other men did the same and led by Sir Francis, we marched indoors and into the midst of the wedding party. "Well, well. So these are the rascally conspirators. Good morning, Master Littleton. You're looking well. I doubt if you'll seem quite so healthy much longer; nasty damp places, dungeons. Which of you is Magnus Whitely? I don't believe I've had the pleasure."

For a moment, there had been a threat of resistance, mainly from the Grimsdales and their mining relatives, who had bristled up at once at the sight of a crowd of armed men marching into the room. The sight of swords being drawn discouraged them, however. They backed away against the wall. Will Thwaite, who had come back inside with us, seemed completely bemused. "What's going *on*? What's all this about conspirators an' murder?"

"I beg your pardon. I should have introduced myself. I am Sir Francis Knollys, from Bolton Castle."

Sir Francis paused, glancing toward the stairs. Pen's voice, raised in sobbing protest, could still be heard from the upper floor. "What's happening up there?"

"My son's on his honeymoon," said Thwaite. He seemed more bewildered than ever. I had not hitherto been certain that the Thwaites were really quite unaware that Andrew's marriage had been linked to a scheme to free Mary Stuart but now I saw that it was true. As far as the Thwaites were concerned, I had offended their friend Magnus and he had agreed to bring them Pen Mason as a way of making a little money while being revenged on me. They were innocent of treason, if not of much else.

I started to say something of this to Sir Francis but I was interrupted by a hoarse scream from overhead and a crash as though someone or something had fallen over heavily. Will Thwaite swung around to face the stairs. The maidservant Rosie clutched at the nearest arm, which belonged to one of the younger miners. Another scream came. It died away into a horrible bubbling, choking sound.

It hadn't been Pen. I was as sure as I could be that that dreadful noise had not been made by Pen.

A shadow moved at the top at the stairs and Andrew blundered into view. He started downward, lurching, keeping upright by fending himself off from the wall and the banister with hands which left red marks behind them. He was naked except for the blood that ran in a stream from his gasping mouth and pumped from a huge wound close to his heart, veiling the front of his body in scarlet.

Before he was halfway down, his eyes went huge and blind and he sagged, losing his balance. Will Thwaite, crying out, ran forward with outstretched arms to catch him as he fell headlong.

Thwaite sank at the foot of the stairs, holding his son in his arms. He put a hand behind Andrew's head and shook him, calling his name, and Sir Francis went quickly to kneel beside them, resting his hand on the boy's neck where the great pulse of life beats as long as life endures. Presently, he shook his head and stood up. Will Thwaite, still cradling his son, stared up at him and then back at Andrew's face. "It isn't true! It can't be true! Andrew, *Andrew,* answer me, it's your father! *Andrew . . .*"

A sound from above made us look up once more. Pen was coming down the stairs. She seemed to be unhurt and she was still dressed, but she too was splashed with blood. She was carrying a sword. Its blade was stained with red and between her crimsoned fingers I saw the glint of amethyst.

"It's the sword that he was wearing," she said, in answer to our questioning eyes. Her voice was a monotone, as though she had been shocked beyond the power of expressiveness. Halfway down the stairs, she stopped, because Will Thwaite and Andrew were in the way. She spoke to us from where she was.

"He took it off when he undressed and I picked it up and told him that I'd never wanted to marry him and we *weren't* married. I said to him: 'I shouted *I won't* at the very altar; why didn't you listen?' But he took no notice. He laughed at me. He said we were man and wife all the same and I'd got to sleep with him whether I liked it or not. He was going to force himself on me . . ."

Her voice had gone up now, becoming shrill. "Gently, mistress, gently!" said Clem in a kind voice.

Pen looked at him. As though he had asked her to explain, she said: "He told me to put the sword down and he came toward me, still laughing—he didn't expect me to do anything to him; I could see that. I backed against the wall and then I couldn't go any farther and he came near enough for the swordpoint to be touching him and told me not to be silly. Not to be *silly.* He was going to . . . going to . . . and he told me not to be *silly*! It's heavy." She looked down at the sword. "But I was holding it in both hands and I was so frightened and so angry—I lunged. It went into him. The blade was so sharp! I only meant to hold him off, to make him jump back, but it ran him through! He . . . he screamed and then he turned and stumbled out of the door . . . there was so much b . . . blood . . ." She was beginning to cry. Her eyes shifted to Sir Francis. "I heard your voice . . . is . . . is he dead?"

"Aye." Very gently, Will Thwaite laid his son down. Rising to his feet, he faced her. "You murdering bitch," he said. That he didn't shout but said it quite softly somehow made it doubly menacing. "You've killed my son. My only son. My only hope for tomorrow. *You've killed him.*"

"B . . . but I didn't m . . . mean to kill him. I didn't!" The tears were streaming down her face and with her spare hand she was leaning on the banister for support. "I j . . . just wanted to hold him off. He was g . . . going to rape me!"

"*Rape* you? You were his wife! And," said Will Thwaite grimly, "t'murder of a man by his wife—that's got a name, that has. That's petty treason and the woman burns for it." He swung around to face Sir Francis. "Isn't that t'law? Tell her!"

"It's also the law that a forced marriage isn't valid!" I said loudly. "Pen never said *I will.* She said *I won't* at the top of her voice and no one listened."

"She and Andrew were declared man and wife by an ordained priest and that's enough for me!" snapped Thwaite. He turned again to stare at Pen. "T'law's clear and even Sir Francis here can't deny me when I tell him to take thee into custody. Thee'll go to t'stake for this, my lass, and I'll be there when t'faggots are lit and . . ."

"Except," said Pen shrilly, "that Father Bruno *isn't* an ordained priest and Andrew was never my husband in any sense whatsoever."

"*What?*" shouted Thwaite.

Father Bruno, who had been standing back in the shadows, pushed his way forward. "Mistress Mason—which is still her name—is quite correct. I am not a priest and never have been." He spoke without a trace of Italian accent, though there was a tinge of the English countryside in his voice.

The daylight was full by now. For the first time I could see Father Bruno properly. He smiled at me and my jaw dropped. *"Brockley!"* I said.

"Brockley?" said Sir Francis questioningly.

"Yes!" I had even seen Brown Berry in the byre and noticed his hairy fetlocks, but because of the bad light I hadn't recognized him. "This is Roger Brockley, my manservant. He went off a couple of days ago saying that he had an idea about protecting Pen, but . . . but . . ."

"Walnut juice to stain my face and a black dye for my hair," said Brockley. "I stopped before I got to Fernthorpe to use them, and while I was at it, I clipped my hair and shaved the top of my head to make a tonsure. I took the cassock and a prayer book and this silver crucifix I'm wearing from the chapel at Tyesdale. I'd raided Agnes Appletree's stores for the walnut juice and the black dye. She keeps such things for coloring cloth. It was the best I could do. I reckoned that if I could get myself into the Thwaite home as a priest, they might use me if it came to the point of forcing a marriage on Mistress Pen. Then the marriage wouldn't be legal and couldn't bind her."

"I might have known!" I gasped. "I had no idea where you'd gone, what you were doing, what had happened to you. I should have known you wouldn't fail us. Oh, *Brockley!"*

"What's all this? Is he saying he's not a priest? That he's . . . ?"

"He's my steward, and he's certainly not a priest," I said to Master Thwaite. "Pen hasn't by any stretch of the imagination killed her husband. She resisted rape, that's all. A woman's entitled to go any lengths she likes to fend off a man who wants to take her against her will."

"Is *that* t'law?" Thwaite demanded, turning to Sir Francis.

"I knew who Master Brockley was before that so-called ceremony began," said Pen. She brushed her knuckles across her wet eyes, and though her voice shook, she spoke with determination. "I recognized him the moment I went close to him. That's why I knelt to pray beside him."

"And what I said, when everyone thought I was praying," said Brockley, "was that if she would let me conduct the service, it wouldn't be lawful and the Thwaites would have no hold on her afterwards. I said I would bring help as soon as I could, and meanwhile, she had best smile and be complaisant and—do what she must—and soon she would be rescued."

"Only I couldn't! I *couldn't*!" Pen said. "But I didn't dare tell Andrew about Brockley—he'd have said I was lying and anyway, that was before I understood that Sir Francis had come and I thought that if Andrew *did* believe me, I'd put Brockley in danger. But I'd have spoken out at the inquest, in public, and I'll still do that if I must. Andrew and I weren't married. We were *not*!" She looked down at herself. "I'm all over blood," she said wonderingly.

Then the reaction came. She began to shake. The sword she was still holding dropped from her hands, falling onto Andrew's body where it still lay at the foot of the stairs. I ran forward, meaning to jump over him and get Pen into my arms but Clem Moss was ahead of me.

He leapt onto the stairs and caught hold of her as her knees gave way. She sagged against him, sobbing. Two of Sir Francis's men, moving suddenly, as though released from some kind of paralysis, hastened to lift Andrew's corpse out of the way and Clem, picking Penelope up, carried her down the last few stairs and placed her gently on the settle. "Easy. Easy!" He sat down beside her and his voice was warm and soothing. "There, there. If there's an inquest, I'll bear witness that you were deceived and takken by force to be used against your will and against t'law and I'll call out any man of t'jury that brings owt but a verdict of right and just killing against you."

Sir Francis let out a snort of something very like laughter, but Will Thwaite simply stood there, his face bloodless. "So there's no justice for Andrew? Thee'll all stand against me, an old man that's got no son, no future . . ."

"As a matter of interest," said Brockley inquiringly, scratching at his black tonsure as though it itched, "why were you so wild to get Andrew married to Penelope? You even tried to kidnap her before she'd reached Tyesdale and that was before you'd seen her. It must be Tyesdale that you wanted but what's so wonderful about Tyesdale?"

From where he stood, backed against the wall beside the staircase, Grimsdale suddenly laughed. "Coal!" he said.

"Coal? What do you mean?" I turned to him in astonishment. "There's no coal on Tyesdale. I know there are some old workings on it—like the ones on Fernthorpe land, where Pen was imprisoned. But they're abandoned. They were no use."

"They're *old*. I was never happy with that report. I had a *feeling* about it," said Magnus Whitely sullenly. "Two months back, I had another survey done. There's coal all right, and plenty too, and near the surface at that. You go into those old workings and you'll find *new* digging inside one of them. I told the men to be secret, so the rubble that was dug out was shoveled into a tunnel where the lode really *had* run out. There was another tunnel that told a very different tale. Oh yes, there's coal on Tyesdale. The prospector's bill hasn't come in yet, though I've got the report. I kept that under my mattress. Your prying eyes never found *that*. I took it away with me. Tyesdale's worth a *fortune*. If you'd let us alone, or let Pen get married to Andrew . . ."

In Clem's arms, Pen's sobs grew momentarily louder but subsided as he whispered to her and patted her shoulders.

"They'd have shared it between them, I suppose," said Brockley contemptuously. "Littleton, Whitely, and the Thwaites. *Now* it becomes clear. The Earl of Leicester," he added thoughtfully, "will probably have a seizure when he realizes what he kindly gave away to Mistress Pen!"

"It seems," said Sir Francis grimly, "that there is a fine tangle to undo. But the first step is to take a number of these people into custody. Mistress Stannard, what were you saying about Master Thwaite being unaware of the scheme concerning . . . a certain lady?"

Thwaite looked at him in evident confusion. "I think the Thwaites genuinely know nothing of it," I said quietly. "I think they were only concerned with getting hold of Pen—and her coal mine."

"There'd have been grandchilder, too," said Thwaite. "My lad were a bridegroom this morning and now he's dead."

Andrew's body was still on the floor, where Sir Francis's men had laid it after shifting it away from the stairs. Once again, Will Thwaite sank down at its side and gathered his son into his arms.

He was a horrible man, a barbarian. I hated his squalid home, his gap-toothed mouth, and the spittle when he talked. I hated him and Andrew alike for their greed and their ruthlessness and their cruelty. I hated Will more still when, as I passed close to him, going to help Clem lead Pen away, he caught at my arm and said: "I'll maybe go t'law yet and get a rope round t'bitch's neck if nothing more."

Yet I pitied him, too, as he crouched there, clutching the body of his only child and weeping.

Enough so that I paused to whisper to him: "If you will let Pen go in peace, I will not point the finger at you when we take up the body that's buried in your old mine, and carry him to a decent churchyard."

He blanched and held his burden tighter. "No use pointing fingers at me, girl. It were Andrew that slew t'lad and that were only by accident."

I had seen it happen. I could even remember the build of Harry's slayer and I would have said it was a younger man than Will Thwaite. In all probability, I had just been told the truth.

"But you can't prove it wasn't you," I said softly. "Not if I chose to say so. So leave Pen be. And I'll say nothing."

I turned away. We left him still holding Andrew's corpse and crooning to it as though it were an infant he wished to soothe to sleep.

I suppose barbarians, too, can know what it is to be bereft. If so—I knew about grief. My mother. Gerald. Matthew. I had endured and survived because I was still young. Will Thwaite was not. His future hopes, all his proud dreams, had died with Andrew. Nothing lay before him now but an empty old age, and grief might well bring his decline on before its natural time.

According to Dr. Lambert, with whom I had begun to study Greek along with Meg and Pen, the Ancient Greeks had a word for the fate which had befallen Will Thwaite. They called it hubris.

26

The End of Enchantment

On the way back to Tyesdale, I noticed that the imitation Italian priest who was riding with us on Brown Berry had a most unclerical sword at his side. It was in its sheath but the violet gem in the hilt was instantly familiar. "Brockley, where did you get that sword?"

"It's the one Pen used, madam. I went upstairs before we left to collect my own saddlebags and belongings, and collected the sheath and sword belt for this while I was about it. Will Thwaite isn't going to argue. We can send the sword home to Harry's parents."

"Thank you, Brockley."

I was thankful beyond belief to see Tyesdale again and not only for my own sake. I was exhausted, but Pen was in a worse state than I was. Clem rode beside her all the way, talking to her in a calm and reasonable manner, but the girl had just killed a man and wouldn't, I thought, get over it quickly. She shivered constantly, although Clem gave her his cloak, and I think she cried the whole way. She almost collapsed as she dismounted.

Mercifully, Sybil was there to take charge of her and Sir Francis did the necessary explaining. I left Sybil, wide-eyed with horror, but kind and practical as ever, to look after Pen and give her a dose of my sedative, while I stumbled upstairs and surrendered to the ministrations of Dale, who helped me to bed, brought me some porridge and mulled wine, pulled the coverlet over me, and sat beside me until I slept.

Mary Stuart was gone. I had gathered during the ride home that Sir Francis had not brought all his men to Fernthorpe. Three of them had taken her back to Bolton. Thank goodness for that, I said. I could have my own bed again. I presume that Sir Francis also took some rest but he was up and active when I woke, later that day. "I take it," he said when I joined him in the hall, "that your remarkable ward is still abed?"

"Yes. Sybil gave her some of my sleeping potion. Pen has been very brave," I said. "Foolish to start with, but then brave and determined. There—won't be any charges against her. I have seen to that."

"Ah. You threatened Thwaite, did you? But according to you, he really is innocent of treason. We didn't arrest him."

"I still—er—managed to frighten him," I said circumspectly. I added: "Pen will suffer greatly, you know. What she did wasn't in her true nature. She was terrified and desperate. She'll remember it in nightmares for all the rest of her life."

"I agree with you. Don't worry. I too spoke with Thwaite before we left. He certainly seemed frightened. Natural enough in the circumstances, but I take it that you helped to petrify him. There will be no inquest on Andrew Thwaite. His father seems anxious to cause no trouble and avoid getting into any. His family had enough of that in the past! He said he would give it out that Andrew died of a sudden consuming fever and see that the maidservant, Rosie, never says otherwise, either."

"What about Littleton and Whitely?" I asked.

"They and their helpers—except for the woman, Madge Grimsdale, who probably had to do what her husband told her— will be tried, but only for plotting Mary's release. It will be claimed that she never left Bolton. From the start, I thought it best that as few people should know as possible. The only ones who do know are my own men and a couple of trustworthy women servants. I arranged for the Douglases to go hawking and spend a night with friends at a distance. From now on, they'll be denied access to Mary, so she will have no chance to tell them."

"Sir Francis," I said, "you never told me how it came about that the dogs lost my scent last night. I remember asking you when you arrived at Fernthorpe, but in all the uproar, you never had a chance to answer."

"That!" Knollys snorted furiously. "I'm truly sorry, Mistress Stannard. It was a shocking failure on our part. I was concerned with keeping my men back. I didn't want to risk your companions glancing behind them and glimpsing them in the moonlight. We let you go out of sight and trusted that the dogs would do the tracking—only, over in one of the laborers' cottages, there was a bitch in season. Your dogs smelled her and after that they cared nothing for your scented pebbles. They led us to her instead! We didn't know we were off the line till we were at the cottage and they were throwing themselves against the garden fence. We dragged the brutes away but their hearts weren't in the work after that and we never found the scent again. And then we got lost in the mist."

"So that was it! Our maidservant Bess did tell me once that her father had a bitch and that our dogs usually sired her puppies. What brought you to Fernthorpe at all, then?" I asked. "I've never been so glad to see anyone in my life as I was glad to see you. Whitely and Tobias were going to flee to France and Whitely meant to murder me before leaving, because I knew too much."

"Fernthorpe was the only lead we had," said Sir Francis. "That was where Mistress Pen would be taken unless you helped the plotters. You wanted us to lay the trap there in the first place, I recall! Kind of you," he added dryly, "not to say *I told you so!* Once we had managed to find our way again, we made for Fernthorpe because it was the only place we could think of. Your man Roger Brockley did splendid work in pretending to be a priest. A remarkable fellow!"

"He has had some education," I said. "He even has a little Latin. I'm sure that helped to make his performance convincing."

"Indeed, yes. Mistress Stannard, there was another priest at Fernthorpe and I understand that he was hired from a family called Holme, who live in a house known as Lapwings. Is that household involved at all? The men I left at Fernthorpe to question the captives report that according to Robinson and also to Whitely and Littleton, she was merely paid for Robinson's services as a priest, and nothing more. Is that correct?"

I thought of Mistress Holme and her five frightened daughters, the girls for whom she was so desperate to find husbands. There had already been two deaths, those of Johnnie Grimsdale and Andrew Thwaite. There were several prisoners possibly facing death, and a grieving father. Madge Grimsdale had not been kept in custody, but I wondered if her husband and her last son would ever come home. It was enough.

"I imagine so," I said. "I heard that, too, but nothing more."

"Lapwings wasn't by any chance the safe house that Lady Mary was being taken to?"

"Sir Francis . . ." I looked him in the eyes. "Lapwings," I said, "is occupied by a widow and five young girls. The man of the house, now deceased, was among Mary's supporters. No doubt he left his family with a sense of loyalty towards his . . . his attitudes. But I think that they will reject those attitudes now, out of sheer terror. I doubt if they are still a danger to Queen Elizabeth."

"Humph!"

I had done my best for the Holmes. I could do no more. Uncertain of what Knollys's *Humph* meant, I changed the subject. "When I came to Bolton," I said, "I spoke to you, did I not, about an attempt to kidnap my daughter, and the death of a young man called Harry Hobson?"

"You did, yes."

"Penelope was held prisoner in an old mine working on Fernthorpe land," I said. "I was taken to her there. In that working, I saw a mound of rubble that looked suspicious. I moved some of the rubble, and yes, there's someone buried there. I think it could be Harry. I believe the Thwaites were behind the attack, along with a few local men under their sway—possibly including some of the Grimsdales. But I think the man who killed Harry was Andrew Thwaite who is now dead. I don't want to pursue the matter, though I do want the body retrieved."

"You obviously want to leave a good many stones unturned."
Knollys eyed me thoughtfully. "But you may be right. I feel
much to blame for this whole debacle. I should not have let
Mary leave Bolton at all, and I shall incur Her Majesty's displea-
sure if I ever admit that I did!"

"Then, perhaps, if the stones—apart from those in the old
mine workings—remain unturned . . . ?" I suggested.

"We've got eight men in custody, if you count Father Robinson," Knollys said. "Well, eight's a good haul. But the folk of this
district had better be careful henceforth."

No one ever contradicted any part of my story. Harry was
found, as I expected, in the old mine; his body was taken out
reverently and laid to rest in proper fashion in Fritton Churchyard, and the gloomy vicar, accepting what Knollys told him,
provided a most dignified funeral service for a young man killed
in an encounter with unknown robbers.

As for the Holme family, I saw the records of the trial later and
there was no mention of them at all. Knollys was not a cruel man.

Even through my haze of exhaustion, I had noticed Clem's kindness to Pen. I also recalled that as we rode into the courtyard on
our return, I had heard her say to him: "I'm thankful to be
home." It seemed that she had begun to look on Tyesdale as her
home.

She had had a terrible shock, but I began to see how she
might be healed. The day after our return, when Pen, still pale
and inclined to be tearful, at last reappeared, I took her on a tour
of the house, talking to her about the various improvements that
needed to be made. The arrival of a bill from the prospectors
who had found the coal on Tyesdale land enabled us to send
word to them, ask for a new copy of their report (Magnus
Whitely having removed the original), and thus discover just
how prosperous Tyesdale could soon hope to be. I also sent her
off to ride around the land with Clem and discuss what needed
to be done outdoors.

She returned looking better, so much so that before long, I

sent her out with Clem again, to ride in the fresh air. I watched her begin to take an interest in her surroundings, to think about the present rather than the past. It was Pen, indeed, who decided that Bess and Feeb, who had for the time being been asked to stay away, should be employed once more.

"We need them," she said seriously. "There are a thousand things to be done and Agnes needs the help."

"Tom Smith will be pleased," said Sybil. "I think he's sweet on Bess."

Pen laughed and I said with some asperity that I hoped the romance would prosper. "I'd like to hear of one with a happy outcome, I must say," I told them.

Clem was listening when I said it. He didn't comment, however. Wait a little, I said to myself. Play the fish with care.

I had nothing against Tom Smith marrying Bess Clipclop and either bringing her south or staying in Yorkshire with her. I quite liked the girl and if she or Feeb or both of them had spied on us, I knew they had only been doing what their parents told them, and that the parents in turn had probably been bullied by Whitely.

I still felt very tired. It was an exhaustion of the mind as well as the body, born of homesickness as well as sleeplessness, and it lingered on, day after day. I ached to go home to Hugh. I had borrowed the services of a courier from Sir Francis Knollys and sent a long letter home, explaining most of what had happened and sending Hobson's sword back to his family. But for the moment, I knew I must stay where I was. There was still much to do at Tyesdale before it would be fair to leave Clem in charge. Besides, I was waiting for someone.

Seven days later, just before dinner, he arrived.

I didn't recognize him at first, since he was now over twenty and I hadn't seen him since he was thirteen. At first, when I went down to see who the young man was who was dismounting in the courtyard, I merely thought that he looked vaguely familiar. Then Pen came flying out of the house, ran down the steps with a glad cry, sketched a curtsy, and threw herself into the arms of the newcomer. "George! Mistress Stannard, it's my brother George!"

"Your letter reached Lockhill safely," George said to me, hugging her. "I set out as soon as I could. I spent last night at Bolton Castle. I saw Sir Francis and I hear that two men I thought were my friends are now under arrest for laying a plot concerning Mary Stuart, and I know they tried to force Pen into a marriage she didn't want. I know what happened at Fernthorpe. Sir Francis questioned me. He is satisfied now that I had nothing to do with any of it but he obviously thought I might have."

He frowned at me over Pen's head. "I'm glad to see her safe, and since you sent for me, I take it that you've been on her side, whatever that exactly means. But I'd like a fuller explanation from you."

"Come indoors," I said. "I'll tell you what you want to know."

In the parlor, sometime later, I said quietly: "I am aware that you wanted a Catholic marriage for Pen, and perhaps a family with—shall we say, a willingness to find Mary Stuart acceptable as a queen? Like Sir Francis, I wondered if you were part of the conspiracy. When I wrote to you at Lockhill, it was only partly to summon you to Pen's aid. It was also to find out where you were. If you were at Lockhill, you could hardly be involved. The plot was created at very short notice, during the few days before I wrote to you. An exchange of letters between Lockhill and Tobias or Whitely would hardly have been possible. They could only have done it if you were here in Yorkshire. Tobias had been in touch with you earlier, I know, when he was thinking of marrying Pen himself. You might have come to the district. I wanted to make sure that you hadn't. I told the messenger to find out, at Lockhill, whether you had just returned from an absence."

"I see," said George. "Well, he did as he was bid. He talked to my mother and to the servants there, who all told him that I had been there without interruption for months, which is true. My mother sends her good wishes to you, and is wondering why you sent for me so urgently."

"I didn't want to alarm her needlessly," I said.

"Thank you for that." George's voice was chilly. "Mistress Stannard . . ."

"Yes?"

"I do wish my sister to marry into the faith in which she was reared." He sounded remote, as though I were a public meeting. "I do indeed hope that when God brings about the turn of events which I believe he *will* eventually bring about, and sets Queen Mary on the English throne, Pen will be with people who are glad to offer Mary their allegiance. But while Queen Elizabeth rules, I will never turn traitor nor would I wish Pen to be connected to traitors. My mother," said George, suddenly abandoning his orator's voice and becoming human, "would kill me if I did either."

I laughed. "I remember once hearing your father declare that he would never touch a treacherous scheme because his wife wouldn't let him! Your mother hasn't changed, it seems." I became serious. "George, I am sorry that Pen has had such a frightening experience. It wasn't the sort of thing any young girl should have to face. I have to say, though, that it is high time a husband—a *congenial* husband—was found for her."

"I agree. I gather that as well as running off with Tobias Littleton, she had some kind of infatuation when she was at court."

"Yes, she did. I think . . ."

A tap on the door interrupted us. I called to whoever it might be to enter, and to our surprise, Pen came in, accompanied by Clem Moss. Clem was very tidily dressed and had an air of formality about him. He bowed with great politeness to me and to George Mason.

Then he said: "I have come—Mistress Penelope and I have come—to ask permission of you, sir, her brother, and you, Mistress Stannard, as her guardian, to marry."

"He'll be doing well for himself," said George. "A younger son, a steward, marrying the lady of the house and, incidentally, marrying a very valuable parcel of land with a potential coal mine on it. I know he says that he decided he wanted to pay court to Pen before he knew the full value of Tyesdale, but who's to say that's the truth?"

"Oh, it is," I said. "When he arrived at Fernthorpe along with

Sir Francis and Pen was in a panic over what might be said at the inquest about Andrew Thwaite's death, it was Clem who tried to comfort her. He went to her at once, and that was before anyone knew about the coal. I think he means what he says."

Which had been frank and to the point. "I like Mistress Penelope and she seems to have takken to me. She's my kind of lass. I like it that she's been properly educated, and I like her honest looks. I've had my fill of pretty kitten faces. Mistress Pen and I can work side by side to make Tyesdale thrive, if thee'll give us the chance."

Clem, clearly, was not concerned with the fact that Pen wasn't a beauty. He had recognized the real Pen and valued her.

"I've been thinking for some time," I said, "that it would be a suitable match. She enjoys his company and he keeps her from brooding about what happened at Fernthorpe. I've been hoping that Clem would approach me before I approached him."

We were in the parlor, George Mason, Roger Brockley, Sybil Jester, and myself, a conference in session. The young couple had been sent away, Clem to get on with his work as a steward and Pen to sit sewing upstairs with Meg and Fran Dale while I discussed their future with Pen's brother and my own most trusted companions.

Brockley, who had got rid of his walnut juice complexion by now but still had a jet-black tonsure, which didn't suit him, said: "He's a steady fellow and he knows how to run a manor. He and Mistress Pen won't need to pay a steward; he can do that himself. That'll save them money, until the coal mine becomes profitable, which will take a while. I've had a look at Whitely's ledgers and documents myself now. He's milked Tyesdale of a fortune!"

"I have a comment," said Sybil. We turned to her. "From what I've observed," she said, "she hasn't fallen in love with him, but she likes him very much and feels safe with him. That might be better for her than marrying the kind of man she *does* fall in love with. Which, so far, have been a tutor old enough to be her father, a married linguist in Sir William's Cecil's household, and Tobias Littleton, in romantic thrall to Mary Stuart and prepared to stop at nothing to serve the wretched woman. He valued a fugitive queen under suspicion of murder a great deal more than he valued Pen. Clem, on the other hand, does value Pen. He's not a courtly lover but he knows her worth. He'll take care of her."

Sybil was not a talkative woman, but she had a remarkable knack, when she did talk, of speaking to the point.

"Even Pen," she added, as we all thought this over, "may well be tired of the catastrophes that falling in love has brought her. She is growing up—very rapidly, especially over the last few days. I think that in Clem Moss, she sees a wise choice and a chance of reliable happiness."

"And once she's wed to him," said Brockley, "Clem won't let her gaze wander. There's good stuff in that lad. I've got to know him pretty well since we've all been back here."

George threw up his hands. "Well, my mother put Pen's marriage in your hands, Mistress Stannard. In the end, you're the one who should decide. That's what guardians do and you've been appointed her guardian. What's your opinion?"

"When I first met the Moss family," I said, "I'd have said no. But as far as Clem is concerned, I've changed my mind completely. I say yes, with all my heart."

We summoned the pair to tell them the news, and to begin planning how the marriage should be organized. This would be no hasty dawn ceremony with coal-dust smudges on the face of the bride and a dubious priest to officiate. It would be held at the parish church in Fritton and banns would be called for three Sundays beforehand in the manner preferred by the Church. The bride would wear the blue velvet gown and the lace-edged ruff that I had so carefully brought for her; her brother would give her away and her mother would come from Lockhill to meet her prospective son-in-law and shed the traditional tears as her daughter took her vows. The feast would consist of . . .

We had gone that far with the joyful details and I was watching with great relief the new brightness in Pen's eyes, when Clem suddenly said: "Mistress Stannard, I'm that overset by all these plans and by knowing Pen and I are to be wed, that I'm forgetting things! I'm right sorry. A messenger rode in just before tha sent for me and Pen, and gave me a letter for thee. Jamie's seen to his horse and Agnes is giving t'fellow food and drink—but here's t'letter."

He pulled it out of his belt pouch and gave it to me. My name was written on it and to my delight, the handwriting was Hugh's. "Excuse me," I said, and broke the seal.

The letter thanked me for mine, which had reached him safely, though, Hugh said, it had been too long in coming. He was sorry to learn of the trouble I had met and deeply grieved to learn of Harry's death. He was himself well, though missing me.

But then the letter went on:

Here at Hawkswood, we too have had trouble. That aged servant of yours, Gladys Morgan, has angered the vicar by expressing some opinions not in accordance with his notions of piety. She doesn't see why she should accept the aches and pains of age as the will of God. I have aches and pains myself and am inclined to agree with her, but that isn't all. She has also interfered with the local physician—prescribing her homely medicines for his patients and so on. And now a young woman in Hawkswood village has died suddenly. She wasn't taking any of Gladys's potions but she and Gladys had quarreled just before the woman died and the physician and the vicar are convinced that Gladys put a curse on her.

I think I have smoothed matters away for the time being but I am worried. There is a good deal of local feeling. I am sending Gladys back to your home at Withysham for the time being, but, Ursula, I pray that you come home soon.

In any case, you have been so long away that the house seems to echo with emptiness. Come back, my love, and put us all to rights.

Your most loving husband,
Hugh Stannard.

And so, in the end, I did not see my ward, Penelope Mason, go to the altar in her gown of blue velvet and her lace-edged ruff, though she wrote to me, telling me what a happy affair her wedding had been; how the sun had shone and her mother had wept and smiled both together; and how smart Clem had looked; and how Cecily Moss had boomed at everyone all through the marriage feast; and how Clem was the most kind and delightful husband any girl could wish for; and how the mining work was soon to begin, and new wall hangings bought for Tyesdale, and how Agnes Appletree had made all the furniture shine with polish, and Father Robinson—who had been released and had returned to Lapwings—had come privately to say the Catholic Mass for Clem and herself in the Tyesdale chapel . . .

She wrote, too, of the smaller, simpler ceremony that took place on the same day and united Bess Clipclop to Tom Smith. Tom stayed in Yorkshire with Bess, whom he didn't think would settle happily in the south. He was a strong lad and proposed to become a miner and work in the Tyesdale coal mine when it was started.

I was glad for them all, but I had left Tyesdale the day after Hugh's letter arrived. I had missed Hugh so much, and I had always been afraid that Gladys would get herself into trouble again and I knew I must go south at once, to look after them both.

I knew I would have to go to court on the way, to make my report to Cecil on the errands I had performed. The inquiry into Darnley's death might not be until October but I would be expected to make my report as soon as I reached the south and I would also be expected to make it by word of mouth and not in writing. I fretted at the delay, but hoped it would be a matter only of one day.

I also accepted a further day's delay by going out of my way to visit Bolton. I felt obliged to let Sir Francis Knollys know of my departure, in case my testimony was needed for the trial of Tobias Littleton and Magnus Whitely, and indeed, while I was there, I made a witnessed statement that could be used if required, describing how they had attempted to force my hand by kidnapping my ward.

I did not ask to see Mary, nor did she ask to see me. Perhaps she didn't know I had arrived. She knew when I left, however, for the next morning, when I and my companions were mounting in the courtyard, I saw her watching me out of an open window overhead.

She did not call out to me or even raise a hand in farewell;

nor did I acknowledge her. Her face was very sad. It was so very much the face of the prisoner, left behind in captivity. It was a captivity that would last for nearly twenty years, and though neither of us could have known that at the time, I think she had already begun to despair.

The end of enchantment is a sorry business. It's like awaking from a beautiful dream, the kind of dream you don't want to leave. But if you try to fall asleep again, to recapture it, you never can. You may still remember it, its beauty and its magic, but memory is all it is.

I would remember the enchantment of Mary Stuart for the rest of my life but never again would I experience it. I knew the truth of her now. I could feel her eyes on the back of my head as I turned my horse away and finished saying farewell to Sir Francis, and rode out of the gate, but I would not, could not, look around.

Before I was a mile from Bolton Castle, my thoughts had fixed themselves once more on Hugh and Gladys, neither of whom possessed any magic. Dear Hugh was down-to-earth and practical, and as for poor old Gladys, she was always her own worst enemy, with her brown fangs and bad temper and useless curses. She positively invited accusations of witchcraft, though in fact she had as much power of enchantment, for good or evil, as an old, ill-natured, spavined horse or a broken plow, rusting in a barley field.

But Hugh was my rock and my windbreak and Gladys was my responsibility. I was going home, to be sheltered by the one and to give shelter to the other. I intended to press on at the best possible speed, to make up for having to go to Bolton and to the royal court, and all my mind was fixed on the journey ahead and what I would find at the end of it.

A mile, just one mile from the gates of Bolton Castle and I had forgotten Mary Stuart.

DATE DUE		
FEB 1 0 2004	SEP 2 1 2004	
APR 2 1 2004	JUN 0 8 2005	
MAY 1 1 2004		
JUN 0 1 2004	NOV 0 7 2005	
JUN 2 3 2004	MAR 0 6 2006	
JUL 1 3 2004	JUN 1 6 2007	
AUG 0 5 2004	NOV 3 0 2007	
AUG 2 5 2004		